PRAI

MW01487758

The Epicenter of Forever

"With the perfect mix of dreamy romance and affirming self-discovery, *The Epicenter of Forever* is the kind of novel that cracks your heart wide open and leaves your emotions trembling long after the last page. Williams's writing is wonderfully rich, her characters layered, and the rugged MMC—did someone mention 'biceps'?—is as swoon-worthy as they come. But I double dare you not to fall in love with the small California mountain town of Grand Trees. You won't want to leave."

—Lauren Parvizi, author of *Trust Me on This*

"Perfect for fans of Annabel Monaghan, Mara Williams's *The Epicenter of Forever* weaves together old hurts and new love. Eden is an instantly relatable protagonist, and I loved watching her navigate her divorce, her relationship with her mother, and her growing feelings for Caleb and the people of Grand Trees. Insightfully written and emotionally rewarding, I devoured every page."

—Emma Barry, author of *Bad Reputation*

"What a cozy, heartwarming, and searingly hopeful romance. *The Epicenter of Forever* took me on an enchanting ride full of emotional longing, gorgeous prose, idyllic nature, and sweeping grand gestures. With a thoughtful portrayal of fractured family dynamics and beautiful examples of how to heal—all set amid a budding yet soul-deep romance I could not get enough of—Mara Williams has to be on your radar."

—Clare Gilmore, *USA Today* bestselling author of *Never Over*

"Atmospheric and romantic, *The Epicenter of Forever* is a heart-swelling book about going back to your roots to make way for a hopeful future. Mara Williams crafts a story of a woman still in pain from long-forgotten wounds, a family torn apart by past mistakes, and a man who would help them all heal—set against a lush California forest backdrop. Readers will fall hard for Grand Trees and all of its quirky residents just as they'll root for Eden and Caleb to find their happy ever after. An enchanting small-town romance that is sure to warm your heart!"

—London Sperry, author of *Passion Project*

"Poignant, heart wrenching, and filled with steamy tension, *The Epicenter of Forever* is a lyrical, evocative portrait of reconnection, rewriting memories, and risk-taking beyond the narratives we and our families have set for ourselves. You won't be able to set foot in Grand Trees without feeling completely enraptured by Eden and Caleb's love story and Williams's thoughtful prose."

—Katie Naymon, author of *You Between the Lines*

"Swoony, tender, and addictively steamy, Mara Williams's *The Epicenter of Forever* provides a beautiful exploration of the way love in all its forms can heal past hurts that had me desperately turning the pages while praying it would never end."

—Amy Buchanan, author of *Let's Call a Truce*

"A rich, layered story about forgiveness, family, and starting over, *The Epicenter of Forever* is the kind of book that teaches you something about yourself and will leave your heart racing. Williams weaves her signature wit and lush prose through a California landscape filled with big trees, bigger feelings, and love that shakes the world. This was the most magical, immersive, heart-pounding read I've had in ages. *The Epicenter of Forever* is a triumph of emotion from a stunning voice in fiction."

—Isabelle Engel, author of *Most Eligible*

The Truth Is in the Detours

"Why does childhood sweethearts to estranged friends to lovers have to go *so hard*? I loved all the history between Ophelia and Beau in Mara Williams's *The Truth Is in the Detours*, and I loved watching them fall for each other as adults with all the complications that come with having more life experience. By the time they finally hooked up, I had been dying for it to happen—these two were always meant for each other! Mara Williams is definitely a romance writer to watch."

—Alicia Thompson, *USA Today* bestselling author of *Never Been Shipped*

"Clever, funny, and wonderfully romantic, *The Truth Is in the Detours* tells the story of a woman who finally gets to know herself. It delivers all the best story elements: delicious banter, tension, a road trip, gorgeous California settings, and hot romance. I devoured this sharp story. Mara Williams is a talent."

—Sierra Godfrey, author of *A Very Typical Family*

"A rare gem of a book that captures the beauty and pain of grief, love, and finding yourself, while still feeling like a hug. With sentences that sing and settings that feel like characters, *The Truth Is in the Detours* is the perfect blend of frenemies-to-lovers road-trip romance that will steal your heart and set it racing, and a woman's journey to finding herself as she searches for the truth about her family. An outstanding debut."

—Holly James, author of *The Big Fix*

"Mara Williams's debut is everything I love in a frenemies-to-lovers romance: delicious tension, fleshed-out history, and so much pining! The slow-burn romance between Ophelia and Beau delivers (and then some), and the mystery regarding Ophelia's mom kept me riveted to the pages. Williams levels it up even further with masterful writing and vivid imagery that truly allow the reader to feel like a third passenger on the road trip. I could smell the salt water and feel the sand between my toes like I was right there with them. *The Truth Is in the Detours* is a must-read for this summer!"

—Meredith Schorr, author of *Roommating*

The
Epicenter
of
Forever

ALSO BY MARA WILLIAMS

The Truth Is in the Detours

The Epicenter of Forever

a novel

MARA WILLIAMS

LAKE UNION
PUBLISHING

Published by Lake Union Publishing, Seattle
www.apub.com

Amazon, the Amazon logo, and Lake Union Publishing are trademarks of Amazon.com, Inc., or its affiliates.

EU product safety contact:
Amazon Media EU S. à r.l.
38, avenue John F. Kennedy, L-1855 Luxembourg
amazonpublishing-gpsr@amazon.com

ISBN-13: 9781662528941 (paperback)
ISBN-13: 9781662528958 (digital)

Cover design by Sarah Horgan
Cover images: © Lana Brow, © harkani, © Max_Lockwood,
© saturevibes / Shutterstock

Printed in the United States of America

For anyone mourning a dream but daring to dance anyway.

For my parents, who taught me to dream big and paid for all those dance lessons.

And for Kenny, who supports this wild dream of mine and defies his two left feet to dance with me.

CHAPTER 1

I must have fallen for a billion little lies to wind up here, unexpectedly face-to-face with my ex and his pregnant girlfriend barely a week after our divorce.

As my failed marriage flashes before my eyes, I tally every deceit and decide the cruelest one was his bullshit reason for leaving. *We only hit one note,* he said with a single suitcase in hand. Of course, I didn't know he was lying then, even though the truth should have been obvious. Cheating, after all, is part of my origin story.

"Eden, wow," Jeff says now in the polite tone reserved for acquaintances. "What a surprise. It's nice to see you."

I have no idea how I feel about seeing him because I can't look away from the woman holding his hand. I'm disappointed in myself that my first thought is a petty one: She's pretty but not beautiful. She has mousy brown hair that frizzes at her temples, flat blue eyes framed by blunt lashes, and overplucked brows. I'm not sure I'd notice her if she weren't flaunting the evidence of Jeff's betrayal with a full abdomen that does the math for me.

My second thought is a devastating one—I bet this new girlfriend, round with the baby Jeff refused to give me, must play him a motherfucking symphony.

"You too." I accept Jeff's hug. I don't think to hold my breath, forgetting scent memory is the most stubborn. I'd bought him this Tom Ford cologne on the last anniversary we celebrated together.

Memories of that day invade like an occupying force: Baker Beach at dusk, take-out coffee cooling in my palms, fog so thick we couldn't see the bridge.

"Eden, this is Nadia. Nadia, this is Eden."

Nadia. Nadia. Nadia. The name is familiar but less potent than the cologne.

"It's nice to meet you, Eden." Nadia extends her hand.

It's disorienting to live in two worlds at once. Internally, I'm devastated by the delayed realization that my marriage ended in infidelity. I'm furious that Jeff fed me a half-truth drenched in a sad metaphor, and I fell for it. But externally, I'm politely shaking the hand of the woman he must have been sleeping with while I did his laundry and bought his mom's birthday present. Worst of all, my irrational composure validates Jeff's frequent complaint that I'm incapable of passionate emotions. And maybe he's right. I should be yelling, screaming, crying. Instead, I'm undergoing a system reboot.

Cassie emerges from the restroom and steps into the cramped café lobby. Her gaze darts from me to Jeff to Nadia, drawing immediate conclusions.

"Jeffrey, what a surprise," she says. "Who's this?"

Jeff's face goes pale. Somehow, I didn't suspect he was a cheating scumbag, but I can tell he's scared shitless by the look on Cassie's face.

Cassie extends her hand to Nadia, and Nadia takes it, giving a good impression of nonchalance if her left eye weren't twitching.

"I'm Cassie, Eden's best friend. At their wedding, I gave a speech about what a nice guy Jeff was. But I guess even smart women get duped by assholes."

"Cassie," Jeff warns.

Cassie cocks her head toward Nadia's pregnant belly. "Yours?"

Jeff looks at me before pursing his lips and nodding.

"Congratulations. When are you due?" Cassie asks Nadia, the hard edge of her voice smoothed to velvet.

Nadia hesitates, looks at Jeff, whose gaze is ensnared with mine, and stutters, "Friday."

Cassie spits out a laugh. "Nice, Jeff. So this is why you bowed out of our friend group? Not because you wanted Eden to have her 'support system,' but because you were trying to hide that you'd knocked up someone else? What happened to not wanting kids?"

"Cass," Jeff says.

"Don't 'Cass' me. You made it clear we're no longer friends. At least now we know why."

We're drawing the attention of a family waiting for a table. A teen in sweatpants and an oversize T-shirt gawks openly while her parents avert their gazes. Sunday brunch in a crowded San Francisco café does not permit discretion.

"Cassie," I hiss as I tug on her arm. "Let's go."

"No, stay. We'll go," Jeff says, ever magnanimous. "Enjoy your brunch. Try the matcha waffles, Edie. You'll love them."

Cassie's incredulous laugh attracts more stares from nearby guests. I wish Jeff would let us leave, that he would grant me this one kindness. But Jeff, I see now, is not kind. I thought he was, but I confused politeness for kindness. Jeff holds the door open for Nadia, and the bell chimes as her name finally rings a bell in my brain.

"She was your physical therapist." The words escape without my permission, loud enough that Jeff turns. This time, his wince is full-body—a slight shudder.

Jeff whispers, "I'm sorry, Edie," but looks away. He places his hand on the small of Nadia's back—a gesture I feel against my own skin like a phantom—and escorts her out.

"Eden, party of two?" the host calls from behind us.

"That's us." Cassie puts her hand around my waist, holding me up as we walk. I slide into a booth across from my oldest friend as the host places menus in front of us.

"What a cockmuppet," Cassie says. "I hope he catches his dick in his zipper again and has to be examined by a room full of med students.

I hope Carmex stops manufacturing that lip balm he's obsessed with, and his lips crack until they bleed. I hope he stubs his toe and gets a paper cut every day for the rest of his miserable little life."

I wish I could express outrage like Cassie. I wish I could *feel* as deeply as Cassie, but my emotional muscle was torn in two a long time ago and never healed, forcing me to watch my most dramatic moments happen from a distance. I'm lucky to have Cassie feel them for me. She is unapologetically herself—definitive, direct—voicing thoughts I can't articulate out loud. Even my appearance is less decisive. Whereas Cassie is a striking brunette with a rich tan and chestnut eyes, my hair is not quite brown or blond, straight or curly. My eyes can't make up their mind between green, blue, and hazel, and my complexion changes with the weather.

"I can't believe that slutbag," Cassie continues. "Pretending he's the bigger man. 'I'll let Eden keep the house, friends, and favorite corner coffee shop,' when really he was trying to protect his precious reputation while committing Douchebaggery 101." She throws the menu open.

I'm barely listening to Cassie's rant. Instead, I'm scrolling through my phone, checking old entries in our shared calendar, trying to figure out how long ago he started physical therapy and met the woman he left me for. I freeze when I land on September, eighteen months ago. The appointments are blocked out three times a week for a year. Jeff knew Nadia when we bought the couch we'd saved up for, when I had an emergency appendectomy, and when I replaced my IUD because he still hadn't changed his mind about children. I was hoping he'd come around. And I waited, wasting so many years.

How much of a sham was I living?

Cassie grabs my hand. "Maybe this is the turning point in the story, you know? It's the big twist, and now you've pulled his mask off, you know he's the villain, and—"

"This is not an episode of *Scooby-Doo*, Cass."

"But—"

I hold up both hands and loosen my shoulders. "I'm fine. Fuck him."

"Yeah! Fuck him," she roars, a deep, guttural sound. Heads turn, and a middle-aged blond woman glares at the back of Cassie's head, covering her son's ears. "How does it feel to say that?"

"Shh." I dart my focus across the dining room, wary of the attention we're attracting.

"Don't shush me. This is a powerful moment. This is your moment." If this is my moment—sitting down to brunch after learning my ex-husband impregnated the woman I didn't know he left me for—my life is sadder than I thought.

"I think . . ." She pauses, a rarity in conversation with Cass. It typically means she's not sure she should say what's coming next. Her track record suggests she shouldn't but absolutely will. "The hardest thing about the divorce is you didn't understand it. You two were solid, and then you weren't. And Jeff's explanations didn't add up. Maybe this is closure. He's just a standard-issue cheating scumbag. Now you know." She lifts her shoulders in an apologetic shrug and chews her bottom lip.

My phone rattles on the table. I should ignore it. But the alternative is listening to Cassie tell me about the hardest part of my failed marriage while her adoring husband waits for her at home. I don't check the number before I answer. It could be a telemarketer selling an extended warranty or asking me to take a survey. Either option is preferable to Cassie's well-intentioned but clumsy psychoanalysis.

"Hello?"

"Eden Hawthorne?" a reedy voice asks.

"That's me." I plug my other ear and whisper into the phone, hoping to avoid additional judgment from our fellow diners.

"This is Adelaide Chan." *Adelaide, Adelaide.* I scan my mental Rolodex for the name, but it's escaping me just like Nadia did a moment ago. I think shock kills brain cells. "Your mom's friend? I'm her neighbor." Or maybe I keep all artifacts related to my pain locked away in the same faraway vault. "I hope I'm not out of step calling you, but I think you should take a trip out to Grand Trees to visit your mom."

The suggestion erupts across my nerves like a lit fuse. If seeing Jeff threw me into darker days, mention of my mother drop-kicks my heart into pitch black. Mom and I aren't estranged exactly. We talk—sometimes.

When I don't respond, Adelaide continues, "Caleb's been helping out, you know. But Abby had a cold all week, so he didn't want to expose your mom, what with her diagnosis. And I didn't realize how much he's been doing or how bad it's gotten. Caleb just handles it without complaint. But I learned a lot this week, and I thought it was about time for you to visit and convince your mom that treatment will help."

My attention snags on "diagnosis." I can't keep up with this woman's monologue, complete with a cast of characters I've never heard of. I don't even know what questions to ask.

"Diagnosis?" I mutter.

"She says there's nothing to be done, but I went to the library, looked up some articles online, and there are good treatments available. Since Sonny died, I think your mom has given up. And I get it. When my husband died, it took me years to accept that I still had a life to live. But you know your mother. She's as stubborn as they come and . . ."

Cassie frowns and mouths, "Who is that?"

My head feels like it's been pressed in a vise, my temples pounding, and my skin stretched taut and thin. I slide out of the booth and move to the exit, searching for air as Adelaide prattles on about people who all seem to know my mom in ways I don't.

"I'm sorry." I emerge into the cool morning air. "Diagnosis?" I repeat, begging for context but unable to admit I know less about the woman who raised me than this stranger on the phone.

"Well, yes," Adelaide says, clueing in, and sympathy coats her words like buttercream. "The Parkinson's, dear."

CHAPTER 2

It's Friday—Nadia's due date—when I pull into Grand Trees. The town sits at the southern edge of the Sierras, home to giant sequoias and pine forests but not far from the white sand and cacti of the Southern California desert. It's a tumultuous vista of all the American West has to offer. For a time, it was my favorite place on earth, back when I used to believe in its magic. When I used to believe in magic at all.

It took me all week to convince myself that I could withstand a couple of days here, and my resolve has frayed with each mile eaten up by my tires.

Somewhere in the recess of my mind, Jeff's betrayal and Adelaide's call are connected. In order to process my most recent heartbreak, I must finally stop running from my first. It's as if Grand Trees extended its haunted branches across the state to drag me back into its fold. *Look,* it whispers through its windswept limbs. *This is where your life derailed. You must retrace your steps to get it back on track.* Or it could be a cruel cosmic joke, and the universe wants to kick me while I'm down. Or maybe I'm just a coward who's running to avoid thoughts of Jeff and his imminent fatherhood. Maybe running is the only way I know how to cope. Perhaps home and here are the two poles that control my gravity.

I'm starving after the seven-hour drive. It must be nerves, because I've done nothing but snack since I forced myself into the car. I bypass the restaurants that Mom and I once frequented and head toward

Nowhere Saloon. It's been here as long as I can remember, even though Mom never took me inside, which is part of its allure, I suppose.

I park along the curb and gather myself before stretching my right leg. It still gets stiff on long drives. I take several steps before coaxing the limp back into hibernation.

Pushing through the double doors, I take in the brick walls, brass bar rail, worn leather booths, and dim overhead pendant lights. I navigate through the sea of revelers to settle at the bar, climbing onto a swivel stool at the corner. It's a mixed clientele. If I had to guess, most are tourists. I feel like I'm back in the Bay Area when I catch fragments of a conversation about tech stocks.

A group of men crowds me while watching a basketball game. They gesture aggressively toward the television as if they can sway the officials from here. An older group across the bar checks out a hockey game on the smaller screen over my shoulder, and a quartet of women in their twenties waits as the bartender pours colorful cocktails. When a roar erupts from the crowd beside me, I pivot to the TV, but my gaze lands on a man standing alone, leaning on the mahogany bar with one elbow. He's broad shouldered and imposing, with dark waves poking out from under a beanie, his jaw hidden behind a scruffy beard, which is unkempt but can't hide his soft mouth. My perusal catches on a white scar that bisects the fullest part of his upper lip, creating the illusion of an off-center Cupid's bow. My instinct is to look away, but then I remember I can admire an attractive man. I can do more than that, actually. God knows Jeff did a shit ton more than that. I'm single now, although out of practice and a little gun-shy.

The bartender makes her way over to him, and when he whispers something to her, the shell of my ear warms in response. She nods once before pouring a beer from the tap. His gaze shifts, and I flush when he catches me studying him, but something in his steady stare is more powerful than my embarrassment. As our eye contact lingers, a bolt of lightning electrifies my nerves. It's exciting and unnerving to be watched by a stranger and have the confidence to let him.

I'm startled by something wet on my cheek, a splash of beer from the drink my neighbor just slammed on the bar. I drag my gaze away from my mystery man, and my clumsy seatmate turns as I wipe the liquid off my face.

"My bad." He hands me a napkin.

"No problem." I take it from him and wipe the spot below my eye.

"They really need to get a rebound. They're getting killed on the boards, you know?"

I bob my head in a gesture that's neither a shake nor a nod.

"Games are won on defense."

"Right," I say, because he probably is, even though I don't know or care. Jeff loved basketball. His team, the Warriors, is playing. Maybe he's watching from the delivery room, shouting at the small TV while Nadia breathes through contractions.

"I'm Darren."

"Eden." I shake his proffered hand but turn back to my phone immediately. I'm single, but I still have standards. He's a close talker, and the smell of the beer on this guy's breath kills the burgeoning sparks of desire my mystery man ignited.

"As in *Garden of?*"

I force a smile and don't respond, hoping he'll go back to the game. Making an obvious joke about my name is such a self-absorbed move. It assumes I haven't already heard that joke about a hundred times, as if I haven't lived with my own name until this moment. Eden's not a biblical reference, at least not directly. Dad's an amateur horticulturist. He's told me that my birth was the only thing more magical than coaxing an orchid to thrive.

There's a commercial break, so Darren's focus returns to me. Well, not *me* precisely: my breasts, which are not on display. And even if they were, the display would be minimalist. He looks back at my face.

"Are you in town for the Mud Run, too?" he asks. Nothing about that question surprises me. Darren has that restless middle-aged bro quality, like an old high school athlete trying to reclaim his former glory.

"No." I return my attention to my phone again, hoping he gets the point. He might be a perfectly nice guy, but I have no need to find out. I sneak a glance at the end of the bar and see the mystery man is gone.

"What brought you here, then?" he asks with half his attention on the game.

"Family." I wave to the bartender. But no luck.

"Visiting home. Nice." Darren leans closer. He's wearing so much cologne, it's aggressive. It's a spicy, antiseptic scent.

"Something like that."

"Well, if you need to get away from Mommy and Daddy, you should come by the race tomorrow. I'm running in it." He leers at me but keeps one eye on the game.

I offer a noncommittal nod as he high-fives a friend in celebration of a buzzer-beater to end the half.

I start tomorrow's crossword puzzle on my *New York Times* app. He doesn't take the hint because then he says, "And I'd love to have a pretty cheerleader at the finish line."

I look toward the end of the bar, hoping to grab the bartender's attention. I really don't want to give up this seat. But this guy has gone beyond chatty, leaped over flirty, and has landed somewhere near creepy.

Darren leans perilously close to my personal space. "Let me buy you a drink."

I shift away. "No, thanks. I'm just here to grab food to go," I say, which is a lie. I wanted to linger, stall, and take enough time to rebalance my blood sugar before heading to my mom's house and whatever awaits me there.

Darren laughs, and it's a condescending chuckle. "You can stay for one drink. C'mon, lighten up."

"I'm good," I say evenly.

But he waves to the bartender, his long arms grabbing the attention of the tattooed beauty with a purple pixie cut. "Let me guess," he calls over his shoulder. "Rosé?"

"I'm going to head out—"

"I'm sorry I'm late," someone beside me hums. I do a double take because the words seem intended for me, spoken by the man who just squeezed in beside Darren, who lowers his arm and inspects our new guest.

I startle when I realize he's the hot lumberjack who had been standing beneath the TV earlier. I wait for him to apologize, laugh, and say he thought I was someone else, but he doesn't. His whiskey-colored eyes widen in a conspiratorial look before he rests his forearm on the bar. "I hope you weren't waiting long."

And that voice. There's gravel in it; it's so low I have to lean forward to hear his words, but the vibration lands somewhere deep in the center of me, rattling something alive. My heart does a stutter step when he whispers in my ear, "Need a rescue?"

I pick up the hint, taking my chances that this knight in rugged armor might have noble intentions, even though I am, obviously, a pathetic judge of character. I nod.

The knight gestures to the far wall. "I have a booth." And it sounds like a proposition, one that I wouldn't take if I weren't so captivated by whatever his voice is doing to my insides.

I pause a few beats, calculating my odds, before sliding off the stool. He points to the far corner, and I lead the way through the labyrinth of bodies as Darren glares at us.

"Thanks for the save," I say.

"Consider it your Grand Trees welcome." His voice is dry and raspy.

A half-empty mug of beer is resting on the tabletop, and he gestures to the far side.

"Do you do that often?" I slide into the booth.

"What?" After he settles across from me, he takes a swig of his beer, and I watch as he swallows, mesmerized.

"Rescue women from drunken bros?" I unzip my fleece and set it beside me on the bench.

"It's a first for me. But we sold our town's soul for the tourist revenue those meatheads bring in. It's the least we can do."

I should have guessed he's a local. He certainly wears the uniform, a soft charcoal flannel open over a navy thermal. But these days, even city boys wear hiking attire to stare at a screen all day. Jeff's favorite brand was Patagonia, even though the outdoorsiest thing he ever did was drag the trash to the curb. This guy wears it like it's meant to, filling out the chest and shoulders like he chops wood, shovels snow, and volunteers as a firefighter to carry people from burning buildings. The crew neck of his thermal grazes a tree branch of a clavicle that's putting in some work to support those sizable deltoids. Even his hands are brawny, and his forearms flex below his rolled cuffs as he spins his beer on the tabletop.

You don't see guys like him in my world, working from home as a nonprofit fundraiser while mourning my failed marriage. To be honest, I don't see many guys at all in my world.

I gesture toward his beer, dragging my gaze away from the distraction of his physical form. "What's the secret to ordering something around here? I've been trying to get the bartender's attention for ten minutes."

"I'll get you a drink." He watches me over the rim of his mug as he takes another sip. His eyes reveal nothing but seem to drink me in.

"No, no. I didn't mean to imply—"

"Don't worry about it. I'm not trying to pick you up." He offers a tease of a smile, hinting at the transformation his face might make if he unleashed a full grin. "I saw that idiot strike out. I don't like my odds."

"Oh . . . uh," I stammer, and he chuckles, seemingly enjoying my awkwardness. He spins a large menu on the table so it's facing me.

"I'm just waiting for a to-go order, and then you'll have this booth to yourself. Let me know what you want. I know the secret to getting the bartender's attention."

I bet he does. My gaze trails to his calloused fingertips, his forearms, his shoulders. "Does it require having a beard and biceps?" I ask before ducking my head to scan the menu. Am I flirting? I don't flirt. Well, I haven't in fifteen years, at least. His silence on the opposite end of the table is telling. He just said he wasn't interested. And I'm not interested in men on principle. My face heats in embarrassment.

"Well, that," he rasps, "and her cell." His thumbs hover over his phone. "What are you having?"

I feel the pressure to choose quickly. Comfort food seems like a solid choice before heading into an uncomfortable confrontation with Mom. "The grilled cheese and tomato soup combo. And sparkling water."

He fires off the text and settles back in the booth, taking a long sip of his ale. He studies me for a moment, removing his beanie and rubbing a hand through his hair until it's a tousled mess. If I had to guess, I'd say he hasn't had a haircut in months. Probably hasn't trimmed that beard either. He's a far cry from the guys back home with their beard wax, expensive trimmers, and impeccable grooming. They can't compete with those amber eyes of his, though, which seem to be stripping me as I inspect him.

He's not wearing a ring. If he works with his hands, as I suspect, he likely wouldn't wear one anyway, so he could be married. But I would bet my house that he doesn't have a girlfriend. Girlfriends inspire boyfriends to groom themselves, even if they give up once married.

"Where do I know you from?" he asks abruptly.

The question catches me off guard, and it must be a line because we have not met. I would remember him.

"I thought you weren't trying to pick me up."

He shakes his head. "Seriously. I know you from somewhere. Are you a seasonal?"

"A what?"

He leans onto the table, hands clasped and forearm muscles engaged, as his gaze picks me apart. "Do you come on summers and holidays?"

Not since I was a teenager, and that was too long ago for either of us to remember.

"Nope, and I don't think we've met." But he's so certain. I strip away the years on his face to find the younger version of him without the fine lines around his eyes and the overgrown beard. I'm drawing a blank. It's hard to picture the boy underneath all that scruff. We're probably about the same age, give or take a few years. Was he one of the few locals who attended summer camp? Mostly, I got to know a rotating group of kids who, like me, came from out of town. Maybe he was a counselor one summer?

"What's your name?" He drags his gaze across my face, and I stammer before a paper bag lands on the table between us.

"All right, Sunshine. Two burgers, fries, and one potpie. You taking the potpie to Nicki?" I glance up at the bartender. She has two full sleeves of ink. She's wearing a white crop top, high-rise Levi's, and a small black apron tied around her tiny waist.

"Yeah." That rasp returns to his voice before he clears it. "Thanks."

Nicki? Hmm . . . Maybe there is a woman in his life. Which is fine, considering he was clear about not being interested before trying to convince me we knew each other way back when.

"You're good to her. Give her my love, okay?"

"Yeah. Will do."

She turns to me. "And you ordered the grilled cheese, right? It'll be out in a few."

She has the bone structure for beauty risks, like those tattoos she might someday regret and the close-cropped purple hair that would make me look like a Teletubby. "Yeah. Thanks. And separate checks, please."

She offers a perfunctory smile and strides away.

The man saws at his bottom lip as he grabs the bag off the table. "All right," he says, still studying me. "Enjoy your trip." He slides out of the booth, and I hurry to offer another thank-you as he slips through the crowd. The hand he holds up is the only proof that he hears me.

When the meal comes, I eat quickly so Darren won't notice I've been left alone. The cheddar and mozzarella are melted to perfection between golden sourdough bread, and the tomato soup is just the right balance of tangy and sweet. It's the comfort food I need to fortify me for the confrontation to come. When I ask for the check, the pretty bartender waves me away.

"Already taken care of. He said to tell you it's your official Grand Trees welcome."

CHAPTER 3

After I eat, I drag myself back to the car to do what I came for.

The landscape of Grand Trees is too familiar. That first summer Mom and I left San Francisco to spend six weeks among the sequoias—me as a pint-size camper and Mom as the art teacher—I was escorted by the flutter of butterflies in my gut and watched as the cityscape shifted to meadow, then mountains, then majestic redwoods. When we left Grand Trees for the last time seven summers later, our escorts home were my fury and Mom's shame. But guilt rides shotgun this time, with my adolescent outrage still coiled tight in the back seat, ready to steal the wheel if I let it.

Mom lives at the end of a one-lane road on the outskirts of town, right at the border of the summer camp property. I have a hard time thinking of the house as Mom's, even though it's been two decades since she left us to move in with Sonny.

Muscle memory guides me along the route. I remember each turn, having identified the landmarks as a child, with my forehead pressed to the window, counting the moments until we arrived. Sonny hosted weekend parties for the summer camp staff, and I tagged along with Mom. While the other campers headed home, filled with formative memories and promises of new pen pals, I was the cool kid invited into the inner circle. We'd celebrate with Sonny's improvised songs on guitar, and I'd dance as he sang. I adored Sonny, until I didn't. Until

I was filled with shame that I didn't notice how friendly he and Mom were becoming.

I make a slight right when I spot the abandoned fishing skiff on the side of the gravel drive. I almost miss it—the once-white boat is corroded, and the hull is a pure rust color. It bleeds into the background, becoming one with the redwoods, a reminder that the forest will return everything to dust eventually.

I slow to a crawl as I skate over potholes and kick up gravel against the fender. Finally, the house comes into view, and the nostalgia catches me off guard. It's built around a tree that survived a big fire, which ravaged these forests and created a clearing with one strong ponderosa pine at its center. It always felt sacred to me, as if the nearby trees gave the ponderosa a wide berth, grasping branches and spreading out in a concentric circle like a ritual.

Sonny told me that the house was enchanted. He insisted the whole town was magic—that once it became part of you, it would burrow into your bones. He was right, I suppose. Grand Trees has stayed with me, but not in the way he meant.

Parking beside a newer-model black truck, I grip the steering wheel and brace myself for this reunion. Once out, I climb the porch steps and lift the hummingbird knocker, and noise explodes in its wake. A threatening bark comes closer and closer, matched by raised voices and rapid paws on wood.

"Houdini!" The shout startles me as if it's the first chant of a code phrase I'll need to answer to gain entry, which wouldn't be off brand for Sonny's tree house.

The paws screech to a halt, and the barking ceases immediately. "Houdini!" the voice says, quieter now, before "Kennel." I hear softer paws that prattle before fading out.

Finally, the door swings open, and my heart does a little hiccup.

There's a beat of silence before he narrows his eyes. "I knew I knew you."

His words are both an epiphany and an accusation.

But I still don't know who this guy is or why he's in the doorway of Sonny's—I mean, Mom's—house. The dog barks again; the mystery man hushes him with a quick command.

"Caleb? Who is it?" My stomach drops at the sound of Mom's voice coming from inside the house. I'm not ready for this. Not even a little bit ready for this.

I shake my head, and my knight frowns, studying me with those liquid eyes. He wasn't warm at the bar, per se, but in comparison, now he's an iceberg. His huge body is rigid, and his stance is wide, as if blocking the threshold. He folds his arms across his chest like a challenge, and I whisper, "I'll come back later," because I'm suddenly too disoriented to confront Mom tonight.

"Delivery," he shouts toward inside. "Just a second, Nicki."

Nicki? Nicki? Nicolette Hawthorne never tolerated anyone calling her Nicki. But I guess she hasn't been Nicolette Hawthorne in a long time.

To my surprise, Caleb steps onto the porch and closes the door behind him. "I don't know what your deal is—"

"My deal?" I rasp, taking a step back from his threatening posture. "You don't know me."

"You're Eden, Nicolette's daughter, who hasn't bothered to pay her mom a visit in twenty years." That deep voice is venomous now, but I still feel it like a bass line nudging my body alive. "And you show up on her porch without an invite and then scurry away like that sweet woman is someone to be scared of."

Who the hell is this guy? As if it's my responsibility to visit my mom. As if I'm the one who did *her* wrong.

"I don't know who you think you are to lecture me about my relationship with my mother, but you obviously have been fed some bullshit. It hasn't been twenty years. I came to Sonny's funeral." But even to my ears, it sounds like a weak excuse. "And I'm here now."

"But are you stayin'? 'Cause if you were planning on running out of here like you did at the funeral, I think I'll just tell Nicki the delivery driver had the wrong address. I don't want her heart broken."

"*Her* heart broken?" How dare he spin this, and how does he know I left the funeral early? "Again, who the hell are you?" I can't help but yell.

I didn't even yell at Jeff when he walked out. Or when he walked into my new favorite café with his pregnant mistress. But this guy. The Grand Trees Welcoming Committee, who pegged me as a damsel in distress and had the audacity to pay for my meal without my permission and then lecture me about my mother. He thinks I'm the villain? This man deserves to be yelled at.

But he doesn't even flinch, his frame on guard in front of the colorful patchwork of Sonny's front door and the hummingbird knocker I once loved so much. When he speaks, it's with forced calm, barely a growl.

"I'm the guy who watched your mom paint your portrait for the last twenty years. And I'm the guy who's been taking care of her since Uncle Sonny died. And the fact that you don't even know who the hell I am says about all I need to know about you."

Uncle Sonny?

The front door swings open, slamming into Caleb's back as all hell breaks loose.

"Houdini! Houdini, stop!" a young voice calls before a wild mass of fur and paws pummels me. I lurch back and run into the porch railing. I'm accosted by a tongue longer than on any domesticated animal I've ever seen. He gets in two licks to my face before someone catches the dog around the collar and yanks him back. The dog is howling, and I feel a sensation resembling slime trickling down my neck.

When I steady myself, I notice a coltish teen with her hand on the dog's collar as he jumps like a freshly caught fish on the line. The girl has stick-straight dark hair with blunt bangs and limbs she hasn't grown into. "I'm so sorry," she says between pants of breath. "We're still training him. But he's friendly, I swear. He just doesn't have"—she pauses as the dog unleashes another howl—"any chill."

I wipe my face and brush my shirt, but it's hopeless. I have a fur coat and dusty paw prints perfectly aligned over my boobs. "It's all right."

The girl cranes her neck to Caleb as the dog twists and squirms, trying to wriggle free. "Dad, can you help me?"

"Houdini, down," Caleb says, and the dog drops to his belly and gazes up at him with hearts in his eyes. I guess Caleb's voice has that effect on everyone.

It also dawns on me that this jerk could have prevented my assault with one stern command. I glare at him, and he raises his brow in challenge.

The girl looks from Caleb to me and back.

"Abby, can you give us a minute, sweetheart?" His tone brooks no argument.

But I'm done. We don't need a minute. I need to check in to the bed-and-breakfast, take a shower, sleep off this strange day, and visit tomorrow after a full night's sleep.

Just as I turn, I hear shuffling from inside, a dragging gait, and the door creaking open again. "What are you two doing out here?"

I look up to see my mom in the doorway, her face falling when she meets my gaze.

"Eden?" she whispers. She stopped dying her hair, so the silver falls across her shoulders like a shawl. Her blue eyes are cloudy, so unlike the twinkling sapphires I knew so well. And there are deep grooves around her smile. When did I last see her? Last year? The year before? And then I realize it's been three years. The funeral. I haven't seen her since Sonny died. And she's aged about ten since then.

She steps onto the porch, and Caleb grabs her hand, steadying her as she comes to me, wrapping her thin arms around my shoulders in an embrace that steals my resolve to leave.

"Who is she?" Abby stage-whispers to Caleb.

But whatever he says is lost to the sound of Mom's relieved tears as she burrows her face in my neck.

CHAPTER 4

"We just finished eating, but I can throw something together." Mom drags me across the threshold. *Drags* is not quite right, really, but she's surprisingly effective at steering me, even though I'm holding her up. She hasn't even asked me why I'm here, as if it's perfectly normal for me to swing by on a Friday evening.

"Thanks, but I've eaten already."

"Okay, then, you can stay for game night. Do you have a game picked out, Abby?" Mom glances over her shoulder at Abby and Caleb, and I catch a whiff of the honeysuckle scent of her perfume. *Home,* I think, before I remember and dispatch the instinct.

"Sure do, Grams," Abby calls back.

My pulse thunders in my ears. *Grams.* This girl calls my mother Grams. Jeff is having a baby that's not mine. My mom has a granddaughter who isn't mine either.

We shuffle into the house, where the sunset bleeds through the windows and barrels through the hole in its center where the tree grows. The familiarity of the home sends conflicting signals to my brain, homesickness and horror battling for control. The cylindrical glass structure encasing the trunk reflects the varied colors like a prism. *Sunset and sunrise,* Sonny would say, *are when you need to be closest to nature.* At camp, the sunset was honored every night. We'd hike to Colibri Peak and have ten minutes of silence as the sun descended, or sing meditative songs in the amphitheater, where the crimson light would beam down on us like a benediction.

Here in this house, you don't need to pause to notice its beauty. The sunset demands attention like a ballerina taking center stage. The first floor is a single open space that curves around the tree. Mom nudges me toward the dining area. The house is the same in many ways, but the muted bring-the-nature-in design Sonny favored is punctuated by Mom's bright artwork on every wall, vivid oil paintings on canvas without a theme to ground them. When I settle Mom at the head of the live-edge dining table, I note a collection of portraits on the wall behind her. They're all me. As a baby, toddler, child, and several of me as a teen, as if I got stuck at that age in her mind forever.

In the biggest one, I'm in costume. It's my first professional tutu, and I'm posing in a simple épaulement. It's the long, straight line of a girl who didn't know how lucky she was.

I feel Caleb's gaze on me as I inspect it. I dart my focus to him, and he's unabashed. His expression is biting. *I'm the guy who watched your mom paint your portrait for the last twenty years.*

She painted the same version of me over and over and over again—the me I was before she broke me. If I could wield a brush, I would have painted me, too.

"Edie, honey, sit here." My mom's smooth hand curls in mine and coaxes me into the seat to her right, giving me a view of several portraits of Sonny—his head thrown back in laughter, his body curved over the neck of his guitar, leading the campers at the nightly campfire.

Abby settles at the table, shuffling a deck of cards like a dealer in a casino.

"Would you like a glass of wine?" Mom asks, pointing to a bottle on the table.

"No. No, thank you," I say. The last thing my fragile nerves need is alcohol.

"Oh." Abby gasps. "That's you." She points to a canvas, and I notice Caleb is still staring at my portrait. It feels like a violation that I've been hanging here on exhibit all this time. I don't know if I should be flattered or horrified that Caleb and Abby recognize me from those old portraits. I couldn't have been more than fourteen in them.

"Oh dear." Mom laughs uncomfortably. "Abby, I'm sorry, honey. This is Eden, my daughter. And Eden, this is Caleb, Sonny's nephew. And Abby is his daughter. You've heard me talk about them, of course."

But I haven't. I know I haven't because when we speak, it's like she's in denial that she lives in Grand Trees. She can't casually mention people from the town and simultaneously pretend she didn't ditch me to move here. In the intervening years, Mom mentioned Sonny only twice—once to tell me he proposed and once to tell me he was gone. She never mentioned a nephew or a child. Mom doesn't know I'm divorced, and I didn't know she had a new family, which is a surreal discovery. I have tried so hard not to imagine her here with Sonny because it felt disloyal to Dad, but I have worried about how she was faring since Sonny's death. I just couldn't bring myself to return after my failed attempt with the funeral.

"We do game night on Fridays," Mom says. "What are we playing tonight, Abby?"

"Asshole." A grin blooms on Abby's face.

"Language," Caleb warns.

"It's the name of the game," she protests without the slightest bit of fear.

"Actually," Caleb says, "we should let Grams catch up with Eden." He stands behind Abby, with his hands resting on the back of her chair.

"But we play every Friday," she says.

"Don't leave on my account," I say. "I have a room at a bed-and-breakfast. And I had a long drive, so I can't stay late tonight." It was once a five-hour drive from San Francisco to Grand Trees, but years ago, the main highway was wiped out in a landslide, and the detour added another two.

"Oh," Mom says. "You came all this way to stay at a motel?" Her voice is soft, a little pleading. Does she really expect me to stay here? Really?

For a brief moment, I'm grateful we have an audience. Perhaps I can delay the uncomfortable conversations until tomorrow, when I'll have to confront her about why she didn't tell me about the diagnosis, and why she's unwilling to seek treatment. I can do my duty, change her mind, and get out of here by Sunday.

"Dad, can we still do game night? Please?" Abby tilts her head back to gaze at her father, flashing a smile I suspect typically works.

"Fine," he says. "But not too late. We have the festival tomorrow. And no more swearing."

Abby perks up, straightening her spine and dealing cards to each of us until the deck is empty. "We're playing A-hole." She enunciates slowly, and Caleb's jaw tenses as he flashes her a warning. "Have you ever played?" she addresses me as Caleb sinks into the chair between Abby and Mom, perched on the end as if he might change his mind.

I shake my head, and Abby launches into a description of a game that sounds familiar, actually. "Oh, wait. I have played this."

I remember it vaguely as a drinking game I'd played in college but omit that part. Caleb sighs when I cast a glance in his direction.

"I know what you're thinking," he says, and I wonder why he thinks he can read my mind, irritated at how presumptuous he is. "But we play without alcohol."

I organize my hand and ignore the weird tingle when I realize he did, in fact, read my mind. "What are the stakes?"

"Pride," Caleb says.

Noted.

My mom grasps my forearm, releasing a relieved sigh. "I'm so glad you're here, Edie. How long are you staying?"

"The weekend."

Mom releases me, placing her palm flat on the table. "Okay," she whispers. "Are you sure you can't stay here?"

I feel Caleb's focus on me, and it's strange because I barely know him, but I can imagine the expression on his face, as if whatever answer I give will be the wrong one.

"Next time, Mom. I can't show up unannounced and have you host me." I hope my forced smile looks natural.

"Next time." She pats my arm once again. "I like the sound of that."

"Youngest goes first," Abby declares, throwing two threes onto the table.

Abby looks to be somewhere between twelve and fifteen. She has a complexion I would have envied at her age, with a mouth full of bright-orange rubber bands stretched across metal. She also has a wide-open earnestness that pop culture would have me believe is impossible in adolescence, due to social media and technology destroying their childhoods. She resembles Caleb; they have the same coloring, full lips, and prominent brows. But otherwise, they couldn't be more dissimilar. Abby, even with her braces, has a face that is begging to smile at any opportunity.

On my turn, I play three jacks, winning the hand and clearing the pile.

"Look at the newbie." Abby giggles.

"Beginner's luck." I start the next turn with a single three, and play resumes.

Mom's hands shake slightly as she studies her options before playing two fours.

Abby wins the next turn, clearing the pile with a two, the most powerful card in the deck.

"What grade are you in, Abby?" I ask when the table grows too silent.

"Seventh," she says. "Only one more year of middle school. Thank God," she groans. "It's like the world's worst social experiment. Someone should set a reality show in the halls of junior high."

"Well, it's only up from here." I offer her a sympathetic smile that betrays my real feelings about growing up. "You're twelve?"

"Thirteen," she says, proud. "I keep telling my parents I only have five years till college."

"Hey now." Caleb nudges her shoulder with his. "Slow down, kid."

I notice the mention of "parents" plural, but no one elaborates. Is her mom around? Are she and Caleb together? Maybe she's the pretty bartender from earlier. I remember how they leaned close, how he whispered in her ear. But that couldn't be right. Wouldn't she have been suspicious that he saved me from a lecherous tourist and paid for my meal? No wife is that naive, other than me.

"Abby's so smart she has to take some classes at the high school already. She wants to be a lawyer when she grows up." Mom plays her turn.

I notice Caleb tracking me as I watch the tremor in Mom's hand.

"I want to sue all those evil corporations destroying the world," Abby says.

"Wow, that's ambitious," I say.

"Or a vet," Abby says. "I have time, I guess."

Caleb chuckles before he plays three aces and wins the hand.

Abby groans. "Dad, you always win. It's so annoying."

"I don't find it annoying," he says.

Abby folds the score sheet into a paper airplane and launches it at his head. He grabs it out of midair.

We play for a second, third, and fourth round before Caleb slides out of his chair. "Anyone want something to drink?"

Abby asks for a soda, and Caleb shakes his head. "It's too late for that. Water?"

She rolls her eyes. "Fine."

Caleb heads toward the kitchen, and Houdini scampers out from under the table to follow. I almost forgot he was there, but he sprints to catch up, fixing himself against Caleb's heels.

"What kind of dog is he?" I ask as Abby shuffles.

"He's a mutt. I want to get him DNA tested, but Dad says that's bullshit science." She deals the cards with the dexterity of a pro.

"Language," Caleb yells from the kitchen.

"I'm just repeating you," she calls back. "You're the one with the foul mouth. We think he's German shepherd, Lab, and pit bull, or maybe husky or something."

"And maybe wolf." Caleb returns with a tray in his hands.

"Seriously?" I watch the animal as he trots back into the room on Caleb's heels. He has tufts of wiry hair mixed in with fluff. He's both adorable and awkward.

"Whatever he is, he's definitely first-generation domesticated." Caleb sets the tray on the table before sliding a water glass in front of each of us and a bowl of pretzels beside me.

"Thanks," I say. Perhaps we've graduated from contempt.

Houdini jumps up and puts his paws on the table, hunting for scraps.

"Off," Caleb says, and the dog skulks away to a corner of the carpet, circling three times before landing with a harrumph of protest.

"They rescued him after that big fire last year in the next county over. So many people left, didn't rebuild, and abandoned their dogs. How sad is that?" Mom sorts her hand as the tremor intensifies. I catch it out of the corner of my eye as I try to reconcile this diminished woman with my mother, the bold artist who uprooted her life to paint a lifetime of art pieces in her encore, who left her family for a man so full of life it was contagious.

In her weakened state, it's hard to pin her as the villain of my story. She's wrapped in a shawl, the sheath of fabric cascading to her wrists. The skin of her hands has thinned to a topography of veins and age spots, hiding the precision with which she held a paintbrush, the finality with which she waved goodbye.

"Winner goes first," Abby demands. "Dad," she nudges.

"One more hand, and then we're going to let Grams get some rest."

I win this one, with a decisive victory over Caleb's three kings in the final play, and restrain myself by offering only a self-deprecating shrug.

"All right, Abs. That's our cue to leave," Caleb says.

"What, you losing?" Abby laughs. "And to a girl?"

He pushes his chair back and stands, stretching his arms overhead. I look away as his shirt rides up to show a dark happy trail. I don't want to see more, because it's clear it wouldn't dampen my attraction to this surly man who hates me and is probably happily married.

"Are you calling me a caveman, kid?"

"If the barefoot fits." Abby cackles, and Caleb picks her up by the waist in one arm, spinning her until Houdini gets into the mix, howling and jumping on his hind legs in an arc. Caleb tosses Abby onto the couch with an effortlessness that doesn't escape my cavewoman brain.

"Just for that, you're doing the cleanup while I help Grams upstairs."

Abby's still giggling as she rolls off the couch.

"C'mon, Nicki." Caleb extends an arm to Mom.

"I can get myself upstairs. I'll use the handrails."

How could that not have crossed my mind? The floating spiral staircase hugs the tree, curling around the glass enclosure like a vine. Those steps require a sure foot. I know. It was the excuse I gave for not visiting when she first left. Not that I needed an excuse. She knew exactly why I didn't want to be here.

"I'm sure you do. But humor me, please." Caleb's tone is all sugar for her. This is a man who is selective with his kindness.

Mom sighs but relents, sliding her arm in Caleb's as she stands. "Eden, we have the festival in the town square tomorrow. Caleb's picking me up at nine. You'll come, right?"

It's not like I have a bunch of options. I'm here for Mom. If she's going to a festival, I'm going to a festival. If I only meet her in crowds, I can't confront her about her diagnosis, which might be her strategy. "I'll be there."

CHAPTER 5

When I find a table in the dining room at the B and B the next morning, I can see the crowd gathering across the street in the town square. There are pop-up tents lining the lawn while Top 40 hits blast through portable speakers.

"What brings you to Grand Trees?" the innkeeper asks as she pours coffee and hands me the menu. Her black hair is threaded with silver and woven into a thick braid draped over one shoulder. She's wearing a gingham apron over a gray cotton dress, with a collection of bangles roping up her forearm, and a name tag that says CARMELA.

"Just visiting for the weekend." I don't feel like getting into this conversation with a stranger, who probably isn't a stranger to Mom. I don't need those dots connected before breakfast.

She cranes her neck out the window, following my gaze to the square. "It's not much of an attraction for out-of-towners, but there will be ice cream later."

"What is it?" I ask.

"An emergency preparedness festival."

Are they selling hand-crank radios and fire extinguishers? "I don't think I've ever heard of an emergency preparedness festival."

"Well, this town is perched on a restless earthquake fault, and we've dodged fires that have destroyed sister towns. We fret about landslides during heavy rains and cross our fingers that the levee holds. Somehow, it's sprinkled with fairy dust. But who knows how long that'll last."

She glances at my face and cackles. "Oh goodness, I've scared you. I'm like an anti-tourist commercial." She puts on her best impression of a movie trailer voice. "Come to Grand Trees for the magnificent redwoods. Stay for the mortal danger." She grabs her stomach as she breaks into more laughter.

But I know all about the town's vulnerability and providence. Sonny would weave the town's unique history and geology into campfire stories. He was the town's protector, and I wonder who's looking out for it now.

"Forget I said all that," she continues. "You should check out the hiking trails along the lake. Dog Ear Hollow is gorgeous this time of year. And Maxine's across the way there has a sommelier that'll introduce you to the best wine you've ever tasted."

After I polish off a plate of pancakes and three cups of coffee, I don't have a choice but to head to the town square. At its center is a verdant park punctuated by a white gazebo with spring flowers blooming in planter boxes. Three sides of the park are lined with shops built at the turn of the last century, displaying character and disrepair in equal measure. But the fourth side is a slab of concrete buildings so plain it stands out like a redacted line of text on an antique scroll, a scar on the otherwise picturesque scene. As Sonny once told me, an earthquake rattled the town in the seventies. The original brick buildings were built on the fault and fell like dominoes. They were replaced with retrofitted buildings that may withstand the next big one but won't win any design awards.

It's still brisk even though spring is waking from this prolonged winter. I forgot how the cold lingers in the mountains. I zip my green fleece to my chin and bury my hands in my pockets. As I reach the first booth, a familiar face greets me with a wide grin.

"Eden," Abby says. "Oops, can I call you that? Or do you prefer 'Ms.'?" She chews her bottom lip. "I don't know your last name, though."

"It's Hawthorne, but please call me Eden." One benefit to my divorce is Jeff can no longer guilt-trip me about keeping my maiden name.

Abby relaxes into her metal folding chair. "Okay, good. My dad tells me it's respectful to call adults by their last names, but my mom hates it when people call her 'ma'am' or 'Mrs.' because it makes her feel old."

"What's this booth about?" I ask so I don't drill her about her parents' relationship.

"Oh." Abby sits up straight and takes on a practiced tone. "This is one of the kids' booths. We have cartoon maps of Grand Trees"—she spins one toward me—"and crayons. The little kids color them in to show where to meet in case of fire, flood, earthquake—that sort of thing."

I study the map, which is designed like a kids' place mat from a chain restaurant.

Abby continues, "But the older kids are supposed to make an evacuation plan and sign up for alerts on their phones."

"Alerts?" I ask.

"There are warning systems for disasters, and everybody with a cell phone can subscribe. I can help you." She reaches for my phone.

"That's okay. I'm just staying the weekend."

"But you're going to visit again, right? And your mom lives here. Maybe you want to know if something happens to her when you're not here?"

Abby's a tough sell and makes a good point. I hand her my phone.

She waves it over my face to unlock it. "There are earthquake, fire, and flood warnings." Her thumbs move over my phone with the skill of a digital native. "The earthquake alarm will only trigger if there's a big one. Like over 5.0, I think."

"Whose idea was this festival?" It's distressing and apocalyptic, but resourceful, I suppose.

"My dad." She sighs as she types a few more keystrokes and hands me my phone. "I begged him to do a music festival instead, but he was like, 'No, let's scare all the little kids and make them think the world is ending.' That's much better than live music."

"I told you, Larry Styles isn't coming to Grand Trees." I turn to the sound of Caleb's voice, which trails over my skin like fingertips. Today he's in a heather-gray T-shirt and frayed jeans, with gooseflesh pebbling his forearms. And he's looking everywhere but at me.

"It's Harry Styles," Abby says, as if this dad joke is as old as she is.

"He ain't coming here either, kid. So we may as well do something useful." He leans in and straightens the coloring pages until the edges are aligned. "Your mom's looking for you."

"Not very hard, obviously. I told her I was volunteering at this booth."

Caleb gestures over his shoulder toward the far corner of the square. "She's chasing your brother and sister around by the Paper Horse. Go. I'll watch the booth."

Brother and sister? How many kids does Caleb have? How many surrogate grandchildren does my mother love?

Caleb looks about my age. Early thirties? Thirty-five tops. There isn't a single silver thread in his dark-brown hair. The faint lines around his eyes appear to be a product of sun exposure rather than age.

He must have started his family young. And kept going. I wish I were a better person and didn't feel a pang of envy—jealousy, if I'm being honest—when I meet people my age with babies, toddlers, tykes, and teens. I even covet Abby's mild attitude, eye rolls, and impatience for her dad's gentle ribbing.

I realize my feelings are misplaced. I recognize my jealousy of strangers is really anger at Jeff for asking me to sacrifice my opportunity to have children and for being unworthy of the sacrifice. But mostly, it's disappointment in myself for agreeing to that bargain in the first place.

Abby stands, pushing the chair back. "Okay. But did you talk to Mom?"

"She's thinking about it," Caleb says.

"Thanks, Daddy." Abby steps out from behind the booth and wraps her arms around his waist. Caleb kisses the top of her head.

"No guarantees, kid." He presses the words into her hair.

"See you later, Eden." Abby scurries away, skipping every few steps like a much younger child.

As Sabrina Carpenter's voice drifts over the speakers, Caleb shifts his focus to me. The cheery pop is an ironic background to his sour expression.

"Your mom is helping assemble the emergency packs in the gazebo." Caleb nudges his head in that direction as if he hopes I might skip away like his daughter. Instead, I face him.

"How long has she been sick?" I whisper, although we're alone over here.

"Who?"

Now I understand why Abby rolls her eyes at him. "My mother."

"What do you mean?" He shoves his hands in his pockets. This man is infuriating.

"The shaking, lack of balance. How long ago was she diagnosed?" I'd researched Parkinson's disease after I spoke to Adelaide, but I still don't know enough.

"You should talk to your mom, Eden. If she didn't tell you, I'm sure she had her reasons."

I don't appreciate his insinuation that her reasons were valid. "I will talk to her. But she's evasive, and I can't take her word for it."

Caleb assesses me, staring for several moments before he relents. "The movement issues have been going on awhile."

"What's awhile?"

"I don't remember when we first noticed symptoms, but she didn't get diagnosed until three years ago, right before Sonny . . ." He trails off.

"Three years ago?" I raise my voice, grasping the corner of the table for support.

Caleb nods slowly, managing to make the gesture accusatory. "Why'd you come finally?"

"Adelaide. She said my mom's refusing treatment, and she thought I could convince her."

Caleb sighs. "Of course she did. Well, we've all tried to reason with her. But there's no cure. You know that, right?"

He delivers the news like he's telling a child there's no Santa Claus, like I'm naive and he's mature and pragmatic. And it's every bit as cruel as those sanctimonious parents who think they're doing their kids a favor by ruining the little bit of magic they have.

"I know. But she can't go on like this, living all alone in a tree house in the woods with stairs she can't climb in a town she can't escape in the next disaster."

Caleb folds his arms across his chest. "She's not alone."

"Right. She's with her new family now. She's got a nephew I didn't know about and grandchildren I didn't give her. I noticed all that even though none of it makes any goddamn sense."

Caleb's eye twitches as he stares me down. He does a good job of giving me time to replay what I've just said. I've revealed too much about all the confusing baggage I've lugged here.

"I'm sure you've talked to her. But I'm her daughter. I have to try," I say, calmer.

"Eden?" I turn my head at the sound of Mom's voice, yelling from somewhere behind me. I spot her at the top of the gazebo and wave, but Caleb speaks again before I can go to her.

"Knock yourself out." His voice is dry as dust. "But before you go riding in on your white horse, remember we'll be the ones taking care of her when you ride back out."

I glare at him, affronted by his accusation but also reeling from the potential truth of it, before I hear Mom's voice again. When I spin around, she's on the stairs of the gazebo, making her way to me, her grin warm and eager.

I ignore Caleb behind me, keeping my focus on Mom as I approach, so I have a clear view when her hand slips from the handrail, her foot skips a stair, and her body crumbles down the final steps to land on the bricks with a sickening crunch.

CHAPTER 6

Caleb gets to Mom before I do, sprinting by me to reach her in long strides. By the time my incompetent leg carries me forward, a sea of strangers surrounds Mom, and I can barely push through the crowd.

Caleb is at her side, performing an amateur examination and asking quiet questions as several others stand vigil. But as soon as I crouch beside her, Mom fakes a smile and says she's fine. She lies to me all over again. And my irritation with her—for the years of distance and avoidance and silence about her illness—battles with my worry.

The wait for the ambulance is interminable, even longer than it used to be. With the main road washed out, the detour is a one-lane road with switchbacks and infrequent turnouts. Every time Mom winces in pain, it reduces my tolerance for this town—for all its fuck-yous to modern conveniences and hubris about its invincibility.

When the paramedics do finally arrive, I don't even argue when Caleb climbs into the ambulance after her, taking the rightful place I forfeited.

"Where are they taking her?" I ask before the doors shut behind them.

"County." Caleb doesn't spare me a glance, his focus still on my mom.

"No." Bile rises in my gut at the thought of going back. "Not there."

Caleb looks at me now, his face hard. But he shakes off my concern as the doors shut with a decisive click.

"Is there another hospital you can take her to?" I ask the paramedic before she steps to the driver's door.

"Sorry, ma'am. It's the closest."

I need to follow the ambulance. I need to take every step toward reconciliation available to me while there's still time. I know it. But knowing the right thing and doing it aren't even related.

Abby is at my side as I stare at the retreating ambulance, frozen in place. "Eden, can I please go with you to the hospital? Please? My mom can't go because she has the kids. But I have to go. I have to. Please, please."

Her desperation snaps me out of my trance. Tears fall down her pretty face, a backpack slung over one shoulder while she grips the hand of a towheaded little girl.

I remember being her age and the intensity of every emotion.

"Of course you can," I say, committing to facing more ghosts.

She lets out a hiccuping breath. "Thank you." She flings her arms around my neck, and in my surprise, it takes me a moment to reciprocate. "They didn't let me go with Grandpa Sonny and . . ." She breaks into tears again.

"She's going to be okay. She is. It's just a fall." The irony of those words catches me by the throat, but I swallow and hold my own tears at bay while Abby clutches me.

"Don't cry, sissy," the younger girl says.

"You cry all the time." Abby's voice is muffled against my shoulder. But this makes them both giggle. Abby pulls back just as a woman approaches and drapes her hand on the small of Abby's back.

The woman has blue feather earrings that hang below the edge of her chin-length blond hair. She wears no makeup but has flawless skin, and in an instant, I know where Abby got that lucky trait from. She steps beside her two girls and swings the little one onto her hip, around her very pregnant belly.

I wish my current panic would deaden my receptors for that particular trigger, but instead, it makes me wonder whether Nadia had her baby yet and if Jeff held her hand in the delivery room and cried when he welcomed his child into the world. Did he tell Nadia all the ethical reasons he didn't want children, or did he reserve that long list for me?

"Mom, can I please, please go with Eden to the hospital? I can't wait around without knowing if Grams is okay. Can I go, please?"

Abby's mom extends a hand to me. "I'm Lina. You're Nicolette's daughter? Eden? I'm so sorry about your mom." Lina's voice is low and lyrical.

"Thank you." I take her hand in mine. "If it's okay with you, I don't mind taking Abby."

"You have enough to worry about. Are you sure?" A toddler who looks just like the little girl crashes into Lina's legs, wrapping his hands around the bend of her knees.

"Dad will be there. I won't bother Eden, I promise," Abby pleads.

"They probably won't let you into her room to see her," Lina tries as her younger daughter dives out of her arms and tackles the boy. The toddler slams the girl until she flips him, pinning him to the grass with a roar.

"Are they okay?" I ask, although neither Lina nor Abby seem alarmed.

Abby spares a glance before muttering, "They're fine. Mom, can I go, please?"

Lina rests one hand on her belly. "Yes, but call me when you know anything."

And that's how Abby and I wind up racing out of town on the one-lane road, heading toward a place I was lucky to escape. The landscape has been scarred by new disasters in the years since I left. A broad crevasse cuts along the embankment, evidence of a landslide in recent years. Shoots of wild grasses and lupines push through the raw earth, seizing opportunity from calamity. Roots of an upturned pine splay like fingertips, uncovering the underbelly of a regal creature toppled by a tremor, flood, or drought. Grand Trees has always been the fault line between fairy tale and nightmare.

I'm grateful Abby joined me, because she doesn't let me wallow or worry—she's too busy talking.

"My dad says that Grams is awake and doing okay." She fires off a text and looks up from her phone.

I exhale. "Good."

Abby fidgets with a stack of handouts from the festival, folding one piece into a paper airplane before making a fortune teller like the ones I played with as a kid. "Do you believe in magic?" she asks.

"Magic?"

"Not pulling rabbits out of hats or cutting a woman in half. Just things you can't explain."

"I'm not sure."

"Grandpa Sonny said that Grand Trees is magic, and it takes care of its people. But now that he's gone, I wonder why it didn't take care of him." She glances out the window, but before I can respond, she jumps in again. "Why don't you visit more? Grams is always talking about you. She says you're busy saving the world, but this is the first time I've even met you, which is kinda strange. I mean, I'm thirteen. And you only live in San Francisco, right?"

"It took me seven hours to get here yesterday." California is vast, of course, but even I know that's a pathetic excuse, and I'm ashamed of myself for the evasion.

But I can't spill all the reasons Mom and I aren't close. Anger is a strange thing. My resentment had cooled to ash over the years, but every time I reignite our relationship, I kick up all that residue. We become coated in it, our lungs fill with it, and we choke on the dust.

"And I'm not saving the world. I'm just a nonprofit fundraiser. I raise the money so others can save the world."

"Isn't that the most important part? Money is power, right? The people screwing up the world have all the money. If you take money from the powerful people to help the powerless, then bam—you save the world."

This kid has it all figured out, and I envy her for it.

Abby looks at her phone again, her thumbs flying over the screen before she tucks it in her pocket and folds a piece of paper into an origami crane. "What do you fundraise for?" Abby asks. "And how do you get people to give you money?"

"I worked for the Red Cross for a long time. But I'm an independent consultant now, so I fundraise for a variety of causes: disaster relief, cancer treatment, food banks, the arts."

"Okay, but how?"

I love her curiosity and tenacity. She'll make a good lawyer. "I'm hired to do big campaigns: when a food bank wants to buy a warehouse, or a health charity wants to raise millions for research. Sometimes I'm hired to put on an event to pitch a bunch of rich people in a ballroom. Or they need me to fill in when their head fundraiser leaves or coach a new CEO about how to work with donors. It varies."

"How do you get people to pay you to ask rich people for money? 'You need money? Pay me to get it.' It's like holding them for ransom or something."

An hour ago, I didn't imagine I'd be laughing or thinking about anything other than how broken my mom looked at the bottom of the gazebo, but Abby has managed to do both.

"For every dollar they pay me, I raise multiple times that amount."

"Seriously?" Abby gapes.

"It's what I'm hired to do."

"You make it rain is what you're saying." She rubs her fingers against her thumb, and I chuckle. "Where do you work?"

"I travel to meet donors wherever they want me, but I work from home most of the time."

"It sounds pretty flexible."

"It is. I can't complain."

"So you could come to Grand Trees to visit Grams more often if you wanted to."

I see what she did there. Our little lawyer. I fiddle with the radio, trying to coax any station to come in, but there's only static. I flip it off.

She continues, unfazed by my silence. "My dad hasn't seen his parents since he moved in with Grandpa Sonny in high school. But his parents were awful, so that makes sense. But Grams, she's the best. Don't you want to visit her?"

I don't think Caleb would want me to know any of this, and I feel guilty for consuming this information, even if it is offered without provocation. He moved in with Sonny as a teen? Sonny lived alone when I knew him, so it means Caleb moved in after my mom left us. It means Caleb was her surrogate kid and my substitute. No wonder Mom didn't mention him. She's always had a great discipline for omission.

"It's complicated," I say.

"Adults always say that. *Complicated*. It's not like I can't understand complex concepts. I'm taking geometry in seventh grade." She crosses her arms and sinks into her seat. "Sorry. I didn't mean to be disrespectful or anything. It's just my mom's favorite phrase, and I hate it."

"I think when adults say that, it's a way of saying they don't want to talk about it."

"You don't want to talk about why you don't visit Grams?"

"Not really," I admit.

"Well then, you should have said that. It really isn't complicated."

When I sneak a glance at my interrogator, she's grinning at me. And somehow, she makes me laugh again. A real, deep laugh that brings tears to my eyes. I wipe them away to stay focused on the one-lane road. "Fair point."

"Grams has more paintings of you upstairs. My favorite is the one of you in your wedding dress. It's of the back of your dress and the veil, and the sun is setting, and it's so pretty." She releases an appreciative sigh.

This well-meaning girl has the instruction manual for all my emotional injuries. It's a talent. And she's undeterred by my silence. She flips the heating vent toward her face. "What does your husband do? Does he save the world, too?"

I could tell her I don't want to talk about it, but I'm afraid she'd use a legal loophole to find the answer on cross-examination. I practice the words that still feel so foreign to me. "We're divorced, actually."

Abby pulls her feet up, crisscrossing them until one knee rests on the passenger door. "That sucks. Divorce is the worst. But you don't have kids, right? It really sucks with kids."

I swallow a laugh because if I don't, I might cry. I can't even fathom what heartbreak she'll introduce next. "It sure does."

"Thanks for taking me to the hospital." She grabs another piece of paper from the festival and folds it into a star. I breathe a sigh of relief that we'd managed to find a conversational off-ramp before she asks me why I don't have children or whether I still do ballet.

"I don't mind," I say, even if she does have a laser pointer to all my points of pain. She's surprisingly comfortable around adults, especially relative strangers. I never was. Perhaps it was the ballet training, which was steeped in deference to authority. It's made it hard to exist in the real world as a woman, a people pleaser, and someone allergic to confrontation. Abby will have a head start in navigating this world.

"I like hospitals. I know that's weird, though," Abby says when I've been silent too long.

"Why?" I'm thankful I can ask a question now; this hot seat is burning.

"Well, my brother and sister were born at the hospital, so those were pretty good memories. New babies are the best, better than when they become toddlers and ruin all your stuff. But also, the hospital vending machine sells Butterfingers."

I laugh. "A plus for sure."

As we hug the river embankment, Abby looks out the window and picks at her cuticles. The skin is red and raw, with several scabs along her knuckles. "And like now," she continues. "I hate that Grams got hurt, but when someone you love is in the hospital and you can be with them, you know you're in the right place with the right person, you know?"

"I've never thought about it like that." Life is a series of competing priorities, and I suppose there is comfort in fate forcing your hand.

"I always feel I'm in the wrong place. When I'm at my dad's, I feel left out of all the family time with my mom, my stepdad, and my little brother and sister. But when I'm at my mom's, I miss my dad and worry about him being all alone."

I snap my head to Abby, taking in this new information. Caleb and Lina aren't together, and he must not be the father of the younger kids. I think of Abby's beautiful mom, pregnant with another man's baby, I presume. I guess Caleb and I have that in common, at least.

It also might mean Caleb is single—and it unsettles me that my nerves ignite at the thought.

CHAPTER 7

The hospital must have had a facelift in the intervening years because it doesn't look the same. But my bones remember. I enter on shaky legs, trying to convince myself that my memories are not welcome today. I envision shrugging them off my back as I walk through the automatic doors.

Caleb meets us in the lobby soon after we arrive, taking Abby into his arms as she dissolves into more tears. He rocks her gently back and forth, and she settles, wiping her eyes with the back of her hands when he pulls away.

"They're doing X-rays. She may have broken her wrist and a few ribs. We'll know for sure soon. But she was alert and lucid during the ride."

"Good." I sigh. "That's good."

"She really is going to be fine, Abs," Caleb says, low, soft, patient, so dissimilar to his tone with me.

Abby scans the waiting room nervously, leaning into our small circle as if she's about to tell us a secret. "But Dev's grandparents both died last year. One right after another. And you know how Grandpa and Grams were. What if she gives up because she doesn't want to live without him?"

Caleb hooks his palm around her nape, pulling her in for another hug. "She won't," he whispers. "It was just a fall. Bones heal."

The Epicenter of Forever

I step back out of respect for their privacy and so I don't break down as well. This moment—this entire day—is why I haven't visited. But it's also revealed all the reasons I should have. I missed my chance to make peace with Sonny, to decide whether I should. But I can't miss my chance with Mom. There may not be another one.

After a moment, I walk back over to them. "I want to see her. Can I go back?"

Caleb glances at me for the first time, his face hardening. "Yeah. Just get me when the doctor comes." His curt words land in stark contrast to the warmth he lavished on his daughter.

"Thanks again, Eden," Abby says. "I'm sorry I talked too much."

I squeeze her shoulder. "You talked just the right amount."

I find the room down a narrow hall. Mom is asleep when I peer behind the curtain. A nurse looks up from the IV drip and smiles as I slide into the red plastic chair at the bedside.

"We just gave her something for the pain. She'll likely be asleep for a while."

"Thank you," I say, but he's already slipping out, and my voice is so thin I'm not sure he heard me. I wrap my hands around the bed rail. The width and curve are so similar to a ballet barre that I release it and tuck my hands under my thighs. Mom's wrist is in a brace, and a few bruises are already blooming on her breastbone, visible above the neckline of her hospital gown. She looks almost childlike, the blankets tucked around her slight frame, emphasizing her frailty.

I should have come sooner. I should have figured out how to forgive her, but it would have meant exonerating—or condemning—myself. I never could figure out how our culpabilities intersected, whether we absolved or indicted each other by facing the truth of our own crimes. But I'm thirty-five. And I've lived more of my life without her than I did with her loving hand to lead me. I'm ready to fix this. I don't know if forgiveness is possible, but acceptance must be. And I have to hope it's enough to heal us both.

Her love was the richest of my life. If it had been tepid to begin with, maybe we could have found our way back to normal. We would have gone on to have the relationship Cassie has with her mom—formal, forced. Or the relationship Jeff has with his—obligatory, reserved.

But indifference was never an option for us. I loved her fiercely. And afterward, I hated her violently.

When I was in third grade, a new girl moved into town and took over my life one friend at a time. I told Mom I was too sick to go to school. Mom fed me soup and brought me tea, allowing me to languish under a soft blanket and watch the Disney Channel. But, of course, I hadn't fooled her. She was patiently waiting for me to talk. I finally confessed over afternoon ice cream, and Mom told me no one could steal my life without my permission.

I think Mom's been waiting for me to be ready to talk for two decades. But it doesn't matter whether I'm ready. Time is working its hand on her, and she may not be able to resist it much longer.

~

Three hours later, we learn Mom fractured three ribs and two bones in her wrist and required five stitches along her shin where it caught the edge of the brick landing. She's bruised and broken, but there's no sign of concussion or internal injuries. She should be okay, but they're keeping her overnight for observation.

Caleb and Abby meet us upstairs when Mom is admitted into a semiprivate room. The second bed is empty, so there's space for all of us, and Mom's current nurse isn't a stickler for rules.

I watch the clock. It's old and original. The stark white face, bold black numerals, the numbing sound of the second hand nibbling away the hours. The sound is a flashbulb memory. A marker of all my time eaten up by injury here. I steer my focus away.

Abby does all the talking while Mom enjoys a drug-induced sleep, waking only briefly to say she's just fine and doesn't know what all the fuss is about. I sit beside Mom in a plastic chair, and Caleb leans against the far wall, arms crossed over his broad chest, baseball cap slung low on his forehead, glaring at me. I think Cassie would call his look smoldering, but she reads too many romance novels. And I read too many mysteries, so I suspect the look is actually murderous.

"Hi." A young woman in black slacks and a midnight-blue blouse pokes her head through the doorway. Around her neck is a name tag dangling from the hospital-issued purple lanyard, but she's not in scrubs. Administration, I assume, and here for payment. It dawns on me that I have no idea about Mom's insurance situation. "I'm Tanya, a social worker here at the hospital. I would like to speak with Nicolette's attorney-in-fact."

"That's me. I'm Caleb Connell."

"Wait," I say as Caleb steps away from the wall, arm outstretched with the manners he reserves for everyone but me. "Why do you have power of attorney?"

Tanya glances between us, her expression morphing from professional warmth to trained impartiality as she accepts Caleb's proffered hand.

"You are not an attorney, Dad," Abby whispers.

"Do you have somewhere we can talk?" Caleb asks.

"I'm her daughter," I say. "I need to be updated as well."

Tanya looks to Caleb, and I recognize the subtle request for assent. It's the way a donor would check in with the highest-ranking man in the room to confirm whether what I've said is true, even when that man couldn't recite any of the information I'd fed him in advance. Caleb nods, and I'm relieved he didn't take the opportunity to keep me in the dark, but I hope he doesn't expect me to thank him for doing what's right.

"Sure." Tanya smiles. "Of course."

"Stay here with Grams," Caleb says to Abby, softening the command with a quick kiss on the top of her head. She's chewing on her bottom lip and picking at her cuticles again. "And press that if she needs anything." He points to the call button.

Tanya leads us past the nurses' station and down a few corridors. The linoleum transitions from sage to daffodil to eggshell before she gestures for us to enter a tight, white, windowless room. I sit in one of the four chairs crammed around a small table, but Caleb opts to stand, leaning against the wall, which makes it feel as if he's hovering over me.

"I understand Nicolette had a fall." Tanya takes the chair across from me, setting an accordion file on the table.

Caleb says, "She's usually pretty good about asking for help. But she was rushing to see her daughter and—"

"So it's my fault?" I snap, turning to glare at him.

"Didn't say that," Caleb mumbles.

Tanya leans forward. "With her condition, her balance may be deteriorating, and the shifts could be so subtle she doesn't realize she needs help until it's too late."

"She's stubborn," Caleb says.

Tanya offers a soft smile. "That's not surprising. People with degenerative illnesses are losing control of their bodies. Resistance often comes in the form of stubbornness about what they can control."

"She's refusing medication," I say, irritated that we're litigating the accident instead of discussing ways to stabilize her condition.

Tanya's expression is compassionate, but I recognize it to be the trained countenance of a professional. "I encourage you to speak with the attending physician. Unfortunately, I can't provide medical advice."

"Right," I say. "But you could speak with her about it. She might need a professional to help her get over her anxieties about treatment."

"I thought you wanted to speak to her yourself because you didn't trust I had," Caleb says to me. "And now you're off-loading the responsibility so you don't have to deal with it after all?"

I whip my head toward him, my worry turning to rage. "I thought a neutral party might be helpful since you coerced my mom into signing over power of attorney."

"Coerced?" Caleb barks.

"How do I know you don't have something to gain if my mom doesn't take life-prolonging treatment?"

"Are you kidding me? You show up here after—"

"Why don't we all take a seat." Tanya's voice is stern, and I'm impressed with her command of the room, even as I seethe at Caleb's nerve.

Caleb yanks on the chair, pulling it away from the table before he settles. It's way too small for his frame, and I almost want to laugh at how ridiculous he looks. He's a giant in a child's chair. But then I remember he's an ass. And nothing about him is funny.

Tanya takes a deep breath, one of those intentional inhales used by yoga teachers, and I suspect she wants us to imitate her. But I don't. And Caleb sure as hell won't.

"Caring for an ill relative is difficult. Even the most tight-knit families struggle with these critical decisions."

"We're not family," Caleb says, and I'm offended, a little hurt, even though he said the words before I could.

"We're only related by marriage," I say, and then add, "distantly." I don't know if you can be distantly related by marriage. But at this point, I want to put distance between us in any way I can. I'm an only child. I never assumed I'd have to make medical decisions for my mom in partnership with her second husband's handsome jackass of a nephew.

"Well, either way, you both are invested in Nicolette's care and want what's best for her, so she must be well loved. As she recovers from the injuries, she will need full-time care, either in a rehab center—"

"She doesn't want that," Caleb says. "She wants to be at home."

Tanya folds her hands and rests them on the table. "That's good that you know her wishes. Is there someone who can care for her? At least until the bones heal?"

"I can," Caleb says, just as I blurt, "I'll do it," without thinking about what I'm offering, without intending to enter an irrational competition with the most infuriating man I've ever met.

"Great! A partnership is perfect for this scenario." Tanya puts a chipper punctuation on the rash agreement.

What have I done? How many months will it take for her to heal? How can I possibly survive in Grand Trees for that long? How can I commit to staying and caring for Mom indefinitely?

Caleb turns an icy glare on me, ready to battle me for this, and I straighten my shoulders. Something about his indignation compels me to fight back, even though I'm not sure I want what we're fighting over.

CHAPTER 8

Tanya escorts us back and leaves us alone outside Mom's hospital room. I'm sure she's happy to have the matter settled and relieved to be done with us. Caleb hasn't said a word since I offered to stay, which is a relief. I don't think I have the emotional energy to bicker with him. I've barely come to terms with what I've offered and don't want to cave.

I head to Mom's door, but Caleb flicks his chin toward the window seat across the hall, an irritating gesture that I follow anyway. He sits in the corner, and I do the same but only manage to put a foot between us.

"You can't take care of her. You don't even have a relationship with her," Caleb says.

And good Lord, I thought he was going to apologize.

"You know, I'm sick of your shit. I could say the same about you. But just because I don't understand your relationship doesn't mean it doesn't exist." Our bodies are contorted so awkwardly in this intimate window seat. I'm sitting upright and prim, arms crossed tight over my chest. He's pushed against the opposite corner but manspreading shamelessly, as if his crotch can't be sacrificed to our mutual goal of staying the hell away from each other.

"But the difference is, I see Nicki every day, and I've seen you once in twenty years, and only from behind when you skipped out on Uncle Sonny's funeral."

I didn't skip out; I just didn't linger for the reception. I went to the service through a mounting panic attack, but I'm not going to tell him that. "Yeah, well, I'm here now. She's my mother. And I'm taking care of her."

His thigh is too close for comfort, and I hate myself for noticing how strong and capable it is. I can see where his IT band bisects his quads and hamstrings, prominent even under his worn Levi's. It means nothing. I notice strong legs. Unscarred legs. But my mind flashes to a vision of straddling those impressive thighs, and I have to blink it away. Where the hell did that come from?

I think he catches me staring, and he glares back from under his filthy baseball cap. "You don't get to decide that."

I stand, pacing in front of him, and he watches me like a predator. "Because you have power of attorney? How'd that happen anyway? Are you lying in wait for an inheritance? Taking advantage of a frail old woman and hoping for a buck?"

He stands, blocking my progress. "Don't even try to accuse me of that," he says, jaw clenched. "I've been here for years, taking care of your mom while you shunned her."

"Who are you to judge anyway? Abby says you don't talk to your own parents."

The look on his face is a douse of ice water on my anger. It's a microsecond of pain, as if all his facial muscles recoil for a heartbeat. It's there and gone so quickly I could convince myself I imagined it, but I know it. I feel it. It's how I wipe my own face clean after taking an emotional blow. I likely made that same expression on the ride here, when Abby landed so many unintended punches.

I just found Caleb's open wound, but it brings me no pleasure to exploit it. He doesn't respond, watching me like he's acknowledged the hit and is planning his counterattack.

I release my arms and face him. I don't know why this man antagonizes me so—to the point that I hardly recognize myself. Maybe there is a way to appeal to reason and troubleshoot this together.

"How could you stay with her?" I ask. "Where would Abby stay?" Sonny's house was built as a bachelor pad. The stairs lead to a massive loft bedroom with a 360-degree view of the forest, but there are no other bedrooms. I—or Caleb, if I lose this battle—will be sleeping on the couch for the foreseeable future. But Caleb can't have his teen daughter live in flux for months.

"Upstairs. And I'll take the couch." It's as if he's had these answers at the ready.

"Where will my mom stay?"

"In my old room. I've been trying to convince her to move down there anyway."

"What room?"

Caleb sighs and sits, pulling off his cap and running a hand through his unruly hair. He really needs a haircut. And a shave. "Sonny added a bedroom off the main level. He built it after your mom moved in, for you, actually, but you never came." Caleb looks away; maybe he doesn't relish confirming how badly I broke Mom's heart. "I moved in at sixteen. I didn't have anywhere else to go."

This small gift of vulnerability, after I'd launched an emotional strike just a moment ago, defuses me. This man has done everything he could to make my last twenty-four hours difficult. But I've had a front-row seat to his loyalty, kindness, and tenderness with the people he loves. He's not an asshole. He's just determined to be an asshole to me.

I take my seat—tree-trunk thighs be dammed—and remove all the starch from my posture. "I don't know how much you know about what happened between my mom and me."

"I know she left your dad for Sonny, and you disowned her," he says.

Something tells me he doesn't know everything, though, because I don't think he'd be judging me so fiercely if he did. I bite back my frustration at his ignorance of the truth my mom refused to tell.

"Look, I get it," he continues. "It's easy to want a villain. But your mom isn't one, and you've been punishing her long enough."

He has all the power here, so I have to temper my fury. I don't take the bait. "So let me do this," I say. "Let me do what's right."

Caleb leans forward, and I sense his contempt softening, the first tug on a tangled chain that loosens the knot rather than tightens it. I see the Caleb that other people probably see—attentive, curious, and thoughtful.

I continue, "Besides, you'd have to uproot Abby and bring Houdini, who will likely knock Mom over."

As I advocate for this plan, I also convince myself I need to face these demons finally. For years, I've waited for an epiphany and change of heart. I thought forgiveness would arrive like a gift I could hand to Mom with a tidy bow. But now, my only hope is to steal it from the clutches of the town that gave birth to our rift in the first place. I need to reconcile with Mom before it's too late.

He watches me for several soundless moments. Hospital monitors beep in the background, and calm voices drift in from the nurses' station. Caleb stands and walks toward Mom's room, forcing me to follow. He stops abruptly and turns back to me when he reaches the doorway, and I almost bump right into him.

"It's your mom's decision. She gets to make the call anyway," he says.

"Do you really want to put her in a position to choose between us?"

He raises his chin, implying he thinks he'd win. "I don't want to put her in a position to be devastated if you bail."

"I think you have your facts wrong, because I'm not the one who bailed on her," I snap.

"But you are the one who condemned her for it. And if you think for a second you can take this opportunity to make her feel even worse about herself when she's at her lowest, I swear to God I'll—"

Abby pokes her head out of Mom's hospital room and clears her throat. She darts her focus between us and whispers, "Grams is awake," like an accusation.

CHAPTER 9

We shimmy into Mom's hospital room, bookending either side of her bed.

"How are you feeling?" I ask when I take in her distressed expression. "Do you need more painkillers?"

"Abby, honey, can you ask the nurse if I can have something small to eat?" Mom asks.

Abby steps toward the doorway, casting a worried glance on her way out.

"They haven't fed you?" Caleb asks, his face hardening.

"I couldn't eat if they forced me," Mom says. "I just wanted Abby out of the room. She doesn't need to hear you two arguing about me any more than I do."

Caleb and I share a look from across the bed, chastened.

"We weren't—" I start.

Mom shushes me like I'm back in kindergarten. "What on earth are you two bickering about?"

Caleb speaks first. "The hospital wants you to have full-time care until you heal."

Mom frowns. "The doctor said it may take three months. I can't impose on anyone that long. That's ridiculous."

"You'll need your wounds cleaned and dressed," he says. "You'll have meds to take. And it's going to be a while before you can do things for yourself."

"And I want to stay with you," I say, beating Caleb to the headline.

"Oh, honey," Mom says. "You can't do that." But there's a subtle giddiness that betrays her refusal, a tug of a smile, a glimmer of hope that I might be sticking around. It makes me feel even guiltier for my long absence.

"That's what I told her," Caleb says. "I don't think it's a good idea."

"And I told him it's the only plan that makes sense," I say between gritted teeth.

"But what about the Red Cross? You can't miss work that long," Mom says.

"I haven't worked for the Red Cross in a few years. I'm a consultant now. I can work from anywhere."

"Oh." Mom blinks, and I read a mix of relief that I can stay and shame that we know so little of each other. Abby bounds back in the room, her errand regrettably short. "And Jeff? You can't live apart from your husband." She pats my hand with her good arm.

When I freeze, Abby chimes in from the doorway. "They're divorced, Grams." She says it in a tone that accuses Mom of suffering from dementia.

I should defend Mom's memory. I should confess that I never told her—about work or Jeff. But I can't talk about it with Caleb's hard stare on my face. And I can't look directly at Mom as her pity makes landfall.

"I can do this, Mom, really. I want to."

"But she doesn't know your routines. She doesn't know you," Caleb says.

"Caleb," Mom scolds, giving him a meaningful look. What it means, however, I don't know. They have a shorthand I can't read.

"I will learn." I face off against Caleb over Mom's hospital bed.

"You'll have to stay the full three months," he says, but this subtext I can read. *Don't let her down.*

"I'm planning on it." Three months is an eternity, but I will not let this man chase me away.

He taps his hand against his thigh. "I'll come over every day to check on her."

"I'll appreciate the help." See, I can be accommodating.

"Caleb," Mom whispers her warning this time.

He lets out a long breath. "Fine."

And for some reason, I feel like we need to shake on this agreement. I extend my hand, and he takes it, absorbing my entire palm in his strong, calloused grip. I mean to pull back quickly, but time is suspended. Because this touch is . . . well . . . it is decadent. It feels like that dream I have sometimes. Where I'm onstage and begin a pirouette that doesn't end. As long as I spot my head at a point on the balcony, I can spin and spin and spin, staying in the euphoric revolution without care for physics or reality.

The handshake—if you can call it that—lasts too long. A minute. A day. An eternity. A perfect amount of time.

Mom tsks. "Don't try to intimidate her with a death grip, Caleb. Stand down."

Her voice snaps me out of my trance, and I pull away as the nurse walks back in.

"I'm sorry, folks, but visiting hours are over. She should be released at about eleven tomorrow if all goes well."

We say our goodbyes and hurry out into the cool night air. Caleb insists on following me back to the inn because *the road is dangerous* and *there is no cell service* and he *doesn't want to be responsible* if I become stranded on a one-lane road in the middle of the night.

I drown out the scents and scenery along the route by playing an audiobook I've listened to a dozen times—the twists already uncovered, the surprises safely revealed. There's comfort in knowing how things end.

~

In the morning, I let myself into the tree house with the spare key under the mat and wait for Caleb to arrive with Mom. My resolve and bravery dissolve as I step over the threshold. Of all places to be stuck for months, this is the last one I'd choose.

I leave my small suitcase in the entryway. In it are two outfits, one pair of shoes, and a travel toothbrush. There's no time to make the fourteen-hour round-trip trek to gather my stuff. Besides, I'm afraid that if I go home, I won't have the courage to come back.

I step into the living room. Sonny's instruments—acoustic and electric guitars, bass, ukulele, banjo, harmonicas, and bongo drums—are still near the fireplace. At camp staff parties, he'd put on a show, using the raised hearth as a stage. Mom would sing with him every year, even though I don't ever remember her singing at home.

Sonny taught me to play guitar one summer, and I practiced until my fingertips bled. I remember wishing my ballet teachers could be more like him—patient, warm, praising.

Beside the fireplace are more portraits. I stumble on one of a young man. He's clean-shaven, baby-faced, staring straight ahead. It's the eyes—and that white scar across his full lip—that give him away. Mom is a beautiful artist. Even in an abstract piece, she captures the soul in oil. And something about this painting takes my breath away. Young Caleb, bare of animosity and armor, looks fragile.

My phone jars me from my exploration. Cassie is calling, and I notice several missed texts from her over the last hour and realize what I've done. I forgot about our weekly Sunday brunch.

"Oh my God, Cass. I'm so sorry."

"Are you okay?" Her voice is high pitched and panicked.

"Yes. I'm so sorry. I forgot to tell you I was out of town."

"What? Where? For how long? I've been worried your car broke down. Or you were dead in a ditch. Or you met some hottie and eloped in Vegas. Or you got mugged. Or you ran away to join a commune in Portland to raise alpacas. Or you got amnesia and forgot about me since . . . You. Haven't. Returned. My. Calls. All. Week."

"Cass—"

"You haven't talked to me since you ran out on brunch last week. I know you're upset about your ex-dickhead, but I'm the person you're supposed to talk to—"

"I'm at my mom's."

Cassie is never silent. She has an endless bank of words at the ready no matter the crisis. And it's telling that she's quiet now.

"Whoa," she says after I've pulled the phone from my ear to ensure she's still on the line. "That's some breaking news."

I catch her up in a breathless rush. The diagnosis. The fall. The injuries. My impulsive offer to stay and help her recuperate. Cassie listens without interruption. It is a novelty. She waits until I breathe out a tired sigh before she asks follow-up questions: How severe were Mom's injuries? What's the timeline for her recovery? What stage is her Parkinson's? How do I feel about being back? When she's satisfied by my answers—as perfunctory as they are—she asks, "Now tell me more about the hot nephew."

My skin flushes, and I turn to the open bedroom door as if someone could have heard her, which is ridiculous. I'm here alone, and she's not on speaker.

But just in case, I whisper, "I did not say he was hot."

"You didn't have to. You used a dozen nicknames." She slips into a terrible impression of my voice—deeper and raspier than hers—so she sounds like an elderly smoker with a Jersey accent. "Angry lumberjack with splinters in his ass, knight in rugged armor, heroic asshat, muscled jackass, bearded bastard, fuckable fuckface—"

"Hey, I did not say that last one." Somehow, I'm laughing.

"Artistic license," she says. "But I don't think I've ever heard you mention a man so often in the span of ten minutes. And you were married to one for more than a decade. Ooh, boy." Cassie whistles.

"Because he's hell-bent on punishing me." I know I sound petulant, but he makes me feel like a child—scolding me for my inability to deal with my shit and fix what broke between Mom and me.

"Have you been a bad, bad girl?" Cassie says in a sultry voice.

"Cassie," I groan, but I know what she's doing. She doesn't let me wallow. Her hug is therapeutic, but her humor is salvation.

Before I can protest, I register the squeak of the front door. It's too early for Caleb and Mom, so I peer down the hallway. "Cassie, gotta go. Someone's here."

"If it's the nephew, snap a picture and send it to me. Love you to Neptune."

"Love you to Pluto."

I shove my phone in my pocket just as a woman appears in the entryway, carrying two multicolored canvas bags on each shoulder.

"Hello?" she singsongs. She sees me and rushes over, her floor-length tie-dyed skirt fluttering around her ankles. "Eden, I'm so glad you came. I bet Nicolette is thrilled to have you home." She wraps me in a hug that smells of eucalyptus and vanilla.

It takes me a moment to reciprocate this stranger's embrace, but she does a little swaying dance as she hugs me, which is infectious.

"Are you Adelaide?" I ask.

She pulls back and laughs. "Oh, yes. I'm so sorry. We spoke on the phone last week, remember?"

As if I'd forget the impetus for upending my life. "Of course. Thank you for calling me."

Her long black hair is pulled into a taut ponytail, and she brushes aside a few wisps that have escaped. Her eyes are hidden behind round transition lenses, and she's wearing several layers of gauzy fabric—skirt, shirt, cardigan, and scarf. It's impossible to tell how old she is; she could be anywhere from forty to seventy. Her energy is timeless.

"Let me get this food in the freezer and then we'll get to work."

There's no time to ask what work she's referring to before she hurries to the kitchen and the front door swings open again. A pack of people filters in, but I only recognize Lina, Abby, and the two little ones. Everyone is carrying casserole dishes or cleaning supplies.

"Good morning, Eden." Abby shuffles by while chasing her sister, who makes a beeline for Sonny's drums, pounding her little fists on the rawhide.

I smile at Abby and squat beside her sister. "We didn't officially meet yesterday. I'm Eden."

The little girl looks up and grins as she beats a frantic rhythm.

"Fiona, say hi," Abby says.

"Hi," she yells over her music. Fiona has fine blond shoulder-length hair with errant strands that fall forward into her eyes. She's wearing penguin pajama pants, a ruffled pink Easter dress, and yellow rain boots. I love this stage—the stubborn independence, willful individuality. When Jeff's niece, Aarya, graduated from baby to toddler, she decided I was her favorite. She'd slip into my lap with a picture book and giggle when I'd make voices for every character. She made me doubt my own reassurance to Jeff that, yes, I was still okay remaining childless. Until I wasn't.

"Let me guess. You're four?" I ask.

"And a half," Fiona says, in between beats on the drum.

"And a musician," I say.

"Nope. I'm a peacock."

"Obviously."

She smiles so broadly that her nose scrunches up, and her freckles bunch together in a new constellation, but then she darts away. Abby drops to the floor by the guitars, sitting gracelessly with her legs splayed out in front of her. "You're really gonna stay?"

"I am." It's helpful for me to say it out loud.

"That's cool." Abby seems both younger and older than her years. Too confident and observant to be just thirteen and too earnest and sweet to be a teenager. She points to her brother as he storms over. "That's Benny."

He looks like Fiona but with a bowl cut and Kelly-green glasses. He doesn't stop running long enough for introductions. But his dad pauses to say hello. Ian is tall and thin, with tortoise-frame glasses and an easy smile. When he shakes my hand, he grasps it in both of his, finds my gaze, and says how happy they all are to have me here. He's warm and friendly and about as different from Caleb as I can imagine. But he darts away after the briefest of conversations when Benny topples the banjo, triggering an avalanche of musical instruments.

"Eden?" At the sound of my name, I scan the room to find Adelaide striding toward me, carrying a bucket and several hand towels. "We have very little time to get this place ready for your mama."

Over the next hour, Adelaide introduces me to everyone at least twice. I officially meet Carmela, the innkeeper who served me breakfast yesterday, her husband, Bob, a dead ringer for Santa Claus, and Dakota, the pretty bartender from Nowhere Saloon, as well as a dozen others.

Everyone is put to work. Carmela transfers Mom's clothes and essentials from the loft to Caleb's old bedroom. Bob fixes a loose step on the porch while Dakota supervises a group of teenagers organizing the donated meals. And several others disinfect surfaces that were pretty clean to begin with.

I'm good with names. It's an occupational hazard because nonprofit fundraising is a people business. But this lightning round of introductions is making my head spin. I'm too tired and overstimulated by the chaos. And I'm uncomfortable because I don't know if any of them know about my history with Grand Trees. But if they do, they're operating with collective amnesia.

Adelaide completes the introductions while subtly showing me where everything is. Thank goodness I didn't have to ask Caleb for the tour. He'd insert an *if you'd have visited, you would already know where the extra sheets are* accusation at every stop along the way.

"And you'll sleep up here," Adelaide says after I reluctantly follow her up the spiral staircase. My panic escalates with each step. I've never been up here, and I avert my gaze from the wall of windows across the back as my palms start to sweat.

"Oh, no, I'll stay on the couch." I paste a smile on my face.

Adelaide quirks her mouth to the side and squints. "You can't do that for long. Your mom will want you to be comfortable."

"I'll be plenty comfortable there, and I'll need to be close to her." There is no way I can sleep in this room. I steal a glance at the glass wall—and the shadow of the ravine in the distance—and feel my stomach turn.

"Grams!" Abby's voice carries from downstairs, before a chorus of "welcome home" confirms Mom's arrival.

CHAPTER 10

Caleb settles Mom into the Eames chair near the fireplace, propping her injured leg on the ottoman and draping an afghan over her lap. He squats near the chair, fussing over her and ignoring the pack of people clamoring to greet her.

And then it's pandemonium. The work party scrambles to finish, and Mom is brought three glasses of water, ice for her wrist, a heating pad, two more blankets, and a neck pillow.

But after an hour of the meet and greet, I can sense Mom's physical discomfort. I'm just about to call an end to the impromptu party, but Caleb beats me to it.

"Thanks so much for all the help, everyone, but Nicolette needs her rest. I'll send out the schedule tonight."

I don't know why it irritates me that Caleb takes charge, but it does. Apparently, I am petty when it comes to Caleb Connell.

His words are a decree, and everyone scatters, collecting their belongings, saying their goodbyes, giving kisses, and promising to visit. I commit to calling if I need help or more food, which, by the looks of it, will be two years from now. I accept hugs from strangers and practice their names to commit them to memory.

Lina and her family are the last to leave. And when they do, Caleb walks them to the door, chuckling with Ian, heads bowed as if they are old friends. Their blended family strikes me as rather cozy. Perhaps

Caleb's not bitter like I am. While I lament the life I lost, Caleb's slipping lollipops to his ex-wife's new children and hugging her goodbye.

Abby leaves with her mom, taking all the noise with her. It's utterly silent as soon as Caleb and I are alone.

Mom is asleep in the chair, but her face is pinched in a tight scowl as if the pain is following her into slumber. I stand at her side, lost in thought and inwardly panicking about whether I'm cut out to be a caretaker. I know more about being cared for.

"Let her sleep." The edge in his voice is back, apparently reserved for me.

Caleb heads into the kitchen, and I sigh and follow him. He's rinsing glasses at the sink with his back to me, his broad shoulders bunching under the thin cotton of his T-shirt as he moves.

When I've been staring too long, he glances over his shoulder at me with the briefest, barest hint of irritation.

"You don't need to babysit me. I got it," I say.

The house is already clean, thanks to the Grand Trees community. But I grab a rag and run it across the kitchen island anyway. It's a solid slab of honed marble, the same hunter green as the pine tree growing through the house. Everything in here is an extension of the outdoors. The cabinets are a rich cherry, the walls are covered in raw-wood siding, and generous windows bring the outside in. It's gorgeous today—sunny, bright, with crisp cerulean skies. It coats the kitchen in joy, starkly contrasting the tense mood in here.

"I have to give you all the discharge instructions," Caleb mumbles into the sink.

Right. I should have thought of that.

"But I have to get back to Houdini, so you'll get rid of me soon enough." His voice is so low I have to strain to hear him. Perhaps his volume is purely considerate—Mom is asleep, after all—but it seems like a power move on his part.

I step beside him to dry the glasses he's washed and move to the cabinet to put them away. Take that, Caleb. I know my way around here now. I'm not entirely useless.

When he finishes the last dish, he leans against the counter, watching me, his arms folded across his chest. I wish he'd stop doing that. His biceps taunt me from that position. And I don't know what he's thinking with that murderous smolder on his face.

"How long have you been divorced?" The question comes at me while I'm on my tiptoes, reaching into an upper cabinet. I freeze, forcing my fingers to push the glass until it's steady, and take a deep breath before answering. I want to tell him it's none of his business, but I don't want to reveal it matters to me.

"It was finalized a couple of weeks ago." I keep my voice neutral.

"Is that something Nicolette forgot? Or did you forget to tell her?"

I turn, bracing myself for battle. This guy has a skill for using my anguish against me. "I didn't want to worry her." That's not entirely true. And by the look on his face—narrowed eyes, chin raised—Caleb knows it.

"Well, she is worried. She talked about it the whole way home."

I can't do anything right with this guy. I'm a terrible daughter for hiding this from Mom. I'm a horrible person for upsetting her now. I don't respond.

"Maybe you should let her know you're fine. Anxiety can't be good for her recovery."

"Noted." I'll keep lying to her. That should be easy enough.

"But in case you're not okay." He unfolds his arms and wraps his hands around the counter ledge behind him. "It does get easier."

"Thank you." But what I want to say is *Fuck you*. Because what the hell does he know? Does betrayal ever get easier? I'd expect Caleb to be the last person to assure me that I'll heal. He's still judging me about how I failed to move on from the last deception that upended my life. I'm not exactly a poster child for forgiveness.

From what I hear, forgiveness is a precursor to healing. So I have a feeling this wound is going to fester. It is my superpower, after all.

"How long have you been divorced?" I ask, because knowledge is currency. I'm not giving this man anything he hasn't given me.

"Officially? Five years."

I do the math. The same math I did last week while looking at Nadia's swollen torso. "Fiona is . . ." She told me she was four and a half. That doesn't leave much space for the arithmetic of fidelity.

"Ian's," he confirms, although the genetics are apparent now that I've met him.

Maybe Caleb and I aren't so different. Perhaps we can find some common ground.

"My husband . . ." I exhale and start again. "My ex-husband is having a baby. Any day now, actually." How is it that his stern face and harsh assessments coax my confessions? Cassie would have some theories, I'm sure.

Caleb watches me, and there's something about his stare that makes me think he can see right through me to my skin, bone, heart, hurt.

"Were you separated?"

I shake my head. "We separated eight months ago. I didn't know at the time about the baby or the woman." I laugh, although there's nothing funny about it. And the way his body recoils in pity is even less funny. It's secondhand embarrassment for my trauma.

"Yikes," he says. "Is that why you're so anxious to hide out here?"

I don't know why I keep trying with this man. In my attempt at connection, I wind up pointing to my open wounds, so he knows where to pour the salt. I snap back, "Is your failed marriage why you're so insistent on hanging around here, too?"

Caleb takes off his baseball cap and runs a hand through his haywire hair from back to front until he covers his face in one broad palm and sinks against the counter. "I didn't mean that the way it sounded."

"It sounded insensitive." And I realize, I may not like Caleb all that much, but I do like myself in opposition to him and the fight he ignites. I like saying what I mean and telling him to fuck off when he deserves it. To hell with biting my tongue and keeping the peace. I did that with Jeff, and he left anyway. I swallowed my fury at Mom, and she left, too. "I already told you why I'm here, and I'm not putting up with your attitude while I put my life on hold to do what's right. If you plan to be here, too, I suggest you get over whatever you have against me or keep it to yourself."

"Okay." Caleb raises his hands, palms up. But I'm not ready to accept his surrender.

"Because there was a good reason I never visited. There was a good reason I didn't want to be here specifically—in this town, in this house. Being here isn't easy for me. And I don't need you making it harder. If you can't do that, just stay away."

He takes a cautious step closer. "Okay," he repeats.

"You'll stay away?"

Caleb shakes his head, slowly, as if he's a hostage negotiator. Any minute now, I expect him to reach for my metaphorical gun. "I promised Sonny I'd take care of her. And Sonny and your mom were the only people who ever took care of me."

And there it is again, the faintest vulnerability. I fight the urge to exploit it. As much as I like this new fight I've found, I take no pleasure in cruelty.

When I don't respond, he adds, "But I can be more careful with my words. I'm not always good at that. I'll try."

I nod once, and he offers me the barest smile. It is a careful truce, or perhaps just a ceasefire. But either way, the heat of my anger has cooled, and the silence stretches between us, taking on a new shape, filled with memories of his touch yesterday. I sneak a glance at his hands, recalling how rough and raw his palm felt against mine.

I don't remember when, or if, I was ever as attracted to someone, especially against my will. Was I ever this drawn to Jeff? I loved him, the soft-spoken, steady man who cooked us dinner, organized our pantry, and changed the oil in my car before I noticed it was necessary. But my body didn't flush when he looked at me. I didn't obsess about the veins on his arms, the curve of his shoulders, or the slope of his bottom lip. There was little lust left at the end, and it's hard to remember how much there was to begin with.

There's no justification for the attraction I feel to Caleb; he's proven himself unkind and callous where I'm concerned. But he's looking at me, stripping me with those liquid eyes, as intoxicating as the liquor they resemble. His gaze flicks to my mouth for half a heartbeat, and my lips feel like they're on fire.

Caleb grips the counter with one hand, his knuckles white. And I'm probably making him uncomfortable by telling him off one minute and ogling him the next. Where has calm, collected Eden gone?

"So, those discharge instructions." My voice sounds about as low and sultry as Cassie's terrible impression of me.

He doesn't respond immediately, holding me captive with a lingering look. But I glance away, spotting a collection of pill bottles on the counter.

"Did she talk to the doctor about ongoing treatment?" I lower my voice, although we've been whisper-hissing this whole time.

"She's going to have to see a neurologist for that. We saw the orthopedist this morning," he says.

At the mention of the orthopedist, I'm again thankful she didn't need surgery. I would have insisted we transfer her to a better hospital, and that would have been a battle with Caleb, Mom, and the hospital. But we dodged that bullet.

"Are there any neurologists around here? How far does she need to travel for treatment?"

"The clinic is an hour away, and she hates the doctor. Something about him being a condescending prick."

I snort. "But if that prick can give her meds to slow the progression—"

"I know." He sounds resigned and frustrated, and I sense he's already had this conversation with Mom multiple times. He shifts to face the counter and drags the pill bottles to the edge, spinning them so the labels are facing out. "But first things first. We need to deal with her pain and prevent infection from her stitches. And maybe when you get her more relaxed on the good stuff here, you can convince her to see the neurologist again."

Caleb goes over the medications the hospital prescribed, all of which are clearly labeled on the bottles. But he takes his job seriously, so I pay attention. He pulls the hospital paperwork from his back pocket and flattens it on the counter, waving me closer as he reads the fine print aloud. Again, this is unnecessary, but there's something sweet about his diligence. He's so close that his arm brushes mine as he flips to the next page. He smells like Dove soap and fresh lumber and something distinctly male. And his body is inviting, even if his disposition isn't.

"I'll be by every day. And others will help, too. Adelaide, Bob, Carmela, Dakota, Lina, Ian . . ." He trails off. "You won't be doing this alone."

"That's kind, but I've got it."

He rests his elbows on the counter, leaning over as if he's exhausted, and he probably is. It's been a long twenty-four hours. "You think that now, but it's a lot. When Sonny was sick . . ."

I don't know much about Sonny's decline, but I know he wasn't sick long because he never recovered from his stroke. Mom brought him home, and he died a few months later.

I have wondered since whether I would have come if Mom had called earlier. Would I have faced my anger at Sonny's bedside? Would I have tasted the words of forgiveness? But she didn't call me until he was gone. Mom and I have mastered the art of avoiding hard truths.

"I'm sorry about Sonny. I know what he meant to this town. And what he must have meant to you."

Caleb nods and returns to his full height, his posture locking into place like armor. He reaches into the drawer at his hip, finding a pen before scribbling his name and number on the discharge instructions. He pushes it toward me before he heads for the back door.

"I'm five minutes away. Call me if you need anything."

He hesitates with his hand on the doorknob. "I know I was a dick for what I said about your divorce and hiding here, but I guess I meant"—he looks out over the forest—"this isn't the worst place to come when your life goes to hell. Grand Trees can heal you if you let it."

Maybe he's right. But unfortunately, I know how easily it can break you, too.

CHAPTER 11

I don't know how healing this place is. It's somber, quiet, and a little lonely. At home, my life has a steady melody that distracts me from my solitude. I can hear neighbors walking their dogs, ice cream trucks rolling by, and music from my neighbor's garage band. But as Mom sleeps, the only sounds are the wind through the trees and the birdsong Sonny could have identified.

When Mom wakes, she's in pain, and I wish I had paid closer attention to Caleb's instructions instead of his pheromones, because I can't remember which pill is long lasting but slow acting versus quick release but short term. I didn't prepare myself to change the dressing on her shin, but she's bled through the gauze, and I don't have a choice. I hate the sight of blood and tending to open wounds—physical or emotional. I think I've gone white, and my mouth fills with saliva. I have to swallow rapidly and coach myself through my panic. It's only a small gash.

"It's okay, honey. I'll have Caleb do it tomorrow." Mom speaks in short bursts in a shallow voice as I kneel before her.

"We don't want it to get infected. And I wouldn't want Caleb to think I can't handle it." It fortifies me to remember I have something to prove and someone to prove wrong.

"He's all bark," she says. "Sorry that he's giving you a hard time."

"I can hold my own with him." I sound more confident than I feel, however. That man rattles me like no other.

"Well, you let me know if I need to intervene."

I laugh. "He's not some big kid bullying me on the playground. I'll be fine."

Mom holds motionless as I unwrap the soiled dressing, use the ointment, and force myself to inspect it carefully. She's so bruised along her shin, her chest, and her arm. Mom's always been clumsy, more from hyperfocus and distractedness than physical limitations. When I was a kid, I remember noticing all the bruises she'd earn by turning a corner too sharply, the scratches she'd acquire by stepping into a rosebush to analyze the texture of the petals. But she was never so fragile.

I rewrap her leg in the clean gauze, taking great care to be gentle, no matter how quickly I want this to be over. I don't relax until the pain medication kicks in and the tension drains from her face.

As I'm cleaning up the bandages and ointment, she asks softly, "Why didn't you tell me about Jeff, honey?" and I pause with my back to her as I turn to the kitchen.

"Why didn't you tell me about your diagnosis?" I blurt, even though it's not the time to get into it, or maybe it's exactly the time, while the evidence of her illness is all over her.

"There was nothing you could do about it." Each word is a labor from her wounded ribs, and I know neither of us has the energy to address all the elephants in the room.

"Same, I guess." I cast a quick glance over my shoulder. "Can I get you anything else?"

"No, honey." And that's the last of our conversation for the day. She sleeps in fits and starts. I pull out one of the premade meals for dinner, and we eat in silence. I think we know each potential conversation is a quagmire. At least we're choosing to be gentle with each other. It's an implicit agreement that neither of us can handle difficult conversations yet. Maybe when she's stronger.

Mom doesn't even argue when I help her into the downstairs bedroom, seemingly unsurprised that her found family moved her from the bedroom she shared with Sonny, handling her belongings without her permission while she was at the hospital.

But once she's settled for the night, I move on to something I can control. Work. I reach out to clients to reschedule in-person meetings and answer a few emails, which is easier to face than calling Dad. I want to put that off.

I come by avoidance naturally. I didn't recognize it was part of my familial DNA until Jeff pointed it out. *If one of you forgot to put pants on for Thanksgiving dinner, no one would acknowledge it,* he said after a particularly polite Sunday dinner with my dad. *You act like you're strangers,* he said the first time he met my mom.

There are some advantages, though. Neither of my parents asked if we were planning to have children. Dad didn't even ask why we divorced. We give each other a wide berth in this family. When there are land mines anywhere you step, you learn how to tiptoe.

But I have to call Dad. He will often drop by my house unexpectedly, under the guise of checking on the native flowers he'd planted for me after Jeff left. But we both know what he's really checking on, even if we're not direct enough to discuss the details of my divorce or how I feel about it.

I head out to the porch and pace along the rickety boards while the phone rings.

"Edie." His voice is timid but warm.

"Hi, Dad." I keep my volume low, steeling myself for this conversation. I wish I could sidestep the subject of Mom like I usually do, but I can't lie to him. There's no way for me to hide my long absence. "I came to visit Mom this weekend."

He swallows unnaturally, and I'm immediately guilt ridden. He's never been able to conceal that the pain of her leaving is still raw. "Oh?"

"I was just coming for the weekend, but—"

"Is everything okay?" he jumps in, panic lacing his words. They've been apart as long as they were married, but Dad never moved on. Mom is the most perilous land mine of all.

"I need to stay here a bit longer. Mom . . ." I filter through the available options—*had a small fall, had a minor injury, needs some extra help*—and remember how good it felt to say what I meant this afternoon. I think of how easily I communicated with Caleb and decide to tell Dad the truth. The full truth. And let him take responsibility for his own emotions. I finish, "Had a bad fall yesterday and broke several bones."

His gasp, and the following rattle in his throat, make me second-guess my bluntness, but I continue, sharing everything.

He doesn't speak for several minutes, and I don't press him because some habits die hard, and bad habits rarely persist because they're effective. But the silence is quicksand, and I want to yank him from it, pull him out of his old heartbreak, and force him into the here and now.

If only I could have done that years ago. If only he could have done the same for me.

"You'll take good care of her, Eden, won't you?" He doesn't want me to acknowledge the tears caught in his throat, so I do the Hawthorne thing and pretend I don't.

"I will," I promise, even though I'm still not certain I have it in me.

"If you need help, you call me. I'll come."

I'll never call him, and he knows it, but acquiescence is easier. "Sure."

And then he's silent again, and I worry he's put himself on mute so I won't hear him cry. Back when she left, we didn't have that luxury. I'd hear him through the thin walls when he thought I was asleep.

"You know what, Edie?" And for the first time, he invites me to listen to the tears, to the grief, to the longing. "I always thought she'd come back. I know it's silly. I'm an old man. But I thought there was still time. That someday, we'd be together again . . . because I never stopped loving her."

It's the truest thing he's ever said to me.

"I know, Dad." I've always known. It's a weight I've carried. Because I'm the reason everything fell apart. If I would've bitten my tongue, we could've kept pretending Mom was faithful and their marriage was fine. Maybe Mom would have stayed. Perhaps she'd be living in the city right now, seeking treatment instead of mourning the loss of the second love of her life.

"I was furious at first," Dad says. "I didn't know how to handle that anger, and I froze her out instead of dealing with it. And then after she left, all my anger melted away and I was drowning in regret."

I hate that this trip is dredging all this up for him. Grand Trees is pulling us both back in time. "But you have nothing to regret. You didn't do anything wrong."

He sighs. "Oh, sweetheart, I wish that were true. I refused to forgive her but wouldn't let her go either. That wasn't fair to any of us."

Dad excuses himself soon after, and I am guilt ridden that I'm not there to tend to him, too, and frustrated that it's always fallen on me to do so.

As a kid, Mom ripped me apart, and Dad chose the only functional piece of me as his. But now they both need me, and I don't know if I can stitch myself back together so I can be helpful to either of them.

∼

In the morning, I'm startled awake by something wet, and warm, and smelling of day-old fish. I scramble against the couch cushions as my eyes fly open.

"Houdini, off," comes a loud voice.

But the dog jumps onto my stomach—paws, tongue, and fur having their way with me. I let out a guttural groan from the pain of being trapped under eighty pounds of animal. Houdini lets out an excited howl.

"Houdini." Caleb barrels into the living room just as the dog in question pins my arms under his forelimbs and drags his tongue over my neck. Caleb tugs on Houdini's collar and pulls him off, but the dog's nails catch on my blankets, yanking them into a heap on the ground. It's then I remember I'm essentially naked. I packed in such a hurry that I forgot pajamas—or loungewear of any kind—so I'm sleeping in a tank top and underwear.

"Oh, holy hell." Caleb turns away and releases the dog, who hops on me again, and I squeal as his nails make landfall on my bare skin.

I wrangle him by the collar, but the dog must think this is good fun because he's leaping and flailing, and trapping me and exposing me anew, like we're both in on this game. I shriek when Houdini pins me between his paws, hovering over me with a long trail of drool suspended from his jowls.

Caleb issues commands punctuated by expletives and scrambles blindly for Houdini as he squeezes his eyes closed to avoid my nakedness. All the while the drool lengthens and thins, inching toward my nose.

"Caleb." I regulate my voice, hoping to lull Houdini. "Please get him off of me before he showers me in drool."

"I'm trying," Caleb says but swipes aimlessly at the air as Houdini dodges.

"Oh my God." I laugh. "Just open your eyes."

Caleb grumbles but does as he's told, wrapping his arms around Houdini's torso and lifting him from me in one heave. But I see the moment his gaze catches on my bare leg, and his face freezes before he turns away to shuffle Houdini out of the house.

It gives me just enough time to wrap a sheet around my body like a toga and step behind the couch for good measure. When Caleb faces me again, he looks like he's just survived a barroom brawl. He presses his back to the front door as Houdini cries from the porch. The dog shoves his mug in the window, dragging his tongue across the glass in a desperate attempt to lick his way back inside.

And then I lose it, the laughter starting low before it topples me. Caleb can't maintain his stern expression and grins at me. It's a lot—how his face changes. The smile takes over. His eyes crinkle at the corners, his mouth breaks apart, his cheeks rise, and he's so beautiful that I feel winded.

Abby got her smile from him. Not her mother. That broad, lovely smile I adored in her at first glance—it's his.

It's a moment before I realize I've stopped laughing and am staring at him like an idiot. His face straightens, and it's like the sun disappearing behind clouds.

He clears his throat. "I didn't know you'd be sleeping on the couch and . . ." He trails off, and I fill in the blank with *half naked*.

I clutch my makeshift toga tighter around my chest. "I didn't want to be far from my mom in case she needed me." And I wasn't about to sleep in Sonny and Mom's bed.

"I'm just checking on Nicki before heading to work. I shouldn't have let myself in."

"You have a key?"

He fishes it out of his pocket and holds it aloft like he's a suspect surrendering a weapon. "I'll leave it."

"No, no, it's fine. It's just good for me to know."

His face flushes the barest shade of pink, and I'm sure he's remembering me in my underwear—my fuchsia thong, I realize—and my face turns crimson.

I haven't shaved my legs, or anything else, and it wasn't like I was posing in flattering angles as I defended myself against the benevolent wolf dog, who's now standing on his hind legs and whimpering in the porch window.

Caleb spares him a glance. "I think he likes you."

"He's coming on a little strong. He might want to work on his game." Houdini howls and hops on his hind legs, slamming into the window in his attempt to reach us. Poor guy. I don't think he knows what he did wrong.

Caleb's smile cracks again, making me want to keep joking with him and finding ways to please him.

"I seem to have a habit of rescuing you from overzealous admirers." He gives me a real smile, this one intentional, and it's like he's offered me a carefully wrapped gift in the palm of his hand.

"You must be shocked that some males aren't repulsed by me," I tease.

Caleb's Adam's apple bobs in his throat on a hard swallow. "Not even a little bit." His voice is such a low timbre that it makes me shiver.

My embarrassment fades, replaced by a flush born of a different emotion entirely.

"Eden? Caleb?" Mom's voice breaks through the ruckus. "Is everything okay?"

Caleb gestures toward the room down the hall. "I'll go help Nicki."

"And I'll go"—I motion to my suitcase, open on the floor—"put some clothes on."

Caleb blushes again, this time deeper, and hangs his head as we shuffle by each other. "Sorry," he reiterates. "I didn't see anything." But he avoids my gaze, and we both know he's lying. There's the embarrassment, of course.

But also, I couldn't miss the look of shock on his face when he saw my mangled leg.

CHAPTER 12

Every evening, the people of Grand Trees turn up in a rotating schedule meant to brighten Mom's spirits and ease my caretaking load. But really, they bring chaos.

On the nights Abby is with him, Caleb stops in with her in tow, but we avoid additional awkward interactions because we are never alone. Adelaide swings by at least once a day, and the other folks I met on Sunday take turns checking in. There's enough food to feed a cavalry, and there's always a work party at the ready to do the cleaning, so there's little for me to do, but it's still exhausting.

Their polite curiosity about my job, my home, my friends, and my failed marriage feels like an extended interview.

On Thursday evening, the entire town shows up. There are more names than even I can memorize. I don't know if they got their signals crossed and were all accidentally assigned to tonight's shift or if someone sent out an SOS that we needed reinforcements. And maybe we do. Mom's silence has felt like melancholy. She's been withdrawn, and I'm ashamed to admit I don't know whether it's normal for her. But I know that injuries can spark depression. Mom has lost so much in the last few years, and now her independence is slipping away. We're not able to talk about real things yet, and I don't know how to get there. I want to, even if I have no experience turning that want into reality.

Adelaide pours drinks, serves appetizers, and insists that Abby provide musical accompaniment. Because, of course, Sonny taught her to play guitar. And piano. And she has a singing voice that rivals his. It makes me miss him. And missing someone who died while you were estranged is a special kind of torment.

I always understood how Mom fell in love with Sonny. I loved him, too. He was light and sound and joy and optimism. He was everything Dad was not. And because I made that connection—even after the discovery of their affair—I felt complicit in Mom's betrayal. I couldn't still love Sonny. I couldn't forgive him and still be worthy of Dad's love.

Being back here, in this house, surrounded by the community that Sonny built—it's all too much. I need fresh air. I find my way into the kitchen and escape out the back door, but I hadn't thought this through. The expansive deck extends over the ravine, and the perilous elevation makes me lightheaded. I hurry back toward the door when Adelaide calls to me from where she's perched with a group of people in a circle of Adirondack chairs. They're a murmur of soft voices rising from the half-light of the firepit.

"Eden!" she calls. "Oh, Eden, I have a question for you. Come sit with us, dear."

I should make an excuse and seek solitude elsewhere, but I'm finding it hard to speak, so I walk on shaky legs toward the edge of the deck, shoving my hands in the pockets of my fleece jacket. The night is cool and dewy. The towering pines watch over the landscape like sentinels, the same pines that hovered over me during my darkest time. Adelaide pats a chair beside her and I drop into it, focusing on her face, with my back to the menacing view.

"We were just talking about how cut off we are out here, and the county supervisors have basically written us off. But Caleb has all these ideas to make us safer. The festival last week was one. But we need to cut down all those dead trees up at the camp next to the state land, get the main highway back open, and convince the old town holdouts to clear overgrown vegetation, and . . ."

I look around the circle as Adelaide barrels on without taking a breath. I didn't notice Caleb sitting across from me because his face is refracted through the blaze, but I see him now. His eyes are fixed on me, laser-like, but his body is relaxed; he's leaning against the armrest, his chin in his hand, foot hitched on his knee. He has no business being so fucking hot.

"But it all takes money," Adelaide finishes. "And I was just telling everyone that you're a grant writer."

"Not really. I do work in fundraising, but I'm not technically—" I start.

"But you know how to raise money." Adelaide's expression is hopeful, and I realize this is not small talk.

"Yes," I say cautiously.

"Well, we're looking for some help, and I bet you're just the hotshot we need."

"Okay . . ." It's a prompt for more information about what exactly they could want from me, hoping to wrap up this conversation so I can go back inside.

Adelaide claps her hands together, a grin breaking loose across her round face. "Oh, that's wonderful, Eden. Thank you so much. We've been lost trying to figure out how to fill out all those forms, but I bet this will be a piece of cake for a professional like you."

Shit. What did I just commit to? She reaches out and clasps my hand between hers. This woman is dangerous. My life gets upended every time she begins a monologue. Ian is grinning at me, a knowing smile from someone who may have been roped into things by Adelaide a time or two. I bet everyone in town has been a victim.

"Some things are just meant to be." Adelaide glances at Caleb. "Don't you think, Caleb? You two will make a perfect team."

"Oh, they will." Ian appears to be enjoying this spectacle. I'm so confused by his relationship with Caleb. I couldn't sit beside Nadia around a firepit and pretend we're friends. "Maybe you two should start with the camp project. Spend the spring outlining the plan before the kids come back this summer. Have you ever been there, Eden? I'm sure Caleb would give you a tour."

"I spent every summer there as a kid." My words come out dry as kindling.

"Oh, that's right. I forgot you were a Colibri Camper," Adelaide exclaims. "Caleb, you should take Eden with you the next time you do your rounds. Show her all the improvements and your new ideas so she can visualize them."

"You run Camp Colibri now?" I ask Caleb from across the fractured light of the fire.

"Just the land and buildings. Ian runs the program." I have to strain to hear him above the crackle of flames. He and Ian are not just friends—they're business partners?

"I don't have the patience to manage all that acreage," Ian says.

"And Caleb doesn't have the patience to manage all those people," says Bob, who's sitting to Caleb's right. He laughs and nudges Caleb with his elbow. "Can you imagine dealing with all those entitled parents?"

"Oh, tsk, Bob. Caleb's all teddy bear." Adelaide is indignant on Caleb's behalf. "He has plenty of patience for people."

I try to school my expression but fail, and Caleb catches me cracking a smile. He raises his brow at me, and I bite my lip, looking away. Caleb's patience is selective. For Abby, my mom, his unruly dog, and his ex-wife's new husband, it's limitless. For me, it's nonexistent. But even at his best, his surly disposition isn't suited for customer service.

"I'll stay with Nicolette so you two can get started." Adelaide charges ahead. "Tomorrow? How does tomorrow work?"

"I have to head over there anyway. What about you?" Caleb asks me, and he sounds like he's calling my bluff.

Everyone's watching the exchange, expectant, while Caleb waits for me to back down.

"I'm free tomorrow afternoon," I say.

"Great," Adelaide says. "I'll swing by after lunch."

And that's how I agree to visit Camp Colibri for the first time in twenty years—with Caleb Connell as my escort.

CHAPTER 13

Sonny's house shares a property line with the far edge of Camp Colibri, connected by one of the more remote trails, but the entrance by car is three miles away, along a sequence of switchbacks I anticipate like lyrics to my favorite song. When I pull into the dusty lot, I park beside Caleb's black truck in front of the welcome hall, an old log cabin with a tin roof and a cheerful sign with a blue hummingbird and hand-carved letters: Welcome to Camp Colibri.

I brace myself before stepping out, stalling by cleaning up the mess Abby left on the floor of the passenger seat on the way to the hospital. I don't have the heart to toss her creations—an origami crane, a folded star, and a fortune teller—so I shove them in my glove compartment.

When I stride up the flagstone path, I'm hit with a wave of nostalgia so potent that my breath catches. It smells exactly the same, an olfactory trigger that sends me right back to my childhood. A whole lotta heartache rushed straight at me when I crossed the town line last week. But this scent sparks a kindling of happiness, too. I've been holding my rage like a shield; the memory of my joy is the sword that can pierce it.

The brick patio is bordered by a halo of towering pines, with rustic cabins nestled beneath the emerald branches. There are no counselors or campers. No nervous energy. The camp is in hibernation. It reminds me of Friday afternoons when kids would pull away in their parents' minivans, and I'd stay behind to help Mom clean the art room, take inventory, pick up trash on the trails, or shadow Sonny as he oversaw it all.

During the week, I slept in the cabins with the other kids. But I spent every weekend with Mom in her summer rental. We'd choose books at the Paper Horse and paint each other's nails while watching DVDs borrowed from the video store, now a French bistro. Dad would call to tell us about the summer classes he was teaching at the university, and we'd tell him everything we'd been up to. Or at least, I'd tell him everything. Mom was more selective, apparently.

But Fridays were my favorite. I loved the stillness of the typically bustling space, like an empty theater. There's something sacred about stepping out from the wings in solitude, finding center stage, imagining the spotlight, and hearing the echo of your own footsteps. The empty camp was like that: hallowed, as if the campground was exhaling and reclaiming the tranquility. And all the beauty and charm were just for me.

It's fitting that this is how I'm seeing it again after all these years. I tilt my head to the sky. Clouds are collecting overhead, but the sun barrels through a patch of blue, and it feels like a spotlight. I close my eyes, raising my arms, palms up, breathing in the scent of pine, and replaying memories that are more joyful than I've allowed myself to trust.

"Eden?"

My eyes fly open, and I drop my arms. Caleb is so close I take a step back, squinting into the light. One side of his mouth quirks into a smile.

"Hi," I say curtly. "What did you want me to see?"

His smile falls, and he settles back into his standard posture: stance wide, arms crossed, a hint of a scowl. "You don't know why you're here, do you?"

"Adelaide," I say, as if that explains everything.

Caleb sighs. "I could tell you weren't listening."

"I think I get sensory overload when Adelaide starts talking," I admit. And Caleb shakes his head but waves his hand in a *come along* gesture, and I follow him.

"We could've done this without a personal tour, but you're here now, and I have to make my rounds anyway." He stops beside the door to the welcome hall and glances at my feet. "You all right for a hike?" It's then I notice the heavy daypack slung over his shoulders.

"I can walk just fine," I snap, but my leg rewards me with a dull, phantom ache—my own rebellious body calling me a liar.

"Good to know," Caleb says. "But I was talking about your shoes."

I look down at my canvas sneakers, chastened. Maybe I need to dial it down a notch. Once someone's seen my leg, pity and lowered expectations follow. But perhaps I jumped to conclusions with Caleb. "Oh, yeah. I'm good."

He watches me skeptically, not looking away as he calls, "Houdini, come on, boy."

Houdini appears around the corner of the welcome hall, head lowered and tail tucked between his legs, taking a cautious step onto the landing.

"Look at you, playing coy after coming on so strong the other day," I say, and Caleb snorts as I sink down to my haunches. "What's wrong, Houdini?" He slinks over and rests his chin on my thigh. "Is he in trouble or something?" I scratch his ears.

"He's just been acting weird the last day or so. Anxious for some reason."

"Ah, that's rough."

Houdini whines in response and nestles his muzzle against my stomach. I whisper into his ear, "I know how that feels." He tilts his head as if he's really listening to me, and then he licks my face. "Cheap shot." I laugh as I stand. But Houdini leans his body weight into my legs, and I lose my balance before Caleb catches me by the elbow. And there it is again—a jolt of lightning at his touch. We make eye contact before he releases me. Does he feel it, too? I wish I could read him.

"Let's head out," Caleb says.

We walk in silence for the first twenty minutes, which is for the best. The nostalgia has me by the throat. We pass through the lower grove, where I had enjoyed so many hours building fleeting but intense friendships. We skate around the amphitheater, home to Sonny's sing-alongs, improv contests, game nights, and dances. Along the river trail, I spot the park bench where I had my first tentative kiss with a boy named Roger. There's an old willow, bent and bare now, that once held a rope swing.

The sleeping cabins are new and sleek; the buildings look like they were photoshopped over my memories. But the footprint of the camp is the same. I catch sight of the ropes course in the distance, and I peer through the trees where redwood posts rise above the clearing, with tightropes strung between them.

"Was the ropes course here when you were a kid?" Caleb asks.

"Yeah," I say. "But I never tried it. I wanted to, though."

"Why not?" Caleb asks.

"By the time I was old enough, I was too serious about ballet to do anything that came with a risk of injury. I had to sign a contract with my school." I'd come down and watch my friends and high-five them when they were done. But I was used to it; I spent so much of my childhood on the sidelines observing others take risks I couldn't. I didn't ski, ice-skate, or play sports. I was so careful. The irony of my later injury was another layer to my grief. This camp was the only place I was able to be a kid. But it was also the place that destroyed my childhood.

"Whoa," Caleb says, frowning. "That's intense. How old were you when you had to stop having fun?"

"I started dancing when I was three, but I don't think I had to sign my life away until I was ten or so." Most of the time, it wasn't a sacrifice. I had a goal. And my body was the vehicle that would get me there.

Caleb glances at my leg, a well of questions perched on his lips, but he quickly looks away. "Abby has the fastest recorded time on the high course."

"I bet." I follow as he starts up the trail. "She's a cool kid."

"The coolest."

At least we agree on something.

Houdini hangs close, frantically herding us as we climb the Poppy Ridge Trail. It's one of the longer hikes, and Caleb takes several detours, checking out the trees and shrubbery and making notes on a clipboard while I hang back.

"Come here." Caleb crouches beside a pine and presses against the bark with his thumb. Houdini is at his heels, sniffing around the trunk.

My feet crunch along the pine needles, and I avoid a patch of poison oak as I make my way over.

Caleb snaps a few photos with his phone before shoving it in his pocket. "This tree is showing signs of a bark beetle attack, but it looks to be fending it off."

I guess Caleb isn't a fan of context, but I play along. "How can you tell?"

"See these globs of white sap?" I nod. "That's the tree's defense. If the sap was brown or red, I'd know the beetles had gotten in."

"And this has something to do with why I'm here?" I ask.

He spares me a glance as he stands. Houdini lifts his leg against the side of the tree. "Last year, bark beetles killed a whole batch of trees, weak from drought. It cost a fortune to remove them. Dead trees are kindling during fire season. And climate change makes all of these issues worse, so managing these lands is gonna get even more expensive."

He doesn't wait for me to respond while he swerves around a few stumps to check out another ancient ponderosa.

"And this is what you need money for?" I ask.

"For starters. We also need a fire station and the main road repaired. We've been sitting ducks in case of emergency since that landslide."

"Isn't that a state or county responsibility?" I ask as I pat Houdini's head. His ears are folded back like he's scared of something.

Caleb is focused on a tree, scribbling notes on his clipboard after noticing subtle marks and blemishes. "Yeah, but I gotta put pressure on them to do their jobs. CAL FIRE and FEMA give grants for fire prevention and disaster preparedness. And the camp is a nonprofit, so we can apply for some. The town can as well, but the council is all volunteer, and I'm the only one who knows how to work a computer."

"Ah," I say. "That's where I come in." I scramble to keep up with him as he veers back to the trail. "You know, I'm not technically a grant writer."

"But you know how to raise money."

"Yes, but I don't write many government grants."

"Well, I'm not in the Forest Service either, but here we are." He stops and turns to me with a hard expression. "Are you saying you won't do it?"

And ugh, this guy. Adelaide voluntells me to undertake a complex governmental grant process while I care for my sick mom and keep my consultancy alive from hundreds of miles away, and I'm the jerk for hesitating. "I didn't say that. But I don't want you all to think I can save this town from the apocalypse. I have to set reasonable expectations."

He hitches his backpack higher on his shoulders, dragging his thumbs under the straps. "We're not looking for a hero. We just pitch in for each other around here."

I hear his admonishment. I've seen the way this town pitches in for each other, and my mom and I have been recent recipients. "I'll do what I can."

We stare at each other for a brief moment. Every time he looks at me like this, a flash of electricity pulses through my body, even when my blood is boiling in anger. He looks away first and heads back to the trail through knee-high grasses. I follow, navigating the overgrowth.

Houdini jolts past me and charges up the trail, barking at something in the distance, his hackles raised. Caleb jogs uphill to reach him and scans the area.

My foot is beginning to throb. I haven't been disciplined about stretching since I got here, because all my routines are out of whack. I take a moment to extend my calf before rushing to meet them, forcing myself to walk without a discernible limp.

The wind picks up in the clearing, tickling the wildflowers and shaking the branches of the pine trees in the distance. The clouds are thickening, darkening, and inching toward us.

"Houdini's afraid of his shadow today," Caleb says. "And it looks like it might rain. We should hurry." He leads us up the final climb, telling me about the seedlings he hopes to plant and his plans to transition all the buildings to a fire-resistant design like the new sleeping cabins, which are made of faux-wood steel siding and designed to withstand wildfires. It's more words than I've heard him utter in one stretch. I feel like I should be taking notes.

Finally, we reach the summit, Colibri Peak, which leads to a steep, rocky trail to the east side of Grand Trees Lake. But what I remember as a barren and treacherous cliff is covered in a thick coat of California poppies and purple lupines, draped like veils toward the shoreline. The lake's surface appears obsidian against the darkening clouds.

"I didn't know how beautiful it could be up here." I'd only been here in summer, so I've never seen it in bloom.

"It hasn't looked like this in years." Caleb offers me his open canteen. I take a small sip. When I hand it back, he takes a swig before pouring some into a bowl for Houdini. "We had our first good rain this winter after a long drought. These flowers are celebrating."

The breeze picks up, and a group of poppies waltz in response. "That should help the trees recover, too, right?"

Caleb shrugs. "Yes and no. The drought damaged roots, made them shallower, and it's hard for the trees to handle all that water at once."

I pull my phone from my pocket and snap several photos of the landscape. I can add photos of this view to the applications.

"I have contractor bids and budget figures in the maintenance office. We can grab them on our way down," Caleb says as I linger over the view.

He leans forward, assessing me. I'm worried I might have something on my face.

"What color are your eyes?" he asks, scanning me like a painting.

I'm struck dumb by the heat of his attention. When I don't respond, he continues. "I thought they were blue, but now they look green. And when your mom paints them, they're iridescent and sort of every color at once."

"I think it depends on the light," I manage, trying to keep the vibrato out of my voice so he can't tell what his focus does to me. He holds my stare until my breath falters and I feel my body sway toward him.

He nods toward the ledge, breaking the trance. "Like the lake."

I follow his sightline. The lake is tempestuous right now—a little surly and mysterious. I appreciate being compared to its power. When I look back to Caleb, he waves me forward and waits for me to turn toward the trail, taking the rear this time.

Caleb and Houdini can probably move faster on the descent, but downhill is harder for me; I have to compensate for all that pressure on my shin and knee. Caleb jogs off the trail and comes back with a branch, handing it to me for a walking stick. I want to protest, but it will be helpful. I hate him a little for being right.

As we make our way to the first crop of pines, it begins to drizzle, and Houdini and Caleb hurry down the slope behind me before a roar of distant thunder launches a deluge. Fat drops of rain slide down the back of my jacket and soak my jeans. Water blurs my vision before Caleb leads us to a building hidden within a patch of trees. He rests a hand on the small of my back, guiding me toward the cabin, while Houdini charges out and paws at the doorknob.

Caleb calls out, "It's locked," and chuckles.

"Can he open doors?" I ask as Caleb hunts for the keys in his pocket.

"He didn't get his name for nothing."

Houdini releases a long howl as thunder—closer this time—claps overhead.

Caleb swings the door open and waves me in, but Houdini scrambles in first, rushing under the desk at the far end of the space. Caleb closes the door behind us. "Sorry." He looks me up and down.

My teeth are chattering and I must look like a drowned rat. "It wasn't supposed to rain today."

It appears to be one of the old drafty counselor cabins converted into an office space, with bare wood walls and narrow clerestory windows along the ceiling. The perimeter is lined with metal filing cabinets and open shelving, the desk is covered in piles of paperwork, and there's an entrance to a small bathroom in the corner.

Caleb grabs a couple of towels from a storage shelf and hands me one. I recognize them as the standard-issue beach towels we used to bring to the lake. It smells like mothballs and dust, but I'm not picky. I wring out my ponytail as Caleb does his best to dry himself off.

"I have quotes from contractors in here that'll help with budgets and pricing. We can race back to camp as soon as there's a break in the rain." He riffles through a stack of paperwork, collects it into a neat stack, and drops his backpack onto the desk chair to load it all inside. "Okay. I think that's everything."

But as he slings his pack over his shoulder, Houdini lets out a guttural cry, and the ground comes alive, rolling under us until I stumble backward, catching myself on the shelving behind me.

CHAPTER 14

I don't see Caleb move, but he's on me in a minute, wrapping an arm around my waist and pulling me under the bathroom doorway.

It's over before I register the earthquake. It's a small one, I think, but Caleb is still pressing me against the jamb with a hand on my hip, the other gripping the upper casing to stabilize us, and he's hovering over me like we just lived through the big one. My face is even with his neck, and I'm so close I see the way his pulse riots in the hollow of his throat, and I feel the tension of his fingers as they dig into my skin through my jeans. I'm stunned still by the realization that this man just dragged me across the room and pinned me against the doorjamb—and I liked it. I really, really liked it.

I thought I was more evolved than that.

I want to tell him everything's okay. The earthquake was minor; I've felt similar ones over the years, and damage is typically minimal. But he's breathing rapidly and scanning the room. I follow his gaze. Nothing is out of place but a few toppled water bottles on the shelves.

He doesn't move, so neither do I. I'm a lecher for reacting to his proximity while he's panicking about the mild tremor. I place a hand on his forearm, trying to center him in the room, where everything's fine, versus whatever catastrophe is unraveling in his head.

"We're okay," I say. Houdini growls in response.

For the first time, Caleb looks at me, and our gazes collide. His eyes are glazed, as if there is a disaster playing out behind them and he can't see beyond his personal movie screen to focus on reality.

"It was a small one." My voice comes out like I'm soothing a child.

Caleb blinks, shaking his head slightly, and I register when he comes back into his body, because he moves away and releases me abruptly. I sink against the door casing and exhale, both relieved and disappointed by the new distance.

But just as I get my legs under me again and duck out from the cage of his protection, Houdini jumps on the desk and begins a plaintive howl. I catch a strange sound from outside, and it builds steadily, like kindling catching fire, but louder, more resonant.

"Shit." Caleb looks up to the ceiling.

"What?" I ask, and we've switched places, because I'm panicking and he's found his calm.

He gathers me back into him, one hand on my neck, the other around my back, and he yanks us down until I'm crouched and he's kneeling over me like a force field.

A boom rattles the cabin, and Caleb cradles me tighter. He waits another few seconds before he releases me and sits up.

"That was close," he says.

He moves to the door in hurried strides. He tries to open it, but it doesn't budge. He presses his shoulder into it, grunting as he barrels into it once, then twice.

"Caleb, what is going on?" My patience is fraying.

Houdini's howls reach a desperate crescendo. Caleb drags a chair to the door, stepping onto it so he can peer out the clerestory window. He drops his forehead against it, and his breath fogs up the glass.

"That was a huge pine that just came down. And it's blocking the door."

"What?" My mouth is dry and my voice shallow, and I need to find some new words.

"I'm pretty sure we're trapped."

"At least it didn't crush us." I recall that he threw himself on top of me to protect me from it. My body heats from within, remembering the weight of him, but I shiver as the warmth collides with the cool air on my damp skin.

He steps down, grabbing his cell out of his pocket, and I do the same.

I call my mom, but the call fails. "Do you have service? Is there Wi-Fi?"

Caleb fiddles with the light switch. "The power must be out. It's erratic at best up here."

I step onto the chair, but I can barely see through the high, narrow window. Branches and leaves are smashed against the dusty glass. I step down to push futilely on the door.

Caleb releases an irritated laugh. "Are you trying to fact-check me? Did you think I was making it up and trying to hold you hostage?" He steps back, looking affronted, before removing his soaked hoodie and dropping it on the chair. He has on a fitted thermal underneath, a russet color just like his eyes, which are sparking at me in irritation.

"It was just reflex. Like when someone says, 'What stinks?' you can't help but smell it. It's instinct."

"Why would you want to smell something that stinks?"

I ignore this. "What now?"

Caleb scans the space and bites his cheek. "I don't know. The windows don't open, and they're way too tight to climb through even if they did. If we shattered one, we'd cut ourselves to hell and get wedged in there anyway."

"So we're just what? Stuck here forever?" We're both drenched. Rain is pummeling the tin roof, and a giant tree is blocking our only exit.

"Yes, Eden. This is our life now, until we run out of water or kill each other."

I step into the bathroom, looking for an exit route he may have failed to mention, but there are no windows, no doors. We are trapped.

Houdini howls as I lean against the door, and Caleb crawls under the desk to soothe him, whispering in a low register and stroking his back until the dog's cries soften.

I close my eyes and listen to the rain outside, hoping the sound will settle my panic. But the prattle of raindrops isn't as comforting in our current predicament as it is when it drifts through my speakers to lull me to sleep in the city. It reinforces that I'm soaked, cold, and helpless.

But I remind myself that I'm not hurt. We have shelter, water, and a bathroom. It's not the same as the last time I was stuck on this land, even if my overactive nervous system doesn't believe it.

When I open my eyes, Caleb is standing in front of me. He shoves his hands in his pockets, and I watch the way his jeans dip. I swallow and try to focus on his words.

"People know we're here. We're not trapped forever, just until someone comes looking, which won't be long."

But hours later, we're still waiting. Caleb found a box of old camp T-shirts, and we changed out of our wet clothes and into the shirts and beach towels as skirts. I stayed in my soaked outfit and resisted for an hour but relented when I began shivering uncontrollably and my modesty felt more like a death wish. I emerged from the bathroom with the blue-striped towel held together with white knuckles.

My shirt is hunter green and made of cheap, stiff cotton. Caleb's is bright orange and two sizes too small. It leaves nothing to the imagination. Well, actually, I still have plenty of imagination to spare, because the way this shirt hugs his biceps is indecent, and it rides up his abdomen to reveal a trail of dark hair along taut skin. I'm trying really hard not to look. And to his credit, I haven't noticed him staring at my exposed leg. The scars have faded, but my calf is smaller on the right, and the scar tissue creates an uneven surface. I don't wear shorts or short skirts because I hate the unwanted attention.

Caleb is petrified that the earthquake was just a prelude to something stronger, so he insists we huddle in the corner where there are no tall shelves to crush us. We're sitting against the far wall with Houdini curled between us.

"So you don't like earthquakes." I swallow a bite of a stale granola bar. I'm still reeling from Caleb's reaction. The instinct to protect me was—I'm not ashamed to admit—hot. But his terror was real.

Caleb scoffs. "Who does?" He strokes Houdini's back in a soothing rhythm. He loves that silly dog.

Jeff didn't like animals. Or kids. I told myself it didn't matter. As a childless, petless couple, we could go on spontaneous romantic getaways, travel overseas, experience the world. But we rarely traveled; we were never spontaneous. I convinced myself that being kid-free meant Jeff would have more love and time for me, but I learned too late that his desire to ration himself was selfish, not generous.

And more importantly, I want a dog. I want kids. I want a man who wants these things. I want a man who knows that love can't be rationed. It can only be shared.

Caleb leans down and whispers something in Houdini's ear. It's unintelligible, but the tone is cajoling and kind, and it makes my heart race.

"How's a California boy so scared of earthquakes?" Because, yes, no one likes them. But you live here long enough, you grow accustomed to occasional tremors. The last big one in San Francisco was before I was born, but I was raised in its shadow—collapsed freeways, condemned buildings, a city punished by a vengeful earth.

"I grew up in Texas."

"Don't you have hurricanes, tornadoes, and floods there?" I need to distract myself from the thirst trap that is Caleb soothing his anxiety-ridden dog.

"Yeah, but in a quake, the earth literally gives way. That's the stuff of horror movies." Houdini whimpers in his sleep. "See, Houdini agrees."

I thought it was an old wives' tale that dogs could sense earthquakes, but after Houdini's behavior, I'm a believer. I scratch under his ears.

"You were trying to warn us, weren't you, good boy?" He lifts one ear, like he's answering me.

"There was a quake the night I first came to Grand Trees. I didn't know what the hell was going on. It scared the crap out of me."

"You moved here as a teen?" Caleb had told me that in a moment of vulnerability at the hospital. He said he had nowhere else to go, but Abby said he didn't speak to his parents because they were terrible, not because they were dead. What would bring him halfway across the country in search of a new home at such a young age?

He's quiet for a few moments, while the rain pelts the roof and the wind drags the downed branches against the window. Finally, he says, "Yep."

Well, that was enlightening. We sit in silence again. So much for using this time to get to know each other and maybe find common ground.

Caleb laid out extra towels on the floor, but the cold seeps through. There's nothing comfortable about the accommodations or the company. My leg is asleep, and my butt is following suit. I need to get up and stretch, but I can't hazard a wardrobe malfunction while trying to stand, so I settle for shifting to my hip and crossing my other leg. It means my bad leg is exposed.

"Does it hurt?"

Most people ask what happened, but this isn't any better.

"Yep," I say, and he releases a wry laugh. I think he recognizes the mimicry.

"You favor that foot sometimes." He's undeterred.

"Nice of you to notice." Most people don't until they see the scars, and then they have a million questions or look away and pretend they didn't see.

"When you're tired, or you've been sitting too long."

And my hackles flare again. Why can't I ask him a mundane question about where he's lived, but he feels safe to ask about my leg? "Or someone takes me on a surprise hike?"

"You could've said no. I gave you an out."

"So you were lying when you said you were asking about my shoes."

"Your shoes are also crap. You should wear better shoes."

I release an incredulous laugh, wrapping my towel tighter around my waist and pushing to stand. To hell if I flash him. Maybe he can find another imperfection to dissect. I pace to the other end of the room, but my entire body is screaming at me. It's cold and drafty away from the shared body heat of Caleb and Houdini's corner.

"How much longer do you think they'll be?" I don't want to commit to the cold corner, but I need to make a statement, so I pace in front of the door.

"Thirty minutes."

"Really?"

Caleb laughs. "How would I know? There could be blocked roads due to the storm. Not to mention the earthquake."

"It was so small it was hardly an earthquake," I say. "It didn't even trigger one of those alerts Abby added to my phone. Yours didn't go off either. And those are for large quakes." But maybe cell service went out before there was a chance for a warning. I don't really know how it all works.

"It brought down a tree," Caleb protests, waving to the blocked door as if it's the smoking gun.

"It was the drought, or the beetles, or the rain, or the lightning—probably all of the above. We don't know it was the earthquake."

"It didn't help," he grumbles.

I lean against the desk and sigh. "Sonny was wrong. This place isn't magic. It's cursed."

"This place is blessed," he says. "And then you show up, and we have broken bones, freak storms, and motherfucking earthquakes."

"Wow." I make an exaggerated expression of awe. "I am very powerful. I wonder what else I could curse. Maybe you should be nicer to me so I don't put a hex on you."

He chuckles, and I catch another rare smile that changes his face from austere to elated. "I'm plenty nice to you," he says, the smile still in his voice. "I could have let you get crushed by that tree."

"I didn't need saving." But I watch him, cuddled in the corner with his eighty-pound puppy, an arm draped over the dog's spine, soothing the anxiety out of him. This man is a protector. He's built for it. The towel is too small to cover him completely, so there's a slit extending up to his thigh. It's obscene. His leg is dusted with a light coat of hair, his upper thigh paler than his calf, and the length of it is muscled and strong. He looks like he could deadlift the tree blocking our escape. I think he catches me staring, because he clears his throat, and I dart my focus away. "But I appreciate the gesture. You could have taken the opportunity to let nature do your dirty work."

He barks out a laugh. "I guess I missed my chance." He's looking right at me—and wow, that grin glows even in the fading light. I feel his smile under my skin like the first embers of a fire. "Unfortunately, I promised your mom I'd be nicer to you."

And just like that, the moment passes. "We missed game night." I note how late it's gotten. "You weren't supposed to pick up Abby, were you?"

He shakes his head. "Lina was planning on picking her up from school and dropping her at your mom's. And I bet the whole town is there by now, planning the rescue and worrying."

I don't like the thought of Mom worrying about me. I hope she trusts we're okay. I sink to the floor, but Caleb grunts. "I don't like you sitting in front of those shelves."

"There's not gonna be another earth—"

But he talks over me. "It's warmer over here without the draft from that vent." He points a finger toward the ceiling above me. "You made your point by walking away. I won't ask you any more personal questions."

I should be relieved. But for some reason, I'm struck by a wave of disappointment. I don't know how long we'll be stuck here, or why I'm so curious about Caleb, but I don't want to sit here in silence. I traipse back over, finding my spot beside Houdini, who shifts to rest his chin on my thighs.

"Traitor," Caleb mumbles.

The wind picks up, and branches scrape against the cabin. Houdini whines, lifts his head, and shuffles off to hide under the desk again. I feel the absence like a gust of refrigerated air. His thick coat was welcome insulation.

"Can you believe we met only a week ago?" Caleb asks.

"Happy anniversary to you, too. I'm touched you remembered." My tone is sarcastic, but his words warm my body like a glass of wine.

"Don't be flattered. It's just that I'm starving, which reminded me I met you while picking up Friday dinner."

I roll my eyes, even though it's too dark for him to see the gesture. "Alcohol would really come in handy about now, too."

Caleb chuckles and shifts until he's stretched out on the floor beside me, his palms clasped and resting on his stomach.

"Are you going to sleep?" I ask. Is he really accepting we'll have to spend the night in here, half naked and freezing?

He opens one eye. "Do you have a better idea?" When I don't answer, he settles into a prone posture as I huddle in the corner, upright and uncomfortable.

There's no way I can sleep next to him, in this cool, dusty space on a bare wood floor while the wind threatens to finish the job of the fallen tree. And I resent him a little for being able to.

CHAPTER 15

"Hey, Eden, wake up." Caleb's voice is gruff, more texture than sound.

"What?" I grumble. Everything hurts—my hip, neck, leg, back—and I can't feel my toes. The ground is ice against my body, and the towel has come apart at my waist. I yank it closed.

"You're shivering so loud it woke me up."

"Sorry." I force my jaw closed to stop my teeth from chattering. I contract into a tighter ball, pulling my knees against my chest. Leave it to Caleb to be inconvenienced by my misery.

"Eden." He sits up so his face is even with mine. "We could huddle closer. It'll help."

He's impossible to read. Is he repulsed by the idea? Is he being a hero? Do I care as long as I'm warmer?

"I don't think"—I have to stop as my jaw clenches shut—"that's a good idea."

"You're freezing." He pauses. "You can just use me for body heat. Promise I won't do anything inappropriate."

The suggestion is so tempting. The chill in my bones is painful, and my back spasms as my shivering intensifies. I'm just afraid I'll receive the comfort in a way he's not offering it.

"C'mon, you're miserable." I catch the glint of his irises in the faint light—those whiskey eyes I'd noticed from across the bar—and I cave.

"Okay," I whisper, scared to say it too loud. I slide until I'm lying sideways on my other hip, my back to his front. When he scoots closer and wraps his arm around my waist, his heart hammers against my shoulder blade, and I feel the relief of him in every cell in my body. He keeps a modest distance so there's an inch or two between our hips, but my back is cramping from the biting cold, and without thinking, I pull him closer, sinking into him like he's salvation.

His breath catches, but he doesn't pull back. Instead, he tucks the top of my head under his chin so we're connected everywhere. I'm still shaking, but the tremors are slowing, the battery on my chill dying with every inch of him that makes contact.

"My feet are freezing."

He slides his leg over mine and traps my feet between his calves. This man aims to serve; it cannot be comfortable for him. Jeff used to complain about my cold feet and would pull away if I strayed too close to his side of the bed. But Caleb clutches me tighter, rubbing my toes between his warm skin until I regain sensation. He is the afternoon sun on white sand. He's a warm towel fresh from the dryer.

"Better?" His voice sounds strangled, as if he's holding his breath.

"Getting there. Thank you."

He squeezes my waist. It's almost imperceptible, but I feel the subtle affection like an ache. I haven't felt another body this close to mine since Jeff left. I haven't been held like this in . . . maybe ever. And Caleb's body is so unfamiliar and new. It's an impenetrable wall and a down blanket all at once. My body releases one last involuntary shiver, and I exhale with the relief of it.

"So, umm." Caleb sighs and his breath tickles my cheeks. "My body may react. If it does, I'm sorry. It's involuntary."

While my ego takes a hit at his insistence that he doesn't find me, specifically, attractive, the thought of him hardening makes me flush. I squeeze my legs together and clear my throat.

"I get it. It's fine. It's a small price to pay to steal your body heat."

He chuckles softly. "I'll try to be your nonreactive heating pad."

"Just remember you don't like me. That should help."

He shifts and brushes my hair until it falls over my shoulder—I assume to get it out of his face—but the indirect touch makes the tiny hairs on my skin stand on end.

He whispers, "I don't dislike you, Eden."

I laugh. "Sure."

"I'm just protective of my people. And sometimes, I let my loyalty get in the way of civility."

I make a contented sound in acknowledgment. I honestly don't care why he's been such an ass, because right now, he feels so divine that I'd forgive him anything.

"I'm sorry I made you uncomfortable earlier. By asking about your leg."

"It's okay."

His body is wrapped around mine, bringing feeling back to my extremities and reminding me how amazing it is to be held. To feel skin, and breath, and the texture of fine hair and the vibration of voice. Maybe I'm too easy. But fear of frostbite—and a man's hard body as salve—will do that to you. I sink against him a little deeper as my body releases another thread of tension.

"If it makes a difference, I have a bunch of scars, too. The one most people see is the one on my lip."

"Bar fight?" I tease.

He's silent for a few minutes before he answers. "My stepdad sliced it open against his wedding band when I was ten."

I pinch my eyes closed, trying to drown out intruding images of young Caleb terrified, hurt, and betrayed by someone who should have cared for him. But my body reacts viscerally. It's like I just plummeted several stories in an elevator; the air leaves my lungs, and my stomach gets stuck near my throat. "Caleb," I say, a little breathless.

"I have a four-inch gash on my rib cage. That time, he threw me against the garage wall where the garden shears were hanging. And there's another under my chin when he pushed me down the stairs and

I sliced it on the edge of the tile. I have some hearing loss in my left ear, but I don't remember which hit caused it."

"Caleb." I have no other words, just his name as a prayer or maybe an elegy. I can sense my tears coming. My nose is burning and throat tightening in sharp warning.

"You asked me when I moved here. And I think you were really asking why."

"Yes," I admit, my voice small.

"I moved here when I finally got big enough to fight back. I was sixteen, I think. After our first fair fight, my stepdad gave my mom an ultimatum. Him or me. She chose him." He clears his throat. "I couch surfed for a few months, got into some trouble, and overstayed my welcome with friends. Finally, I remembered my mom had a brother in California. I took the bus and then hitchhiked. I didn't know where Sonny lived but knew he ran this camp up in the woods. I got here in the winter and came straight here, but it was deserted, so I broke into one of the old cabins."

"And there was an earthquake?" I ask, remembering what he told me earlier.

"Happened in the pitch dark that first night. It wasn't big, but I was alone and . . ." He trails off. "Well, Sonny found me the next morning. He could have called the cops because I'd broken the lock to get in. But instead, he and your mom took me in. And this place healed me."

I find his arm across my waist and thread my fingers through his. He doesn't even hesitate before squeezing my palm, his breath catching.

"I guess my point is that scars don't really mean anything. They just show what happened to you, not who you are."

I breathe in his words, which land like a truth just out of reach, wishing I could believe them. But for me, my scar *is* who I am. I was a dancer, and then I wasn't.

"I'm sorry about what happened to you," I whisper, and he nods against my hair. "I broke my leg when I was a teenager." I've given this same answer a few dozen times to strangers. To friends. To colleagues.

But Caleb's calves are pressed against that broken leg, and I want to give him more. His soft hair tickles the incision the doctors used to staple me back together after they set the bone, the same incision that got infected a week later. His shin bone presses against the other scar where my tibia stabbed through my skin. His inner thigh clutches the knee that never fully straightened afterward. His hips warm the muscles that had to fight twice as hard to support me, trying and failing to give me the strength I needed to be who I once was.

"It was a compound fracture of the tibia and fibula. I had a botched emergency surgery. They didn't align the bones properly. Then the incision got infected and I had sepsis. They almost had to amputate. But I was lucky." I swallow the words that were bestowed on me so many times in those early months and made me feel ungrateful for still having a leg that would never allow me to do what I loved. "I had to have several more surgeries, one to fix the first and another for skin grafts since the infection damaged the tissue."

My stomach turns, the nausea creeping in at the memory. Cassie says it's my trauma response. I threw up for weeks after that first surgery. There wasn't enough medicine in the world to quell the queasiness.

"And you were a dancer." He offers a breadcrumb to my own story. His voice could coax a genie out of a bottle. The hum of it is an elixir.

"Ballet."

"You were good. So good they had you signing contracts at ten."

"I was good," I confirm. There's no use in equivocating. "Ballet is elitist and terrible in a lot of ways, but I loved it. You have to have the right feet, the turnout, the body proportions, flexibility, strength, and aesthetics even to have a chance to train at the highest levels. I started at a neighborhood school, and my ballet teacher pulled my mom aside after I'd been there a year. A few weeks later, I had an audition at the San Francisco Ballet School, and I grew up there. My time here at camp was the only time I wasn't training full-time." It was holy to me. To us. And I thought Mom came here every summer for me. But I was wrong.

"Did you want to dance professionally?" he asks.

"It's all I ever wanted to do."

"And you couldn't after the injury?"

I shake my head, and my hair catches on his beard. He brushes it away, and the lingering feeling of his fingertips on my nape sends shivers down my spine. "Maybe I could have recovered if there weren't so many complications, but even then, it would have taken a miracle because the injury was so extensive. So my leg made ballet impossible."

I think of the day, a year after the accident, when I placed my hand atop my kitchen counter like it was a ballet barre and forced my way into first position, which was once as easy as instinct. But with my palm on the white tile, I couldn't straighten my leg, couldn't support my weight. As a dancer, I knew my body like poets knew their words, but this new body was foreign to me.

My favorite teacher often said that *it's not about perfection; the magic is in the attempt.* But I couldn't even attempt mediocrity anymore.

"So it wasn't really a broken leg. It was a broken heart," Caleb says.

My tears burst to the surface, shocking me. They slide over my nose, across my cheek, and into my ear. I don't move to brush them away, fearing Caleb will pull back from me. I can't risk ending the spell of his body pressed to my spine, his words pressed to my hair.

But these tears aren't born of the grief Caleb so succinctly spoke aloud. These tears are born from being understood. These tears are clean like the rain pattering against our cabin in the woods. They are a release.

"Yes," I say.

"Well," he says, and I could be wrong, but I think he presses the softest kiss to the top of my head. "I'm sorry about that. Heartbreaks are the toughest breaks to set."

I sniff the tears away, and Caleb tugs me closer.

"But I know something about healing them," he whispers.

This makes me chuckle, and my laughter is wet from my tears and filled with gratitude for his kindness. "Really, how's that?"

"You gotta fill your life with things you love more than you loved what broke you."

CHAPTER 16

Caleb's body does react, and I wake to his reaction pressing into my backside. I should be ashamed for not jumping away, but it's so cold in here. And he told me it's not personal. It's biology. So I hold still and replay the memory of our quiet confessions.

I have no idea what time it is, but it's full dark outside. The rain has stopped, the wind is gone, but we're still stuck. Houdini yawns and whimpers. He must have curled up on the other side of Caleb, because he isn't under the desk.

The side of my body pressed to the floor is in agony. But the rest of me—sandwiched against Caleb's muscle and warm skin—is relishing the closeness. With Houdini stirring, I expect Caleb to wake and recoil. Instead, he spreads his broad palm across my stomach and pulls me tighter against him with a subtle thrust of his hips. And oh. I'm here for it. But I think he's asleep. My conscience jumps into action, and I try to roll away. Caleb's arms are strong, though, and there's no give. He has me around the waist, sealing me to him with his signature stubbornness. I feel the outline of him against my ass and . . . well, I'm not sure I could resist it if he were offering.

I'm embarrassed about the heat that's building between my legs. It's just been so long. And he's so incredibly hot, and surprisingly sweet when he's not being an asshole.

His hand travels under my T-shirt until his calloused palm is splayed against my bare rib cage like he's claiming me. I'm really going to move away. In a minute. In a few minutes. But until then, I'm going to cement the texture of him into my long-term memory.

There's a faint sound of voices from outside, before the crunch of pine needles, and then a shout, followed by Houdini prattling to the door, whimpering.

"Over here," someone says, and then there are so many voices.

"Caleb! Hey, are you in there?"

I need to yell and let them know they've found us, but then I'll have to admit I've been taking advantage of Caleb's "reaction" while he lay comatose behind me.

"What?" Caleb's voice is rough with sleep. "Shit," he says into my hair. "Eden, I'm sorry." He slides his hand out from under my shirt and jerks his hips back. It's then I realize we'd been under the same towel, and I'm exposed. He tosses it to me and stands in his boxer briefs, turning his back so he can adjust himself.

I should look away. I really should. But it's so dark in here that I can see only a vague outline of him anyway. He moves to the door. "Hey! We're here. We're okay, just stuck."

"You had us worried," someone says. It's a male voice I can't place.

Caleb laughs. "Well, you could have fooled us. It took you long enough."

"So ungrateful." When the guy laughs, it clicks. Ian. "If Eden wasn't in there with you, I might be tempted to leave you for the night."

"Is everyone else okay?" Caleb asks, still unconcerned about his ass on display in those tight briefs. And since he's not guarding his modesty, I don't feel bad about enjoying the view.

I wrap myself in the towel and walk toward the voices.

"Yeah, the earthquake was small, and the storm wasn't too bad in town," Ian yells.

"Told you," I say.

Caleb smirks at me. On one side of his head, his dark hair is smashed flat, on the other it's standing straight up, and he has a crease on his cheek. There are also dark bags under his eyes. But somehow, he still looks irresistible.

"But there were a couple of trees down on the road," Ian continues. "And we checked every goddamn trail out here searching for you. What the hell are you doing in the maintenance office?"

"Picking up paperwork." Caleb glances at me, and I feel the heaviness of his gaze as potently as I felt his palm on my skin earlier. Maybe it isn't just biology after all. Because he adjusts himself again with a small wince and mumbles, "Sorry," before turning back to the door, waiting for our rescuers to get to work.

"Is that what they're calling it?" A woman's voice this time. And the voice is so familiar it makes me giddy, like a flipped switch. It sounds like Cassie, but it couldn't be.

"You okay in there, Eden?" Ian asks.

"Yes." I swallow. "I'm good."

It's then I hear the voice again, and it's the laugh that confirms it.

"Cassie?" I yell.

"I drive all the way out here to drop off your favorite hoodie and fuzzy socks, and you repay me by going missing like a *Dateline* episode."

"Oh my God, Cassie," I squeal. "You're here."

"And this is the thanks I get? Giving me a heart attack? This trip is worse than that norovirus nightmare in Cabo last summer. I did not want to have to explain to Lester Holt how you lit up the room."

Caleb looks at me, bemused. "Who is that?" he mouths.

"My best friend."

Houdini jumps up and paddles his paws against the door like he's running on a vertical treadmill.

"I'm surprised Houdini didn't get you out of there," Ian says.

"Maybe they didn't want to get out." Cassie, naturally. I drop my forehead to the door, and Caleb chuckles beside me. "Do you two need more time?" she asks.

"Cassandra Moreno, we are freezing and hungry, and Caleb is a big dude with a giant mean streak. If you don't get us out of here right now, I will share your seventh-grade school photo on Instagram. The one with the drool mark from your headgear."

Cassie guffaws, and Caleb says, "Cassie, don't believe anything she says about me," with all the charm in the world.

"As long as you believe everything I tell you about her," she singsongs.

Caleb scans me up and down, smiling briefly. "Deal."

"I hate to break it to you two," Ian says, "but it's going to take a while to get you out of there."

It takes another three hours to be precise, three hours during which Caleb is not cradling me in his arms under a layer of beach towels. Instead, we're up and pacing, trying to distract ourselves from the whir of the chain saw and the chatter of conversations we can't make out. By the time we emerge, everyone in Grand Trees has been alerted and is waiting outside the cabin, and the sun is rising, no evidence of yesterday's storm in sight.

Cassie envelops me in her enthusiastic embrace as soon as I step from the door. For all her teasing, I can tell she was, in fact, worried. She arrived at Sonny's house to surprise me with two suitcases full of everything I could possibly need and found a houseful of traumatized townsfolk organizing a search party.

Meanwhile, Caleb is attacked by Abby. She jumps into his arms like a wild monkey, a whir of tears and squeals and a rant about how scared she was. I catch Caleb's blissed-out expression as he greets his daughter—eyes closed tight, arms wrapped around her spine—and I know he loves her a billion times more than whatever broke him. All these people showed up to find him and rescue him. He's filled his life and loved so big that his heart had no choice but to heal.

The heart's a muscle, I realize. Instead of exercising it, I let it atrophy; I loved small with what was left of mine. It's why all the surgeries and physical therapy in the world couldn't fix me. It's probably why I married a man who felt safe, who—even when he did the worst thing—couldn't break me any more than I already was.

I hug Cassie tighter, so thankful she was already lodged in there before my heart stopped working properly. "I love you, Cass."

"Ah, I love you, too." She drops her voice. "And because I love you, I hope you took advantage of your near-death experience."

I pull back. "What?"

Cassie doesn't have a subtle bone in her body, and Caleb is watching us. I sense his stare, even though I refuse to make eye contact.

She nods toward him. "If the world were ending, I don't even think Justin would fault me if I hit that."

CHAPTER 17

"Your problem"—Cassie places a stack of my shirts in my mom's dresser—"is you let go of all the things you should hang on to and hang on to all the things you should let go of."

"How do you explain our thirty-year friendship, then?" I tease.

"It means I'm the lucky beneficiary of your poor choices." She closes the drawer and reaches for the pile of sweatshirts, placing them carefully in the next drawer. "You should have broken up with me when I made you wear matching pink overalls to homecoming."

"I can't stay up here, Cass." I gesture around Mom and Sonny's bedroom, where she's strong-arming me to move into. I won't be able to sleep in their bed, surrounded by paintings of the two of them together and mementos of their life—staring over the dark abyss of the forest.

"Your mom says she doesn't need your help at night anymore, and you can't sleep on that couch forever. You need to let this go. What would your therapist say?" she huffs as she continues to unload the outfits she brought me.

"I don't have a therapist."

"Exactly." She closes the drawer with a click and leans against it, folding her arms across her chest. "That's why you have no choice but to listen to me. You're here. That's a good first step. Now, spend some actual time with her. Have the tough conversations so you can get to know her again. She was so worried last night. She loves you, Edie."

"I know." Cassie's right, of course. For years, she pushed me to visit Mom, go to therapy, and deal with my shit. I've always preferred to shove it in a box and avoid it. But my box is full, and I can't close the lid anymore.

I open the second suitcase to avoid the conversation and find a bright-pink gift bag. Digging inside, I lift out a scrap of scarlet with black lace by my pinkie finger. "What the hell is this?" It's not clear which part of the body the lingerie is meant to cover.

"A gift." She grins, the dimple on her right cheek taunting me.

I drop it into the bag as if it bit me. "Only you, Cass. 'What could Eden need while tending to her injured mother? Oh, I know—stripper underwear.'"

"I thought the big angry nephew might like 'em. And now that I've got a good look at him, he does seem like an ass man."

I snort to cover my blush; I still feel him pressed against my backside, hard and tempting. I look down to avoid eye contact and explore the gift bag filled with bralettes, panties, and a couple of teddies.

"So far, my problem has been needing more clothes, not less." I decide not to tell Cassie about Snugglegate or the sneak attack by Houdini that left me naked and Caleb mortified. She never lets anything go, especially if she finds it funny, sexy, or perverse.

"Oh, and I bought you these." Cassie dangles something above my purse. I step closer before I see her stuffing a strip of condoms inside.

"Cassie." I laugh. "What the hell?" I reach for it, but she swings it out of my grasp.

"Just looking out for you. You know, have fun but be safe." She drops my purse on the side of the dresser and wraps her hands around my upper arms. "I'll tell you what: I'll sleep up here with you tonight. We can put on face masks and binge a show on my laptop. You don't even need to model one of those negligees for me. I'm a sure thing." She winks at me before returning to her task.

I laugh but can't deny the king-size bed looks especially appealing after a sleepless night on a cold floor.

"You sure you have to leave tomorrow?" Having her here is a balm to my soul.

"Sorry. That drive is brutal, and I have a meeting with my boss on Monday at eight a.m. *in person*. I miss when I could roll out of bed and onto the Zoom screen. Now I have to wear hard pants, makeup, and deodorant." She sighs dramatically. She works in marketing at some big firm in the city and hates it. "I checked out flights, but they're expensive and likely use tin-can planes, and it's still a two-hour drive in a rental car. Why isn't it easier to get here?"

"You know I love you for coming all this way," I say. "Even if it's just to lecture me and bring me inappropriate underwear."

"I also brought you your emotional support hoodie." She reaches into a suitcase and tosses me my favorite Cal sweatshirt—the stitching on the satin yellow *L* is peeling away from the blue fleece. I yank it over my head and slip my thumbs through the makeshift holes in the cuffs.

"Can you do one other thing for me?"

"I draw the line at asking Caleb if he likes you. We're not in middle school anymore. But you can send him a note. 'Do you like me? Check Yes or No.'"

"Hilarious," I say, before sobering. "Can you check on my dad every once in a while? When I told him about my mom, he . . ."

"Shut down?" she guesses.

I nod. "He sounded so sad and probably feels weird about me being here."

"Sure," she says. "You know I love Len. I'll be happy to visit. I'll make up an excuse about needing book recommendations or help with my houseplants so he doesn't think I'm babysitting him."

I exhale a sigh of relief as I grab a stack of jeans and place them in an empty drawer. "Thanks. I'd appreciate that."

"But," Cassie says, "your dad's emotions aren't your responsibility. And you have to promise you won't let his hurt keep you from reconnecting with your mom."

I look away as I close the drawer. I know she's right, but old habits die hard. In high school, my dad encouraged me to call my mom, told me I should visit, but his despair was so consuming, I didn't want to contribute to it. Besides, my anger was as potent as his sadness. We were in it together.

"I won't," I say, hoping I can keep this promise.

When Cassie and I collapse in bed later, the promised laptop perched between us, cued up to a reality dating show that Cass assures me is the best worst thing on television, I don't think of it as Sonny and Mom's room. I don't envision the yawning abyss of the forest taunting me from the wall of windows.

And I think maybe there's a corollary to Caleb's rule about healing from heartbreak: The secret to letting go of traumatic memories is to make beautiful new ones in their place.

~

Cassie wakes me with a steaming latte in a mug the size of a soup bowl, placing it on the nightstand before she perches on the side of the bed. "I brought you a three-month supply of Four Barrel coffee and a handheld frother. You may be light-years away from the city, but you are a bougie coffee snob and would perish without the good stuff."

"I was wrong about you," I say. "You're really coming through for me."

"Just this once. Don't get used to it."

She's been the most consistent joy in my life, but I smile and tease her. "Never."

"Nicolette is downstairs with her coffee and reading a thriller on her Kindle. She seems better today."

"Oh, shoot, what time is it?" I scramble for my phone. "She needs her morning meds."

"Already taken care of." Cassie smiles, but it's brittle and forced.

"What's wrong?" I press myself up on my hands until I'm resting against the headboard.

"Nothing's wrong. I just need to tell you something."

Her tone has the solemnity she's reserved for only a few sober moments in our lives, and I'm scared of what she's about to say, because I'm not ready for the nausea and dread. Not when she's packed and prepping to leave.

"I'm pregnant," she says finally, her eyes glistening with trapped tears. She looks so pained that I panic.

I scoot toward her and wrap my hand over hers. I always assumed she wanted to be a mom and would have a bunch of kids. We're thirty-five. It's not like either of us have a lot of time to equivocate. "Cass, this is good news, right?"

Cassie blinks rapidly and brushes the tears aside with her free hand. When she speaks, her voice is thick. "Yeah. Yes. I mean, Justin and I have been talking about it for a while. Maybe it wasn't planned, exactly. But not not-planned either, if you know what I mean. I stopped taking the pill a year ago, and we've been using the lazy pull-out method and fucking like—"

I raise both hands to stop her. "Got it. But why do you seem upset?"

She inhales and holds her breath for several seconds before speaking on an exhale. "I was going to tell you at brunch that day. And then, well, I didn't want to do that to you after Jeff, but I also didn't want to keep it from you. I just . . ."

That nausea makes landfall, and my stomach roils. I'm such a mess that my favorite person in the world didn't want to share her good news. Life-altering news. Beautiful news.

"Cassie." And now I'm the one with tears caught in my throat. "I am so happy for you. You are going to be the best mom." I wrap my arms around her and we both cry—happy tears, mainly. And if my emotions are more nuanced, it's not because I'm ambivalent about her pregnancy, it's because I'm disappointed that my best friend thought she couldn't share this with me. "You'll take your marketing expertise and become a mom influencer with a million followers. You'll be funny, even on no sleep, and hot, even with spit-up in your hair."

She snorts, which brings on a fresh wave of tears. "Not so effortless so far. I just puked twice in the bathroom."

"Oh, Cass." I draw her closer.

I ask all the requisite questions. How far along is she? Nine weeks. Will she find out the sex? No. Has she told anyone else? Just one of her sisters. Has she seen the doctor yet? Yes, and she likes the sound of the heartbeat even more than John Legend's baritone. I manage to stay in the moment, stay in *her* moment, and not acknowledge that my heart is throbbing a little along the seams, or stretching to accommodate the promise of more love.

Or maybe both.

CHAPTER 18

The clouds roll in later that afternoon, chasing Cassie out of town and replacing clear skies with ashen, which is fitting. The light dims when Cassie leaves a room. But this time, the colorlessness of her absence is like a black hole. I walk Cassie to her car and send her off with enthusiasm to mask my melancholy.

As I trudge up the porch steps, I have to steady myself against the rail. Cassie is going to be a mother; I'm going to be an auntie. I'm ecstatic for her. But I'm also keenly aware that, as she takes the next step on the path she set for herself, I'm starting over—or maybe still lodged in purgatory, unable to begin again. I'm like Miss Havisham, letting cobwebs grow in my hair through inaction. My life has been in a holding pattern since Jeff left, and if I'm honest with myself, long before that.

As I wait for Mom to heal over these next few months, I can't fall through another trapdoor and get stuck further. I need to feel alive, whole. I need to be well enough that my closest friend trusts me with her good news.

Cassie got the process started for me: clothes, necessities, good coffee. But I need to move my body, which has always been the fulcrum around which my mental health pivots. I head upstairs and grab my laptop, checking out the Be Well fitness interface. A friend of mine from undergrad started the alternative-wellness app a few years ago, which uses your location to curate a set of nearby fitness activities for any age, skill level, or ability. I reset my address to Grand Trees to check out some local options before an idea takes root.

Mom. My artsy, hippie, new age Mom. What if I can convince her to concentrate on wellness to mitigate her Parkinson's, versus the medicinal treatments she's refused so far? Maybe exercise can be the gateway nondrug to the drugs she needs. If she feels a bit better, she may want to feel a lot better. I know something about that. Hope doesn't have a chance until there's a tear in the cloak of despair.

I open a new browser and reload the site, this time creating a new profile. I input Mom's details—age, diagnosis, strengths, interests, and location. The results are spare. At the community center, there's art therapy, which is out. Asking Mom to take an elementary art class would be as demoralizing as asking me to struggle through basic ballet. The negative comparison to your former self is crushing. The local trails are too precarious for someone with balance issues. The high school pool is an option, but there's no water aerobics.

But then my brain snags on another idea. I change her location to San Francisco and wait as the wheels spiral, caught in the tailspin of slow internet. When the page loads, limitless results fan out before me, fifteen pages of inspiration: a movement disorder clinic at UCSF, Stanford's Parkinson's exercise clinic, physical therapy, light therapy, and even boxing. One option crashes through the screen like a wrecking ball: San Francisco Ballet's dance classes for people with Parkinson's. I shut my laptop as my head spins at the cosmic irony of Mom taking classes at SFB to support her recovery.

But setting that splinter aside, what if she came home with me? I live alone in a three-bedroom, two-bath house; there's plenty of space for the two of us. It's a single story and well equipped for someone with mobility issues. I work for myself and could build her care into my schedule. We'd have world-class clinics and hospitals within arm's reach in any direction we spin. She loved San Francisco once. Maybe she could love it again. Maybe we could love each other again there—where we were happy—away from where everything fell apart. Maybe we can reconnect away from the place where we imploded.

I know it's a long shot that she'll agree. She's so connected to Caleb, Abby, this town, and her memories of Sonny. But if she keeps refusing to see the local doctor, moving may be her only option at some point. And if we strengthen our relationship over the next few months, if we're able to put the past behind us, I can introduce the idea gently. Perhaps if I invite her home once she and I are more at ease with each other, she'll consider it.

After scrolling through the results from Be Well, I fall down the deeper rabbit hole of Parkinson's treatment, studies about therapeutic advances, and the extensive list of medical experts practicing in and around my home, which could become our home. I'm filled with something I haven't felt in an eternity when it comes to Mom—hope, for her, for us. Possibility and promise that our future can be better than our past.

When I head downstairs, it's already late afternoon. I find Mom reading in the Eames chair. She sets her Kindle on her lap when she spots me.

"Hi, honey."

I must showcase how amped up I am by the ideas I just gathered, because Mom studies me like she's trying to read my forecast. Her pale-blue eyes are like witch's orbs, cloudy and reflecting her worry back to me. But I know she won't probe, because we don't ask questions of each other for which we don't want the answer.

"You were quiet up there. Were you napping?" she asks, keeping us safely in small talk territory.

But if we can't mention the past, perhaps I should broach the future. It's what I came for, and I've been stalling. I settle on the couch across from her, taking a deep breath. "I was looking into treatment options for Parkinson's."

Her face falls. "Eden, I appreciate you staying to care for me. But I have done all the research I need. My doctor and I decided not to start medications right away. My symptoms aren't that bad yet, and the side effects are terrible." I forgot about this tone—calmly defensive, with precise ending punctuation. In the last couple of decades, once we began a tentative truce, she only showed me her agreeable side. Her warm, easygoing, *I'll say whatever you want* side. Her *isn't the weather lovely* side. But that's gotten us nowhere.

I'm not even convinced she's being honest. I have a hard time believing her doctor would advise her to delay treatment. "Mom, you just fell and broke several bones. You need to take this seriously."

Her posture stiffens, and she sits upright, bracing her ribs with her good arm and taking a shallow breath. "I realize this is a lot for you to absorb because it's all new to you. But I've been dealing with it for a while."

"No, you haven't." I've kept a lid on my feelings since I arrived, while she rested in the hospital, while I've cared for her since. I was hoping her injuries might be a wake-up call. Now my frustration—at her hiding and ignoring her diagnosis—boils over. "You've been burying your head in the sand, and I don't want you to wait until it's too late."

"I think that's a bit dramatic. My doctor and I decided—"

"Have you been seeing the neurologist?" Maybe Caleb and Adelaide were wrong.

"Yes. I've seen him." She blinks at me innocently, like a child trying to evade capture in a lie. I see right through it.

"Caleb says it was years ago."

She sighs. "He's not a good doctor, Eden. He didn't listen, and he belittled me."

I didn't intend to bring this up yet, but perhaps this is the opening I need to plant the seed. "Maybe Grand Trees isn't the best place for you if it doesn't have the care you need."

"I've been doing fine. I just slipped. It could happen to anyone."

"But it happened to you, and you have Parkinson's, which affects your balance, especially since you've refused treatment."

She purses her lips. "I know all about my condition, the symptoms, and the available treatment."

But she doesn't know all her options. "What if you move to San Francisco and live with me?" I blurt.

The words settle between us like a live grenade, and her eyes go wide. It's a reminder that this conversation is cutting too close to our emotional arteries, and my ill-timed suggestion may just be the nick that causes a hemorrhage.

"I can't do that," she says.

But she could if she wanted to. "My place is big enough. I work from home and can take care of you."

She's silent and still, her focus averted. "I appreciate the gesture, I really do. I love having you here, but once my bones heal, I'll be fine, and you can go home without worrying."

It's not surprising that she's dismissing me, but I can't understand how she's delusional enough to think she won't need help at some point. Does she not remember falling and breaking several bones a week ago? Does she have memory loss, too? But I dial back my frustration and try to speak reason. "Mom, your condition is degenerative, and it'll get worse faster without treatment. You don't know how quickly it will progress or when you'll need full-time care. Even if it's not right away, someday it will make the most sense for you to live with me."

"For whom, Eden? For you? You're young and have your whole life to live. And my life is here."

A life she's disregarding and choosing to cut short. "But what kind of life? You won't be able to enjoy it much longer at this rate. You're deteriorating and choosing not to do anything about it."

Mom looks away, rubbing her good hand on the arm of the chair. "I am comfortable with my choices."

The pilot light of my rage roars to life. It's been simmering, and it doesn't matter how many years are stacked over my hurt, because it always comes back to this: Mom has always been comfortable with her decisions, even when they've devastated me. She was comfortable with her choice to cheat and, ultimately, her choice to leave.

It's difficult not to experience this betrayal—of herself and her health—as a betrayal of me, too. Is she so devoid of regret that she's ready to let fate fall? Doesn't she want enough time to rebuild our relationship? Is she at all curious about whether I may give her grandchildren someday? Was her love for Sonny so intense that she'd give up our second chance and speed up her journey to join him?

But I don't have the strength to ask those questions, because I'm terrified of the answers. Besides, we're not talking about her emotional priorities. We're talking about her health. "I'm concerned you're not behaving rationally or making sound decisions."

"How would you know, Eden?" She's been warning me with her escalating tone, but this side of her is foreign. In my family, conflict was noiseless but perilous. And when everything finally detonated, we burned as quickly as a matchstick. But now, she lights another fuse. "It's not like you've been around much in the last twenty years."

"And whose fault is that?" I snap, before taking a breath, releasing it. I want to start over, edit this conversation toward the intended script. "Sorry. I didn't mean—"

"I think you did," she says. "Believe me, I know what I am guilty of. It took me years to rebuild a life that I could be proud of. And now you're asking me to leave it all behind."

I blink rapidly as my eyes burn, and I stand on shaky legs. "If you think your whole life is here, I guess we have nothing to talk about." I don't look at Mom as I head for the door, swiping my purse from the hall tree on my way out. When I emerge on the porch, the dewy air, laced with pine and campfire, assaults me. I get to my car, swinging the door open and sliding in before I realize I can't leave. As frustrated as I am, I'm not heartless enough to leave when Mom needs me.

I'm not like her.

In the privacy of my car, I let out a sound that's a cross between a wail and a scream. I don't know why the hell she agreed to let me stay if she wasn't willing to work on us. If she's so adamant about refusing treatment or making room in her life for me, why did I bother?

I drop my head to the steering wheel, defeated. I want to flee, if not forever, at least until I can stuff these feelings back into the emotional cage I erected for them ages ago.

I startle upright as a vehicle comes down the driveway and spy Caleb's truck approaching. I immediately drop my seat into a recline, hiding like I once dodged old high school classmates in the grocery store. He pulls up in front of the house, about ten feet from where I'm parked. I don't need Caleb to find me hiding in my car like a weirdo.

Abby's voice carries through my closed window a moment later. "Should we play Catch Phrase? Because Grams can't hold cards yet, and I think that would be easiest. Or Scrabble? Because it doesn't move as fast?"

Gah. I forgot about our game night redo.

During the long hours waiting in that cabin, Caleb told me game night began after Mom was diagnosed. Games help strengthen neural pathways and improve small motor skills and are a type of therapy she can't refuse. Because she can't resist Abby, even though she has no qualms about saying no to me.

Friday was the first game night they'd missed in years, so Abby convinced Caleb they needed a do-over.

"Maybe Scrabble. You get too excited playing Catch Phrase, jumping up and down like it's an actual sport," Caleb says.

Footsteps land on the porch, and the front door creaks open. I'm in the clear; I'll go inside in a minute and claim I was on a walk. But then a huge, hairy face pops up on the driver's side window, and I gasp when its long, pink tongue drags across the glass. And my jig is up. Because then, Caleb's big hairy face appears in the passenger window, his expression impassive. He knocks once on the window with the back of his fist before gesturing for me to roll it down. I sigh, but comply, opening it a crack as Houdini cries on my other side, whimpering at the injustice of being separated by glass.

"Go on in with Grams," Caleb says over his shoulder. "I'll be right there." He turns back to me, shoving his hands in his pockets and tilting his head. "You all right?"

I sit up and release the lever. My seat springs upright aggressively, knocking me forward, and I have to catch myself on the steering wheel. I stare straight ahead when I say, "I'm fine," in a robotic tone even I don't believe.

"Do you hide out here often?" I can hear the smile in his voice. It distorts the resonance of his gravelly tone, making it smooth and soft.

I turn to glare at him, and he grins back, which does not help me. I'm feeling too many things today, and Caleb is the epicenter of emotions I'd rather not have.

"What happened?" It almost sounds like he cares, like maybe, possibly, I've weaseled my way into the inner circle of people he treats as friends versus foes.

I expel all the air in my lungs and slouch against the too-upright seat. "Mom and I got in a fight."

"Good."

"Good?" I snap. I was so stupid. He's not here because he cares; he's here to gloat. Definitely still an asshole.

"From what I understand, you two have caused a lot of harm by holding your tongues. It's good to finally say something honest. Even if it's not careful or polite."

"You're not a fan of polite, are you."

"Polite is lying with better PR. I prefer the truth." He rests one hand on the hood of the car, leaning toward my window. "C'mon. Let's go for a walk. It'll give you a chance to cool down and practice not being polite with me." I shake my head and look back toward the steering wheel. "What are you gonna do? Stay here and sulk in your car?"

"We can't leave my mom."

"Abby's got it. It'll be nice for them to have some one-on-one time. And I should wear out this dog before going inside. I don't want him to jump all over your mom."

As if on cue, Houdini springs off his hind legs, slamming against the driver's door and releasing an aggrieved howl.

"I think he belongs in a zoo." I laugh as the dingo thrashes beside me.

"Nah, he's not nearly tame enough for that," he says. "He belongs with a pack of wild dogs, far away from civilization."

"Alas"—I make eye contact as Houdini gazes longingly at me through my window—"he's stuck with humans."

"I'll tell Abby she's in charge." Caleb rebounds off my car, the matter settled.

"Wait," I say. "Bad things happen when we go out in the woods."

One side of his mouth quirks. "I don't remember it being all bad."

Caleb steps away and doesn't wait for me to respond; thank God for that, because I'm not sure I can. His words send me straight back to the cabin. I'm in his arms, my skin on fire everywhere he's touching me, my body aching everywhere he's not, his hard form pressed against me, his soft words of understanding in my ear. *It was a broken heart.*

When Caleb emerges a few moments later, he restrains Houdini long enough for me to slip out of the car, but I sink to my haunches to receive the dog's overzealous affection. He smothers me in kisses before spinning in circles, his hindquarters jerking in the air like a bull in a rodeo.

"Houdini, heel," Caleb says, and he sprints to Caleb before circling twice and plopping down at his heels.

"He listens to you."

Caleb nods. "When he feels like it. He's feral but doing his best. Okay, Houdini."

Houdini takes off in a sprint toward the back of the house, and I know exactly where he's headed. There are six trails that veer off from this house. But, of course, the dog would choose that one. Dry Creek Loop. Caleb jogs behind him.

All my senses crank up to full blast, and my nerve endings crackle like they're on an overloaded circuit. I freeze.

CHAPTER 19

Caleb is almost to the trail before he notices I'm not following. He casts a glance over his shoulder. "It's just a walk, Eden. There's no rain or earthquakes in the forecast."

This jolts me out of it. "Earthquakes can't be forecasted. And that last rain wasn't expected either," I say. "Can we take this trail instead?" I nod toward a path tumbling out of the sequoias on the south side of the house. It's short and flat, so I have a plausible argument for my choice.

Caleb peers at me with a curious expression, tilting his head, but finally he says, "Sure," and doesn't ask any questions. As he jogs toward me, he whistles to Houdini, who sprints to us, veering just shy of knocking me to the ground as he passes.

The temperature drops by nearly ten degrees when we step under the canopy of trees. The imposing giants insulate the space, blocking out sunlight, sound, and stress. Our feet compress the soft bed of redwood leaves as we enter the forest. But the silence doesn't last long.

"Are you going to tell me what happened?" Caleb asks, glancing at me askance as we walk side by side.

I need him to be more specific, because so much has happened in the past few weeks, and I think I'm reeling from all of it.

"With your mom," he clarifies when I don't respond.

"I told her she should move to San Francisco with me."

Caleb stops. "This is her home."

"It hasn't always been." I match his stance, but as soon as I do, he carries on up the trail. Houdini sprints ahead and circles back, covering miles for every few feet we travel. "I was looking up resources for her illness. And San Francisco has some of the best care—exercise, therapy, dance classes specifically for people with Parkinson's." I leave out the fact that it's at the same school where I trained, how it seems like an omen of some kind—a full-circle opportunity for us both. I fill him in on what I learned and how our conversation imploded. We approach a bend in the trail. This path is flat, sheltered, and benign, and probably no more than a mile. It branches out to other trails in various directions, but Caleb keeps us on the beginner route.

"Okay."

"What does that mean?" I watch Houdini take off after a bird he has no chance of catching.

"Well . . ." He pauses, biting his lip. "I'm working on being more careful with my words."

"Screw it. Give me honesty."

His smile splits apart. He likes that answer, and I like his smile. I *love* his smile. I want to taste it and feel it pressed against the pulse point in my neck. "How would you react if your mom demanded you move here?"

I like him less now. "That's different." I stare at a sequoia in the distance whose trunk is marred by a fire scar, a satiny black hole at its base. And yet, it's still standing tall, undeterred by its injury.

"How is it different?" Caleb sounds like a teacher posing a trick question.

"I have a life there."

Caleb stops, but to my surprise, his face is compassionate when he sighs and whispers my name. That simple reproach is enough.

"Okay, maybe you have a point." I sigh, because he does, but still, I feel the sting of frustration—or maybe it's rejection.

"And maybe you do, too. But she's not going to hear it if it feels like you're threatening her independence."

"But you agree she should move?"

His smile is mollifying. "No. She has her friends, routine, and community who would do anything for her. And she has Sonny's memory."

I look away, suddenly interested in the hole Houdini's digging on the edge of the trail. I admire the dog's ability to attack the world without fear of consequences.

"You don't like that." He ducks into my line of sight.

"I don't like that she's more concerned with holding on to a memory than living the best life she can."

"Hmm." He starts walking again, and I have to jog to keep up.

"What's with the vague reactions? I told you to be honest." I'm out of breath when I catch up, finally stepping into stride with his longer legs.

His gaze skates over me. "I think most people hold on too tightly to memories." My forearm brushes his, and the contact is like flint and stone—our flesh charged and arcing toward each other. I take a half step away. "It's harder to live in the moment."

This feels like a dig, even if it's not intentional, because it rings true. Too true. I always have one eye on the past. "Houdini, on the other hand, is always living for the moment." I nod to where the dog is on his hind legs, front paws pressed to a tree trunk, staring at some animal well out of his reach. I catch sight of a fork ahead; the trail marker says DRY CREEK LOOP.

It's just a path, like any other.

I don't want to live—or not live—for a memory anymore either. Perhaps I need to lay it to rest so it stops haunting me. When we reach the marker, I veer us onto the route, shoving my hands in my pockets so Caleb can't see them shake. I breathe slowly to steady my pulse and keep my focus on the trail ahead, counting each footfall as it lands on the bed of needles. It's quiet, and I feel powerful, like I'm sneaking up on my past, ready to pounce on my demons.

The detour will drop us off at the back of Sonny's house, right where Houdini tried to start our walk. It's only a few more paces, a few more breaths, a few more heartbeats until we're there, and I halt and take a cleansing inhale.

"Eden?" The softness lingers in Caleb's raspy voice. "You okay?"

I refuse to let the ghosts in these forests haunt me anymore.

I close my eyes. "My accident happened right here." When I open them, Caleb is studying me so intently that I have to catch my breath from the sheer impact of his attention. "It was dark, and I got turned around. Instead of taking the trail back to camp, I hooked a right and fell into that ravine. I was stuck until they found me, and I remember thinking I'd die down there." But when the shock wore off and the pain intensified, I hoped for it. Afterward, I was told I must have been trapped for a few hours, but it felt like days.

"Eden." It's just an exhale, and I feel more than hear it, because he's suddenly so close. "You should have said something. I never would have brought you here."

"I wanted to come."

"Okay," he says, but it sounds like a question. He stays close, as if he can protect me from my own memories. I turn to face the ravine, and Caleb stays at my back, his warmth giving me the courage to stare out over the site of my loss. It's a steep slope to the creek bed, which was dry that summer. Gnarled tree roots and sharp boulders cover the short hillside, with logs and river rock at the bottom.

I always wondered how Mom could fall asleep each night overlooking the scene of my nightmare. And yet, it's different than I remember. The shadows, the sounds, the stillness of that night may always haunt me, but the scene before me is serene. There's a steady trickle of water flowing through the bed, wiping the slate clean, and fooling me into thinking nothing bad could have happened here.

Everything changes, I realize. Even landscapes. Even memories.

"I avoided this place for so long," I say. "I probably gave it too much power."

"I get it. I've never been back to Texas."

I don't know who extends their hand first, whether I reach back or he reaches forward, but his fingertips tease mine, and our bodies barely brush as we wind our hands together until he's holding on to me so securely that even here, I feel safe.

"I shouldn't have given you such a hard time when you showed up. It was brave of you to come."

I release a humorless laugh. "I don't know about that."

"I do." He squeezes my hand, and an electrical pulse fires up the length of my arm, lands in my chest, and simmers there. "And I tried to chase you away."

"Like a dog barking at the mail carrier."

He chuckles behind me, ruffling my hair. On instinct, I step back and settle so my back connects with his chest, the barest graze. His breath catches, and I exhale, feeling something akin to relief. I've been aching for contact since we drew apart in the cabin.

"Thank you," I say.

"For what?" His voice is shallow, a little shaky. I think he's confused that I've touched him on purpose, no longer under the cover of survival.

I'm confused too, but I think I like it.

"For helping me make a new memory here. A better memory." The beauty of the landscape comes into focus—the stately trees, the burbling creek, the silhouette of Sonny's tree house, and the mountain covered with wildflowers. The last glimmer of the sun's rays bleeds through the leaden skies, coating us in copper.

"Being here with me is a better memory?"

"Better than being at the bottom of a ditch with my bone sticking out of my leg? Surprisingly, yes."

The sound of Caleb's laugh pierces me right in the solar plexus. I turn to face him with a flare of recognition, of nostalgia. I may have been waiting for the sound of his laugh my whole life. It's an audible joy that seeps into my blood like the first notes of the orchestra before the stage lights rise.

I want to feel that laugh against my neck, taste the sound on my tongue, and cover myself in its fiber. I want to give this beautiful, horrible place an even happier memory. When I slide my hands around his neck, his laughter dies immediately. He bites his bottom lip, but his smile is stubborn. He leans down and rests his forehead on mine.

"You're funny, Eden Hawthorne." His voice is like fine-grit sandpaper, stripping away my defenses, making my nerves raw and tuned for sensation.

"No one thinks I'm funny."

"I do," he says, but it's only breath, and I feel it against my lips, a moment before his mouth skates across mine, featherlight. My skin erupts in goose bumps, and I fight a shiver as he takes a second pass, even softer, as if asking me for permission, as if I have a choice. Every cell in my body is screaming yes.

I tighten my hands on his nape and angle my chin so we can slip together. When his full mouth catches mine, it's like sinking into quicksand. I nip at his upper lip, which is unbearably soft except for where his scar cuts through his Cupid's bow. He brings his hands to my waist, stabilizing me and restraining himself, before I coax his mouth open with a soft sigh. The moment his tongue meets mine, the caution is gone. He slides a hand to the small of my back and threads the other in my hair, cradling the back of my head, before he kisses me like he means it.

And this, *this* is what it feels like for every nerve, every fiber to sing. Each touch feels like *yes, there*. His soft lips belong *there*. His rough hands are *yes*. We're performing choreography we've already learned, perhaps in another life. We're a duet with perfect musicality and timing. And the intimacy, the rightness, is so shocking I have to settle my breathing, turn down the chorus in my head that screams *yes, now, more*.

I want to savor this kiss and take all of him now. I want to toss aside our clothes and strip him slowly to relish each new patch of exposed skin.

He nudges my thighs apart with one of his. He's hard and urgent against my stomach, but there isn't enough friction. I slip my hand under his sweatshirt to find an undershirt and release a frustrated little gasp before tugging it free to reach the silken skin of his waist. He's so warm, and I'm dying to absorb every inch of his heat. He drags his mouth to my jaw, my neck, whispering something I can't hear as he tilts my chin for access. And this, too, is *yes*. *God, yes*.

I forget to breathe when he scrapes his teeth across my collarbone and splays his hand on my rib cage. He tugs me closer, and I squirm against him, pressing to my toes and arching to find the shape of him through our jeans. And this, too, is *yes*. He's a *yes*. I groan when he grips my thigh with firm fingertips and hitches my leg over his hip, giving me just enough of him to know I won't be satisfied until I have all of him.

Through my lust haze, I'm vaguely aware of the sound of Houdini's footsteps before he unleashes a howl, but the sound is traveling farther and farther away. When I pull back, startled, Caleb coaxes my mouth to his again, swallowing my concern with a kiss.

There's another sound in the distance, but before I can register it, Caleb releases me, eyes wide, and I blink several times, trying to come back into my body.

He's a mess. His hair is all over the place, his lips bee stung, and there's a satisfying flush blooming on his neck. My gaze catches on the impressive display in his pants before I hear, "Dad? Are you out here?"

Oh shit. And I realize I'm at the stage of life where it's more troubling to be caught by your children than your parents. Caleb wipes his hand over his mouth and adjusts himself before he tucks in his shirt. I do a physical tally of my own appearance, smoothing my hair and straightening my sweatshirt, and we make eye contact as I take a deep breath.

I don't see Abby, so hopefully she didn't see us.

"Dad?" she calls again, and her voice is closer now. "I'm hungry. When's dinner?"

Caleb presses a quick kiss to my forehead before he clears his throat and walks toward the trail outlet. "Right here, Abs." He sounds almost normal.

I wait a moment for the sensation to return to my legs and brush a fingertip to my forehead, feeling that lingering intimacy long after he disappears around the bend.

CHAPTER 20

Game night is awkward.

The only salvation is that Mom must think it's due to our fight, and Abby doesn't seem to notice. Either that, or she's trolling us.

Abby lays down her Scrabble tiles and exclaims, "HARD." Caleb coughs into his fist as she looks at him, puzzled. "Triple word score," she continues, proud and oblivious.

I jump up from the table with my water glass in hand. "Does anyone need anything from the kitchen?"

"But it's your turn," Abby says.

"I've got you." Caleb swipes the glass from my hand, eyes twinkling.

I reluctantly sink into my chair and take stock of my tiles. Because this game is trying to destroy me, my only options are MOAN and MOUNT. I decide the latter is less dangerous, but maybe it's worse?

I think that kiss melted my brain.

Caleb returns and slides a fresh glass of water in front of me as I lay down my tiles, but I don't announce my play. I can't look at him or my mom, and I can barely face Abby. She could have caught us. What was I thinking? Well, I wasn't thinking, obviously. I've spent one week in Grand Trees, and I'm behaving like the teenager I was when I left. Or that teenager's rebellious cousin. I never let infatuation make me foolish. I didn't date the wrong boy. I certainly didn't hump the wrong boy in clear view of the people who should be the last to know about it.

Because Mom and Abby cannot know about this, whatever it is. I can't predict how either of them would react, and I'm not sure how I feel about it yet. There's no sense in disrupting this strange, fragile, extended family dynamic because of my impulsivity.

I haven't kissed anyone but Jeff in more years than I care to count. So maybe a fling isn't such a bad idea for my battered heart. But is it a good idea to get involved with someone tethered to Grand Trees and all the trauma the town conjures for me? Should my first flirtation postdivorce be with someone so tied to Mom? If I pursue this attraction, it could complicate everything I came to do: find peace with this place and rebuild my relationship with my mother.

When I look up from the Scrabble board, Caleb is watching me, chin in hand, gaze traveling over my face as if he's asking himself the same questions. Or perhaps he's reading my apprehension.

Mom plays her hand, and Abby adds the points to the score sheet as I attempt to look away from Caleb. But the intensity of his expression hooks me like a snare, and I can't catch a full breath. I know his taste, the texture of his hair, the grit of his beard against my skin. And whether or not it's a bad idea, Caleb is the only idea in my head as the memory of his touch possesses each nerve.

I'm grateful when Caleb puts us out of our misery on his next turn with a benign, but game-winning, JUKEBOX.

Abby groans. "You know, some parents let their kids win. You are allowed to do that."

Caleb chuckles. "And you're allowed to beat me fair and square. You should try that next time." He bats her ponytail, and she twists her mouth, leveling him with her sternest glare. Her face is too sweet for real sass, but she gets an A+ for effort.

"Do you see how he treats me?" Abby looks from me to my mom, mouth agape.

Mom laughs, her sober expression finally breaking. "He didn't take pity on this little old lady either."

"Ian lets me win," Abby says.

I bristle, expecting Caleb to react in jealousy or offense and ready to come to his defense.

"That's because Ian is nicer than me." Caleb stands and plants a kiss on the top of her head. "I'm going to help Grams, and then we have to head home."

"Did Mom give you an answer yet?" Abby asks, grabbing his arm.

"Not yet. But I'll talk to her again this week," Caleb assures her. I'm curious about what he needs to speak with Lina about. I have a vague recollection of Abby asking something similar last week at the festival. What conversation is so fraught?

I don't argue with Caleb when he helps Mom into her room, offering me a reprieve from caretaking while she and I cool off. We've managed to avoid speaking directly to each other since our fight. Caleb and Abby have been effective buffers.

I clear the dinner plates as Abby puts away the game board. She follows me to the kitchen, carrying the drink glasses.

"Have you recovered from your night with my dad?" Abby giggles.

My face heats and I stammer. "What? I haven't . . ."

She tilts her head in confusion as she places the glasses in the sink. "In the cabin. He's a big baby about earthquakes."

"Oh, right." I catch my breath. "He really is."

She laughs. "I knew it. He told me he was all brave."

I flip on the faucet and scrub the remnants of Carmela's enchiladas from our dinner plates. Abby grabs a towel and stands beside me, drying as I wash.

"He was," I say, defensive on his behalf for some reason. "He acted as a human shield when he heard the tree falling."

"Ah," she says. "That's noble. I guess he's not the worst."

I laugh. Teenagers. That's some high praise right there.

"He does that for me all the time. But not, you know, literally," she says. "Like with my mom. She's stricter and sometimes kinda stubborn." Her sentences all sound like questions.

"Oh." I hand her another plate. The kitchen window faces the ravine, and I can see the end of Dry Creek Loop, just paces away from where I mauled Caleb a few hours ago. Whether it was ill advised or not, I'm grateful that the kiss is the first thing that comes to mind instead of the accident. I'm editing this place, redlining terrible memories and rewriting better ones. I look away as Abby continues.

"I spend about half my time at each house. And my dad is super flexible with the schedule, but my mom isn't. And I want to change it. But it might hurt her feelings coming from me, because I want to spend more time at my dad's. There's no room at my mom's, and when the baby comes, I won't get any sleep. And I have school and homework and swimming, and . . ." She trails off. "It's just easier at Dad's."

I cast a glance at Abby. Her shoulders are tense, and she's picking at her cuticles again. This must have been what they were talking about earlier. Custody. I was old enough to choose where I wanted to go when Mom and Dad split, so it wasn't an issue for me. At fifteen, my word was gospel, and at that point, I didn't care about hurting Mom's feelings. I relished it. I never bounced around in an overnight bag or felt like a wishbone being pulled between two homes. I was just left behind.

I don't know which is worse, honestly. At least I wasn't conflicted or guilty. Not until years later.

"It's not that I don't love my mom or want to be with her and Ian," she adds in a hurried rush. "It's just . . ." She sighs. "Dad's house is home, I guess. And sometimes it feels like Mom started over, and there isn't enough room for me there."

I'm amazed she can be open and vulnerable with me, a near stranger. I'm not as transparent with my closest friends and family. But maybe my distance is exactly why she's sharing with me, and I don't want to let her down. "I don't know your mom well, but it sure seems like she loves you very much and that you are just as much a part of her family as your younger siblings."

Abby stretches to place the stack of plates in an upper cabinet. "I know I'm lucky that way. My parents get along. They share custody without any drama. They both love me, blah blah."

I chuckle at her flippancy. "But it sounds like it's still hard for you."

"It's just easier at my dad's because he's easier going."

I cackle. "Your dad. Easygoing?"

"About the little stuff? Totally. I can leave my room a mess, and he'll shut the door and let me clean it when I'm ready. If I tell him a teacher is unfair, he believes me. Some days, when I'm overwhelmed, he'll let me stay home from school, or we'll have a Daddy and Abby day."

There's a balloon inflating in my chest, creating pressure and static everywhere. I smile, pushing past the weird fondness blooming without my permission. "But he doesn't let you win at Scrabble."

She rolls her eyes. "He never lets me win at *anything*."

The man in question strolls into the kitchen, shoving his hands in the pockets of his worn jeans, with a subtle smile in place. "Are we still on this?" He chuckles, and the sound makes me warm all over because I know what his voice feels like against my skin. "I let you win the most important thing."

"Oh really? What's that?" Abby asks as she gives him the side-eye.

Caleb crosses his hand over his chest. "My heart."

Abby groans as my stomach does an idiotic little flutter. "Oh. My. God. You're so cheesy."

"It's in my job description. C'mon, kiddo. We gotta go." Abby hangs the dish towel on the oven handle and waves at me as she follows him. Houdini rouses from his corner near the sliding glass door, scampering behind her.

Caleb turns to me at the spiral stairwell. His gaze skates over my mouth once before he gives me a look I can't read. "Good night, Eden. I'll see you this week?"

I nod. Good or bad, that much is certain. I can't avoid him, and I have to finally admit I don't want to.

CHAPTER 21

Nowhere Saloon is noticeably empty when I arrive on Monday evening. This afternoon, I sent Caleb the first draft of a grant application, and he texted back.

Want to meet to review? I have some updated numbers.

He'd taken the liberty to ask Adelaide to stay with my mom. I wondered if it might be a ruse to see me, because who meets in a bar to go over budget information? He could just as easily have come to the house. What is this? A date? An excuse to get me alone? An opportunity for a rerun of last night's make-out session? I didn't have the nerve to ask any of those questions and, frankly, was relieved to get out of the house. Mom spoke about a dozen words to me today in total, and they were all transactional as I tended to her injuries.

Is that too tight?

No.

Do you need help getting up?

No.

Rinse and repeat. All day long.

I'm grateful to see a friendly face when Dakota approaches me with a smile and makes me the perfect margarita. Not too sweet, and just strong enough to release my tension and settle my nerves in advance of seeing Caleb after letting him kiss me senseless. After dreaming about that kiss all night long.

As I wait, I drink the margarita a little too quickly and scroll on my phone to avoid watching the door. I open Instagram, where I have a billion notifications. Cassie must have had insomnia last night, because she sent me a dozen reels sure to corrupt my algorithm, all with an obvious purpose: a handsome lumberjack chopping wood, the iconic GIF of Chris Evans splitting a log with his bare hands, and a bearded hottie licking a spoon. I roll my eyes and return to my feed when my gaze snags on a recommended follow, because there, in a cheery profile photo, is Nadia.

My stomach turns as I stare at the thumbnail picture of her profile. I should put my phone away and ignore the temptation. I should lean on my superpower of avoidance.

But I hover a finger over her face and cut myself open with one swift swipe. Her profile is public. The most recent post is captioned "Jeffrey Gill Jr. We are loving all seven pounds, three ounces, and twenty inches of him." It's a slideshow of a cherubic newborn, swaddled in the hospital-issued blanket and striped hat. The baby is squishy and pink and perfect. This one photo is enough self-harm, but I scroll until the knife is at my throat, poised over an artery—until Jeff appears with the tiny bundle in his arms. Jeff, asleep on the hospital cot. Jeff and Nadia together, proud grins as they hold their baby. Nadia nursing the baby in the hospital bed as Jeff leans in.

In tidy, filtered shots, I see the life I could have had. A new baby. A faithful husband. The chance for Cassie and me to raise our families together.

I gave it all up for him, and then he gave it to someone else.

I can't name the emotions roiling in my gut—it's some combination of embarrassment, bitterness, and sorrow. And anger, mighty and misplaced. On an intellectual level, I know my anger should be reserved for Jeff. But I'm also mad at myself. For trusting someone who'd cast me aside, for choosing him in the first place, for convincing myself that the ache I felt when holding friends' babies was a remnant of evolutionary instinct and not my own body calling me a liar for denying my dreams.

My dreams had never come true, and somewhere along the way, I decided to ignore them in favor of an achievable reality. Instead of choosing someone who made me giddy, I settled for the simple man I thought couldn't hurt me. Maybe I chose Jeff precisely because we hit only one note—like a metronome.

At this point, I don't care that he slept with someone else. But I'm pissed that I wasted most of my childbearing years while he can still litter his sperm all over fertile soil and impregnate other women until his dick withers to dust.

"You okay?" I look up to see Dakota's pretty blue eyes awash in concern.

"Yeah." I pull some cash from my wallet and set it on the bar top. I need to get out of here before I embarrass myself, before I cry on a barstool in front of strangers or seek solace on Caleb's shoulder again. I don't want to be this fragile person or waste any more tears on a man who didn't love me enough to deserve them.

"You look a little pale," Dakota says as she fills a lowball glass with two shots of vodka.

"I'm fine. But could you tell Caleb I had to leave?" I swivel on the stool and stand, one hand on the bar to steady myself.

"Of course." She eyes me, a little suspicious.

I'm not usually so emotional. It must be Grand Trees. And the unexpected detours my life has taken. I imagined thirty-five as a moment of security, of being firmly planted on a stable landing. Instead, I'm here, revisiting past hurts while coping with fresh ones.

I race to the back exit, toward the small gravel parking lot, and reach into my purse to grab my keys when the door is thrown open. I stumble straight into Caleb, who catches me by the elbows, steadying me.

"Whoa." His fingers curl around my bare arms, but his grip is soft. "Are you leaving?"

"Sorry, yeah. Tonight's not going to work for me," I stammer. "I'll email you about the grant."

"O-kay." His words are elongated in irritation. He steps back and drops his hands. "Thanks for letting me know."

"I told Dakota to tell you." I lose conviction as his irritation clears and something akin to hurt washes across his face.

"I'll see ya." He steps to the right just as I move to my left, before we both shift to the other side. I deflate, losing all momentum for escape. He looks over my head when he steps back to the right, gesturing for me to pass. When I do, he doesn't carry on down the hallway. I turn back with my hand on the knob.

"I'm sorry, Caleb. I'll incorporate your edits as soon as you send them."

"That's fine. I get it."

"You get what?" I think we're having two different conversations.

He turns to me slowly but still doesn't meet my eyes. "I can take a hint, Eden."

"I'm not . . ." I trail off. "I'm just having a terrible day, and I'd be shitty company, and I need to go be miserable without making you miserable, too."

His eyes narrow as if he's assessing my honesty. I'm not sure whether I can commit to walking out on him if I stand here much longer. Even skepticism looks good on him. He's in a pair of dark jeans and a green thermal that makes his eyes appear amber. I think he might have brushed his hair. His dark-brown waves are pushed off his forehead and curl slightly around his nape. And he definitely trimmed his beard; it's short and neat, and there's a hint of dimples underneath. Lord help me.

"I'm always shitty company. I'm a miserable bastard about 90 percent of the time," he says.

I snort. "Give yourself some credit. I think it's only about 80 percent." During the other 20 percent, he's letting me warm my feet between his calves and grope him in the forest.

"I wouldn't mind being miserable with you," he says.

Something detonates in my stomach—sparklers or fireworks or perhaps an atomic bomb—and it's potent enough to turn me to goo. "I think that's the nicest thing you've ever said to me."

His laugh, loud and unabashed, is a light source, a texture, an energy of its own. "Will you let me buy you a drink? Or is there something in there you're scared of?" He waves toward the bar.

"I just downed a margarita and then ran out," I admit. "I'm not sure I can go back in there and retain my dignity."

"Did you have another aggressive admirer?" He runs his hand through his hair, returning it to its natural state of chaos. The messy look works for him, too. I think he's the most gorgeous man I've ever seen up close, and I'm kinda impressed with myself that he kissed me last night.

He really kissed me.

I clear my throat. "Nope. Just that bad of a day."

"Did you and your mom get into it again?"

I bite my lip to keep from spilling my humiliation all over this hallway. I've shared enough sob stories with this man. The baby photos of my ex-husband's love child need to stay in my emotional vault.

"Wanna get out of here?" He moves until his proximity arcs like static. I look up at him and nod dumbly.

Caleb cups my elbow and leads me outside. I don't question him when he moves to his truck, stopping to open my door like we're on a date.

Are we on a date?

Did I almost stand him up and let my jackass ex-husband get in my head and ruin the first bit of fun—of joy—I've had in months?

I slide onto the bench seat as Caleb jogs to the driver's side. The truck's interior smells like him, his soap mixed with lumber and a hint of leather.

"Where are we going?" I ask, but I'm not sure I care. The sun is setting, and a beam of light is streaming in from the driver's side window, bathing him in gold.

"Any requests?"

His place, his bed specifically, but I let that intrusive thought die without speaking it aloud.

"Surprise me." It seems like the safest option, or at least the one that absolves me of culpability. "But I'm not dressed for anything outdoorsy."

"I noticed." His gaze skids over my navy maxi dress and white sandals. I'm even wearing earrings and applied mascara and lip gloss. "You look beautiful," he adds, so quietly I almost miss it.

He pulls out of the lot, his elbow resting on the open window and his other hand on the steering wheel. He casts a glance my way, and it occurs to me how stiff I must look in comparison. I'm sitting upright, both feet planted firmly on the floor, seat belt cutting across my neck.

We drive in silence for several miles as he maneuvers along a windy road into the hills.

"Should I be worried you're taking me to a secluded spot to murder me?" I ask when cell service gets spotty and dusk arrives, making the tree-lined road seem ominous.

"If I wanted to murder you, I would have killed you when I had you alone in a cabin in the woods."

"You answered that too quickly," I say. "Like it crossed your mind at some point."

He laughs and glances at me with an expression I can't read. He makes me nervous, but not for my safety. He slows to a crawl and veers off the paved road until he pulls to a stop in a clearing with a perfect view of Grand Trees Lake. The last rays of sunlight tickle the lake's back, and it wriggles, sighs, and shimmers against the affection.

Caleb cuts the engine and shifts to face me. But I'm entranced by the view. I've never seen the lake from this northern side and didn't know we could just drive up to it. At camp, we'd hike to the southern shore; the reward was a serene, sheltered inlet. The western shore is open to the public with kayak rentals, windsurfing, and paddleboats. A broad pine-needle-strewn beach sits in front of a swim area demarked by buoys and floating docks. From here, I can see the rise of Colibri

Peak. I feel like Caleb is sharing a secret with me. Neither of us gets out of the car, and the silence becomes thick and heavy.

"You going to tell me what happened?" he asks.

"Probably not." I don't want to invite Jeff into this moment. I've wasted enough energy on a man unworthy of it. "But can I ask you something?" I release my seat belt and twist toward him. Perhaps he can talk me down from this emotional ledge even if I don't bare my soul. Perhaps he can teach me something about forgiveness and letting go.

"That doesn't seem fair."

I ignore him. "You're really, truly friends with Ian? It's not an act?"

His smile is slow growing, unsure, and perplexed. "Do you think I would or could pretend to like someone if I didn't?"

I laugh. "Fair point. I guess that's why I'm confused. How do you not feel bitter or angry or betrayed?"

"They didn't betray me. They didn't start dating until after we separated."

I take this in. "But even so, how are you chill about them moving on that quickly? How do you work with him and joke with him and hang out with both of them without resentment?" My eyes burn with unshed tears, but I blink them away and clear my throat.

"Are you sure this is about me?" Caleb's voice drops to its lowest, softest register. I've heard him use it with Houdini when he thinks no one is paying attention.

"Maybe not. But humor me." I inhale and regain my composure. "Please."

Caleb reaches out as if he might touch me or pull me into a hug, but he must think better of it, because he rests his hand on his knee and stares out over the lake before sighing. "I guess Lina never felt like mine, but she felt like my responsibility, which makes me sound like a jerk. I cared for her—still do—but not like I should have." He trails off and looks at me cautiously, carefully, as if he expects judgment on my face. Instead, I'm just confused.

"Lina and I were young when we started dating. The relationship ran its course, and we broke up, and a few days later, she found out she was pregnant. Instead of ending things, we had Abby, slid back into a relationship, and got married. But we never really fit. Lina is a great person. She's just not my person. And I sure as hell wasn't hers. The worst type of loneliness is being lonely together."

I think of Abby—beautiful, expressive, wide-open Abby—a product of a loveless marriage and still struggling to figure out where she fits.

"We were both sleepwalking through life. When Ian moved to town to take over after Sonny's retirement, he and Lina hit it off. And she came alive."

"They fell in love while you were married?" I whisper.

He shrugs. "They couldn't help how they felt. But I trust nothing happened until we split. If Ian hadn't shown up, I think Lina and I would have gone on, not being enough for each other. But Ian gave us an out, and I was relieved, honestly." He runs his hands through his hair, destroying the last evidence of the comb he must have used earlier.

"Relieved?" I ask, unconvinced.

He slips closer, his face growing more earnest. "Among other things, I felt guilty I couldn't give Abby the family she deserved and disappointed that I failed. But, yeah, relieved." He pauses. "When people talk about family and kids and happily ever after? No one ever mentions how many ways you gotta fit and how many things you have to agree on. About how to live your lives, how to have fun, how to raise kids, how to manage money, how to dream. And you gotta be in sync everywhere, in front of an audience and in private. Me and Lina didn't fit in the important ways. And in those spaces in between, where there was either too much distance or too much friction, we built resentments that replaced all the oxygen. We tried. But when we weren't talking about Abby, there was a lot of silence. I think that's why Abby talks so much—growing up in all that quiet."

"Or she just has a lot to say."

Caleb laughs. "Well, that's true, too."

Caleb's perspective makes me challenge my own. Did I ignore all the ways Jeff and I didn't fit? How his idea of vacation was lounging by the pool at a four-star hotel, and I preferred to book cheap accommodations and explore. Or how he refused to dance with me at weddings. How I liked the outdoors, and he preferred being inside. The way he didn't like public displays of affection, so he wouldn't touch me except in our bedroom, and even then, not enough. How he hated when I sang along to music, so I bit my tongue when my favorite songs would come on the radio. How when I'd finally treat myself and curl up with a novel, he'd offer some bland business leadership book and tell me to read it instead.

Maybe I confused compromise for contentment, settling for security. Maybe we didn't fit in the important ways, and I didn't notice or was too scared of instability to acknowledge it. Maybe Jeff did us both a big favor. If only he had done it earlier, before I'd given him so much of my youth.

Caleb and I sit in silence for a few moments, watching as the final remnants of daylight slip away and the moon takes center stage, shining a beacon across the still lake.

"I guess life with Lina . . . it just felt . . . single sensory when you want your partner to make your nerve endings crackle."

Caleb gives me a meaningful look, and my skin takes the suggestion, erupting in goose bumps. His words strike me somewhere tender and raw. Jeff may be a cheating asshole, but that doesn't mean he was wrong about us, because I'm not sure he ever made me feel more than tepid contentment. "You only hit one note?"

Caleb turns his chin, squinting at me like I've said something true. "Yeah. That's a good way to describe it."

"Why'd you bring me here?" I ask, not breaking eye contact. The sun is down, but his eyes glimmer. I remember seeing him across the bar over a week ago when I was struck by their unusual color. Some people might describe them as brown, but that would be a lie. They're the color of a rare gemstone, made of copper and gold and sparks of light.

"I come here to think when I'm struggling with something. You seemed upset, and I've noticed how much you loosen up when you're outside." He rubs the back of his neck, his head bowing slightly.

"This isn't where you brought girls in high school?" I joke.

His smile is lazy and crooked. "That would require actually speaking to girls in high school. So no."

"Too cool to make an effort?"

"Too angry to interact with other humans."

I picture Caleb as a withdrawn and petulant kid. It's not that hard to imagine. But I'm impressed by all the connections he's forged since—and the daughter he's raised, who's so secure in her attachments that she connects with everyone without hesitation or reservation.

"I've never brought anyone here," he says.

"I feel special." I am aware of every inch of empty space between us on the bench seat.

"You should." Caleb gives me a soft smile before he slides his hand to my nape and tilts my chin with his thumb. We hold there, connected only by his touch and our locked eyes. "Are you okay, really?" he asks, low and sweet.

My pulse is a drum in my throat, and I'm sure he can feel it against his palm, like a confession of what his attention does to me. "I'm just realizing I've spent my life afraid of falling but wound up at rock bottom anyway."

He makes a soft sound like a hum, thoughtful and seductive all at once. "How do you feel now?" He swipes his thumb across my bottom lip, and I fight a shiver.

"Terrified," I whisper, but I lean forward and capture his mouth in mine.

There's nothing tentative about this kiss, no questions or equivocation. Whatever hesitation we had was put to rest on the trail of my demise last night. He cradles my face in both hands, moving into a kiss so certain, so possessed, that I whimper at the perfection of it. And I lose all sense of time, space, and separation. I slide closer, or maybe he does, until his thigh is pressed to mine, and I wrap my hands around his neck and into his hair. He deepens the kiss just as I demand it, swallowing my small gasp, letting me taste him, bite him, and consume him. I am overwhelmed by how right he feels. Kissing Caleb is like muscle memory, some familiar phantom from a former timeline. There's no surprise, just relief and need.

Twisted this way, I'm frustrated by the lack of contact. Without breaking the kiss, I plant both hands on the backrest and climb onto the bench to straddle him. He spreads his hands and gathers the bunched fabric of my dress before grabbing my hips. When I lower myself, settling in his lap, his fingertips dig into my skin reflexively, and he releases a soft groan. I want to bottle it—that sound and this heady mix of power and powerlessness as his hands roam, and I move against the hard ridge in his pants. He slides his hands up my sides, over my rib cage, until his thumbs swipe over my breasts—gentle, maddening—and I wiggle closer. I'm trapped in my long skirt, and I rise to my knees to yank at the hem when Caleb finds my shins, circling both in his broad palms. The surety of his hands makes me shiver, and I realize, absently, that I'm letting him touch my scars. I don't shrink from him as he skates across the damaged skin, which is numb and oversensitive all at once. He doesn't linger there, though, instead finding my bare thighs with his hands as he trails his lips and teeth along my jaw, my neck, my clavicle. His beard scrapes against my flesh and his hair tickles my neck. It's a delicious mix of sensations and textures. I tug at his shirt, finding skin that's silk over granite.

I am an electrical fire, a misfiring fuse; the blaze radiates from each inch of skin spoiled by his attention to every part of me still crying for contact. He leans forward into my touch, as hungry for me as I am for him. When his hands slip under my dress, hands splayed over my ass, I drag his mouth to mine, and my restraint snaps. I can't get close enough, I can't feel enough. We're tangled in clothes—bunched up, pushed aside, in the way—as I rock against the fly of his jeans. He pulls me toward him, tighter, faster.

Caleb ducks his head and lifts my hips until his mouth is over my breast, a force of suction and wetness through my dress. I gasp, and he pulls away, his eyes glassy and unfocused as he looks at me and says, "Is this too much? I feel a little crazy."

I hold his gaze as I slip the spaghetti straps from my shoulders and fold the elastic top to my rib cage. I'm bare underneath, and his eyes go wide as he takes me in. I whimper when he circles my nipple with his tongue, tugging me into his mouth as his hands roam. I'm impatient and needy and fumble with his belt, relishing the clank of metal and tug of leather before working at his button and zipper. And then I cup him over his boxers, and he opens his mouth over my skin, teeth grazing me, panting, releasing a little groan from the back of his throat. "Eden," he says, but it's more like a prayer.

I sneak under his waistband, and he lifts so we can shove his jeans and boxers down enough for me to free him. He's perfect in my palm—impossibly hard, tempting, and hot. He makes the most delicious sound at my first touch, some combination of my name and gibberish. But I'm not prepared when he tugs the layers of fabric twisted at my waist so that there's nothing between us but the thin scrap of my underwear.

I feel feral and free, like a forest fire ready to burn this place down. He pulls the elastic of my underwear aside and circles me with expert, calloused fingertips, but it's still not enough. I'm aching for him. For all of him. And now that I have a taste, I want to devour him.

"Caleb," I say. "Please, please, please." He bites the words off my lips as he pushes two fingers inside me, rubbing me with his thumb in maddening, relentless pressure.

My hand falters in its rhythm—I'm so lost to the brink of bliss. Caleb knows how to touch me, how to take me toward something that's often elusive to me. Thoughts fly in and out of my head, pushed aside by the primal need for *this* and *more* and *all*. I don't care that it's fast, that the last person to touch me was a man I vowed would be the last, that I'm nearing climax in the cab of a truck with a man I didn't know two weeks ago and didn't like mere days ago. I don't care that there's no guarantee but this moonlit moment at the lake, or that I may regret this tomorrow. But regret or not, I know I will replay it and relish that I had him once.

I am close, deliciously close, but I guide his hand away, reaching into my purse as I send a silent thank-you to Cassie for her lack of boundaries. Caleb scans my face for answers, and his brows pinch in confusion, then relief, as I find a condom. He snatches it from me, sheathing himself in a few fluid movements as I rise onto my knees, positioning him against my entrance. His breath hitches—wonder in his wide, shimmering eyes—before he smiles. He holds my face in both palms and watches my reaction when I sink down an inch at a time.

"I swear I didn't plan this." Caleb releases the words between gusts of breath.

"Didn't even imagine it?"

He holds my hips steady, and I sense we're both overwhelmed. I might explode from the pressure and pleasure and clawing need to bring us both to our knees.

"I imagined it," he says with his smile pressed against my lips. "But not half dressed in my truck." He exhales, still holding himself back, letting me lead, but it looks like it's killing him.

I finally settle low, until he's deliciously deep. He kisses me as I move over him, and he slides his hands over each patch of exposed skin. His touch is light and teasing at first, but then he rises to meet me, and our rhythm becomes desperate and greedy—his fingertips dig into flesh as if he's hanging from a precipice. I know the feeling. I match each thrust, straddling wider to take more of him, all of him, as I hover over the abyss of relief, worried it'll topple me too soon and too intensely. I want to keep it at bay and keep him inside me forever. I want to suspend this rash and wild moment. I want to hold on to how it feels to be possessed by a man as self-possessed as Caleb.

But I'm too wound up, and my body is in a hurry, even as my heart hauls it back. Caleb groans with his mouth open on my breast, his teeth grazing my skin, tongue finding the peak and gaze locked on mine, until it's all too much, and I burst into flames. I scream his name like an incantation, a chant, as my orgasm tears through me, cresting and cresting before I come down in shuddering waves. I lose all sense of control—my limbs limp and hips heavy—and Caleb holds me steady as he drives into me once, twice, three times, before he buries his face in my neck to muffle the sound of his pleasure.

Reality comes back to me in a fragmented array. The starbursts behind my eyes fade to black, sensation returns to my limbs, and I hear the wind through the trees and the soft surf of the lake. I feel the scratch of Caleb's beard on my shoulder and the warm gust of his breath against my neck. He hums and drags his mouth along my throat until we're kissing again. This kiss is slow, a half measure of soft lips and the give and take of a quiet conversation. He wraps me in a hug so tight and intimate, that I wonder how we got here. But also, how did it take so long? Caleb feels inevitable. From the first glance of his intense gaze from across the bar to every combative, comforting moment since, I've wanted him. And despite the absurdity that we're two adults who just had sex in a truck on a random Monday night in spring, nothing about this feels wrong or off or uncomfortable.

I drop my head into the crook of his neck and lift my hips so he can pull out of me. I breathe in his sweet, salty scent—wood, soap, and something primal. His proximity makes me drunk.

"We just had sex in your truck," I say, a laugh caught in my throat.

He groans but then chuckles, grabbing my ass and shifting me higher onto his lap. "We did. You make me a little unhinged."

My inner thigh scrapes against his open belt buckle, my foot hits the steering wheel, and my bad leg is throbbing at this awkward angle, and I don't care. His hand travels up my back until he grips my neck, nudging my mouth to his again.

"Same. I'm not usually this . . ." But I don't know how to finish the sentence, because I don't want to admit how restrained, careful, and measured I've been.

I like this new freedom to feel, to let this beautiful, complicated man own me, to permit this unleashed version of myself to take what it wants when it wants it. He smiles against my lips, and I think this is my favorite version of Caleb, too. His hands skate over me, carefully adjusting my underwear and dress so I'm decent, unfolding the skirt until it hangs behind me. As diligently as he pulled me apart, he puts me back together. But I don't think I'll ever be the same. I've never had sex like this, driven by need and left sated and calm.

"I like you," he says, and I can't help but laugh. He's surprisingly cute.

"You let me defile you, so I suspected you might, finally."

"I've always liked you." He kisses my jaw, my cheek, my temple, resting there as he speaks into my hair. "The first time I saw you, I lost my train of thought. You were stunning, and I felt like I knew you or I was supposed to."

My heart hiccups, stuttering to a stop before flooding me with warmth. I remind myself that he recognized me from the portraits lining the walls at the house he grew up in, and maybe from a quick glance at Sonny's funeral. It's not deeper than that. But it doesn't explain why I felt the same way, why I couldn't look away from him, why I've never felt this drawn to anyone. I can't say these scary words aloud, so I wrap my arms around his neck, holding on to the moment like it's mine to keep.

"After we met the first time, you left the bar without getting my name or number."

"I thought you were just here for the weekend," he says. "And I knew I'd want to see you again."

"Well, you're in luck. We can't seem to go a day without running into each other now."

"I want to do more than run into you in your mom's kitchen. I want to take you out, take you home, and take my time with you." When he talks to me like this, I'd be willing to strip and let him take me all night, right here, but he's not done. "And I don't want to wonder where we stand. I don't want to worry this was just some impulse of yours after a bad day."

His candor is a key in the lock of my reserve, tempting me to be honest as well. "I've been wanting to do that for a while," I say. "But this could get complicated. This is a small town, and I don't know how my mom would react."

"And I've never introduced Abby to anyone."

The weight of the responsibility falls over me like a bucket of cool water, and I shiver. "Never?"

He shakes his head. "She's been through a lot."

I kiss him. The kiss is for all the times I wanted to before I could, for all the times his unexpected kindness made me breathless, for all the ways in which he's such a better man than most. I kiss him because, in a different universe, he's the father I'd want for my kids, and I'm glad sweet Abby has him in this one.

"Then we'll just keep it to ourselves until . . ." But the reality intrudes like a ticking clock. Until when? There's no use in telling anyone and confusing Abby and my mom, because we can't last. "But I'm not going to be here long."

He's silent for a moment, pulling back until he's looking into my eyes. He's lit up from the moon, all soft light and shadow. "I'll take however much time I can get."

Time. Time is simple. I'll give him as much as we can salvage, in secret or sunlight. But as my body shivers from the aftershocks of him, as my mind reels from the vulnerability he's voiced, I worry I'll have to give up more than my time. I'm afraid he might take my heart in the process.

CHAPTER 22

There isn't much time to be found, it turns out. Caleb works various jobs: He maintains the camp facilities and forest, leads the town council, is a volunteer firefighter, and is the person everyone calls when something goes wrong. He's part arborist, part handyman, part town hero. And Lina relents, letting Abby stay with him every weeknight so she can focus on school.

It means I see Caleb every evening, with Abby in tow, but I don't see *my* Caleb. Not the one who kisses me like it's his calling, whispers sweet words into my skin, and makes me feel like a much younger, more impulsive woman. While watching him from across the room—interacting with Abby, caring for my mom, cuddling with Houdini—I remind myself that I'm going home as soon as Mom's better. I can't afford to fall headfirst for a guy whose identity is Grand Trees itself.

We work on the grant applications while Abby does her homework, but we're never alone. I have to restrain myself from sitting near him, touching him, staring at him. I am an expert at bottling my emotions and sealing them tight, but Caleb makes me porous.

It's easier to guard myself with Mom. I've had years of practice. I'm treading lightly, hoping I can rebuild trust before attempting another tough conversation. I need to show her that I'm here and all in—or, at least, I want to be. If I convince Mom, through my care and commitment, that I want what's best for her, maybe she'll trust me enough to listen and get treatment, prolonging her life and our chance for reconciliation. If I had the courage to frame it that way, would it make a difference? Would she be willing to extend her life to share her last years with me? I'm not sure I'm ready to hear an honest answer. I'm afraid to ask.

As I change her dressing on Wednesday morning, Mom looks especially pained.

"Am I hurting you?" I ask, giving some slack on the bandage.

"No, honey. I just . . ." She trails off, and I freeze and watch her choose her words. "I'm sorry about the way I reacted the other day. It's hard getting older and feeling like a burden—"

"You're not a burden, Mom."

She smiles, but it's melancholy. "I am grateful for your offer. All I've ever wanted is to be closer to you."

"Then why won't you consider it?" I wince as I say it, like I'm begging. It pains me to offer myself up to her rejection again.

She pats my shoulder. "You're young and should be building your life, not caring for me. I couldn't do that to you after I . . ." She darts her eyes away. "Maybe there will come a time when I'll need more support, and we can cross that bridge when we come to it."

It's something, at least. Not now. But someday.

She clears her throat and continues, "But once my bones heal, I want you to get back to your life and focus on *you*."

Perhaps I jumped to the wrong conclusions about her motives. Her refusal felt like another rejection, but maybe it was meant as a kindness.

I squeeze her hand with my free one.

"And about you," she says. "I'm worried. What happened with Jeff, honey?"

"Oh." I've been dodging this conversation. Telling her the truth about his infidelity might sound like an accusation. Offering a half-truth may be a kindness of my own. "It turns out we weren't right for each other. Jeff just figured it out before I did."

Mom offers a warm smile. "It was amicable, then?" I sense she's distancing my divorce from hers to ensure my recent wound didn't open an old one.

I nod—a full lie—but I'm committed to this kindness.

"Well, then, this can be a fresh start for you. If you still loved him, it would be . . ." She looks over my shoulder, her face awash in an emotion I can't read. "Well, it's hard to start over when half your heart is still beating for someone else."

I can't take that bait. I assume she means me, but she didn't have to leave at all. A mother should never leave. I swallow back a retort so I don't ruin this fragile progress.

I want to find a way to set aside my lingering anger and learn to love her purely again, without falling prey to these stubborn resentments. I want to do what I came for—forgive her and rebuild our bond. But I'm afraid Mom and I can't heal our relationship without digging into the hurt, and I'm not strong enough for that.

After my surgeries, I went through painful physical therapy. My body had sealed the hurt into the fibers of my muscles, nerves, tendons, and skin, leaving me with limited mobility and debilitating pain. But breaking through the scar tissue was more excruciating than the accident itself, as if the trauma had settled into hard, lumpy adhesions, and it put up a fight as it escaped.

For now, I suppose I'll avoid the tender spots and do my best to make progress on our relationship without unearthing more agony.

~

Late Thursday afternoon, I'm working on a client project, huddled over my laptop at the kitchen counter, when Caleb arrives alone, sneaking in through the front door and scanning the space before sprinting to me. "Where's Nicki?" he mouths.

"In her room," I say, concerned, until he spins my stool and cups my face in his hands, kissing me so fiercely I have to take fistfuls of his shirt to keep myself upright. He presses me against the counter, tipping my chin higher as he sinks his mouth into mine. He catches me on a gasp and drags his hands to my jaw, my neck, my bare shoulders.

Warmth floods me, and I am desperate to be alone with him, to explore his body, find every freckle and flaw, to experience his weight on me.

But it's over as soon as it starts, and he steps away, my lips stinging in his wake.

"Hi." He drags his focus away from my mouth.

"Hi." I'm dizzy from the kiss, but the front door swings open, and I come back to reality. Abby and Houdini barrel in, with noise, chaos, and pine-scented air in their wake.

Under the counter, Caleb tangles his fingers in mine and squeezes once before stepping aside to receive Houdini's exuberant entrance.

"Eden, do you remember your worst teacher ever?" Abby stomps over, swinging her backpack onto the counter.

"Umm . . ." I'm still rattled by the kiss and its abrupt end.

"Because whoever it was, my social studies teacher is worse. He gave us a pop quiz today on something we learned three weeks ago." She emits a little growl and slumps onto the stool beside me. "That's like ancient history. I didn't even know *you* three weeks ago." She drops her forehead to the counter, her arms dangling limp at her sides.

"BE, even before BC. That's not ancient history—it's before history." Caleb's head is buried in the fridge.

I laugh, and Caleb winks at me over his shoulder.

"What?" Abby lifts her head with a blank expression.

"BE. Before Eden," I clarify.

Abby rolls her eyes, looking between us as if we've grown extra appendages. "You guys are so weird."

"I'm sorry, Abs." I slip my hand over her ponytail. It's wet and tangled from swim practice and stuck to her neck. I smooth it down her back. "That does seem unfair."

"He's evil," she says. "And I have another three tests tomorrow."

"You always stress and then ace it. Just skip the stressing part." Caleb moves to the pantry, pulling out a bag of chips.

Abby and I both groan in unison.

"What?" he asks through a mouthful of Lay's.

"Boys," Abby says, just as I say, "Men, always thinking they can solve our worry by telling us not to worry about it."

"Like, duh. If I could not worry about it, wouldn't I have figured that out already?" Abby rolls her eyes.

Caleb swallows and looks from his daughter to me, then back, before whispering, "Uh-oh."

"What's wrong?" Mom asks from behind me. She moves so quietly that the sound of her voice startles me.

"The two of them are ganging up on me," Caleb says.

"Did you deserve it?" She tilts her face to his with a teasing grin. She used to look at me like that—adoring, doting.

"Yes," Abby and I say in unison, and Mom laughs while Caleb glares at me.

"How are you feeling, Grams?" Abby stands to give her a tentative hug.

"Better, actually, as long as I don't use my arm or touch my ribs or breathe in too deeply."

"Sounds easy enough. Why would you need to breathe?" Abby winces.

Mom pats her hand. "I'm doing fine, sweetheart."

"Well, I'm not. I have to study for seventeen hours. Do you want to quiz me on vocab?"

Mom smiles indulgently. "Of course."

Abby slings her backpack over her shoulder, and the two of them head into the family room, leaving Caleb and me alone-ish in the kitchen area.

I pat the stool next to me. "I need you."

Caleb offers a lopsided little smile and mouths, "They're right there."

The house has zones, but there's no privacy in this great room. I wish the house were divided into alcoves and nooks so I could press Caleb against a door and release some of the tension that's been building since he dropped me off at my car on Monday night, already wanting more of him.

I laugh softly, and shift my laptop closer as he slides in beside me. "For the state application."

His thigh is pressed to mine, and heat travels up my leg like ivy.

"If you say so," he whispers against my ear, brushing a few strands of hair against my cheekbone. It feels like a kiss. He's playing fast and loose with our commitment to keep this private. I snap my focus to him, intending to flash a warning look, but instead, I'm struck by the warmth in his honeyed gaze. It's soft, playful, and irresistible.

He whispers, "Hi," and a swarm of butterflies bats their powdered wings against my ribs. I can't afford to let them carry me away—all this infatuation is making me punch-drunk and irrational. Caleb lives here. Caleb's daughter is here. I need to enjoy this chemistry and let it fizzle before I leave, hopefully with Mom by my side. He bites his bottom lip to fight one of his blinding smiles, and I can't look away until he does, turning his focus to my screen. "All right, you have my full attention."

"Good." I clear my throat. "I need you to help me with this first question." I tap the screen with the back of my pen.

Caleb leans forward, squinting. His lips move as he reads, his tongue poking out to wet them, and I add this to the collection of personal details I'm gathering like souvenirs.

But then he speaks, and I'm reacquainted with the other Caleb. "Skip it. That's a stupid question."

"I can't skip it. It's required," I say. "And I'm beginning to understand why you needed my help."

"These questions are a waste of time. The grant is asking for solutions to fire danger. Why am I going to write five pages explaining what fire danger is?"

"I will write it. I just need you to double-check the data I gathered online and give me some bullet points. I'll make it sound pretty."

"But why?" Caleb's posture stiffens.

"Because that's how fundraising works. Every application begins with *making the case*, with stats and figures that justify the requested dollars. Is it obvious and tedious? Yes. Can it be avoided? Not if you want the money."

"That's ridiculous," Caleb says, growing frustrated.

"You're right. But it's how we have to play the game."

"Dad," Abby calls from the family room. "It's just like school. All of my homework is repeating the stuff the teacher already knows, like geometry. I have to regurgitate the rules the teacher taught me and then tell him why something he taught us is true. 'Why is angle B equal to angle C?'" she says in a low register. "I don't know, Mr. Cassein. Maybe because you told me it was?"

"I hope you don't have that attitude in class." Caleb twists in his stool and leans into me as he does.

"I hope you don't have that attitude with Eden while she's trying to help you," Abby parrots. I snort, and Caleb grumbles.

"You two are going to be trouble together," he says.

"You're outnumbered, dear. You're going to have to stop being such a stubborn SOB," Mom says, and the three of us share a genuine laugh. "And what did I tell you about being nice to my daughter? This silly feud of yours is bad for my health."

"Fine," he moans. "Let's do this stupid task."

I'm touched to hear Mom stick up for me, even though I am well prepared to handle Caleb—his antagonism, at least. As to whether my heart can handle his affection, well, that's another question entirely.

I listen to Mom quiz Abby in the background as Caleb and I work, and I'm distracted by a memory I haven't thought about in years—Mom spending hours helping me catch up on homework, study for tests, and do last-minute projects. If Mom hadn't made me her full-time job, I never would have been able to juggle school and ballet. I'd get home from dance every evening when my peers were going to bed. Mom would feed me dinner and sit beside me until I finished my schoolwork, soothing my tired meltdowns, quizzing me, or patiently explaining a concept I was too exhausted to understand.

Every beautiful memory with Mom has been tarnished. But she's still the woman who drove me across the city to class every day, picked me up each night, and sewed my pointe shoes. She is still the woman who supported my dream as if it were her own—but made sure I was set up to survive when that dream turned into a fickle fantasy.

And I did survive, even if I didn't thrive.

I'm working on it, though.

Within an hour, I have the first draft of a compelling application, and Abby has practiced her vocabulary words so relentlessly that we all could recite the definitions and spelling verbatim: oblique, obsolete, brusque, exult, quibble.

"You're ready, Abby." Mom places the flash cards on the end table as Caleb and I head into the family room.

"Is anyone hungry for dinner?" Caleb sinks into the sofa beside Abby, wrapping his arm around her shoulders.

"As long as it's not another casserole," Abby says. "I need a new texture. Please say we can eat something else."

"Why don't we go out?" Mom says. "I've been cooped up for weeks."

Caleb looks to me to confirm. We have a wordless conversation in a glance. I shrug, like *why not*, hoping my mom is ready to trek into town, postaccident.

Going out on a Thursday night offseason means we're back at Nowhere Saloon; it's the only place open for dinner. But the booths are comfortable, the food is decent, and I don't have to cook or eat another donated one-pot meal, so I'm game.

The dining room is as packed as the day I arrived in town, but not with tourists. I recognize many of the guests from the revolving door of Good Samaritans who have stopped by to check on us.

Bob and Carmela are at the bar and immediately stand to greet Mom, shuttling her into the largest, coziest booth in the corner as we follow on their heels. I sneak away to the restroom as a crowd gathers to welcome her back into civilization.

I say hello to a few people as I pass, pausing for inquiries about Mom and my visit—and struggling to remember all their names—before ducking into the dark hallway. The women's restroom is tucked into an alcove at the back.

When I emerge a few moments later, Caleb is leaning against the far wall, looking even better than he did in my dream last night. He pushes off, reaching for my hips, pulling me into him, and burying his face against my neck. I shiver at the scratch of his beard against my skin and his rough palms at my waist, and I have exactly thirty seconds of rational thought before I risk pulling him into the bathroom.

"Where's Abby?" I ask to remind myself why I shouldn't.

"She's talking to Ian."

"Ian's here too?" I pull back, and it brings us face-to-face.

"He's picking up takeout." He silences me with a kiss. And that's it—my thirty seconds are up. Those damn butterflies are flapping their wings so loud I can't hear the warning bell in my head. I tug on his shirt to bring him closer, and he obeys. He's agreeable when my hands are on him. Is it possible to miss someone you've just met, who also happens to be around all the time? Because I do, and this kiss is a tonic to all the hours I've been forced to keep my distance.

"C'mon, my truck is right outside," he whispers, tugging me toward the back exit.

"Caleb," I groan, and he chuckles softly in return, swallowing my next words with a deeper kiss.

"Oh." The exclamation comes from behind me, barely rising above the rush of blood in my ears. "Oh my."

I pull back a moment too late, and I'm too embarrassed to turn.

"Shit," Caleb whispers, dropping his arms from my waist and hanging his head.

CHAPTER 23

"Well, well, well, aren't you two something to see."

Adelaide. *Shit* is right. I turn, stepping away from Caleb and shoving my hands into my pockets. I'm a caricature of a criminal trying to act natural to distract a witness from the crime.

"Nicolette is going to absolutely love this." Adelaide's grin is so self-satisfied that I wonder if she had planned this entire thing: beckoning me here, roping me into working with Caleb, causing the earthquake, booby-trapping the tree outside the cabin. Hell, maybe she scheduled Jeff's first physical therapy appointment with Nadia. She strikes me as someone who likes a long con.

"Which is why she can't know." It's the first time I've heard Caleb use that stern, displeased tone on anyone other than me.

"Well, then, you two shouldn't have been making out in a public place like a couple of horny teenagers." She guffaws, her eyes twinkling in joy at her discovery.

I am not sure there is a hue deep enough on the color wheel to describe my blush.

"Actually, we'd appreciate it if no one knows," I say. "It's new, and I'm leaving soon, and we don't want to confuse anyone."

Adelaide's responding laugh is jubilant, as if we're a couple of adorable and delusional children. "I think the people you should be worried about confusing are yourselves."

It's harsh, but she's probably right. I've never had a casual, time-delineated relationship, and I worry I chose the worst person to test my capacity for it. My feelings for Caleb are not casual—they are consuming. I can calculate the distance between us every time we're in the same room. I seek his reaction to every small exchange. When he leaves, my mind fast-forwards to the next time I'll see him. If Jeff was the lauded hardcover that sat on my nightstand for a year, reliably putting me to sleep after a few dense passages, Caleb is the page-turner keeping me up all night, making me obsess over what will happen next, silencing reality with fiction. I want to devour him, consume every detail, and discover every twist.

But maybe that's what a fling is; perhaps it's always this intense. Perhaps nothing this powerful can last, because I'll burn through the chapters and reach the last page too soon.

"Adelaide," Caleb warns.

But she raises a perfectly penciled brow, silencing him. "No one's going to hear it from me." She waggles a finger back and forth between us, her smile blooming. "But word to the wise: If you want to keep this little secret, you may want to keep your distance and nix the PDA."

She slips into the bathroom, her laughter drifting behind her.

"Do you think she'll spill?" I ask. Adelaide, as well meaning as she is, is not someone I'd expect to stay silent about anything.

"Nah," he says. "She's always kept my secrets." He runs his hands through his hair and down his face.

"Wait." I laugh. "Do you make a habit of secret relationships?" And then I still. This isn't a relationship. It's a . . . whatever it is. I think I just made the first fatal flaw of a fling. My face heats again. It's a wonder embarrassment can't kill you.

But Caleb smiles—bright, toothy, beautiful. "This is, in fact, a first." He reaches for my fingers, tangling ours together. "Adelaide, or Mrs. Chan, was my high school guidance counselor. She retired last year."

I snort out a laugh. "No way." That answers that mystery, at least. Adelaide looks ageless.

"I got into a bit of trouble back in the day, but she didn't say a word to Uncle Sonny. She gave me chance after chance."

Another page turns, and I want to curl up in his stories. "Then why are you worried?"

"Because we're still here. Like this." He raises my hand to his lips, pressing a kiss to my knuckles. "Even though I know she's right, I can't seem to stop touching you." With his other hand, he hooks a finger in my belt loop, tugs me to him, and ducks for a kiss.

I give in for a heartbeat as the heat of him pours from my mouth to my chest, and desire pools deep in my center. But he's telling me I need to be the willpower. I need to dog-ear the page for later, set him aside, and let reality intrude until I can enjoy him in private.

I press one more kiss to his lips and step back. His hands trail after me, holding on to me, stretching until I drift out of reach.

When we emerge from the hallway, there's a crowd tucked around Mom: Abby, Bob, and Carmela. Ian is perched on a chair at the far end of the booth.

Caleb and I were careless. The entire town is here tonight.

"Why do you two look guilty," Mom asks, and we both freeze. "Did you get into another argument?"

"Just a minor face-off, but it's all good because I won this one," I say, and it's the right answer, because the table erupts in laughter.

Ian stands. "Eden." His smile is warm and genuine as he reaches in for a hug, patting my back amiably. "Did you and Caleb manage to stay out of trouble this week otherwise?"

My mind is awash with every conceivable reason for this question: He knew we stripped down to nothing in the cabin, or he spied us in the hallway, in Caleb's car, or in the forest? Maybe Caleb confided in him?

"Umm, I . . . well," I mumble.

But he breaks out in a laugh. "Just wanted to make sure you didn't get trapped during one of those aftershocks."

Oh, right. Whew. "I figure I'm safe if I stay away from Caleb in confined spaces." Which, apparently, I am very, very bad at. I'm lucky Ian assumes I'm joking rather than admitting my new favorite hobby.

"Where's the fun in that?" Caleb's whisper slips under the din of voices. He leans in and says, "I'm good in confined spaces," as he brushes past me to accept Ian's handshake hug.

When I look away, I catch Adelaide's gaze as she emerges from the hallway. She shakes her head as she approaches with a knowing grin plastered across her face. She slides into the booth beside Carmela as a waiter I don't recognize comes to take our order.

When Ian says his goodbyes, his arms filled with take-out bags, Caleb and I slip into the two chairs perched at the end of the booth. It saves me from eye contact but keeps him at touching distance, which has proven dangerous.

I don't follow the conversation, which is mainly gossip about town residents I haven't met or don't recall. But my dinner is good, and Caleb keeps his thigh pressed to mine as a promise. And honestly, that may be why I don't follow the conversation.

"Are you with your mom this weekend?" Adelaide asks Abby as she tucks into her burger.

"Yeah. I think my dad needs a break from me." Abby giggles.

"Never." Caleb gives her the side-eye and a sly smile at the same time.

"He's been asking me to play the quiet game more often than normal this week."

Caleb frowns. "Lies."

"Nicolette." Adelaide reaches across the table to grab Mom's good hand. "You look like you're doing well, why don't you and I spend the day together on Saturday? I'll treat you to a facial at Josephine's."

Mom looks at me, unsure. "Oh, I don't know."

"A change of scenery will do you good. And surely Eden will let me borrow you for the day," Adelaide says.

Caleb nudges my knee. Adelaide is working some meddling matchmaker magic or trying to lay a trap. This woman.

"What do you think, Eden? You won't feel like I've abandoned you?" Mom says, and we must both hear the subtext at the same time because her eyes widen, and she looks away before I answer.

And that's the crux of it, isn't it? She wants my absolution, and I want her acknowledgment.

But neither of us will get what we want if we're unwilling to address it.

"No, Mom, you should go," I say, which is another echo from all those years ago.

CHAPTER 24

While I'm caught off guard by Adelaide's thinly veiled intervention, Caleb seems ready to seize the opportunity. From under the table, he texts me.

To be clear, I am free all day on Saturday.

I don't respond. Admittedly, I'm in a weird place after Adelaide caught us red-handed, and Mom inadvertently asked the question she should have asked two decades ago, spilling our baggage all over the booth at Nowhere Saloon. When Mom and I get home, I help her get ready for bed as if nothing happened. We offer niceties, but neither of us confronts the issue.

I pace for an hour as I debate the merits of spending the day with Caleb on Saturday. Adelaide's warning rings too true to ignore. I have no experience with cavalier.

I also have little experience with genuine passion, or what it might do to my stability.

I didn't come here to make my life more complicated. I came here to be a responsible daughter and untangle the past's hold on me. I came here, essentially, to move on from Grand Trees and find a path forward for Mom and me. Frankly, I'm doing a horrible job of both.

I text Cassie just before midnight.

Me: Are you up?

Cassie: Yep. Went to bed at 7, woke up an hour ago feeling like a boxer had punched me in the calf. It was a charley horse. I swear, society gatekeeps 90% of pregnancy symptoms from women. If we knew, none of us would do it, and humanity would die off.

Me: Sorry, Cass. How are you feeling otherwise?

Cassie: Hungry. Tired. Nauseated. Emotional. Justin went out to get me a milkshake, and I cried because he bought me chocolate chip instead of vanilla.

Me: Chocolate chip is your favorite.

Cassie: Apparently, it is not the baby's.

Me: Ah.

Cassie: How's your mom?

Me: Getting stronger.

I console myself that the answer is at least somewhat true.

Cassie: How's your grumpy arborist?

My fingers hover over the screen. But what is the point of this SOS call if I don't ask for the help I desperately need?

Me: Maybe not as grumpy as I thought.

Cassie: Explain.

I struggle to respond, typing out a few lines before erasing them and starting again. Within two minutes of my indecision, my phone rings. And shoot, my ringer volume is turned all the way up. I answer quickly, desperate not to wake Mom.

"Explain," she hisses.

I sigh and pick up the pace of my steps across the loft. The night is jet black behind the wall of windows. It doesn't have any answers for me either. "I kinda slept with him," I spit out.

I have to pull the phone away from my ear when she screams. I hear a scuffle in the background—Justin's groan and Cassie's frantic apology.

"Cassie, did you wake your poor husband?" I giggle.

"Poor husband, my ass," she whisper-hisses. "He knocked me up and has the audacity to sleep like a baby. What about poor Cassie? I'm constipated, up all night, peeing every few minutes, with constant leg cramps and passing gas like a trucker." A door clicks behind her and she shifts to full volume. "Wait. What do you mean *kinda* slept with him?"

"We had a quickie in his truck." I don't pull the phone away in time, and my ear rings from her squeal.

"Yes! I'm so proud of you." She cackles. "When? How did this happen? Please tell me he's as good with those big hands as he looks."

I sink down on the floor beside the bed, cradling my head in my hands. "I don't know what I'm doing."

"But does he? Because he looks like he might be an excellent hands-on teacher, if you know what I mean."

I laugh, but my heart's not in it. "Cassandra," I scold. "He's Sonny's nephew and a single dad to an observant teen. We're sneaking around, trying to hide this thing from the entire town. Because it can't last, and we don't want anyone shaming or encouraging us. And I don't know." I sigh. "I think I like him too much to get involved in something destined to end."

"Edie," she cajoles. "If you're only willing to start something without the power to shake you, you'll never have your world rocked. And you never know how things will end."

"Jeff had his baby."

She clicks her tongue against the roof of her mouth, but she doesn't scold me for the change of subject. "That poor kid. Destined for daddy issues and a six-figure therapy bill." She pauses, her tone slipping into something more soothing. "Even if your marriage had lasted, Jeff wasn't going to be your happily ever after. You need to stop settling for fine when you can have great. Even if great may not last forever."

I hate it when she's right, which is most of the time. "I'm a mess, Cass. I don't know how to deal with being here. Maybe I'm preoccupied with Caleb because it's easier than fixing things with my mom."

"I think you're fantasizing about Caleb because he's a fine-ass man who can throw you over his fine-ass shoulders. Besides, you are a capable woman; you can multitask. You can bury the hatchet with your mom and then let Caleb bury his big—"

"Cassie!" I cackle, and she giggles. But I sober, sighing before I say, "Mom and I got into a huge fight because I told her she should move to the city with me."

"You what?"

"It's the best option for her. There are better treatment options there," I say.

"Well, sure. But she and your dad haven't spoken in twenty years, and San Francisco probably has upsetting memories for her like Grand Trees does for you. Did you talk to your dad about it?"

"He's the last person I'd want to talk about any of this with."

"I saw him on Wednesday."

The night I usually join him for dinner. "Thanks for being my surrogate."

"He asked about my trip there and about your mom. I think he's researching Parkinson's. That man still has it bad for her."

I groan. "I know. But not bad enough to actually talk to her. Why is my family so hopeless?"

"You're not hopeless. Just emotionally repressed."

"I'm not particularly repressed these days. I'm surrounded by all these memories—happy and triggering—and I'm feeling all these old things and new things, and they're all scary and uncomfortable and exciting and unnerving and—"

"That's great, Edie. That's life. You've let yourself grow accustomed to being numb. You should feel things. You should let that hot man make you feel *all* the things."

She makes me laugh, even when she's practicing tough love. "I don't know."

"You do know. You texted me because you want me to be the devil on your shoulder telling you to ride that man until you're raw. But what you don't know is that I'm actually your angel. You deserve good sex. You deserve fun. You deserve to be a little infatuated with a beautiful man who knows what he's doing. Enjoy this. Don't think about whether it's practical. It isn't. Don't think about what happens when you leave. It'll probably suck. But you've spent your whole life living in the future or the past. Just let yourself be in the now."

CHAPTER 25

Caleb picks me up one minute after Adelaide and Mom head off to the spa on Saturday morning, and I push aside my doubts, running to the truck before he has a chance to park.

"You're early." I slide into the cab, but Caleb tugs me closer, swallowing my words with his mouth.

He tangles his hands in my hair and punctuates the kiss with a soft sigh. "I think I was right on time."

"Do I finally get to see your place?" I slip the seat belt on as Caleb pulls out of the drive.

"Not yet. I have somewhere I want to take you, and this is our last chance for a while."

"You don't need to court me, Caleb. I made my intentions clear when I climbed in your lap on Monday." I'm not sure I should call them intentions as much as impulses.

He gives me a crooked smile. "Well, your intentions may have to wait a bit."

But I wore the new underwear Cassie gave me. And shaved my legs.

He must read the disappointment on my face. "Humor me. I promise it'll be worth it."

My phone buzzes in my pocket and I startle, immediately concerned something happened to Mom. When I check it, it's Dad's face on the screen. I place it face down on the seat.

"Do you have to get that?" Caleb asks.

I shake my head, but when it buzzes again, I relent. It's unusual for Dad to call more than once. I take a steadying breath before answering. "Hi, Dad. Is everything okay?"

"Edie." There's so much love poured into my name that guilt eats at me for ignoring his call in the first place. "Everything's fine. Although the city is especially gloomy. I think it misses you."

The Hawthornes are so repressed, we project our emotions on to the weather. "That must be why. San Francisco is always bright and sunny when I'm home."

He chuckles, and my shoulders loosen. "Did you get that photo I sent of your wild roses? They're really showing off this season."

"They're gorgeous, Dad. Thank you for tending to them."

"I sent you your mail and a book from a local author, a fellow Berkeley professor. I went to a reading the other night and got it signed for you."

As a literature professor, Dad's recommendations are rarely the type of light, distracting fiction I gravitate toward. The last one he bought me was dense experimental literature that felt more like homework. "Thanks, Dad. That's thoughtful."

He clears his throat, and by the gesture, I can tell he's stewing about something. "It's an exploration of why people withhold truths from the people they love. I've been finding solace in the stories and analysis. I think you might, too."

This stuns me silent. Since when does Dad dig into—or acknowledge—the lie that sent our lives off course? Neither of us went to therapy. We don't talk about it. We talk around it. I wait to see if he'll say more.

"Are you okay being there? I know that place holds a lot of . . ." He drifts off, stuttering before landing on, "Memories."

I glance at Caleb's profile, aware that I'm making new memories, too. "I am. I think it's been good for me, actually."

"That's great, Edie." But it doesn't sound great, so I wait, letting the wind fill in the blanks.

"And your mom. How's she doing?" he asks with forced nonchalance.

"Better. She's out with friends today. She's getting stronger."

Caleb darts his focus to me, his face impassive. I wish I weren't having this conversation with him within earshot. These two worlds are inherently separate, severed by a seismic shift all those years ago.

"And have you made any progress getting her to seek treatment? I've done some research, if it's helpful. I could maybe send you some links?"

He's breaking my heart by back-seat driving this intervention. Dad doesn't do "some" research. He fixates. I imagine him hunched over a computer, reaching out to experts, dedicating days and nights to his quest, while I can't even make meaningful headway with Mom while living with her. "I'm working on it. And sure, send me whatever medical research you find."

Caleb looks at me again, and it's strikingly similar to a glare.

"Dad, I'll have to call you back, okay?"

"Sure, sweetheart. You take care of yourself . . . and your mother."

When I hang up, Caleb grunts. "Was he seriously concerned about your mom?"

My hackles rise. "Is that so weird to imagine?"

"Well, yeah, after everything he put her through, it is surprising."

I scoff. "After everything *he* put her through? You've got to be kidding me."

"He didn't exactly make it easy for her to move on with her life."

"She seemed to move on just fine. It wasn't my dad's job to give her a pass. If Mom felt guilty, that was on her. And it doesn't mean my dad can't be worried about her health. He's a good, kind man. You don't even know him." I worried this might be a bad idea. Maybe Cassie was wrong about multitasking, because this feels more like compartmentalizing. Caleb and I are on opposite sides of the tragedy that upended my life.

Caleb exhales, and I can see the moment the fight leaves him, which is lucky for him because I was about to ask him to turn his stupid truck around. "You're right. I'm sorry." He lifts a hand off the steering wheel in a gesture of surrender. "Sometimes I get protective, and—"

"I know." I sigh. "But can you please acknowledge you may not know the whole story, because you and I can't do this"—I gesture between us emphatically—"if we're litigating what happened between my mom, my dad, and your uncle two decades ago."

Caleb squeezes my thigh, and I hate the electricity that sparks even when I'm irritated at him. "Yes. I can do that."

"Admit you're wrong?"

"Don't get carried away," he teases. "But I'll admit I don't know *everything*." And just like that, the mood shifts. Guard dog Caleb is a pain in the ass, but his loyalty isn't wholly unattractive.

I clue in to our route, recognizing a series of turns. "Are we going to camp?" I ask, incredulous.

"Trust me."

We arrive in the camp parking lot minutes later, and I twist in my seat and fold my arms across my chest. "Trust you?"

He slides out and looks at me pointedly before saying, "Yes."

"Is anyone else here?" I amble out as he waits at the curb.

"Shouldn't be."

I glance around, checking for witnesses, before accepting his hand. "It's possible that Adelaide's plan was a ruse. She might jump out from behind a tree to catch us in a compromising position and force us to commit like in a Regency-era romance."

"A what?" Caleb furrows his brows with an adorably confused half smile.

"Never mind."

He leads me through the welcome court, his pace quick and purposeful.

"Did you bring me here for another forestry lesson?" I ask.

He tosses me an impatient glance. "No."

Caleb doesn't elaborate as he guides me onto the Ponderosa Path, which leads to the boys' bunks, activity cabins, and sports-and-games fields. A hummingbird floats beside us until it dives into a patch of wildflowers. I check the sky for signs of a storm, but there's not a cloud in sight.

The art room, where Mom taught class and I spent hours under her heel, is a kaleidoscope of color peeking out from a patch of giant sequoias. There's a newer mural on the side of the building, and I dart off course, striding toward it. I freeze when I see Sonny's profile, playing the guitar in front of a sea of adoring children. The painting radiates joy but makes me melancholy.

Caleb clears his throat. "That went up after Sonny died. Your mom was already having trouble holding a paintbrush steady, so she designed it, outlined it, and the whole town helped paint it. Everyone adored him, you know."

"I think I was the only person who didn't," I say, but then hesitate. "That's not true. Maybe if I hadn't loved him, I wouldn't have felt so betrayed."

Caleb hums and steps closer, the redwood leaves crunching under his feet. "He couldn't help falling in love with your mom."

"But he could control who he lied to."

"Fair," he says, but it sounds like an admission made under duress.

"I thought Mom was working here every summer to spend time with me. But she'd brought me here as an excuse to be with Sonny." I don't know how to explain why the affair hit me so hard. That time in my life was too painful to process. When a building collapses on you, you don't know which brick caused which injury. I was battered; we were battered. Recovery and reflection weren't possible; we just had to dig out of the rubble and learn to walk again with new scars. "And it made me feel like their pawn, I suppose. Like I was brought along for cover, and I was an accomplice."

It would be easy to chalk up the affair to the result of a loveless marriage, but I remember falling asleep to the sound of my parents' conversation and laughter on the porch below my bedroom. I was raised witnessing their small acts of love—simple gifts, foot rubs, constant affection. They never ran out of things to talk about, until I said too much, and the whole house fell silent. If I hadn't been so eager to return every year, our lives could have turned out differently.

"That's not your weight to carry," Caleb says.

But the moment I used the agonizing truth as a weapon, I had to carry the weight of Dad's heartbreak, too. "I should have figured it out sooner."

"It wasn't your fault." Caleb's voice is stern, but kind. "Parents hide stuff from their kids all the time. They do it to protect them from things they won't understand. Complicated relationships are at the top of the list of things kids don't need to worry about. We're not telling Abby about us."

"You're not cheating on her mom. And I'm not teaching her guitar and earning her trust while destroying her family."

Caleb bites his lip and looks away with a sigh. Maybe that was a bridge too far. I'm talking about his beloved uncle, who took him in when no one else would. Caleb's version of Sonny is the one that makes sense, and is the same one I thought I knew.

"None of us are perfect, Eden. And the Sonny you knew and the mom you knew weren't fiction. They were just flawed."

I walk toward the mural, noticing new details. The smile lines around his generous grin, his right ear that flared to the side, and the freckle on his temple. Sonny's warmth jumps from the surface. Mom always knew how to capture a person in paint. I haven't asked her about not being able to paint anymore. That, too, would hit too close to my own pain. It's another land mine we can't approach.

"I know it. I just don't feel it yet."

I hear shuffling beside me, and then Caleb's arms are around my waist. He pulls me to him, and I'm hit with a wall of heat. "Yet," he says. "I like that." He kisses the top of my head before leading me back onto the trail. "C'mon. This isn't what we came for."

"Are you going to tell me what we're doing here?" I follow him around the volleyball court and past the archery range.

"Yes."

But he doesn't, and I groan. I understand Caleb better now; he's not the asshole I initially thought him to be. But he's still a brat.

Finally, he comes to a stop by a small storage shed made of weather-beaten wood and coated with dust and spiderwebs.

"I may like you now, but I still don't want to get stuck in there with you."

He inserts a key into the padlock before swinging the door open. I lean against an adjacent tree, worried that he brought me here on a work errand. What a way to spend our stolen time together, completing his to-do list while I'm stalked by difficult memories.

He crouches in the shed and hoists a box into his arms, nodding for me to follow, and then it clicks, a long-stuck key sliding into place.

"No," I say when he drops the box beside the tallest tower of the ropes course.

"No?" Caleb crosses his arms. "You told me you always wanted to try it."

Admittedly, this is sweet of him to remember, but also presumptuous. "When I was a child, yes. Now, I'm an adult who prefers her feet to be on solid ground."

"Hmm." He untangles the harnesses, setting two aside. "I seem to remember you saying you regretted spending your life afraid of falling."

His gaze lands on mine like a laser. How dare he use my words against me. Maybe I was right all along—maybe he is an asshole.

"Do you even know what you're doing?" I wave aimlessly over the equipment as he riffles through it. I'm not even sure what I mean by the question.

"I do, in fact, know what I'm doing. I have a certificate to prove it." He places a helmet on my head, testing the fit before swapping it out for another.

"Why now?" I ask, stalling some more.

"I have a crew coming out on Monday to add another zip line to the course. It's going to be closed for construction until summer."

"Isn't this course designed for children? Will it even support me?" Despite my protest, I secure the helmet when he finds the right size.

He smirks and places the harness on the ground in front of me. "It hasn't collapsed under my weight yet."

"'Yet' is not a comforting word, Caleb."

"It's up to you, of course. I just thought you'd like it. You know, because of your quest to rewire your brain with better memories and all those chances you weren't able to take before."

Why does he have to be thoughtful and considerate? I glance at the tower, noting the narrow metal footholds along the side. I squint against the sun to spot the top. Looking up makes me dizzy, and the punch of blue sky encircled by towering trees is disorienting. I imagine making the vertical climb with nothing but a wire to prevent my free fall.

I remember standing in this exact spot, summer after summer, cheering on my cabinmates as they faced their fears and returned to earth triumphant. They'd rehash their terror as if it were the highlight of the season, often overtaken by emotion with tears or laughter. As a kid, I sat in the audience in real life so I was safe to soar across center stage. And as an adult, I watched my life unfold from the balcony because I was too fragile to fly at all.

"You promise to keep me alive?" I ask.

"Cross my heart." He mimes the movement.

I close my eyes and exhale all the air from my lungs. "Can we start on the low course?"

I'm startled by the press of his mouth and open my eyes to find him studying me, his head cocked to the side to avoid my helmet.

"Anything you want." His scent catches in the wind and wraps itself around me, and he grabs my hand to lead me to the start of the course.

The sun is bright overhead when we ascend and cross the footbridge, a series of wooden planks stretched across rope. I pause in the center of the bridge, steadying myself and taking in a lungful of pine-scented air. There are two handrails, and Caleb and I are both connected to the top wire via harness, but we're so high that my pulse is pounding in my skull. I look away from the forest floor—where tree needles lay inches thick, and ecosystems thrive underneath them. Instead, I focus straight ahead, trusting that my feet know how to carry me forward on a tightrope that feels as thin as thread.

"Are you okay?" Caleb says from behind me.

"I'm good."

From this height, I spot the outline of the town center, the high school campus, and the summit of Colibri Peak. I see a palette of wildflowers, communities of trees, and fresh air. There's no latent sadness as I survey the landscape.

When we descend the wooden stairs at the end of the line, we head to the final obstacle. But I have to do this one alone. Caleb will be on the ground with the belay to lower me after I jump. He straps me in and goes over the instructions.

"You sure?" he asks as I take the first step up the metal footholds.

"You still plan to keep me alive?" My voice is winded as I head up.

"I got you."

When I start the climb, I know he's watching me, even though my concentration is on scaling this tower. My hands are raw, and my thighs are burning, but I ascend, slow and steady. I'm aware of the way my right Achilles tendon is tighter than my left and how I have to rotate my foot for more stability, but I know how to adapt, shift my weight, and usher myself onward. When I reach the last rung, I hesitate, fearful for the first time since Caleb coaxed me into this delayed rite of passage.

"You've got it." Caleb's voice is far away.

I can't visualize how to reach the summit without letting go of the handrail.

"You have to get your foot onto the last step," he yells. But that doesn't make any sense because that's where my hand is. Until now, I've known what to grab on to next. I'll have to let go and hoist myself onto the platform without anything to anchor me. I can't look down at Caleb for reassurance or instructions. And I'm too scared to look up at the cramped pedestal above me. The closer I get, the more I doubt I can balance on it.

"Eden, you can do this. It's just a few more inches, and you'll be there."

Why are the last steps always the hardest?

I reach up, searching blindly for something to grab on to, and my fingertips curl around a small notch in the wood. I hold my breath and release my other hand, finding purchase on the wood. With one swift pull, I get my shoulders over the threshold, and then my ribs, before I find the last rung with my foot and crawl onto the platform on all fours.

Caleb is cheering, but I can't process what he's saying. The air is thinner, the sky is closer, and the earth feels like a memory. I stand, registering the lax tension of the belay and the stability of my feet on the platform. There's no spot in the distance to focus on—the horizon is limitless.

"When you're ready, just jump to me," Caleb says.

I summon my courage to peek over the ledge, and Caleb is barely a spec. I laugh, deep from my gut. "There's nothing 'just' about this," I yell.

"Sometimes the impossible is the easiest thing to do. Once you jump, gravity will do the work for you."

"That's what I'm afraid of."

"But I've got you."

I jiggle my knees so they won't lock and flex my hands, which are clammy and tingly. "Are you claiming to be a stronger force than gravity, Caleb Connell?"

His laugh must catch on the wind, because it shoots straight into my bloodstream like a stiff drink. "I guess you'll have to jump to find out."

I don't count. I don't bargain with myself. I don't ask more questions. Instead, I lean forward, take one bounding step, and soar off the platform.

Caleb hoots and hollers, cheering as he belays me. For several suspended seconds, I am weightless and free, like I belong to this sacred landscape I'd spurned for so long.

I catch sight of Caleb, grinning as he receives me. My feet are barely on the ground before he catches me, lifting me into his arms with an infectious laugh.

"You did it," he says. "You were fearless out there. You didn't even hesitate."

My vision is clouded by tears, born of the crisp wind and maybe something more earnest—the elation of leaping, the joy of finding Caleb on the descent. He brushes them away with his thumbs, studying me.

"I knew you had me," I say.

Caleb cups my face in both hands and drags his lips across mine. He's all hard planes and sharp angles, but his posture softens the moment his mouth presses into mine, instantly melting into the kiss. And this is the Caleb I like best, the one whose guard dissolves, whose softness cannot be contained.

"How long do we have?" he mumbles into my mouth.

Adelaide had a full day planned—facials and pedicures followed by a late lunch at her house. I decide I love Adelaide and her meddling.

"Hours," I say. "How fast can you sprint back to the truck?"

Caleb rewards me with a relieved groan. "I'm taking you back to my place."

CHAPTER 26

Caleb touches me the whole way home—his hand on my thigh, cupping my neck, tangled in my hair. We pass Sonny's tree house and make a quick turn onto a long gravel driveway, parking in front of a strange little house set in a wide clearing. It has an arched metal roof and corrugated siding, somehow looking futuristic and as if it could have been transplanted from the Shire in *The Hobbit*.

"Why do you always drive to my mom's? You could probably walk there faster."

"Because I'm usually coming from somewhere or on my way to somewhere else."

"So what you're saying is, I'm a detour."

"More like a layover, if you want to get technical."

I gasp. "Rude."

His responding chuckle is a texture I want to drape around myself.

We slide out of the truck as soon as he parks, and he meets me at the hood, lacing his fingers in mine.

There's a deep porch swing hanging on heavy ropes, with a thick cushion and soft throw pillows. The breeze activates crystal wind chimes, a calming melody that is immediately followed by the sound of Houdini's bark. He greets us with desperate cries and a wagging tail when we step through the front door before he settles in his bed by the fireplace, digging at the padding and circling three times to plop down.

"Okay, give me the tour. I don't think I've ever seen a house like this."

"A tour?" Caleb asks.

I step back from him, releasing one hand and scanning the open floor plan, which is warm and inviting. "Yes."

"All right." There's a smile in his voice. "Sonny and I built this place with a few of the contractors we use at the camp."

"You built it?" I cast him a sideways glance.

"Well, with a lot of help. It was a kit." He pauses, pulling me into the living room area marked by a leather sectional and a few mismatched armchairs in front of a bank of windows. "Sonny suggested I build something on the edge of his property. And I found this company that makes modular, fire-resistant cottages. I wanted to test them out."

"Ah," I say. "I wondered. The design is unusual."

He chuckles. "It's an acquired taste."

But I take in the quaint space. Every design element and furniture piece is intentional, necessary. The walls are corrugated metal, so there's an industrial feel to it, made warm by area rugs in fall tones, throw blankets, overstuffed pillows, and a square coffee table surrounded by cushions. The kitchen is nestled in the back corner with open shelves and hanging copper pots above a stone island, which is flanked by four stools. A hallway unfurls on the other side of the pantry, and a set of steep stairs is tucked against the opposite wall.

"There's not much to it," he says, but I disagree. It's filled to the brim with character.

"I just want to see where you live."

He leads me to the stairs and waves me ahead.

I climb the ladderlike steps into a loft with low-slung ceilings and porthole windows on either side. Frayed paperbacks spill from built-in bookcases, and two beanbag chairs rest in the center.

"Abby has taken it over for homework and to get away from me, I think."

"Can you blame her?"

He shakes his head and leads us back downstairs, turning into the hallway. "The bedrooms are just over here." It sounds like a suggestion, but I'm committed to this tour despite his impatience.

I peek into Abby's room on the right—it's chaos. She has a full-size bed covered in more multicolored linens and pillows than I can count. There is a bright-red desk tucked under the window, with a mobile of paper cranes hanging from the ceiling above it. Clothes spill out from her closet, and dresses are slung over splayed open doors. Posters, photos, and frames cover every inch of wall space, and a bulletin board is packed with notes, postcards, ticket stubs, and dried flowers.

"This is so Abby," I say.

"Messy?"

"Joyful."

He smiles at that before tugging me by the hips and pulling me across the hallway into the other bedroom. It's a simple space with a king bed and midnight-blue bedding, two mid-century nightstands, brass sconces, and a walnut dresser. It would be sterile if it weren't for the black-and-white wilderness photographs on each wall and the wide window peering over the redwoods.

I want to snoop and investigate, but Caleb has other ideas, and I'm easily redirected. He spins me, trapping me against the wall and kicking the door shut.

His breath is hot on mine, his lips urgent, and his hands slide into my hair, tugging the ponytail free to rake his fingers through the waves. I grip his waist, pulling his hips to mine until the kiss escalates.

Caleb peels off his shirt and tosses it to the floor, and I want to slow time to explore, to memorize every muscle, freckle, and scar. But then he frees me from my shirt, and we're skin to skin, and my brain stops working. His body heat detonates my patience, and I need us to hurry. We undress in a frantic fight of fingertips against fabric as we tumble toward the bed. He pivots us before he drags my jeans off my body.

When I'm down to my underwear and bra, Caleb emits a sound from the back of his throat that I wish I could replay in every future insecure moment. It's a reminder that I wore the lingerie Cassie gave me, a matching barely-there set of black lace and red satin.

"Wait." He steps back. "Wow." Caleb drags his hands down my body, over my neck, my chest, his gaze following in rapt attention. He cups my breasts through my bra, brushing his thumbs over the peaks, until I have to swallow a gasp, and he glides his hands down my torso and over the lace of my underwear. He traces the pattern so softly that it makes me ache. "I like these," he says in a gust of breath as he hooks his thumbs in the elastic at my hip. "But I want to see you."

He moves closer, finding new patches of me to explore—to touch, to kiss—making goose bumps flare across my flesh. He unclasps my bra, and it slips to the floor, but he doesn't stop to look. Instead, he hooks an arm around my waist and, in one swift motion, lifts and turns me so I fall to his bed. I scoot back as he yanks the comforter out from under me until I'm lying on crisp, cool sheets with the light playing across my skin. I see the moment his focus catches on my leg. The scars have faded over time, but I can still spot the original wounds, the flesh that fought against me, the pain that haunted me for years. Caleb bends, pressing a kiss to my shin, to my knee, crawling up my body with his hot breath on my inner thigh, whispering praise into my skin. "You're gorgeous, Eden. Every part of you."

I lift onto my elbow and tug on his shoulder. I want him over me, shielding me from all the big feelings I don't know how to process. I want him to press me down, absorb me, and push aside all the unanswerable questions. But he stays where he is, his arms banded around my thighs, his shoulders nudging my legs open.

For the first time since I climbed into his lap in his truck, I grow self-conscious.

"You don't have to do that," I blurt.

He presses a kiss to my inner thigh and then the other, dragging his warm breath across the most sensitive part of me before tilting his head. "You don't want me to?" The grit of his voice makes me squirm under him, my body rebelling against my verbal protest.

"I don't want you to feel obligated."

He grins a wolfish smile. "I'm not doing anything I don't want to do. And I wouldn't want you to either." He presses another kiss on my thigh, so close to where I want him, before he lifts his head again. "Just tell me if you want me to stop."

He hovers there, teasing me from an inch away, and asking permission. With a shaky breath, I slide my hand into his hair and watch when he closes his eyes, slides his mouth over me, and hums into my skin. My head falls onto the pillow, and my hips tilt reflexively, angling for more. And I wonder how this man knows what I want before I ask, before I know myself. I'm lost to the warmth, the soft friction, the subtle way he moves his tongue over my tangle of nerves, how he teases me until I'm whimpering, begging. He answers my desperation with his mouth open on me, his fingers filling me, until there's nothing but him. Until there's nothing but now. And now. And now.

I come apart by degrees, ready for release even as my body climbs higher. He stays with me, ascends with me until I'm pleading and calling his name, until I fall back on the bed and shiver from the aftermath.

As I open my eyes, I see the rise and fall of my chest, slick with sweat, my nipples pebbled, my skin flushed. Caleb is watching me, still settled between my legs. His breathing is labored, and his eyes are steady as he studies me through the filtered light.

Trees dance in the breeze outside, and shadows waltz across the room, casting him in an uneven glow. I brush his hair from his forehead, and he chases the touch, crawling up my body until he's settled on his elbows above me.

"Just so we're clear," he whispers. "I really enjoyed that."

If I weren't convinced by how eagerly he ruined me, he's pressing the proof against my thigh.

"I'm glad," I say through a shaky sigh. "Because I might want you to do that again soon."

His grin in return is blinding. I rake my nails across his shoulders and over his chest. He's deliciously warm, with corded muscles working as he holds himself steady. His abdominals are all bunched and stacked like masonry. I've never felt a body like his, and I want to get my hands on every hard inch. He lets me explore, biting his lip and holding himself up for access.

When I take him in my hand, he sucks in a breath, and the cage he's created over me bows. He's hot and glorious, moving with me, his temple pressed to mine. He reaches for the nightstand, fumbling in the drawer to retrieve a condom. He pushes my hand away, covers himself, and hovers above me.

"I've been going crazy all week," he says, but I can't answer or tell him *me too*, because it's then that he pushes inside me, stretching me so perfectly that I have to grip his hip, slowing him and holding my breath. "Longer, actually." His voice is tight.

"Since you kept me warm in that cabin."

He exhales, still restraining himself. "Since you showed up on the porch and refused to put up with my shit."

I grab his hip, trying to coax him deep. "Since you saved me from that creeper."

"Since I saw you across the bar," he confesses as he finally sinks to the hilt, trapping my wrists in his fists. I catch his mouth in mine, sucking on his lip until he takes control, his tongue sweeping into my mouth, his kiss stealing my thoughts. There's only sensation—the delicious weight of him on top of me, the slide of his body, the scratch of his beard, the grip of his hands.

He's greedy in this position, keeping me where he wants me, enticing me to meet him with each thrust. He swallows my whimper until it becomes a wail, and then he's everywhere—his mouth on my throat, his hands on my breasts—and I'm lost. Or found. Because I'm shedding who I was, the woman who settled for less than this. The woman afraid to climb to the summit. The woman willing to accept fine forever instead of bliss for now.

"I want to feel you come," Caleb murmurs into my neck before scraping his teeth against my earlobe, sucking a mark into the skin just below it. He presses closer, grinding exactly where I need him, how I need him. And it doesn't take long for me to dissolve under him again, my nails leaving marks on his back, my words lost to the sound of his pleasure. I bite down on his collarbone, and he rewards me with a delicious groan as he buries himself and stills, all the powerful muscles of his torso strung taut. Time is suspended, and I'm afraid I'll remember this snapshot forever—Caleb caught between a sunbeam and shadow, lost to the world for the length of a halted heartbeat.

When he opens his eyes, he searches my gaze. His pulse is a riot in his throat, his mouth is slack, and he offers a lazy smile. He hums, his entire body softening as he kisses me and shifts until we're propped on our hips facing each other, tangled in limbs and sheets. He tastes like me, and him, and this blissful us. And it makes me hungry again.

"I don't want you to leave," he says as our mouths pull together and apart.

"We have all afternoon."

Caleb's lids and limbs are heavy. He's beautiful in the fragmented light, surrounded by a halo of gold, his skin coated in a sheen of sweat, his dark hair a wild mess.

"I meant I don't want you to leave, leave," he mumbles.

Neither do I, I realize. I can't fathom leaving the comfort of his bed today, let alone losing the relief of him when my time is up. I want to drink in more of him and learn all the ways I can drive him wild. I want my mouth on him, his hands on me, his body in mine until I shatter. But if I think about then, it will ruin the now.

If I worry about the crash landing, I'll never trust myself to jump.

CHAPTER 27

Over the next weeks, Caleb and I seize every sliver of time we can—while Abby is at school and Adelaide stays with Mom to play a game or share gossip, while Caleb and I visit landmarks across town to gather information for grant applications. Caleb introduces me to the town as if I'm visiting for the first time, and, in some ways, I am. I knew it as a frequent tourist, but Caleb's Grand Trees is more honest. It's filled with the people who have committed to this secluded, volatile patch of land.

We take his canoe onto the lake, floating in the water while eating peanut butter and jelly sandwiches. We visit Bob and Carmela on their land behind the B and B, where Caleb convinces Bob to cut down a patch of pines infested with bark beetles, but not before patiently explaining the science multiple times and listening to Bob's reservations. We prepare the camp for the annual preseason party, an event for locals planned for the weekend before the summer campers descend. We eat pasta on his patio beside the light of a citronella candle with the chorus of the forest as our background music. We make love in Caleb's cozy cabin as the spring rain prattles on the tin roof and wind chimes sing on the porch.

In between the long stretches of pretense, Caleb and I find moments to be us. We relax into each other with affection that is as comfortable as it is startling. We are polite in public but passionate in private. The stolen kisses and half-dressed trysts make me feel like a new person. Is this what everyone experiences when they fall for someone? I feel lighter, more attuned to the beauty around me, more focused and productive. I feel—more.

As the weeks turn to months, Mom and I get into a rhythm. We're careful with each other, but instead of tiptoeing, we're treading lightly. It may be nominal, but it's progress.

One night as I help Mom get ready for bed, she reaches for my hand. "Eden, honey. I want you to know how much I appreciate you staying with me. I know it's a sacrifice."

"It's not a sacrifice, Mom," I assure her, squeezing her hand, but she doesn't let go. It's cool and soft in my grip. Her skin is a thin layer of satin.

"I love having you here. I've always wanted you here." Her words toy at the border of dangerous territory, but for once, I decide to create a neutral zone and welcome her in.

"I heard you and Sonny built this bedroom for me. I'm sorry I didn't come sooner." I sit beside her on the edge of the bed and glance at the space, at the love poured into the wood siding and plank floors, at how the windows overlook the forest and not the ravine. It mirrors my childhood bedroom.

She pats the top of my hand with a wistful smile. "I'm sorry for a lot of things."

I wait for more, for her to initiate a discussion, but she looks at her lap and grows silent. Maybe it's as close to a proper apology as I'll ever get, and the nearest I'll move to acceptance. It's still better than where we've been. Forward progress is good, no matter how slow.

"Me too, Mom."

When I decided to stay, I wanted to set aside my hurt and build a better future for us. But I'm not the only one who took a chance. It was just as brave of Mom to receive me so readily. It's an act of love to let someone care for you, to be vulnerable and put your life in their hands. Mom could have refused me. Maybe she should have refused me. It would have been my karma.

As a teen, I didn't set out to break Mom's heart by rejecting her attempts to care for me after the accident. But I saw her pain when I rebuffed her. As a minor, I couldn't kick my mother out of my hospital room, but I could—and did—direct my requests to my dad or the nurses. I had lost control of my body and future, and I punished Mom for all of it. When only some of it was her fault.

And yet, Mom isn't retaliating. She's embracing me. She's letting me care for her the way I wouldn't let her care for me.

I hate to threaten our careful peace, but she's given me so few openings, and I don't want to miss this one, narrow though it is.

"Have you given any more thought to treatment? Perhaps I can schedule an appointment with the neurologist and go with you before I leave? Run interference?"

Mom looks out the window and sighs, but she sounds more resigned than defensive when she says, "I don't know, honey."

"Just one appointment. I won't make you go back if it goes terribly."

"The doctor made it seem hopeless." Mom hazards a glance at me, and her expression is fragile. I wonder how much of her resistance is her avoiding the reality of her own mortality.

"So we'll find a different one," I try.

"There isn't another one anywhere near here. But even if there were, with the side effects—and such little prospect for improvement—maybe I'm better off enjoying the years I have left."

I don't know what Mom heard from this local doctor or how accurate his message was, but at least I have a sense of why she made the decision to forgo treatment.

I hold my breath, preparing for the vulnerability of these next words. "That's the thing, though. I'd like us to have as many years as we can."

Mom smiles, and it's wistful. "We have missed too many." She threads her hand in mine. "I'll think about it, okay?"

As I slide into bed that night, I feel something coming loose in me—like my scar tissue is softening, allowing my lungs to expand and take in more air. It gives me hope. Because maybe if Mom and I have a chance to make amends, if I learn how to heal from my first heartbreak, I can allow myself emotions big enough to risk another.

I text Caleb good night.

He texts me a picture of the unused side of his bed with a note.

Caleb: Wish you were here.

Me: Same.

Returning to Grand Trees has been an unexpected unburdening, although I didn't realize I was longing for it until I got here. My return to San Francisco—to the home Jeff and I shared, to the solitary life I had before coming here—looms not as relief, but dread.

But whether I want to face it or not, my return home does loom. It's June, and I've been here for almost three months. I arrived at the dawn of spring, when the weather was brisk and the hillside was draped in wildflowers. But summer is dawning. The days are stretched taut, and unhurried sunsets suspend the stars. This is the Grand Trees I remember—hot, endless, expectant.

Mom's bruising is gone, and her stitches have dissolved. She's still tentative as she moves, but I don't know if that's due to the injury or the disease. She will get her brace off in a few days. She won't need me full-time anymore, once she has use of both hands. Her found family will tend to her, care for her, and let me know when she needs full-time care. I'll have to pick up the battle again then and hope she's willing to move to San Francisco with me at that point.

But for now, I trust Grand Trees to look out for her.

The campers arrive next week, which will keep Caleb busy managing the day-to-day. I'll leave soon after, when it will be easier to slip away.

~

It's early Friday evening. Mom is resting in her room, and I'm preparing dinner when my phone rings. The screen lights up with Dad's profile photo, an unflattering selfie from point-blank range. I slip in my headphones and answer on the third ring. "Hi, Dad. Everything okay?"

"I just stopped by to water your garden and thought I'd check on my girl."

"Thank you." He has the greenest thumb, and I imagine arriving to a house filled with a thriving garden, but I still don't feel the tug of home. "I'm doing well, actually." I slide the pan of seared chicken into the oven.

"And your mother?" His voice is tight, and I suspect this is the real reason for his call.

I hesitate. I never know how to talk about Mom without upsetting him. "She's healing, doing better."

"That's good," he says, but I listen for the unsaid, because I know his speech patterns, his pauses, the words that don't arrive until he's ready. He doesn't say anything else for a full minute, and my pulse races the longer I wait for him to continue. I know I've opened old wounds by coming here. The more upset he is, the fewer words he uses. "I've been looking into things."

I wait again as I dress and toss the arugula salad.

"There are a lot of treatment options here in the city. She could have many good years if she moved home with you."

My dad is quiet and careful—meticulous. I once again imagine him hovered over his desktop researching Parkinson's. He is likely a new expert in a disease neither of us knew anything about just months ago. It kills me that he still cares so deeply about the woman who discarded him. He never dated. Never redecorated. Never lived again.

"I know. But she doesn't want to move in with me. I've asked her."

His silence in response is aggravating. I recognize that my impatience stems from a desperation for him to get over it so I can get over it. My happiness has always been tethered to his.

"Well, you should insist. Try to convince her," he says.

I drop the tongs in the salad bowl and push it away. "Dad," I sigh. "I did. I have. I think I've made progress on convincing her to seek treatment, but I can't drag her back to San Francisco against her will. She reacted terribly when I suggested it."

"Maybe I can talk to her."

There are many things I could say in response, like, *Oh, now you want to talk to her*. It may have helped my mental health had he spoken to her while I was still a child under his care. It would have helped my healing if he had made repairing their relationship a priority. But now? It's too little, too late, and too triggering. He can't reengage with Mom to address something so personal, especially since it has proven to be the third rail.

"I don't think that would go over well. And she has a whole community of people here who have pleaded with her, who are caring for her."

Dad is silent for a long time before he says, "I could help take care of her. I'm good at taking care of people."

I think of those soundless years after Mom left. I remember how gentle we were with each other, how he held me together until I could stand on my own. He is good at taking care of people, but she's not his to tend to anymore.

"I know you are. But she's already refused."

"Well, maybe it's because she's worried it would upset me if she came back. But it wouldn't. It won't. I think if you told her—"

"I don't think that has anything to do with it. She's settled here." I keep my voice modulated, even though his fretting is a familiar frustration for me.

"But I feel responsible. I'm the one who chased her away."

I have to strain to hear him. His voice is thin, and I suspect his throat is constricted with unshed tears. "It wasn't your fault."

"Some of it was. I've had time to think about my part in what went wrong, and I wasn't a perfect husband."

I take a deep breath and pinch my eyes closed. Of course he's had time to think—he's done nothing but stew for twenty years. He's still rattling around in the same house, in a tomb of doubt about his failed marriage. But I don't want to be the audience for his postmortem. Not now, when I'm working out how to feel about my past without his pain compounding my own. "Dad—"

"I didn't support her art. I was too focused on my career, and she raised you almost entirely alone. And then I could have worked harder to forgive her. I could have gone to therapy like she suggested."

This belated self-awareness is a great breakthrough for him, but I shouldn't have to help him work through his conflicted feelings about his marriage when I was the biggest victim of its demise. "I think it's finally time for you to let her go," I say.

It was agonizing to grow up in a household held hostage by heartbreak, and my patience for his lingering pain has been especially thin since Jeff left. I was blindsided when my marriage ended, but I'm moving on, not clinging to hope for a reconciliation. I'm not refusing to live my new life because my old one didn't pan out. Dad's marriage ended ages ago; mine ended months ago. He should be ahead of me in this race toward acceptance. Perhaps it would be easier for him to move on if he saw all the evidence of Mom's life here and knew how easy it was for her to start over.

I would have celebrated his awakening years ago. It would have changed the trajectory of my life had he and Mom put aside their pain to parent me together, or to sit beside each other at my wedding, or to pretend to be fine so I didn't have to choose between them. But now that I've paved the way, it feels like he's profiting off my emotional labor. And perhaps it's petty of me to mind, but I do.

Or perhaps it's regret. If I had dealt with my issues with Mom before now, it may have forced him to deal with his as well. We each enabled the other's inaction.

"I should be the one taking care of her." The vibrato in Dad's voice means I've pushed him too far. "She's my wife."

I take a deep breath and pinch my temples. "No, she's not. Not anymore." I don't typically confront his denial, but pacifying him has gotten us nowhere.

He pauses, and I glance at my phone to see if he's hung up on me. This whole conversation is uncharted; my go-to strategy thus far has been appeasement. I've summoned this directness from somewhere new, rerouting the patterns of our relationship to find new pathways. And I don't know where they lead.

"She'll always be my wife." There's a note of defiance in his shaky voice.

"What are you talking about? She left us for another man. She didn't want to be a part of our family anymore. It was a long time ago, and the sooner you accept that, the sooner you can start enjoying the rest of your life."

My hands are shaking when the timer sounds. I fling the door open and grab an oven mitt, but when I reach for the pan, I hit the back of my hand on the top rack. I swallow a gasp as I slide the pan onto the stove before spinning to run the burn under cool water. When I look up, Mom is leaning on the island, her expression unreadable. I don't know how much she's heard.

"I have to go. I'll call you tomorrow." I place my headphones on the counter without making eye contact with Mom.

"Did you burn yourself?" she asks, but her tone is icy.

"It isn't bad," I assure her, even though it's more painful than it has any right to be. I let the cool water run over my skin.

"Is that really how you see it? That I left because I didn't want to be a part of our family?" She braces herself on the counter with her good hand, and her knuckles are white.

I guess both my parents want to use me as their jury and litigate their choices.

"Mom." I try to sound placating. "I'm sorry you heard that, but it was out of context—"

"There's no other way to take it. Did you mean it?" Her tone is measured, but I sense rage buried beneath.

What the hell does she want me to say? We're standing in the home of the man she left us for. How else was I to understand her choice but as a rejection? How else was I supposed to feel but abandoned? I settle on honesty but with as much neutrality as possible. "You did leave us."

"Physically, I was the one to leave. But you and your father evicted me long before I packed my bags."

My neutrality evaporates. Because this revisionist history is astounding. Before everything fell apart that last summer, we were happy. The night before Mom and I left for Grand Trees, Dad took us to our favorite Italian restaurant. When I went to bed that night, I could still hear them giggling on our porch as I drifted off to sleep. I replayed that moment, that nostalgic sound, for years. How did our family go from solid to shattered in six weeks? "I don't know what you're talking about."

"You didn't speak to me for a full year. A full *year* of silence, Eden. You acted as if I were a ghost in our home. And you learned that little trick from your father, because he didn't speak to me either."

I inhale and exhale with intention. I can't believe I'm hearing this—that she's found a way to blame us. She's the one who broke us. Dad and I just had to deal with the aftermath.

"I'm confused. Do you not remember cheating on Dad for who knows how many years and dragging me along every summer as your alibi?" I shut off the water with an angry flick of my wrist, but my burn throbs in protest. I pace away, turning my back on Mom and staring out over the forest, but I can't focus through my fury.

"I remember all my mistakes—all of them." There's flint in her voice, which makes me flinch. "Yes, I was unfaithful and have lived with that guilt ever since. I groveled to you; I begged your father for forgiveness. I know you probably don't believe me, but I loved your dad."

I whip around, gesturing wildly to the house, the forest, the entirety of the life she chose over him. I don't know how she translates my frantic gestures into an articulate argument, but she purses her lips and takes a beat before she clarifies.

"I loved them both," she whispers. "Desperately. And that's not something I'd wish on my worst enemy."

I don't even know how that's possible. How could she claim to love my father while betraying him? How could she blame our reaction to her rejection as the cause of our destruction? A breeze rushes in through the open windows, and I shiver at the sudden chill. I wrap my hands around my biceps as the sound of rustling leaves replays her words.

"I'm not proud of my choices. I still struggle with self-hatred all these years later. I loved our family. And I hate that I was selfish and risked ruining everything. But you and your father convicted me without a trial. I couldn't fix what we couldn't discuss."

"There was nothing anyone could say to fix it." Some things—families, bones, dreams—aren't fixable.

Mom glides toward me, sliding around the island until she's only a few paces away from where I stand at the sink. "I'm fully aware that we couldn't fix everything that broke that night." Her face is pinched, pained, and etched in deep lines. She's aged too many years since the last time I avoided this reckoning, when she would sit beside my hospital bed with the same look on her face, when she would knock on my bedroom door every day afterward, knowing I'd refuse her. "I understand why you blame me for the accident. I blame myself. Of course I do. But I wanted to make it right. I stayed with you, cared for you for a full year—"

Stars burst behind my eyes, and my rage is so powerful, so sudden and shocking, that I feel faint. "You were my mother. You were supposed to stay forever!"

Mom recoils as if I landed a slap. We're both surprised by my outburst, the unsaid words of my teen self, spilling from the vault where I'd locked them away. Something warm and salty lands on my lip, and I lick away the tear as more join it—hot, fast, and fierce.

"You're right. It was my job to stay and fix it. But I couldn't get either of you to talk to me or go to therapy. I knew it was my fault, but it still killed me to watch you reject me. I felt dead to you both, and at a certain point, I thought you would be better off without me. It was toxic in that home. We were all suffocating on fury and grief. I thought you both might finally heal if I was out of the picture."

"Well, we didn't," I snap. "Believe it or not, your disappearing act didn't help either of us."

"When I left, you were healing. But *we* were broken. I'd lost you. I'd lost your father. And there's only so long I could withstand the punishment." Her expression is resigned, her blue eyes rimmed red.

My vision is cloudy, and I wipe the tears away with the heels of my hands. "I wasn't trying to punish you. But every time I looked at you, I remembered all that I lost. My family. Grand Trees. Camp. Sonny. Ballet. A working leg. I lost everything in one night."

"So did I," she says, and the misery in her words pulls me out of my rage. "I lost my daughter. You were my everything. *Everything.* And you became a stranger to me. At the hospital, I was terrified we might lose you, that the infection would spread, that you'd lose your leg, or . . ." She chokes on the last word. "You pulled through, but I lost you anyway."

Mom blurs in front of me, but I can hear the tears in her voice. A sob bubbles up from my gut, and I'm having a hard time catching my breath or cataloging all the emotions competing for dominance. I'm livid that she's reinvented history to paint herself as the victim. I'm mourning the years we lost because of her lies and my bad luck. I'm bitter that heartbreak discolored every loving memory that came before it. I'm wondering how we got here. How this home, that once was my happy place, has become the scene of our long-overdue confrontation. Most of all, I'm grieving the alternate ways our lives could have unfolded if she had just stayed.

"You left. You can't know what would have happened if you had fought harder for me," I whisper.

It's quiet except for the wind, our tears, and an intermittent drip from the faucet. It sounds like the aftermath of a battle but feels like a stalemate.

"I hated myself for what I did. I prayed every night for forgiveness, that you would come around, but you didn't. I was drowning, Eden. I was in such a dark place. At some point, I accepted I wasn't strong enough to be the villain you needed, and if I stayed, I would lose myself, too. That I wouldn't survive . . ." She trails off, swallows hard.

"I wouldn't be well enough to be the mother you needed if you came around. Sonny was the only person I loved who still loved me back. And I needed his love to stop hating myself—to keep the part of me that loves from being completely destroyed." She taps her fingertips on the counter, a slow, steady drumbeat in tandem with her breathing. I sense she's trying to collect herself and coax her breathing into submission.

I'm too lost in the trees to see the forest, too close to my own pain to empathize with hers. She might have a point, a perspective worth understanding. But I was a child whose life was destroyed. And I'm still trying to console—and forgive—that child.

"I invited you for weekends, every holiday, every summer. But you refused me over and over again." She reaches for my hand, but I pull away like a reflex. "I know I failed as a mother, but I couldn't figure out how to mother someone who wouldn't let me."

There's a noise from the living room, the crash of the front door flung wide, followed by the unmistakable charge of Houdini's paws and Caleb's commands.

Mom and I freeze, unable to make eye contact. I scurry to the sink, flick the water on, and let the cool water run over my burn, which is throbbing in rhythm with my head as I stifle my tears.

Houdini circles my legs, but I don't have it in me to give him the greeting he craves. Caleb's footsteps aren't far behind. "Abby's at Lina's tonight, but . . ."

I don't turn around when he trails off, but I sense the questions on my back and can imagine his expression.

"What's going on?" he asks, his voice in that low, intimidating register he favors.

There's another long stretch of silence before Mom chokes out, "Nothing. I'm just tired."

"Nicki," he admonishes for the obvious lie.

"Caleb," she says, "just leave it. You can't fix this." I catch her reflection in the glass as she walks to her room, her uneven gait heavy on the wood floor. She shuts her door with a definitive click, and my body shivers in the familiar sound of her retreat.

CHAPTER 28

"Eden?" Caleb asks, but I'm fleeing out the back door with Houdini tight on my heels. I don't know where I'm going, but I need to escape this house and its memories and resentments. I jog across the deck and stagger down the steps. Houdini races by me, howling and wagging his tail in delight when he reaches the bottom first.

My mom's perception of events is running like a replay reel in my head, and I worry she's right. I did blame her, evict her, crucify her. I blasted our family apart without considering the repercussions.

It's easy to hate someone after they've hurt you. But it's hard to hold on to that hate when you know you've hurt them right back.

"Eden," Caleb says again, and he must take the steps two at a time because he's on me before I make it across the yard. "Hey, wait up." He brings a hand to my hip and the other to my shoulder, but I keep moving, tumbling back in time toward the trail marker. "Eden. Please."

It's the "please" that does me in. Gone is the demand in his voice, and it's replaced with desperation. I stop, hunched over with my elbows on my knees, my head in my hands as I unleash another sob. He gathers me to him until I'm a rag doll in his arms and his limbs are the sutures holding me together. He rocks me back and forth, his lips pressed to my temple, and I think he's asking questions, or maybe trying to soothe me, but I don't process any of it.

"It was my fault," I cry. "I blamed her. I punished her."

"Hey, hey, breathe." Caleb bends until we meet at eye level.

"I ruined my family. I was so stupid." I choke on another sob.

Caleb's hands are on my face, cupping my cheeks in his palms and wiping my tears, but they're falling too fast for him to catch. He tilts my face to him until he's a kaleidoscope of color. I think he's trying to shush me, silence me, insist I'm okay. Instead, he says, "Tell me."

I catch my breath in a few short gasps before pinching my eyes closed, blocking Caleb out. I don't know if I can tell him. I haven't told anyone—not the whole story. No one asked me questions. There were too many other questions to ask in those first days: Will she dance again? Will she walk again? Will she live?

But I'm asking myself the more important questions now and reliving every opportunity I had to prevent our landslide.

"I don't even remember their names," I say, and for some reason, I laugh at this, at how insignificant the catalyst was: peer pressure.

"Whose names? Eden, tell me from the beginning, okay?" Caleb sounds so patient, so kind, and I want to do as I'm told. I want to do this one thing right—unspool myself before him and indict myself finally for my part in my family's free fall.

"I snuck out that night with a bunch of kids from camp."

"What night?"

"The night of my accident." I take another deep breath and let it out slowly, wiping my face. "I hadn't broken a single rule before, but I wanted those kids to like me."

"The kids whose names you don't remember?"

I nod.

"Okay," Caleb says slowly.

"They were doing a midnight scavenger hunt and invited me." I remember startling at every footstep, jumping at each noise, paranoid the counselors were following us. I didn't want to disappoint Sonny. Disappoint Mom. "We divided into groups, and one of the things we had to bring back was a photo of Sonny's house to prove we were brave enough to hike there."

I replay the memory that infiltrated my nightmares for years. Caleb knows how the story unfolded but must not have heard the catalyst. It doesn't surprise me. This isn't a tale Sonny would want to share with his nephew, or a memory my mom would ever want to relive. But I see the moment Caleb puts the pieces together because he closes his eyes, as if the weight of my past is too heavy for him, too.

"I got there last, just as this girl in our group was pulling out her digital camera. But the light was on in Sonny's bedroom. The rest of the kids ran when they saw him in the window. But I froze—and made the mistake of looking up."

Caleb reaches for my hands, and I'm grateful to have something to hold on to, his calloused skin now familiar in my grasp. I glance at the wall of windows that stretches across the second floor. The glass is dusty, and the reflection at dusk masks the interior from view. But at midnight, it's a well-lit stage in an otherwise darkened theater, where all the performers are larger than life.

"My mom was up there with him." But I don't need to share the specifics—that my first exposure to sex was witnessing my mother's infidelity—her on her knees with Sonny's hands in her hair. At fourteen, it wasn't something I should have seen. And at thirty-five, I still don't want to talk about it. It's taken me a long time to reconcile what I saw and what I wasn't ready to know.

"I must have been in shock at first, but at some point, I ran. My friends were long gone. And I just wanted to rewind time and erase my memory. But I was so rattled that I didn't turn on my flashlight or pay attention to where I was going."

Caleb pulls me into his arms, curling his hands around my spine, building a fortress around the horrors that threaten to spill from my lips: the moment I tripped on the tree root, how I overcorrected and tumbled ten feet over the edge of the trail and landed in a bed of rock with my leg crumpled beneath me. How I could still see the light from Sonny's bedroom, but they couldn't hear me crying for help. How I was stuck there for hours before anyone noticed I was missing.

"When I woke up from that first surgery, my dad was there, holding my mom's hand. And I told him what I saw in excruciating detail. I looked my mom in the eye and called her names I didn't yet understand." My tears stain Caleb's shirt, and he hugs me closer with a hand cradling the back of my head. "That was the last time I spoke to her directly until she left us for good a year later."

As I replay it, I realize Mom wasn't wrong. We spent a year in punishing silence; I cursed her for my loss. But my fall wasn't her fault. I could have made other choices. I could have declined the invite to that scavenger hunt. I could have thrown a rock at the window, yelled, screamed, and confronted Mom and Sonny. I could have turned on my flashlight and walked away. Instead, I ran in the dark despite the danger, after years of eschewing every risk, avoiding all precarious joy in pursuit of my dream. I could have kept Mom's secret, or demanded she tell Dad directly; I could have absolved myself of the culpability of blowing us to bits.

Yes, I was angry at her. I blamed her. But I was even angrier at myself—a lethal combination for an adolescent with nothing left to lose.

"Her crime was cheating, but my accident was *my* fault. And I punished her. I broke my dad's heart and drove her away."

"Shh," Caleb says. "It wasn't your fault. You were a child. Barely older than Abby." He presses his mouth to my temple, my brow, my cheek. "Of course you reacted the way you did."

"I made the worst decision at every opportunity."

"Yeah, well, it means you're human. Messing up is what people are best at, especially teens."

For some reason, this makes me laugh, but it's thick with tears.

Caleb draws my face to his, cradling my cheeks in his hands. "I don't know much, but as a parent of a smart kid, I've learned we don't stop being imperfect when we become parents, and even genius kids have a hard time making good decisions when emotions are high. You can't judge your teen self through your adult lens. Have empathy for that kid who lost everything and forgive yourself for being human."

"But I'm still messing it up. We just got into a huge fight. I waited too many years to hash this out. And now she's sick, and I don't know how much longer she has, and—"

"You're here now, and that's enough."

~

Caleb stays with me, holds me until the sun sets behind the mountains and the balmy air turns biting. When we head to the house, Houdini greets us on the deck with a solemnity I didn't know he was capable of. I squat to receive him, and he leans his body weight into me, giving me eighty pounds of comfort to wrap my arms around. "You're a good boy, Houdini." He rewards me with a wet drag of his tongue across my cheekbone.

Dinner is where I left it on the stove, long cold, and none of the lights are on. Caleb makes my mom a plate and heads in to check on her, and I drag myself upstairs.

Over the last three months, I've claimed this room despite the painful memories it invokes. It isn't a space that keeps its secrets well. Instead, it's unveiled them all—the snapshots of Mom and Sonny, the book *Birds of the Sierras* still open, face down on the dresser beside Sonny's harmonica, and each shelf crammed with the artifacts of their life together. But still, there are mementos of me, too—small portraits, a card I sent on Mother's Day, a painting of me in my wedding gown. She didn't erase me, but she had to move on. Staying here has helped me understand Mom's encore life. Maybe she did love me all along. Maybe she didn't choose Sonny over me. But it's clear Sonny chose her. And I'm finally grateful to him for that.

I kick off my shoes and shimmy out of my jeans before unhooking my bra and pulling it through my sleeves. When I collapse on the bed, I consider cracking open the book Dad sent me, sitting untouched on my nightstand, but decide I'm still not ready to dig into other families' deceptions when I've barely faced my own. Ready to put this day behind me, I crawl under the covers. Caleb creeps up the stairs, Houdini following, and I bolt upright.

"You shouldn't be up here." I glance around as if we're being watched.

"Says who?" Caleb scoffs. He holds up a plate. "Hungry?"

I shake my head. "Just tired."

"You should eat." He sets the plate on the dresser.

"You should go," I say, but he sits on the edge of the bed, one hand on my thigh over the duvet. Houdini rests his chin on the bed, and I scratch him behind the ears. Dogs always seem to know when their people need comfort.

"Do you want me to go?" Caleb asks.

"No." But I withhold my deeper wants—for him to spend every night with me, to wake every morning with him beside me. I've had him naked, inside, over, and under me. I've touched every inch of him and felt his mouth on my skin. But still, I fantasize about that night in the cabin, his body wrapped around mine, holding me together as we slept.

Caleb stands, tugs his shirt over his head, and strips to his boxers before settling beside me. "I'll leave before your mom is up."

Perhaps we're fooling ourselves, but it's enough reassurance for me to pretend it's a good idea. I fold myself into him, resting my head on his chest and tangling my leg between his.

"Is my mom okay?"

"She's like you—emotional and ready to make it right. You two will get there." Caleb presses a kiss to my forehead.

"We seem to have a track record of screwing it up. How can you be so confident?" I inch closer, tracing the outline of his cheekbone with a fingertip. I've never loved someone's face as much as I do his—the angles and slopes, the hard bridge of his nose, the texture of his beard, the softness of his lips.

He hums. "Because you're ready, and it's all about timing."

Is it, though? I've had opportunities to reconnect with Mom in the last two decades. She always showed up, making the long drive at every big moment—graduations, bridal shower, wedding, birthdays, random Sunday afternoons I'd offer as a pittance. She's been waiting. Hoping. Longing. If I had accepted an invitation all those years ago, if I had made my peace and visited, perhaps I would have remembered how much I loved this place, how much I loved Mom and Sonny. Maybe that's what scared me, being unable to cling to the solace of my rage.

"You know"—I drag my finger across his lower lip—"if I hadn't been so stubborn, maybe we would have met sooner." I imagine Caleb and me, both bitter and wounded, and I wonder what our alchemy would have been then.

Caleb opens his eyes and bites the tip of my finger before soothing it with a kiss. "We would have been a disaster. Like flint and steel, burning this whole place down."

I laugh. "It's not too different than how we are as grown-ups."

Caleb chuckles and slips his hand under my shirt, resting it on my lower back. "We're a safe, controlled burn now." But there's nothing safe or controlled about how I feel for him. "Maybe we met exactly when we were meant to."

"You believe in fate?" I ask.

"I don't know about all that. But I think sometimes we're pawns, and we don't know the impact of a move until the entire game is played."

"That's a bit fatalistic."

I feel him shrug. "It helps to know that our tragedies might be blessings. If my stepdad hadn't run me out of town, I wouldn't have found Sonny. I wouldn't have had Abby."

I wish I thought like that, and perhaps I would if my tragedies had led to something beautiful instead of loss and increasing numbness.

Caleb continues, "If things hadn't happened like they did, I wouldn't have met your mom. I was a teen when I showed up here, but I hadn't done any growing up yet. She raised me. Sonny was the best, but he had this . . ." He pauses. "I think Abby calls it toxic positivity."

I snort laugh, and the fondness and warmth are heavy on my heart. Sonny was a glass-half-full-of-magic-potion type of guy.

"I didn't get him at first, with all his campfire songs, animal-print tube socks, and cheesy jokes."

"I bet." I laugh, and it feels good to remember him fondly.

"But your mom and I were in the same place—mourning something too tough to talk about. Trying to start over. I think she had just gotten here after everything went down with you and your dad. We were good for each other. Nicki spoke to me like I was worth something, like my pain mattered, and showed me that not all people wanna hurt you."

I squeeze Caleb tighter. "I'm glad you had each other."

"I don't know what I would have done without her. When I found out Lina was pregnant"—he clears his throat—"I was scared to death. There was a moment where I thought about running. I didn't think I could be a dad. The only model I'd had was my stepdad. And the thought of being like him petrified me."

I cup his face and turn his cheek to capture his gaze. "You'd never be like him."

"Your mom sat me down. Told me that being a parent is the best thing in the world. That it would bring me more joy than I could imagine. That I wouldn't always get it right, but if I left, I'd never regret anything more."

He watches for my reaction, his eyes darting between mine. But I don't know how to respond. Because I forced my mom from our home, Caleb had a mother figure. My mom's regret prevented Caleb's. Because I had an absent parent, Abby had an attentive one. Maybe there is a grand plan. Maybe we are all pawns, and there's some purpose for each loss, some net positive released into the universe when a heart breaks.

But I don't want to be a pawn anymore. I don't want to be too scared to play the game and take the risks. I don't want to just hold on to the thing that won't hurt me. Instead, I want to reach for what will make me happy.

Caleb makes me happy. Grand Trees makes me happy. A second chance with Mom. That might make me happiest of all.

"Maybe we did meet when we were meant to, exactly when I needed you," I say, and it's enough for now. I should take some time to think, to contemplate this crazy change I'm considering—moving here, risking everything for a fresh start.

"Funny, I think I've always needed you." Caleb nudges my chin up and kisses me, and it's slow and decadent, sweet and tender, like we have all the time in the world, like we belong in this tiny part of the universe together. It isn't long before our hands wander, our clothes come off, and I show him the words I can't yet say. The words, I suspect, I've never felt before him.

I kiss my way down his body, taking him into my mouth, tasting him and relishing his gasp and the way his hands fist at his sides when his restraint slips, knowing he wants to be gentle with me. I've never enjoyed this before, usually in my own head and too self-conscious—but I lose my reservations as he responds, ignoring him when he says he's close, offering me an out. Instead, I take him deeper, savoring him as he swells against my tongue and surrenders to his pleasure.

Afterward, when we've explored each other, when I've come apart in his arms on a swallowed scream, when we're sated and spent, he holds on to me like we'll wake up like this tomorrow and the next day and the next. Like we get to choose forever.

"You should stay in Grand Trees," he says, his voice heavy with impending sleep.

"Really?" I'm grinning, and I'm sure he can hear it in my voice.

"Yeah. 'Cause I'm falling in love with you," he says, just like that—like maybe the universe does have a plan, and we're it for each other.

CHAPTER 29

I find Mom in the kitchen when I tiptoe down the stairs in the morning. She's at the counter, trying—unsuccessfully—to make coffee with one arm. I slip in beside her and lift the carafe from the brewer to take over. She darts a glance at me before sliding onto a stool.

"Caleb just left," she says. "I found him and the dog asleep on the couch. I guess he didn't trust us alone together."

"Oh?" I hedge. It's too early to tell Mom about Caleb and me. We didn't make any decisions last night, and I have a lot to think about. Besides, Mom and I have more important things to discuss first. Complicating that conversation by telling her I've been having a secret affair with the nephew of the man she had a secret affair with—well, I can't wrap my head around that yet.

The noise from the coffee grinder gives us a reprieve, a moment of forced silence as I calculate my words. But as the percolator kicks in, I turn to her, gripping the counter with both hands. "I'm so sorry, Mom."

"Oh, honey. I'm the one who's sorry. I'm your mother and should have stayed—to make it up to you and earn your forgiveness. I've laid awake at night for years replaying all the other choices I could have made and the better person I should have been." Her voice is hoarse.

"And I knew it wasn't fair to blame you for the accident. I guess I didn't know where else to put my anger."

"I get it. I do. I put all that pain in motion. Our life was beautiful before that night." Mom glances down at the counter.

"You and Dad had seemed happy." I hesitate, not sure this line of inquiry can lead to anything good, or even if there is a question to be asked. Is it my right to know? Only the two people in a relationship know the truth of it. But for years, I felt gaslit by my parents' marriage, and I couldn't decipher what healthy or happy looked like. "I was confused because it really seemed like you loved him."

"We were happy. And I did love him. There's a part of me that never stopped loving him," she says. "We were so young when we fell in love, and he was my best friend. He was kind and thoughtful and gave me a perfect family. He gave me you. And then life happened, and we lost sight of why we loved each other. I became a full-time wife and mother and gave up my art and pieces of myself. And then, I came here for the summer—for you at first—but it was like the world opened up. Grand Trees reminded me that I was an artist and there was a world beyond my routine. And Sonny reminded me that I was a woman. He made me see new colors . . ." She wrings her hands. "I don't know, that probably sounds selfish and silly."

Sonny played her a symphony. He made her life multisensory. Sonny was her Caleb. But I can't absolve her, and maybe it's not my job to forgive her infidelity anyway. She made vows to my dad, not to me. I don't know how to respond, so I say nothing.

"When I was home with you and Dad, I was fully committed. I wasn't longing for Sonny or Grand Trees. When I was here, Sonny was my world. I know how it sounds, but I fooled myself that I could have both, if only for a few weeks in the summer. Sonny accepted that I would never give him more than that, and I was delusional, thinking that if he wasn't a threat to our family, then my love for him couldn't hurt us."

"But he was a threat to our family. You left."

Mom pats the stool beside her, and I cautiously slide onto it. The heat is gone from last night's argument, but the kindling is still sparking, and if we're not careful, the blaze can roar back to life.

"I did, and I wish I could take it back. Don't get me wrong. I loved Sonny, and I was so grateful for our life together. But I would have given it all up for another chance to have been the mother you deserved and the wife I promised to be to your father." She twists her hands in her lap, and I notice the slight tremor she's trying to keep at bay. "I told you last night that I had been in a dark place after your accident. Looking back, I realize I should have been in therapy and on antidepressants. I wasn't thinking clearly. I wasn't eating. I had some dark thoughts." She shakes her head as if clearing the memories. "By the time I left, I honestly thought you'd be better off without me—that I'd caused so much pain and didn't deserve to be your dad's wife or your mom. I hated myself for what I had done." Tears slip down her face, and she wipes them away before I can. "When I got here, Sonny took one look at me and knew I wasn't well. He took care of me. By the time I got better and started to feel like I could be useful to you again, I'd done so much damage, I didn't know how to make amends."

Thoughts of that time—the complicated web of betrayal, injury, and abandonment—have always triggered my latent rage, but what remains now is sadness and shame, and I try to hear her words. I have to silence the hurt part of me to listen to the hurt part of her.

Neither of us survived that night intact. And the choices we made next were the product of wounded people. She was the mother—the adult—so she had a greater responsibility to do the right thing. But she was human, too. And sometimes our flaws win out over our better natures.

I don't know what forgiveness feels like. I don't know what's on the other side of all the resentment I've harbored. But I'm ready to accept that this was my story—this was our story. Our family's foundation collapsed, and we didn't have the tools to rebuild.

"I shouldn't have punished you like I did, with silence for years and years. And I shouldn't have unloaded on you last night. I came here because I wanted to reconcile but somehow made it worse."

Mom gives me a small smile, and her blue eyes go soft. "You haven't made it worse. I'm grateful you finally said it. You swallowed your anger, and it made us strangers. Maybe we had to unload. All that baggage has been heavy." She laces her hand in mine. "Edie, I love you, and I've missed you. I'd give anything for us to be close again."

I wrap her in my arms, careful not to hurt her but relieved when she pulls me close, squeezing away some of my hurt in the process.

"I love you," I say.

"I love you more." It's an old refrain that stabs me somewhere tender.

We hold each other, our tears mixing together as we whisper apologies and promises. We can't rewrite the past, but perspective might give us a path forward. We're both wiping at tears as we pull apart.

"What would you think about me staying?" I hadn't planned on broaching this with her yet, but I'm emboldened by our honesty, and the words slip out.

"Staying?" She blinks away tears and surprise. "In Grand Trees?"

"I'd have to go back and forth—for work, and Dad and . . ." I trail off, the reality sinking in. Cassie's having a baby, and Dad is aging. It's probably naive and impulsive to flip my life upside down for a man I've just met.

But it's not only for Caleb. I wasn't happy in San Francisco. I was living in the home I bought with Jeff, still sleeping on my half of the bed, rattling around in the life we created that was suddenly silent and oversize.

And perhaps I can convince Mom to seek treatment if I'm here long enough. Perhaps I can live a new life, one I didn't plan, that isn't neat and safe but is full, daring, and unexpected.

"Is this because of Jeff? Are you running from heartbreak, honey? Because as much as I'd love for you to be here with me, I also want you to learn from my mistakes. I never resolved my feelings for your dad. I just ran. It hurt him, it hurt you, and it meant Sonny got only a portion of me, too."

This is more insight into my parents' relationship than either of them has volunteered, but I still don't understand how Mom could have loved them both. I can't fathom how that's possible.

But she needn't be concerned I'm following in her footsteps. "I'm not running from Jeff. I haven't loved him in a very long time." Perhaps I never did.

"Well, good, because that doesn't do anyone any good in the long run. Sometimes I wonder if . . ."

She gets a faraway look in her eye, and I chase her gaze. "You wonder what?"

"I know it's silly, but sometimes I think my guilt contributed to my illness. They say no, but it's not good for your health to leave things unresolved and hostile. All the stewing I did. All the sleep I lost. All the pain I caused everyone."

Her admission feels like the answer to the riddle that's plagued me since I found out about her diagnosis and denial of care. Is she punishing herself? "Mom, is that why you're refusing to get help? Because you think you deserve it?" The words catch in my throat, and I swallow a swell of emotion.

"No, no," she says, but she won't look at me.

"Mom," I plead. "You *don't* deserve this. This isn't your payback, and that's not how illness works. If you won't get treatment for you, do it for me. Give me back the time we lost. Don't punish me by punishing yourself."

Mom's eyes fill with tears. "I didn't realize that's what I was doing."

I wipe away her tears with my thumbs. "I think we've both been punishing ourselves in different ways. We should stop doing that."

She smiles at me, her face lighting up as if a shade has been lifted. "Look at you, all grown up and wise. Your dad did such a good job."

"So did you. I remember everything, Mom. All the late nights sewing my pointe shoes while I studied. All the times you comforted me after a bad class. How you made sure I spent every summer feeling like a kid rather than just a ballerina. The way you were proud but didn't push. I remember dancing with you in the kitchen and the lunches you packed and the notes you'd leave in my backpack. I remember how your love felt like the best and surest thing in the world."

Her tears fall unchecked, but I know they've shifted from grief to joy, because my tears are falling, too. It's a catharsis and cleanse as we give in to the dormant memories of how right it once was between us.

"Let me do this for you. With you," I say.

"I can't have you sacrifice everything to take care of me." Mom searches my gaze with a hopefulness that betrays her excitement. "Your life is in San Francisco. You have your job. Your friends. I'm all you have here."

"It wouldn't be a sacrifice. I'd stay because I want to." I could tell her about Caleb, but I don't want to upstage the breakthrough we've made. I don't want this moment to be about anything but our relationship, her health, and the possibility of us having more time to repair the rift that broke us. "And think about treatment, okay? For me." Her medical options aren't great here, but if I stay and convince her to see a doctor, it's certainly better than the status quo. And who knows? Maybe this town has some magic to spare for us. I think of the words Caleb shared months ago. *Grand Trees can heal you if you let it.*

Mom nods rapidly, blinking back tears. "I will." She cups my cheek in her good hand. "And you're welcome to stay here for as long as you want. But think about it long and hard. It's a big decision, and I don't want any more regrets getting between us."

CHAPTER 30

I help Mom along the stone path to the welcome court, her arm in mine as we're greeted by a few dozen folks who beat us here. Carmela lifts the fruit salad from my arms to ferry it to the buffet table. Adelaide rushes over and shimmies me out of the way, supporting Mom as the crowd envelops her with comments about how well she looks, that her color's back, and that they're glad to see her out and about. There's so much love here, a town full of people invested in her health. Should she decide to seek treatment, the entire community will celebrate her decision.

The camp courtyard is dressed up for the occasion with red-checked tablecloths and mason jars filled with wildflowers sitting atop the old picnic tables. String lights are stretched between the bordering redwoods. Music drifts from the speakers, and the air is thick with the scent of sprinklers on concrete and charcoal briquettes. It smells like summer.

I catch sight of Caleb from across the courtyard, leaning against the gym wall, chatting with Ian and Abby. Abby has Benny on her hip and twirls in circles as he throws his head back and giggles before they spiral away from the tight group. Fiona is more subdued, clinging to her dad with both arms. I haven't seen Caleb since we fell asleep entwined in each other last night, and I'm excited about the possibilities our next conversation may hold.

I know the moment Caleb sees me—his focus is telekinetic—and his smile pulls me to him. I weave between picnic tables, tugged to their quiet corner by the sheer force of him.

"Hey, you," he says on an exhale.

"Hi."

"You're stunning," he says.

My smile takes over my face. "Thank you."

I dressed up tonight in a hunter-green halter dress that makes my eyes look like sea glass and my skin more porcelain than pale. Cassie packed it for me *for a special occasion*, which I assumed would never materialize. I straightened my hair and applied mascara and lip gloss. I am a definite "after" compared to all the "before" months spent in faded jeans and plain T-shirts—the "before" months when Caleb liked me anyway—so I'm pleased to learn he appreciates this version of me, too.

And Caleb is gorgeous tonight even though, or especially because, he is exactly the Caleb I've come to adore—casual, confident, and in his element.

An entire conversation passes between us. Caleb looks like he's undressing me in his head and making plans for later.

Ian glances from Caleb to me and back before he utters a soft, "Oh."

I snap out of it, my face heating under Ian's knowing smile. "Hi," I say, this time to him, my voice finally under control.

Ian grins wider, a little glint in his eye. It's clear Caleb isn't pretending anymore. Maybe we won't have to for much longer.

"Hi, Fiona." I peek around Ian to catch her sleepy gaze. She shifts her face away.

"No nap today," Ian says, an apology for her avoidance. But I wasn't offended. "I'm going to check on Lina. She's due tomorrow but insisted on coming anyway."

"Never argue with a pregnant woman," Caleb says, and Ian chuckles as he and Fiona slip away. I hear Abby's giggle and Benny's squeal, but they've disappeared around the side of the welcome court.

"So much for discretion," I say.

Caleb shoves his hands deep into the pockets of his Levi's, his triceps bunching at the slight pressure, his shoulders rising. He bites his bottom lip, holding back a grin. "Fuck discretion."

I almost do just that, tempted to step forward and kiss him, but Benny barrels between us, and Abby sprints in pursuit.

"Hi, Eden," Abby yells in a blur of long limbs and glossy ponytail.

It pulls us out of our spell. "Perhaps we should save our indiscretions for later."

He steps forward, spinning me toward the party with his hand on the small of my back and leaning in to whisper into my ear, "Promises, promises."

His breath coaxes goose bumps from my skin. I clear my throat and cast him an admonishing look to steer us back to social respectability. "What's the deal with this party?"

"Sonny did a trial run before the kids arrived each summer—a cookout to test the kitchens, barbecues, sound systems, like a rehearsal dinner. And it became a tradition."

"It was one of Sonny's many excuses to party?"

"Basically."

We're swallowed by the crowd as we return to the courtyard. Caleb is pulled away by a man I don't recognize, and I know I've lost him when the man asks about a mysterious illness affecting his trees. Someone turns up the music, and Adelaide declares the food line open.

I fill my plate with three types of salads bursting with color, garlic bread, and more barbecued meat than I can identify. I tuck in beside Mom, Adelaide, Carmela, and a group of locals whose names are rattled off in a blur. Ian mixes up pitchers of a lemonade cocktail that's tart, sweet, and strong, and I'm drawn in by the lure of the enchanted evening among new friends in a place so welcoming it feels like home. My body warms, and my inhibitions dissolve, and I imagine enjoying nights like these for a lifetime. I envision making my temporary life my real life. I think I could be happy here with Mom, Caleb, and the community they've cultivated.

I can see it. I can feel it.

Abby slides in beside me when dessert is served, her plate piled high with strawberry shortcake, a lemon bar, and a brownie. The sun has set, and the string lights set her face aglow in a golden wash. Caleb is ever present in her smile. Her joy is his. And I know I'm jumping ahead—shamelessly springing forward like a middle schooler signing her name with the surname of her crush—but I see in Abby the possibility of our future children.

I can finally admit to myself—wholeheartedly, unabashedly—that I want children of my own. Jeff would debate me on the illogic of procreation—the earth cannot support the booming population, and resources will run out. I would withdraw from the argument because he was right, there is no logic to my innate longing to be a mother. But sometimes our deepest desires are illogical. I want to nurse my newborn, hold my toddler's hand, watch my grade schooler in a talent show, and drop my teen off around the corner when she meets her friends. Maybe it's silly. But I want it. And I'm tired of settling for comfort when happiness requires risk—I'm done being too complacent to reach for what I want.

"You look like you're contemplating the meaning of life," Abby says around a mouthful of strawberries and whipped cream.

"I guess I am," I admit.

"Have you figured it out?" She looks at me with wide eyes.

"Nope."

"Yeah, me neither." She points to her dessert plate. "But I figure I may as well eat dessert until I do."

"You are a wise young woman." I laugh. "What do you have planned this summer?"

"Swim practice at the crack of dawn. I'll do a lot of big sistering once my mom has the baby." She gestures to Lina, who is standing at the end of the picnic table, speaking with Dakota.

Lina has a hand on her belly, absently soothing her unborn child like instinct. She's beautiful pregnant, even though she wears the mark of discomfort—a hitch in her posture, a pinch in her brow.

Abby continues, "And I'll be here helping my dad and Ian. I do a bunch of odd jobs for them on the weekends to get ready for the next group of campers. I'm saving for a new phone."

I feel a fist knocking on a fond memory. I did the same for Sonny. "No vacations?"

"Dad and Ian are too busy in the summers. Sometimes Dad and I'll go somewhere for spring break or New Year's. But we don't go far."

I'm not sure I can imagine them anywhere but here, but perhaps we'll travel together someday. I can show Abby the world so she'll be ready to storm it, and pull Caleb out of his comfort zone in the same way he's done for me.

A few folks have taken to the floor to dance—couples, kids, and teens. Ian pulls Lina out to the center.

"What about you?" Abby asks.

"Me?" I've lost track of the conversation.

"This summer. You're not really leaving, are you?"

I can't have this conversation with Abby. Even if I stay, Caleb will need to decide how to tell his daughter. I imagine a new relationship will be destabilizing for her—she's had him all to herself when she's had to share everything else. "I'm not sure," I hedge.

"Well, I think you should stay. We all like you." She turns to face me fully, hitching one knee up on the bench beside us, and she scans our surroundings as if she's about to do something illicit. "Especially my dad. It's all 'Eden this' and 'Eden that.'" She leans closer, gesturing wildly with her hands. "I think you should ask him out. Look, I know he needs to shave and dresses like a hobo, but he can cook, clean, and play the guitar, and he's always sweet when you get sick and takes care of everyone in this town, and Ellie's and Teri's moms both say he's like cute or whatever." She mimes gagging herself. "But he's a good guy. He even puts the toilet seat down. Benny and Ian do not."

She stares at me expectantly, as if she's awaiting my answer, but my jaw is slack. I do not know how to respond without giving us away or shattering her hopes.

"What are you two conspiring about?" Caleb's voice disrupts the awkward stalemate, and Abby jolts back.

"Nothing. Nothing," she stammers.

Caleb looks at me, his brows drawn together. "I was kidding, but now I'm concerned."

I give him a tight shake of my head, a universal signal of *drop it* before Abby puts us both on the spot and has us married off by the end of the evening.

"All right," he says, still suspicious. But he slides a plate in front of me. "This is Carmela's mint chocolate cheesecake. I thought you'd like it."

Abby catches my eye, giving a knowing look that says, *See, told you.* And then she scrambles off the bench with the subtlety of an amateur sitcom star. "I've gotta go . . . help Mom with Fiona . . . and Benny." She places her palms on Caleb's shoulders and pushes. "Sit here."

She sprints away, leaving her brownie untouched. Caleb rectifies that as he slides onto the bench, swallowing half of it before craning his neck to watch her go. "What was that about?"

I take a bite of the cheesecake, buying some time, because I'm suddenly nervous. Whispering about forever while wrapped in sheets is one thing; planning a future with a courtyard full of spectators is another. "She said you need to shave and that you dress like a hobo. But also begged me to ask you out."

He chuckles, but his eyes lock on mine, twinkling and pleased. "You know, she's a very bright girl. I think she might be on to something."

I swallow another mouthful of cheesecake. Caleb was right. It's a perfect dessert. "Might be?" I tease.

"I could always ask you out first. She has so little faith in me."

My cheeks flush, which is ridiculous since we skipped right over that dating ritual when I straddled him on the seat of his truck. Perhaps I should have considered inviting him out for coffee like a normal person. I look away, spying the growing collection of partygoers on the impromptu dance floor.

"Or I could ask you to dance," I say.

"Hmm." He bites back a smile. "I didn't think you did that anymore."

"Swaying to music is just an excuse to touch you. It's barely dancing."

He scoots closer, and the wind wraps me in his scent. I think he applied cologne, or perhaps aftershave. He smells more formal somehow, but there's something uniquely Caleb underneath the new scent. It's subtle and tempting. I want to move closer, press my face against his neck, and taste him. Caleb licks his bottom lip, gaze crawling over my face, and then he clears his throat as the conversation picks up at the other end of the picnic table. I almost forgot we weren't alone.

"But will you still like me when you figure out I have two left feet?" he asks.

"My favorite dance teacher used to say it's not about perfection; the magic is in the attempt." I climb out from behind the picnic table. "C'mon. Your daughter told me you were a catch. Prove it."

He laughs. "All right. Let's make some magic."

He follows me to the dance floor, extending his hand when we arrive at the edge. I don't look around, refusing to make eye contact with anyone who may be watching with curiosity. He tugs me into him, resting one palm on my back and tucking me close. The eclectic playlist transitions to "You Make Loving Fun" by Fleetwood Mac, Mom's favorite band, as I wrap my other hand around Caleb's neck. I inhale—definitely cologne. It's spicy and sweet. We're barely swaying, but Caleb coaxes me into a gentle rhythm. It would be soothing if my body didn't always go haywire when he touches me. I'm ready to drag him home by the shirttails.

"So when I spoke to my mom . . ." I start, cautious. He'd called this morning to make sure we were okay after our argument, but I didn't tell him this. "We talked about me moving here."

He pulls back, holding my hand close to his chest, his mouth falling open. "Really?"

"Yeah."

"Really?" He grins. "Really, really?"

I laugh; I'm still nervous. This seems crazy, and I don't want him to worry that I'm staying exclusively for him. "I have some stuff to figure out, and we should talk about what it means for us. I know we're new and made no promises. But I'd like to see where it goes. I don't have any preconceived notions for us." A lie, of course, but safer than the truth that I'm daydreaming up names for our future children. "We can take this slow, or—"

"Now you want to take things slow." He wraps me in a full-body hug as we pretend to dance. "Right when I'm desperate to make you mine."

I don't respond—can't respond, because my heart is pinballing in my chest, and my mouth is too dry to form words. My body is a heat map revealing every place he's pressed against me. My emotions are a chaotic mix of fear, excitement, panic—but mainly love, delirious, irrational love. "Or"—I gather the bravery to leap—"we could jump right in."

Caleb's fingertips tighten on my skin, and there's a faint hitch to his breath before he releases it, tickling my hair. "Yeah. I like 'or' better."

We sway under the canopy of twinkle lights, beside his found family, in the sanctuary of my best memories, and the place I hope to make even better ones in the years to come—our bodies connected, our heartbeats in sync—as my mind flashes ahead to every note we'll make together. Major, minor, melodic, but all of them in harmony.

"But let's tell Abby I asked you out, all on my own. I can't have her thinking she set us up. She'll be insufferable," Caleb says.

I laugh, and it emerges as a burst of joy—raw, unfiltered joy. We beam at each other, not even pretending to dance anymore, just staring at one another in a suspended trance. I wonder if he sees what I do, our future unspooling like a promise.

Caleb slides his hands to mine, and the music transitions to a pop song I don't recognize immediately, but the kids on the dance floor do. They squeal and spiral around us like they're in the mosh pit of a live concert. One of them, a young girl no more than five, stumbles into me, and Caleb catches her before she falls to the concrete.

"Whoa, you okay, Skylar?" he asks.

She grins at him, wild-eyed in the way of overtired kids, offers a shy, "Yeah," and dances away.

At the interruption, I pick up my head and catch a glimpse of Mom at the far end of the patio, her back to me as she speaks to someone whose frame is so familiar that a shiver runs through me. But he's cloaked in shadow outside the canopy of lights, so I think my mind's playing tricks on me. It can't be. He doesn't exist here in my nostalgic, anticipative bliss. He belongs in another world, and the two don't collide.

But he takes a step forward, and his face comes into focus. I gasp, and Caleb turns, following my gaze as I make eye contact with my real life on the other side of the night.

"Eden," Caleb says, his voice gruff. "Who is that?"

CHAPTER 31

I charge across the patio, swerving between revelers and picnic tables. My determination turns a few heads. Adelaide is outright staring as I stride by. Caleb follows, asking questions I can't answer.

When I reach my target, Mom grabs my hand, and I can't tell whether if it's for physical or emotional support.

"What are you doing here?" I ask, not bothering with niceties.

"I told the young man at the bed-and-breakfast I was looking for you, and he said everybody would be here tonight. He was nice enough to give me directions. But I admit, I got a bit lost."

"No." I shake my head, and it feels like I have marbles jostling in my brain. The sight of him here is unnatural, dissonant. "What are you doing in Grand Trees?"

"Well"—he smooths the collar of his shirt, running a hand along the buttons—"I thought it was long past time for your mother and me to talk."

"Dad," I say. "You should have told me you were coming. That's not an easy drive."

"I'm not an invalid, Edie. And you weren't very happy with me when we spoke yesterday. I wasn't sure I'd be welcome, actually."

We stand in silence for a moment, because he's right. I've finally made progress with Mom, and I don't need him showing up, potentially dredging up more difficult memories and launching Mom back toward self-flagellation.

What is he doing here? Other than forcing a reckoning of long-suppressed heartbreak just as I hoped to slip outside its clutches. Caleb clears his throat, and I startle.

Oh no. If Caleb hated me on introduction, how will he treat the man who drove my mom from her home with an epic-length silent treatment?

But Caleb extends his hand. "Mr. Hawthorne, I'm Caleb. Welcome to Grand Trees."

I do a double take. Who is this polite man without any hint of aggression?

Dad offers a polite smile. "Please, call me Len."

"It's great to meet you, Len." Caleb waves over to the buffet tables. "You'd be doing us a favor if you make yourself a plate. We always have way too much food. My buddy Ian is manning the bar. If you like your drinks stiff, you're in luck."

Dad chuckles. It's slightly frayed, but he's nothing if not painfully polite. "That's kind of you. I think I will in a bit."

I take Dad in—pressed slacks, dress shoes, his thinning hair tamed with gel. He's a slight man, and he looks older, feebler standing beside Caleb. But Dad always stands tall, his posture honed by years of ballroom classes as a kid. He's out of place in this casual crowd, and it triggers a pang of protectiveness. Mom escaped his silence to come to this boisterous place, and it was never more apparent the punishment she fled—and the refuge she found—than with Dad standing in the center of it.

Mom is gripping my forearm like it's the only thing keeping her upright. I can't remember the last time they saw each other. My wedding? I sat them at the two farthest points of the ballroom. And if they spoke, I didn't witness it. Mom came alone, but that was a lifetime ago. She was able to walk on her own two feet. She went home to Sonny afterward. The frailty of their old wounds is more apparent without the armor of their youth.

And now I know how painful the split was for Mom. I didn't have empathy for her then, but I do now. Because betrayal is painful, but regret is debilitating.

"Nicki, do you need to sit?" Caleb asks, but his words are coded. *Are you okay? Do you want me to ask him to leave?* Caleb's internal guard dog is leashed, but it's not tamed.

"I'm fine. I think Len and I are going to spend some time catching up."

And then she slips her arm in his, and some wheel slips loose in my brain, stuttering to a stop in disbelief. After all this time, my parents—who haven't spoken to each other in two decades—are going to have a long-overdue chat? I did all the hard work, knocked down walls, opened doors, and now Dad gets to walk through and make himself at home? Fourteen-year-old me thinks this is bullshit. How different would our lives have been if they had been adults all those years ago? Instead of now, in the middle of *my* night, *my* epiphany, *my* commitment to move on and create a beautiful new life—damn all the broken pieces of me.

A bigger person might welcome this. But I'm not feeling particularly big right now, and I don't want to risk our fragile progress on my dad's emotional experiment.

"You're just going to catch up? All of a sudden?" I ask.

Caleb steps back—his guard dog upstaged by my feral dog.

Dad's face falls, but Mom squares her shoulders. "There's no statute of limitations on a conversation. Now is as good a time as any."

"Twenty years after your divorce?" My voice cracks on the last word. Caleb is beside me, here to protect me, to protect Mom. Here to be the bigger person, just like he's done in his own divorce for his daughter. I wish my parents had done that for me.

Perhaps it's because the last few days have been so emotional, but this casual chat after years of silence is throwing me for a loop.

Dad looks at me, his eyes soft but his words firm. "I told you, Eden. Your mother and I are not divorced."

"I'm sorry, what?" I look to Caleb for confirmation that this is crazy, but his expression doesn't console me, because he doesn't seem surprised by my dad's words.

Mom places her hand on my forearm and gives me a gentle squeeze. With a wary glance over her shoulder, she leads Dad to a secluded picnic table under a shroud of trees.

"What the hell was that?" I ask as Caleb leads me away, far from the tinny speakers blaring bubblegum pop. "They aren't divorced?"

Caleb's silence says everything.

"How did you know but I didn't? Wait, how is that possible? Sonny and Mom got married." I remember when Mom told me Sonny had proposed and they were planning to elope. I was in college and didn't handle it well. Or perhaps I didn't handle it at all, because I changed the subject.

"They wanted to, but your dad never signed the papers, and Nicki felt too guilty to press him about it, like it was her way to atone for leaving. Sonny was so grateful to have her here, he didn't want to push her or make her feel worse about her choice. They were all . . . stuck. She still wears Sonny's engagement ring, but no, they weren't married. I assumed you knew."

This new piece of history is baffling. I acknowledge that my family's ability to communicate is stunted, but this brings our dysfunction to new levels. Did Dad think he could wait it out and give Mom a couple of decades to come to her senses? Was he going to win her back with silence? My empathy for Mom grows. Dad wouldn't forgive her, but he wouldn't let her go. At least Jeff gave me a clean break, as cold and sudden as it was. It was an end, which enabled a new beginning. And yet, I don't understand how any of them—Dad, Mom, or Sonny—was willing to live in relationship purgatory for so long. Perhaps it was the penance they all paid for how terribly they messed everything up. Mom's betrayal, Dad's denial, Sonny's complicity.

Something comes back to me about Mom's reaction to my divorce. She was relieved it was mutual—that there was no lingering love or regret. She mentioned starting over was easier when you hadn't left half your heart behind. I assumed she was talking about me.

But perhaps she was talking about Dad after all. She literally left her marriage behind, intact, while she built a life with another man.

"Do you know why he's here?" Caleb squints at them across the courtyard sparkling with white lights and beaming dancers. There's a commotion on the far side of the patio, where a group of people is huddled around the buffet table. But it sounds like cheering, so I ignore it, even though my senses are on high alert.

"No. I'm beginning to think I don't understand anything about their relationship." The night is cooling, and I shiver. I cross my arms over my chest. "You were surprisingly polite."

Caleb cocks his head. "Why wouldn't I be?"

I snort. "You chased me off my mom's porch when I showed up uninvited. And he's my mom's evil ex." Although he isn't her ex-husband, apparently.

Caleb steps closer and his shadow bathes me in warmth and his spicy scent. "He's also my girlfriend's dad, so I'd like to make a good impression."

My heart leaps at the admission. I haven't been anyone's girlfriend in so long, and something about it thrills me. By the end of my marriage, the wife title felt obligatory, but girlfriend is a choice—a youthful, giddy, romantic choice. I glance at him, wishing I could see his expression, but he's backlit and opaque, a Caleb-size shape cut out of the evening canvas.

"Dad!" Abby runs toward us at a full sprint, weaving in and out of the crowd and gesturing like she's shipwrecked and waving down a plane.

"What's wrong?" There's an edge of panic in Caleb's voice, a crack I haven't heard since the earthquake.

"Mom's water broke!" Abby releases a hysterical laugh. "All over Bob's shoes!"

"Points for style," Caleb says under his breath.

"I'm going with them to the hospital."

"It could be hours," he warns, but it's futile. Abby loves hospitals. It's the only place she doesn't feel pulled in two.

"It'll be fast. It's her billionth kid. But either way, it'll be fun." She beams before dialing down her smile into something sweeter, more playful. "You know I love you, right?"

"How could you not?" Caleb asks. He's kidding, but I feel the rhetorical question like he's drilling into my soul. Not loving Caleb is beginning to seem like an impossibility.

"Mom has a go bag in the car, but"—she gestures to her outfit: denim shorts, a tank top, and flip-flops—"I have nothing. I'll freeze in the AC, and my phone will die, and I won't be able to post photos of my new sister."

Caleb's voice is dry as dust. "Is this your way of asking me to pack a bag and drive two hours round trip to the hospital to drop it off?"

"Oh, Daddy, you're the best! That's such a good idea," she says, as if it weren't hers at all. Clever girl. Abby wraps her arms around his neck, kissing his cheek before jogging away, returning to the mayhem across the courtyard.

Caleb slumps. "Eden, I . . ." He sneaks a peek at my parents—huddled in the shadows—with an apology hanging on his lips.

"Go." I place my palm on his chest. "I'm fine. Let me deal with my dysfunctional parents. Abby needs you."

"I'll swing by afterward." He searches my face for signs that I'm as fine as I say I am, then places his hand over mine.

I shake my head. "It'll be late. But text me to let me know you've made it home okay."

"Of course." He scans the perimeter before leaning in for the swiftest, sweetest kiss, which stabilizes me, and reminds me of the promise held in that discreet act of affection. Whatever my dad has come to say, whatever the fallout is for my mom, this time I won't have to deal with the aftermath alone.

CHAPTER 32

I glance around the dining room with a mix of nostalgia and dread. Goldie's Harvest Café hasn't changed since the summers I binged their blueberry waffles. It still has the same green pleather booths, fake-wood countertops, and framed photos of every camp cohort along the walls.

"I don't understand why we couldn't talk last night," I say after the waiter pours our coffee and strides away.

"I needed some time to think." Mom's hand trembles as she lifts the mug, and she braces it with the fingertips of her broken arm.

"Think about what?"

"Let's talk when your father gets here."

I snort into my coffee—that expression is like a time warp to my childhood. Mom's evasion is driving me batty, and she's been giving me the same line since last night. The party broke up soon after Lina's dramatic departure. When Mom and Dad returned to the dwindling festivities, Adelaide had put me to work clearing the buffet tables, and Dad took the opportunity to slip away back to the bed-and-breakfast. On the way home, Mom was tight-lipped because some things never change—silence is a stubborn Hawthorne habit. She shuffled off to bed the moment we arrived home, leaving me to count the wooden planks in the vaulted ceiling of Sonny's bedroom.

Mom has been watching the door to the café since we arrived, fifteen minutes before we were supposed to meet Dad. If they're dragging me here to tell me they're finally making the divorce official, it seems like a lot of pomp and circumstance to announce a split I thought had already been finalized. When she straightens her spine and tucks both hands under the tabletop, I turn to see Dad approaching. He's pressed and polished as ever in a short-sleeve button-up shirt and navy slacks. But it's disorienting to see him here; he's a mirage in the wrong timeline.

Dad hovers at the table, as if he's unsure whether the invitation to breakfast was genuine. Mom scoots aside before I do.

"Good morning, Len. How was your stay at the bed-and-breakfast?" Mom's tone is so forced and friendly that she sounds like a Disneyland employee.

Dad settles beside her, tentatively, and his posture is ramrod straight. "It was lovely, actually. It's a quaint town. I understand why you loved coming back every summer."

All three of us freeze, and I can tell by Dad's pained expression that he didn't mean it the way it sounded. But still, we're all aware of the real reason for her visits. I hold my breath, but Mom recovers.

"Carmela and Bob run a charming inn. I'm glad you were comfortable."

Dad fumbles with the oversize menu, concentrating on the page with a focus he typically reserves for classic literature. They trade small talk about what sounds good, whether the fruit plate includes local produce, if the kitchen would make an omelet without butter—as I stare at them, dumbfounded.

But I'm no longer going to play by their rules and swallow the words that need saying. I set my menu aside. "I suppose it's better that you two are on speaking terms finally, but if we're here for superficial chitchat, I'm not interested."

Mom looks at her hands, her shoulders by her ears, and Dad stares over my shoulder, a mock eye-contact trick he taught me before my first oral presentation in middle school.

"What's going on?" I ask.

Mom glances at Dad and then at me. "I've been doing a lot of thinking since you came to town. I know it hasn't always been smooth, and we still have a lot of work to do to heal, and I have a lot to make up for. But seeing you, spending time with you, having the chance to really know you again"—Mom swallows hard and blinks back a sheen of tears—"has made me believe in second chances. And your father's bravery in coming here, in reaching out to make amends, well, he's convinced me that I should seize this opportunity. You're right. I've been punishing myself, and I see how that hurts you, too. I've decided to take you up on your offer."

I look between them, hope building. "You'll seek treatment?"

Dad breaks into a grin, reaching across the table to grab my hand. "Even better. I got her an appointment at UCSF with the best neurologist in the state. And she's agreed to move home with you and start treatment in the city."

I go stock still as I absorb the news I would have celebrated mere months ago, my mouth ajar, my eyes wide. It takes a moment to process the implications, the possibilities, the limitations. But I guess I haven't evolved as much as I thought, because I do not say the words that need to be said. At least, not all of them. Instead, I smile and lean across the table to hug them both. I tell Mom I am overjoyed she changed her mind. That we'll kick Parkinson's ass, or at least throw spikes in front of its tires to slow it down.

I do not tell them that somehow, I fell in love with a man and was busy planning a new future for myself. Here.

Instead, I read through the pamphlets Dad brought along—about the specialized Parkinson's clinic at University of California, San Francisco, world-renowned doctors, surgical options, physical therapy, and support groups. He explains that since they're still legally married, she can use his insurance and have access to the best care.

Mom's eyes well with tears, her lip quivering as she looks at me across the table. "I love my people here. I have loved my life here. But you are the most important person of all, and I want us to have our second chance."

"I want that, too." I ache to rewrite our relationship—my most formative one. "But I told you I'd move here."

"Oh, honey," she says. "I can't tell you what that offer means to me, but you've already given up so much. You've put your life on hold and stayed with me for months. But I am the mother, and I refuse to let you make more sacrifices. That's my job. You can't give up your life. You're young, and have a business, friends, and a home."

"Neither of us wants you to do that," says Dad. And suddenly, they're a united front. As if they rewound my adulthood and pressed play on my childhood.

"But I want to." I sound like a petulant kid arguing with my parents after they've announced they know what's best for me.

"I am touched that you're willing. But I am unwilling to be that selfish."

"It's not selfish." I exhale and rub my clammy hands on my jeans. "When you asked me to move home with you before, I refused because I didn't want to intrude and ask you to give up your life for me. But yesterday, when you said you would move here, I realized you were determined to put aside what's best for you."

I need to tell them about Caleb, about what I want. "It's not like that—"

"It's better for everyone if I move. You get to keep your home and your life, and I'll get good treatment. These doctors may give me some hope. It's all seemed futile until now." She waves to the pamphlets and printouts littering the table. "I know that my condition is deteriorating and it's hard to get the care I need here. My greatest fear is that we reconnect and don't have enough time . . ." She trails off, leaving the rest unsaid. Her lifespan will be shorter, and her quality of life minimal. Our shot at a renewed relationship, abbreviated.

And that's the crux of this, isn't it? I can't sacrifice Mom's life for my relationship with Caleb. I made my original offer before my emotions were muddled. Objectively, this idea is the best option for Mom and me. My life—and her best shot at life—is in San Francisco.

But knowing the right choice doesn't make choosing it any easier. Suddenly, the coffee smells too bitter, and I'm nauseated by the scent of bacon and eggs wafting over from the adjacent table. I'm having a hard time catching my breath, but I'm smiling, pretending, keeping my hurt from my parents' prying eyes. Mom won't agree to come home with me if she knows the real reason I want to stay.

Last night, my future with Caleb flashed before my eyes as we swayed under the fairy lights, and now it's fading like a week-old dream. There's no reality in which Caleb can come with me. Abby is here, and her mom and siblings are here. He's immobile, at least until Abby graduates from high school. And even then, he loves Grand Trees and feels responsible for keeping Sonny's legacy alive.

He can't leave. I can't stay.

I know without a doubt that I'm in love with him—desperately in love with him—but it was foolish to think I could uproot my life and plant shallow roots in the town that broke my body and heart all those years ago. I should have known it would wound me again. That it would taunt me with joy and take it away.

"Oh, honey, why are you crying?" Mom asks, and I look up to see her pale features blurred before me.

Despite the honesty Mom and I have pledged to one another, it's important I get this lie right. I wipe my tears away and plaster on a smile. "I'm just so happy."

Abby sends news of the baby as Mom and Dad are finishing breakfast, and I conceal my lost appetite by pushing eggs around my plate.

I open the text and find photo after photo of a perfect newborn, tucked into Abby's arms, sandwiched between Lina and Ian, with all the kids crowded around the hospital bed.

Abby: My new sister! Maeve Jane. She's already sucking her thumb!!!!

She follows it up with a string of emojis, most of which I don't understand. It's a foreign language.

Me: Congratulations! Give your mom and Ian my love.

Mom leans over to show Dad the photos, and he reacts politely to images of a baby born to someone he doesn't know. I don't press too firmly on my bruise forming from seeing all the babies born as I stall out on my love life, highlighting my short window to have a family of my own closing. Jeff, Lina, Cassie . . . I'm at that age where everyone seems to be sharing baby announcements, so I should be used to it. But my phone dings again with one last picture from Abby. It's Caleb holding the baby in the crook of his arm. And I remember my daydream, the flicker of hope I fanned into a flame over the last few days. And my heart cracks along a new fault line.

I need to talk to him. I have to tell him I'm leaving.

I swallow back my tears and type back.

Me: Adorable. Is your dad there with you now?

Abby: We're in the car on the way back. I'm going to sleep for a week! Do you need him?

Me: Nope. No. Just wondering.

I can't tell him over the phone with Abby in the car. It'll have to wait.

But an hour later, when Mom and I head home, he's still not answering. Impatient and anxious, I head out for a walk, finding the path that leads to his cabin at the edge of the property. But he's not there.

It isn't until I trudge home that I realize my mistake. Caleb's truck is in the driveway. I race up the steps two at a time, swinging the door open, the hummingbird knocker clanging when I slam it behind me. Houdini charges, howling in glee, but I stop dead at the sound of Caleb's raised voice from the kitchen. "This seems like an extreme decision, given this is the first I've heard of it."

Shit. Shit. Shit. Caleb needed to hear this from me.

"But I'm getting treatment. I thought you'd be happy. This is what you've wanted." Mom must understand why this would be hard on Caleb. Losing Sonny, and now her.

And me. Even though she has no way of knowing that would hurt him, too.

"You know I'd drive you to any doctor, any day of the week. Go get treatment in San Francisco, or LA, or anywhere with the best doctors, but then come home."

I'm frozen in place, but I can't hide here forever. Houdini flagged my arrival. Caleb's back is to me, but Mom looks over his shoulder, her focus drifting to mine for a moment. She probably thinks I'm intruding on a personal conversation.

"Eden offered her home, and Len offered financial help."

"Len?" Caleb shouts. "After everything he put you through?"

"You don't know everything, Caleb."

He pushes away from the counter, pacing like a caged lion, running his hands through his hair. When he finally acknowledges me, his expression is riddled with enough anger to overpower every adoring look before it. His eyes flash like the tips of flames. "I know enough."

It's my cue—a begrudging but obvious invitation to the conversation.

"I thought you said you were moving here?" Caleb veers too close to too many truths.

"That's not fair to her. She doesn't want that," Mom jumps in, and I need to correct her, but Caleb and I can't have that conversation with Mom as a witness. If she knew how we felt about each other, I'm afraid she'd sacrifice herself. She'd stay here, fall into the same patterns of inertia, and avoid treatment. And I wouldn't be able to live with myself.

There's no situation in which I can have Caleb and live with the guilt of sacrificing Mom's health to keep him.

Caleb's watching me, waiting for me, and my heart is breaking as the betrayal crosses his face. "Yeah, why would she?"

Because of you, I want to shout. *Because I love you,* my face says. My instinct is to wrap my arms around him and whisper my wants into his ear—to untangle his hurt and place mine in his hands to fix.

This quiet is too loud. I sense Mom's focus on us as we have a conversation she can't hear.

"I want my mom to have the best care," I say, hoping he captures the subtext.

Caleb's gaze barrels into me, his jaw twitching. "Well, since you've got it all figured out, it doesn't sound like you need me." He swipes his keys off the counter, storming away.

"Caleb, wait!"

Caleb doesn't break stride, reaching the front door and slamming it in his wake. I turn to follow, but Mom reaches for my hand.

"Leave him be," she says. "It's between Caleb and me. He doesn't know how to deal with big feelings, so he gets mad, but he'll come around."

I'm not so sure of that. Mom knows him better than me, surely, but she can't know what he's feeling now.

I pat her hand. "Let me try." I don't wait for her to stop me or ask why his reaction has me rattled.

Caleb is already ushering Houdini into his truck when I jog down the porch. He freezes when he sees me and keeps his hand on the open door, a hair trigger away from running again. "So that's it? You're leaving and taking her with you?" I remember this tone—distant, bitter, and accusatory. He's guard dog Caleb again, and I'm the intruder.

I don't come closer even as I feel the pull of his gravity. "What was I supposed to say? That I changed my mind? That the offer no longer stands?"

"Tell her you're staying—that we can take care of her here."

I want that so much. But it isn't about what I want, or what he wants. It's about what Mom needs. "I don't think we can, at least not as well. She's gone years without treatment because there aren't any good options here. And she needs ongoing care. There's no cure, no six-month miracle treatment."

Caleb squints toward the forest as if searching for answers, or possibly just because he can't look at me. "It sounds like you've made up your mind." He swallows hard as he finally catches my gaze. "I thought we had something, but I guess I misunderstood."

I take a desperate step forward, reaching for his hand, but he yanks it back. "Caleb, you didn't misunderstand. We do have something, and I wish there were another way. But I need to do this for her."

I didn't let my mom care for me when I needed her. And I never really healed. I know this is what I need to do to finally heal us both. But I would stay with him if I thought either of us could live with ourselves if I did.

"You don't have to choose her over me just to prove you're not like her."

The accusation hits me like a slap, knocking the air out of me. The comparison is both cruel and too close to home. Every summer Mom left Grand Trees, she chose Dad and me over Sonny. When she finally left San Francisco that last time, she chose him. How many times did Mom face this dilemma? Was her decision as physically painful as mine is now?

"That's not what I'm doing."

"Well, you could have fooled me."

"Caleb, that's not fair. This is an impossible situation." I'm no martyr, and I'm not sacrificing my happiness to prove I'm better than her. I just want to do the right thing. A sob catches in my throat, but I swallow it back because I don't deserve his sympathy right now. I have to leave. But he's the one who's being left, and I'm only beginning to understand what a trigger that must be for him, because he has never been chosen.

"How could you have made this decision without me? Last night, you were going to move here and make it work? And now you're"—he looks over my shoulder toward the house, blinking rapidly—"taking off and taking your mom with you? Where does that leave me? Leave us?"

"I don't know," I admit. I've been in panic mode since my parents sprang this on me. I can't see beyond the fear, the loss, the cost. I'd just started to envision my life here with Caleb, but that fantasy has bloomed so quickly in the fertile soil of my adoration that moving forward without him feels like wandering into the desert—hopeless, lifeless.

"And yet you seem sure of this plan—so sure you made it without even talking to me." His jaw ticks. I want to throw my arms around him and beg him to kiss me and fix this. But he looks so furious that I'm not sure how he would respond. We need some time to calm down and figure this out.

"We can't leave right away, though. It'll take some time for Mom to pack up and say goodbye. We still have a few weeks—"

Caleb barks out an incredulous laugh. "Yesterday, you told me you were staying forever, and now I'm supposed to be happy with a few more weeks. We really are in different places." His gaze lands on me, and I can see the hurt he's hiding behind the anger.

"We aren't. I just need some time to think and—"

"Well, I don't need time. I'm all in. And the fact that you'd go along with this plan without considering me—or us—well, I guess that tells me all I need to know."

He slides into his truck, closing the door behind him with a finality that grabs me by the throat.

CHAPTER 33

After lighting this match, Dad heads home the next day, leaving us to put out the fire. It takes us two weeks to pack Mom up and say goodbye to Grand Trees. And it takes the town several attempts to say goodbye to her, with three going-away parties filled with lamentations, nostalgia, and gifts.

Caleb and I haven't spoken directly since our argument. As painful as the silence is, it may be easier this way because time hasn't offered any epiphanies about how we could make it work while I care for Mom in the city and Caleb raises Abby in Grand Trees. Every time I attempt to figure out a solution, I run into a brick wall, like a labyrinth without an exit. A long-distance relationship would require that I put our future—and my desire to have kids—on hold indefinitely. When would we even see each other while we care for others and are stuck in different worlds? I can't stay. Caleb can't leave.

A few more weeks of pretending would make me fall deeper in love with him and make the inevitable heartache even more acute. As it stands, I'm barely surviving it. Caleb is so hurt that he's acting like the asshole I met when I arrived. It doesn't make me love him less, but it does remind me that relationships are difficult, and it takes two people to make them work. If he won't even speak to me directly, how the hell can we figure out the impossible?

Adelaide spends most of her time with us at Sonny's house, alternating between tears and well-wishes as she helps Mom make decisions about what she can leave behind. I learn the house belongs to Caleb as Sonny's legal heir. But I have no idea what he'll do with it. Perhaps he'll move in or leave it as a shrine to Sonny in the same way Mom has done.

Caleb swings by every day on his way to camp, but he's all business and logistics. He wants to know when Mom's leaving, whether the neighborhood is safe, if my house is appropriate for her mobility issues, how long until she'll see a doctor, and what help she needs from him to move. He directs all his questions to Mom, who doesn't know half the answers. He won't even look at me. And every time he avoids me, it shoots another bullet into my heart.

I save my tears every night for my empty bed, or the shower, when I collapse on the cool porcelain and let my pain escape and circle the drain.

Abby doesn't come to visit, and I overhear Caleb tell Mom that she's having a hard time accepting the move. She doesn't respond to my texts. Abby's outrage and silence must press on the barely healed bruise of my teenage rejection, but I console myself that I'm doing the right thing for my mother.

The day before the move, Caleb finally speaks to me. It's Friday night, what would have been game night if Abby came around anymore. But like he's done every day for the last few weeks, he comes alone and is so stingy with his words that I'm desperate for the sound of his voice. I'm in the living room, wrapping portraits in Bubble Wrap while Mom and Adelaide finish sorting through the kitchen. Caleb didn't say hello to me on his way in but pauses in the entryway on his way out, addressing me as an afterthought. Meanwhile, I've had one ear and eye on him since he arrived.

"Is it all right if I bring Houdini along when I move your mom's stuff?"

I set the bundle of paintings aside and glance up at him from where I'm perched on the floor. "You're coming?" I'm startled, rattled, and thrilled at the idea that I'll get Caleb for one more day, even if he's so cold that he doesn't resemble the Caleb I fell for.

"You need my truck, don't you?" He folds his arms across his chest in a wide stance—guarded, defensive. He's the Caleb I met this spring, the pit bull ready for a fight. But I know better. He's still the same guy who softened among the wildflowers and redwoods, who caught me as I fell to earth, who touched me with reverence and wonder. Every time he stops by, determined to ignore me, it takes all my resolve not to reach for his hand, inhale his scent, beg for his forgiveness with my mouth on his skin. To tell him I'll stay if he'll just look at me again.

But I know I can't stay, so I say instead, "That would be helpful," and fight the sting of tears that are always ready to strike these days.

"Can I bring the dog?"

Houdini is curled up beside me, his muzzle in my lap. I scratch under his chin, and he releases a pleased little groan. "Of course."

"I'll only stay long enough to unload. We won't be in your way long."

I drop my voice, aware that Adelaide and Mom have stopped talking in the kitchen. "It's a long drive. You should stay the night. It'll be late."

"I'm not staying at your house, Eden." He opens the front door, and Houdini scrambles out of my lap to follow him. "I'll be back tomorrow morning at six."

And he's gone.

I'm left staring at the closed door—a habit I'm forming—when Mom and Adelaide join me in the living room.

Mom slides onto the couch behind me, resting a hand on my shoulder. "I'm sorry he's taking it out on you, honey. I was hoping you two would find a way to get along by now, but this threw him for a loop. I suppose it's easier for him to blame you than me."

Adelaide crouches on the coffee table, positioned in my direct line of sight. "He can be hard to win over and sometimes surly, but it takes a lot to really upset him." She levels me with a meaningful look that reminds me of her former life as a high school counselor. "I've only seen him this out of sorts a couple of times. When he showed up here as a kid all angry and alone. And when Sonny died."

I blink back the stubborn tears and fiddle with the packing tape, making an ineffectual attempt at securing the Bubble Wrap to the portraits I'd set aside earlier. I don't need Adelaide to tell me I'm hurting Caleb. I feel his broken heart, skipping beats, out of sync, as mine shatters alongside his.

"But I'm not dying. Well, not quickly anyway," Mom says, missing Adelaide's meaning, as Adelaide intended. "I have a better chance of being around for him and Abby if I make the move and get treatment. And it's not as if I won't visit."

"I'm sure he knows that, Nicolette." Adelaide strikes the balance between soothing and savage. "But you know that boy. He's had a lot of important people in his life who didn't choose him. But there's no one who loves his people more than he does"—she gives me a knowing glance—"and once he loves, he loves fierce and has a hard time letting go."

CHAPTER 34

Caleb sets a box on the floor of the room Mom will now call home and casts an assessing eye over the space. It's spare. Jeff and I never decorated in here. But there's a bed and a blank canvas for Mom to make the room her own.

True to his word, Caleb stormed in at sunrise but surprised us all by bringing Abby along. She is dressed in head-to-toe black and has been hiding in the hood of her sweatshirt like a turtle all day as she moved boxes into the truck, caravanned to San Francisco, and off-loaded Mom's belongings. Abby's been present, but not happy about it. And honestly, I'm impressed with her commitment to protest. She doesn't do anything by half. I'm happy she's here, even if it's just physically. I don't know if Mom could have survived another silent send-off by a betrayed teen.

We left early this morning—Caleb and Abby in his truck, Mom and me in my car. It's been a long, grueling day, and my leg has been killing me. The pain always flares up when I'm at an emotional low.

It's already early evening, and Caleb is rushing to make good on his promise of spending as little time here as possible. In two hours, he has unpacked the truck, assembled furniture, and flashed a laser pointer at every imperfection in my home. He's efficient when he's pissed off. And I'm terrified of the ticking clock—when he'll be out of my life.

"I don't like that ledge in the doorway," he says. "It's a tripping hazard."

"I'll have it fixed."

"Does that smoke detector work?"

"I think so." I stack a box of Mom's clothes on the dresser Caleb just pulled out of my garage and assembled.

He drops his voice. "The hallways aren't wide enough for a wheelchair."

"Hopefully, she won't need one for a long time." I turn to face him. If we're saying goodbye today, he's working hard to make it easier. I still want to kiss him, but I also want to smack him.

Beyond the magic of Grand Trees, maybe I can pretend he's just a pain in my ass.

He's had something to say about everything—that my neighborhood is too hilly (hello, we're in San Francisco!), that my front door isn't secure enough, the shower over the bathtub is dangerous for Mom, the bed is too high, the street parking will make it difficult for her to get to and from the car, among other gripes I've ignored.

"Your house is really sterile," he grumbles, squinting at the span of empty wall space.

"This was a guest room."

"Doesn't explain the rest of the house." He pokes his head into the hallway. "Why is it so empty? Doesn't it make you sad?"

The melancholy invades as if on command. He's right. It does make me sad. But not for the reasons he thinks but because I'll always remember how full my house felt for the one day he was in it. My fingers twitch at the need to touch him once more.

"Hawthorne women, I come bearing gifts." I snap my head at the sound of Cassie's voice.

When I turn the corner, I throw myself into her. "Cassie." I hold back a sob.

Cassie extends her arms, clutching two take-out bags stuffed with something that smells like food from my favorite Chinese restaurant.

"Shoot, sorry. I shouldn't attack you." I jump back and squeal at the sight of her baby bump.

"Attack away. I'm tough, and so is this little bean." She sets the bags on the entryway table and hugs me properly.

"You're really pregnant," I whisper, still in shock that she'll be a mother in four months. We're thirty-five, so it shouldn't be such a surprise; half our friends have become parents already, but it hits differently now that it's Cassie taking the plunge.

"I hope so. It would be tragic if this were an undigested burrito, which is all my parasite wants me to eat." She tugs me tighter, whispering into my hair, "Are you okay?"

I bite my lip and nod. She had the unfortunate luck of answering my phone call two weeks ago and had to listen to the unintelligible ramblings of my heartbreak in real time.

"Nicolette," Cassie sings when Mom emerges from the back patio. She moves to her, giving her a tight squeeze. "Look at you! All healed and ready for our hot girl summer in the city."

Mom guffaws and blushes, and the two of them chat like they haven't spent two decades apart. Sometimes I'm envious of Cassie for her ability to iron out the rough edges with humor, and I'm indebted to her for it today. I'm hopeful for the first time in weeks. I will be okay. My life is fuller than when I drove to Grand Trees three months ago. I have Mom back. My divorce is a distant memory; it's lost its power over me.

But Caleb stretched the borders of my world, and this fuller life is still too empty.

As if summoned, Caleb appears at the edge of the hallway and leans against the jamb.

"Well, hello there, handsome." Cassie grins and greets him like an old friend, stepping closer to wrap him in a hug. He startles, patting her back in an uncomfortable gesture that would make me chuckle if I weren't so sad. They met once, for five minutes after she and Ian rescued us from the felled tree, but Cassie doesn't believe in strangers. I watch as she leans in and whispers something into his ear before pulling back abruptly to wave to the entryway table. "I brought Chinese food. You all must be starving."

"Thanks," he says, "But we've gotta get on the road."

"You're driving back now? Didn't you just get here?" Cassie flicks her focus to me for a beat, but I look away.

"I think we've done all we can." He scans the room and peers down the hall into the kitchen before walking to the French doors that open onto the back patio. "Abby, come say goodbye."

This is it. He's leaving. And taking half my heart with him. I'm paralyzed in place, trying to memorize him—the way his hair curls on his neck, how the soft skin under his eyes turns purple when he's tired, how he bites that scar on his lip when he's thinking, how he kneads his shoulder after a long day.

I don't see Cassie move, but she's somehow at my side, holding my hand. "Let's go set up dinner." She tugs me toward the kitchen and swipes the bags of food off the table.

I trip after her as Caleb says, "Abby, c'mon," firmer this time.

We sneak by Caleb on our way to the kitchen as Abby barrels into the family room, a whir of black and an eruption of sobs. She rushes to Mom, wrapping her arms around her neck and burying her face in her sweater.

We all freeze. I sneak a glance at Caleb, who looks like his chest just caved in at the sight of his daughter's devastation. But I can't comfort either of them. I'm the reason they're in pain.

"Oh, my beautiful girl, I will miss you so much." Mom smooths Abby's hair down her back and holds her tight.

"I don't want to leave yet," Abby cries. "I don't want to say goodbye."

Mom sways, rocking her, whispering words I can't hear, but Abby's hysteria escalates.

Cassie leans toward Caleb. "Maybe you should give her some time," she says, and Caleb pinches his eyes closed and flexes his jaw, letting his head fall against the threshold. "Eden has a pullout couch in the office."

I think he's ignoring her until he asks, "Is there a deck of cards around here?"

Cassie snorts and whispers, "What?"

"I have a few," I say.

Caleb pushes away, striding over to Mom and Abby. "We can stay one night. How does Chinese food and game night sound?"

Relief washes over me—treacherous, dangerous relief—and it gives me a foolish sense of hope.

CHAPTER 35

At the end of the night, Abby is fifteen dollars richer. She won every hand of Texas Hold 'Em, heckling us with each victory. I suspect Caleb let her win, which is very un-Caleb-like. He typically counts cards like a shark. But it was a relief to hear her laugh, to see the light return to her smile, to watch Caleb forget his anger, and to pretend it wasn't our goodbye.

I collapse into bed at midnight, trying not to think about Caleb shirtless on my couch. Although he's just down the hall, he feels miles away—and tomorrow, he'll be gone.

After three months of a star-filled sky, the sounds and lights of the city keep sleep at bay.

But I must fall asleep at some point because I wake to a dim beam of light pouring in from the hall and a blurry figure in my open doorway. I scoot up against my headboard as Caleb closes the door and sits on the edge of my bed, facing away, his elbows on his knees.

He doesn't speak at first, and I suspect I'm hallucinating, so I don't utter a word. If it's a dream, I don't want to wake and risk losing another moment with him. My instinct is to touch him—to press him against my skin and cotton sheets and say goodbye by pulling him inside me one last time. When we meet next—if we meet—we'll be strangers again, and that realization lands like a blunt knife in my gut.

I focus on the long curve of his back as he sits bowed beside me and listen to him breathe. And I wait.

He clears his throat, but his words come out gravelly. "I wanted to tell you that I understand. It hurts like hell, but I get it."

But suddenly, I don't. Why couldn't I have found a solution that didn't propel me to the other side of the state? Why didn't I tell Mom that I was serious about staying? Why couldn't I tell her that I found my soulmate?

"Can you remind me? Because it's hard to remember my noble intentions when you're this close to me."

He chuckles and turns, and my skin flushes at the sight of his smile—warm and wistful in the half dark. Caleb tangles his fingers in mine, and I hold on like I'm hanging from a cliff and he's the rope.

He exhales a shaky breath. "Shit, I've missed you."

My emotions are churning, need and loss and regret and panic threatening to topple the house of cards I've built on my flimsy resolve. I don't want to go back to being strangers. I've never felt so comfortably myself as I have with him. And I worry I'll become a stranger to myself, too. "I think I might miss you forever," I admit.

Caleb closes the space between us and cups my jaw in his palms. "So let's figure this out."

It's too easy to get drunk on him. When he looks at me like this, I believe in fanciful things. When he puts his hands on me, I believe in miracles. He's the magic of Grand Trees that Sonny sang about.

"I want to," I choke out as hope bubbles up in the tide of impossibility.

He leans in, brushing his mouth against mine like we're sealing a promise. But I fear it's transient. I chase it, threading my fingers in his hair and pulling him closer, begging his kiss to convince me that nothing else matters. Every sensation colludes to persuade me—the scratch of his beard, the rough texture of his hands, the uneven bow of his lips, the scent of Grand Trees clinging to his skin. I draw him into my lungs and map the landscape of him.

I want to make it work because we work. Even when we're bickering, at odds, driving each other crazy, we work.

But over the last few weeks, I've twisted my mind around every possibility. Our distance will create a gulf too wide to scale. Physical distance, yes. But emotional distance, too. I know what life is like in Grand Trees—slow and languid. And I know what life is like here—frenetic, consuming. And now I'm Mom's primary caretaker. Even if Caleb and I can figure out how to see each other regularly—and that's a big if—I don't know how we can build a future together when we're living in different worlds, on different timelines.

Caleb pulls back, pressing his forehead to mine. "I can feel you thinking."

"I want to figure it out. But I don't know how." My words are so quiet. Maybe if he can't hear me, he won't be able to confirm my greatest fears.

"I don't know yet either, but we're both stubborn enough to do it."

I laugh, but it sounds like a sob as emotion clogs my throat. "You can't leave Grand Trees. Abby needs both her parents there. And I can't leave the city, because Mom needs to be here."

Caleb traces my bottom lip with his thumb. "So we'll do long distance. I told you from day one, I'll take whatever you are willing to give. Vacations, weekends, or a few weeks in the summer."

I let myself imagine the possibility of surprise visits, Sundays spent in sheets, living in anticipation, late-night phone calls, last-minute cancellations, disappointments, years of stasis.

It sounds like the agreement Sonny and my mom made before chance intervened. Caleb and I deserve more than that.

"And we go on like that for how long? Squeezing in visits around work, Abby's activities, and Mom's treatments? Seeing each other less and less, making apologies and excuses until we resent each other?"

He shifts back from where he's perched on the side of the bed, and I worry he'll walk away, but he turns, slips in beside me, and wraps an arm over my shoulders. I sink against him, resting my head in the crook of his neck, and he places a kiss on my forehead.

"It isn't forever. I could move here eventually."

I can picture Caleb in the city about as well as I can imagine Houdini in the Westminster Dog Show. But even if I could imagine it, it's not possible.

"In five years when Abby goes off to college?"

"Yeah." His earnestness—his certainty—pierces me right in the heart. I want to ski behind the wake of his confidence, but I know how these things play out. Good intentions collide with reality. And I'll miss out on a real life while waiting for the fairy tale.

"I'll be over forty by then." It's a risky endeavor to wait that long to try to start a family. What if I can't conceive right away or at all? I would have to sacrifice the last years of likely fertility and wait for a man to be ready—again.

He laughs. "So?"

"Caleb." I exhale and sit upright, turning to face him. I need to put some distance between us to think straight. The tempting warmth of his skin will make me promise a future neither of us can deliver. "I want kids. I want a family. I gave that up for a man before, and I can't do it again."

"I'm not asking you to give up anything. I want more kids someday, too." Caleb reaches for my hand.

"Women don't have the luxury of someday."

We sit in silence for a while, my hand in his, and I watch his brain working. Perhaps he's hitting a brick wall in the labyrinth, turning back, trying to find a new way forward, but I've walked every path, and I'm just waiting for him to meet me at the dead end I've been stuck at for weeks.

"If you want to make this work, it's going to feel like jumping off that platform. You need to trust we can figure it out."

Trust requires hope, though. It requires faith that the future will be better than the past. Nothing in my life has shown that to be true. And nothing can top the perfect months I've spent with this man. I don't trust it can get better than that.

"When I broke my leg," I begin, tentatively, "I was determined to dance again. But the first time I tried, I realized I'd never be able to, not the way I wanted to, and it killed the love I had for it. I think that was the worst part—the lost hope."

Caleb swipes his thumb across my cheek, catching a tear. "You told me once that it's not about perfection. The magic is in the attempt."

I wrap my hands around his neck and pull him close. It's too tempting to believe that we can make us work. But I'm not sure even he believes it. He wants it, but want isn't faith. He skates his mouth across my cheekbones, erasing my tears as they escape. His lips brush over my eyelids, down the bridge of my nose, and finally land on my mouth as it trembles.

"Yes, but with you, I don't want to just sway to the music. We're so much more than that. I don't want to become some mediocre version of us."

He shakes his head. "It doesn't have to be that way."

"If we're always waiting to see each other, waiting to start our life together, it will be. We can't make each other our priority because we're both responsible for other people. With the miles between us, I don't see how we can make it work without resenting each other eventually. I want to remember us like this. I don't want to ruin us by fighting a losing battle." I can't wait for him for another five years. The only commitment we'd be making would be to break each other's hearts slowly.

The pressure in my chest is rising, and my body is too small to contain the pain. He told me the key to surviving heartbreak is to fill your life with people you love more than the person who broke it. But I'm afraid I'll never find someone I love more than him.

I thread my fingers in his hair and draw him to me, begging him to give him one more night, to leave his scent on my sheets, to imprint his memory here.

"But if the world was ending, you'd come to me, right?" he says.

"If the world were ending, I'd run to you." It's the only promise I can make, the only one I'm sure I'd keep. My mouth opens on his, suddenly frantic, and I climb into his lap, sinking close until I can feel the way his body fits against mine—begs for mine.

We lose ourselves in a kiss, and instinct takes charge. Over the last few months, we've learned and cataloged each other, and we know where our souls meet our bodies. I know he's sensitive at the juncture of his neck and shoulder, and he loves it when I sink my teeth into his collarbone. He's learned that I love to be tempted and teased. And all these intimacies are about to gather dust. Maybe I can let him go if I have him one more time and snap my mental camera shutter on each perfect frame.

But when I reach for the hem of his shirt, he captures my hands in his shaking fist—stopping me. "I can't, Eden."

My body bursts into flames, sparked by rejection and humiliation. I scramble off his lap, but he reaches for my hands, scooting closer as I retreat. He presses his forehead to mine when I drop my head to hide my anguish.

"I need you to do something for me." His voice is tight, and I realize I'm tasting his tears, too.

"Anything."

He squeezes my hands. "I told you I'd take whatever you're willing to give, but I won't survive nothing. If we can't try to make us work, I need you to really let me go. I can't be your acquaintance, and I can't be polite. When I visit your mom, I'll have to stay somewhere else and try not to run into you, because I can't exchange 'how are yous' in the kitchen or handshakes on the porch. When I need an update on your mom's health, I'm gonna talk to your dad or Cassie. It's not because I won't be thinking of you, or missing you, or dreaming of you. I just know my limits. And you're mine."

And this—this is the impact after the fall that I've been fearing. His request breaks me. But this time, it's my rib cage that shatters. Shards of bone are piercing my heart and lungs, making it impossible to catch my breath through my sobs.

I have to let him go. I have to do what he's asking, but this loss may be my undoing.

When he captures my mouth in a featherlight kiss that tastes of salt and sorrow, I know it's goodbye. "I love you," he whispers against my lips.

"I love you," I say for the first—last—time. The words inflate like a balloon in my throat, and I'm choking on all the love waiting to be punctured.

He unfolds my hands from his and shifts away, his weight lifting from the bed like an anchor coming loose at sea. When I catch my breath and open my eyes, he's gone, his shape already absorbed by shadow.

CHAPTER 36

Time stops. And races ahead.

It's been hours, days, weeks, months since our goodbye. My sheets don't smell like him, and he didn't leave anything behind. But my blank walls and cold bed all conspire to highlight his absence.

Mom visits the fancy neurologist Dad found, and she gives us hope and a tentative plan: a cocktail of medications and possible surgery in the months to come. Mom begins physical therapy and dance classes for Parkinson's patients. In exchange, I let her teach me to paint. I am a terrible artist, but she insists she's an inferior dancer and says it makes us even.

I seek comfort in having her home, having the chance to make up for our lost years.

I throw Cassie a duck-and-daffodil-themed baby shower and help her search for baby names. I am relieved I can hold her joy while clutching my grief.

Adelaide brings Abby for a long weekend before the school year starts. It's painful to see how much I've missed in just a few months. She got her braces off, which makes her look even more like her father. Her smile is blinding, both beautiful and torturous. In a blink, she's older, taller, wiser—her girlhood slipping away in a summer. I hang on every word, hoping for news of Caleb: He covered for Ian most of the summer, working sixty to seventy hours a week. He was awarded three of the grants we wrote and will begin forest restoration this fall, which will keep him busier. He's been tired and, Abby says, "a little off." But there's no amount of information that can quench my thirst for him. And Adelaide watches me like the counselor she is, so I retreat. She's kept our secret, just as Caleb said she would. But she's assessing me, judging me, even though I did exactly as she asked. I convinced Mom to seek treatment.

But I also happened to break two hearts in the process.

I know Caleb and Mom talk. There are times when I catch her side of the conversation and feel faint from longing, drawn to pluck the phone from her hand just to hear his voice. But if I cave, I'll have to start the clock over—zero days since I last succumbed to Caleb.

I drift through my white-walled house like the ghost of the girl who found happiness for a season.

Mom mentions how hard it must be for me to live in the house Jeff and I shared. She thinks I'm mourning him. But I barely remember him. How did we spend our time? What did we talk about? Laugh about? Fight about?

I do remember the vibrant colors and textures of Caleb's home. I remember the clean pine scent of the trail that led to him. I remember his laugh lines and scars, his rough hands and soft words. I remember how I'd exhale when he held me.

I've been mourning him longer than he was mine.

But I know I made the right choice, not just for Mom but for me. Mom is thriving—physically, mentally—as is our relationship. I'm finding the rhythm of forgiveness. It's not an epiphany, I realize now. It's a practice. And practicing grace has loosened the ball in my stomach and neutralized my numbness. Absolution isn't a gift I'm offering to Mom; it's a kindness I'm granting myself.

All those months ago, I sensed that I needed to travel back to where everything fell apart in order to begin again. My grief and resentment were poisoning me, killing my ability to connect and care. Over the last few months, I've worked through my scar tissue causing the block. And

I was right—it's a relief to feel alive again, even if it means I experience every pang, throb, and ache from losing Caleb.

~

Mom and I step through the glass doors into the lobby as a trio of young ballerinas step out of the private hallway. Their impeccable posture, willowy limbs, and pink tights peeking out under street clothes would give them away anywhere, but this is their natural habitat.

They sneak past us, giggling, and my chest constricts. I avoided everything dance adjacent for twenty years, but Mom's homecoming has given me an opportunity to heal another wound. Dropping Mom off for her weekly Parkinson's dance class is exposure therapy. On the way here, we passed the War Memorial Opera House, where larger-than-life banners highlight perfectly posed ballerinas in *Swan Lake*. In the lobby, I hear the distant allegros on the piano and the buzz of students talking about class, unmarred by injury or disillusionment. Every Saturday night, Mom shows me what she learned, and I fix her alignment or teach her something new. We dance in the kitchen and laugh at ourselves. She fights for balance, and I struggle to extend my leg. But we dance. And we heal.

An older woman shuffles by with her caretaker. "Are you ready to boogie, Nicolette?"

"Always," Mom says. "I'll see you in there, Linda."

"I filled your water bottle and packed a snack." I hand Mom her tote bag.

She slides it onto her shoulder and smiles at me. "You're such a good dance mom. At least you didn't have to sew my pointe shoes."

"Keep working and maybe you'll earn yours."

She guffaws. "Can you imagine?"

The thought makes me smile, and I check my watch. "I'll be back in two hours."

"Your dad is going to pick me up today. Sorry, I thought I told you. There's an exhibit at the SFMOMA he thought I might like."

"Oh, really?" Their mini adventures around the city are becoming a pattern. Last week, they visited a nursery and brought home an avocado tree for my backyard. Dad stops by every morning, teaching Mom about the native flowers he planted for me after I let Jeff's bougainvillea die. Sometimes, I wake to the sound of their gentle conversation—my childhood in retrograde.

"You're welcome to join us. We just thought you'd like a free afternoon."

"You two should go ahead. I have lunch with Cass, and then I might run some errands." Cassie and I have eschewed Sunday brunch for a weekly lunch on Saturday while Mom is at class.

I smooth a strand of hair that's come free from Mom's top knot. It's not required, but I couldn't bring her to a ballet class without giving her the traditional smooth bun, ballet skirt, and classic wrap sweater. Everyone else shows up in sweats and T-shirts, but ballerina daughters don't let their mothers dress inappropriately for ballet class. That discipline was driven into my DNA.

"Thanks, honey. I love you." Mom turns toward the turnstile that leads to the studios.

"Love you more. Will you be home for dinner?" I call after her.

Mom stops and grins at me from over her shoulder. "We might grab a bite afterward. Do I have a curfew?"

This role reversal is a full one-eighty. "All right. Have fun. Be safe."

She waves, and I watch as she disappears into the back hallway before I exit. It's a short walk to Hayes Street, where I'm meeting Cassie at a café serving all manner of carbs to satisfy her pregnancy cravings. No doubt she'll want to grab ice cream afterward, too.

While I walk, I text Dad to confirm his plans. I don't want to leave Mom stranded if they got their signals crossed. Dad gives me a full rundown of the exhibit and their reservations at some new buzzy restaurant in North Beach. I don't know if their new dynamic is romantic or platonic, and I'm trying not to get too involved. It's long past the point where my parents' marriage should be my concern.

Either way, though, they both seem . . . content. Like the world has settled on its rightful axis after two decades of spinning backward. I know it's not that simple. Mom loved Sonny. She loved the life she shared with him. But my parents cram words into the hours they share, compensating for the silence that stretched taut over twenty years and three hundred miles.

It makes me realize Mom told me the truth all those months ago—she loved them both, the man she married and the man she never could.

It should give me hope that it's possible to find new love while yearning for Caleb from afar. But it doesn't. Because I know, deep in my bones, that my love for Caleb is ivy, wound around my heart, choking any chance for anything else to take root.

And I'm not willing to settle for another small love.

So I am considering my next options.

I spot Cassie at a wood table near the front of the café, sitting in the path of the breeze through the open doorway. Fall in San Francisco notoriously ushers in the warmest weather of the year. Cass typically lives for it, spending as much time outside as she can to soak up the sun like a cold-blooded reptile. But now in her third trimester, she's begging for the relief of winter.

"Hey." I slide my purse over the back of the chair.

"You're sure?" Cassie asks without preamble.

I tilt my head, trying to figure out what she's talking about, and then I remember the text I'd sent her last night, which she never responded to.

"Not really," I say. "But it's time to stop waiting for life to happen to me."

The server places a glass of water in front of each of us and tells us she'll be back to take our order.

Cassie scrolls her phone, and I assume she's looking at the link I had sent her yesterday—a sperm bank that our mutual friends, Xochitl and

Lorelei, used to conceive their daughter. "Honestly, it's a racket. Most men would be happy to knock you up for free."

"Yeah, well, most men aren't screened for STDs, genetic diseases, criminal records, and psychosis."

"You know I'll support you no matter what. I'll give you all the hand-me-downs, let you learn from all the mistakes I'm about to make, and hold your hand in the delivery room. But do you really want to do this without a partner?"

"I don't have a choice." I take a swig of my water and place my napkin in my lap before realigning the silverware.

Cassie winces, and I know what's coming. She's about to detonate a truth bomb as only she can.

"I don't think you're in the right headspace to make this decision."

"I don't have time to wait." I look out the window at the bright-blue sky. I wonder what it's like in Grand Trees right now. I've never been there in autumn. "It could take me years to conceive. Remember how hard it was for Anh?"

"You're thirty-five, not fifty. You have time. Give it a year or two."

If I don't try soon, by the time I have a baby—if I have a baby—Mom might not be well enough to be an engaged grandmother.

"I gave Jeff fifteen." I know women can have babies into their forties, but at thirty-five, fresh out of a loveless marriage and a whirlwind love affair, I can't envision the years ahead as an opportunity for love, partnership, and happily ever after. Instead, I feel the batteries of my biological clock dying prematurely from wasted patience. If I want to do this, I need to do it soon, and on my own.

"But Caleb proves you can meet someone new. You can start again—"

"I won't meet anyone else." When I hazard a glance, Cassie's eyes are narrowed on me. If waiting felt like a viable option, I would have waited for Caleb, not some mystery man without a chance to make my pulse race the way he did.

"You live in extremes, you know that? Maybe you won't feel about someone the way you felt about Caleb, but you could find someone who makes you pee yourself laughing or owns a private jet and sneaks you off to Paris. You don't know what the future holds. But when you can't see it, you think there's nothing there."

Ouch. "Take it easy with the harsh truths, girl. I don't even have a drink yet." I chuckle to stave off a cry, because, man, her tough love is rough.

She folds her hands on the table and straightens her shoulders. "No. You need to hear this. You thought you couldn't dance again because you wouldn't be a prima ballerina. So, you quit entirely. You convinced yourself that romantic love was fickle because your parents' marriage imploded, so you married a bland man you didn't really love. And now that you've finally had your heart broken, you decide to never open up again. But you broke your own stupid heart by clinging to absolutes. If you truly think you will never be happy without Caleb, then be with him in whatever way you can."

The water I just swallowed churns in my stomach. Why is it that the people you love most always know which weapon will wound you? Cassie with the mirror in the café. It's easy for her, though. She heals from heartbreak like a lizard regenerating its tail.

"I can't be with him. Caleb works a bazillion hours and has his daughter to care for. And the longest I can leave Mom alone is a couple of hours—"

Cassie holds up her hand like a stop sign and closes her eyes as if I'm the most tiresome person in the world. "Take your mom with you some weekends. I'm sure she'd love to visit when she's feeling up to it. Or leave her with me, or your dad, who, by the way, is clearly still in love with her and is apparently still her husband." Her voice cracks in a manic cackle. "Or meet in the middle for a quick hookup in a roadside motel. Or in his truck, since that seems to work for you."

"Cassie!" I look around the restaurant and shush her, regretting ever telling her anything. "I can't choose a part-time boyfriend over my chance to have a baby. I gave it up for Jeff, and I'm not doing it again."

Cassie holds both palms up, tilting them like a scale. She drops a hand. "All." And switches them. "Nothing." She releases a long, dramatic sigh. "You're lucky I'm always on your side. Because you are your own worst enemy and need me to protect you from yourself. Figure it out, Eden. Because this self-imposed suffering is painful to watch."

$\sim$

I contemplate Cassie's words as I lie awake that night, waiting for Mom and Dad. When they do finally stumble in, long after the curfew I would have imposed had I taken Mom's teasing seriously, I tune out their hushed whispers and stifled laughter.

Their social life is more active than mine these days.

The streetlights stream in through my thin curtains and splash against the far wall, where Mom has hung one of her new pieces. She started painting again last month, not in her signature realistic style but abstract landscapes with bold bands of calming colors. The broad piece on my wall is a watercolor. By day, it looks like the tree line of a forest from afar. But with the gray scale of night coloring the palette, the painting is also a cityscape in shadow.

Maybe joy and suffering are the same subjects brushed in different hues—not *either or*, but *both and*. Coexistent. They are lovers with clasped hands and entwined bodies.

Maybe in order to have one, you must embrace, accept the other. The beauty is not in the ever after but in trusting the now.

When Mom's hands stopped cooperating, she let her talent evolve. When one life fell apart, she found solace in another. And now she's come home, seeking joy out of what used to be a source of grief. I was furious at her for moving on when our family fell apart, but perhaps I can learn something from her resilience. She preserved her love for me, for my dad, even as she fostered a life with Sonny. And now, she's still mourning Sonny but refusing to miss this opportunity to reconnect with Dad and me. She kept a candle burning for us, and it's growing into a flame.

Mom has no guarantees—not her health, her long-term future, or her relationship status—but she's embracing the moment. She has my dad, a medical team, new friends, her art, and a second-chance love affair with the city that raised her. She's rebuilding her life here, and I am not her only anchor.

As hard as it was to hear, Cassie spoke some truths today. I cut Caleb out of my life because I couldn't have all of him. I'm contemplating having a child alone because I can't guarantee I'll have a partner to share that joy with. I avoided dance because I couldn't perform my chosen discipline at the highest level. I decided that if I couldn't have Caleb in the way I wanted him, I couldn't have him at all.

I wonder whether I've lived my life in black and white precisely because Mom lived hers in shades of gray.

I drift to sleep with the answer just out of reach, as my mind spins toward an elusive solution and my heart swells with possibility.

CHAPTER 37

I wake with a jolt when it's full dark, my pulse pounding in my temples, as a shrill siren blares on my phone. I have a sensation of acute vertigo; I'm disoriented and queasy. I scramble for my phone, seeing the earthquake warning a moment before I realize the ground is rolling under me, rattling my ceiling fan and forcing me to grip the bedposts until I find my bearings. And I know—just as I knew our little tremor in the woods was a small one—this is the big one. My mouth goes dry as it continues, and I cannot ride it out in here.

Mom.

I scrabble from my bed as the quake dissipates, finding my balance before I dart across the hall to her room. I swing the door open to find her fast asleep.

"Mom, Mom!" I rush to her bedside, flicking on the lamp on her nightstand. "Are you okay?"

Her eyes flutter open before panic strikes her face. "What's wrong?"

"There was an earthquake. A big one. You didn't feel it?"

Mom sits up and swings her legs to the wooden floor. She glances around. "Are you sure? Nothing is out of place."

I follow her gaze around the room. She's filled it with knickknacks and art, and everything is in its cluttered place. But my heart is still galloping, warning me of danger just out of sight.

And it lands. "Dad."

Our family home was built on landfill and prone to liquefaction, a term so frightening that I often dreamed of getting trapped in quicksand during my childhood. I race back to my room, hunting in the dark for my phone. Mom follows me, finding the light as I grab my cell. She stands behind me, her palm on my shoulder as I find his contact in my favorites.

I have to hang up and dial again. It rings once, twice, three times before he picks up. "Hello?"

"Dad, are you okay? What's the damage there?"

Earthquakes don't usually bother me. Perhaps Caleb's fear is rubbing off on me, or I've never felt one this big.

"Eden? What?" His voice is groggy, and he clears it. "What time is it?"

"I don't know." My panic is escalating. "Can you check your house?"

"Edie, honey, you're scaring me. What happened?"

"The earthquake. Please make sure your house is okay." My tone is sharp, but I work to soften it. "Please."

There is shuffling on his end of the line. A few moments lapse, and when he comes back, I'm on speakerphone. I hear his overhead fan and the creak of the hardwood floor. "Everything's fine," he says. "The power's on. My pictures are straight. Are you sure you didn't dream it? I didn't feel a thing."

"No." I shake my head, although he can't see it. "My quake alert went off and was still going when I woke up." But even as I say it, I glance around my room, noticing the paintings still hanging at right angles, the snake plant, which tips over at the slightest brush, standing upright.

"I am a light sleeper but slept right through it." Dad yawns. "We should check the news."

I pull my phone away from my ear and put him on speakerphone, but before I can open a browser, he says, "There was an earthquake."

I rub my palm over my face. "I know. How bad? How strong? You should turn your gas off and come here just in case."

"The initial estimate is 6.8."

Mom and I exchange twin expressions of dread. There hasn't been one that big in San Francisco since right before I was born. I saw photos of collapsed freeways and bridges; my childhood was marked with recovery and rebuilding. I expect sirens—some outward sign that the chaos is coming. But it's silent.

"How did you two sleep through it?" I sink down on the edge of my bed, telling myself we're okay. But my heart rate hasn't gotten the memo—it still thinks I'm running sprints.

"Eden." Dad enunciates both syllables of my name. "We didn't feel it because the earthquake didn't happen here."

"What?" I spit out an uncomfortable little laugh. "That doesn't make any sense."

"You're right. It doesn't." His voice drops to the register he uses to deliver bad news—when he told me the doctors had done everything they could for my leg and when he sat me down a year later and told me Mom had left. "The epicenter was in Grand Trees."

CHAPTER 38

"Honey, you're shaking." Mom sinks onto the bed beside me as I check my phone, confirming that the alert that woke me was, in fact, for Grand Trees. I never updated my location after Abby signed me up. I still have the town set as my primary weather zone, too.

I couldn't bring myself to change it, because my heart is still there.

I don't respond; instead, I dial Caleb again. I've lost track of how many times I've tried him since Dad delivered the news, but each time it goes straight to voicemail. I worry for a moment that he's blocked me, but I've tried Abby and Adelaide, too, and Mom has called several friends, with no luck. Mom wraps her hand around my wrist and lowers the phone from my ear.

"No one has service. We will have to wait."

I stand and pace. "Wait? We can't wait. How can you be so calm?" My voice cracks on the last word, and I slump over, hands on my knees.

"Honey," she says, "I'm terrified, but there's nothing we can do."

"I have to do something. I can't sit here." I envision rubble, fallen trees, leaking gas lines, and fire. I can't be idle not knowing whether Caleb's safe. Even if he's unscathed, will he survive after he inevitably plays hero?

"He's scared of earthquakes," I say through a sob. "What if he's trapped somewhere, alone? Or with Abby? What if one of them is hurt, and I . . ."

Mom brings her hands to my shoulders, somehow supporting me with her small frame. She tugs me upright until we're eye to eye. She studies me, her expression growing from confused to knowing as she swims before me, her face a watercolor behind my unshed tears. "Eden," she sighs. "Why didn't you tell me?"

My mouth forms the words, but I barely get out, "What?"

"I didn't understand what was going on with you two." She wraps her arms around me, holding me, swaying me, shushing me as I cry. "But you love him, don't you."

My tears are confirmation enough.

She missed so many of my milestones but is here to soothe my first real romantic heartbreak and hold me up as I fall apart.

"He wasn't mad that you were taking me away; he was hurt that you were leaving him," she deduces, scolding me in the way only a mother can.

"I think it was a bit of both," I confess.

"You should have told me. I would have been overjoyed. It's a dream to have two of your loved ones love each other." She pulls back until we're face-to-face. "That's why you wanted to stay. Oh, honey." She drags her thumbs across my cheekbones, wiping away tears. "I would have stayed if I had known." Mom's gaze travels over my face, and she gasps. "That's why you didn't tell me."

I pull back and try my phone again, sending Caleb another text, which goes undelivered like the last twenty. "Mom, I need to go to him. I promised if the world were ending, I'd—"

"Eden," she admonishes. "The world isn't ending."

"His may be," I choke out. "And he's probably so scared. When we had that little quake, you should have seen how rattled he was . . ." My voice cracks again, but Mom becomes steel.

"Caleb is a survivor. He will be okay. All we can do is sit tight and wait for news."

Dad sneaks in through the patio door as I brew a pot of coffee, still waiting for the phone to ring. I take one look at him and know Mom filled him in. He cradles me in his arms, patting my back in a *there-there* gesture he perfected when I was a kid who needed more comfort than he knew how to give.

"I'm sure your Caleb will be fine," he says when I pull away.

My attention snags on the "your," because he's not mine. I lost all right to claim him. But my body disagrees. I'm keyed up, queasy, antsy, unmoored.

"I need to go," I say. "I can't wait around for news and wonder if he's dead."

Dad and Mom share a look I don't understand before Dad says, "It's a terrible idea to go into a disaster zone, but I can't physically stop you. And if you insist on going, all I can do is stay here with your mom so she isn't worried sick alone."

~

About ten miles from Grand Trees, I come up to a checkpoint blocking the road. There are a few men in uniform, and I want to scream at all of them. Why are they standing around blocking the road instead of helping? But I need to keep my shit together if I have any hope of getting past them.

When I pull up at the barricade, a barrel-chested man in a tan uniform approaches the driver's side. "All roads in are closed, ma'am. It's not safe, and we need to keep it clear for emergency personnel."

I reach for the center console and hand him a card with shaking hands. He takes my outdated business card, scanning it and biting his lip.

"I didn't think the Red Cross could make it out this quickly."

I point to the back of my car. "I came ahead with some supplies."

I have packs of water, batteries, flashlights, and nonperishable food stacked past the window. If he looks in my trunk, he'll find blankets and a portable generator. I raided my emergency supplies and packed everything I thought could be helpful.

He peers through the rear window and back to the card. "All right. Watch out for the flares stationed up ahead. There's a possible landslide."

He shoves my card in his back pocket, and I should worry that impersonating a Red Cross employee will come back to bite me, but I don't have it in me to care. Besides, I didn't lie. I am bringing supplies, and that business card isn't counterfeit; it's just three years old.

He waves me forward, removing the cones to let me pass.

There are several cracks that run through the length of the pavement, so I hug the left lane, dodging tumbled rocks and tree branches littering the way. My radio signal fades as I get deeper into town, and I turn it off. NPR hadn't shared much on the drive here; the extent of the destruction is unknown, and there are multiple reports of fires, collapsed buildings, and injuries within a hundred miles of the epicenter. The reporter shared that the area began experiencing seismic activity, called foreshocks, this spring. I wonder—fuming—how I didn't know the small quake could be a warning of the big one to come.

I hang a right and look for the abandoned fishing skiff that marks the turnoff to Sonny's. It has been crushed by a redwood branch. I pull around the bend to Caleb's. His truck isn't parked out front, which must mean he's safe, that he left here after the quake under his own power. It must. I reject my lizard brain offering other options—that Caleb had to rush Abby to the emergency room, or Houdini to the vet, or he was sleeping elsewhere, in another woman's arms.

But still, I hop out of my car and race up the porch steps. I knock but there's no response, so I try the door, which is unlocked. It's a disaster inside—toppled lamps, artwork thrown from walls, kitchen cabinets flung ajar. The counters and floor are covered with shards of porcelain and glass.

"Caleb? Abby?" I call out.

But a frenetic search of the house confirms that they aren't home. I try Sonny's next. It's standing but didn't fare as well; the porch collapsed, leaving the front door inaccessible. A heavy branch from the ponderosa fell, puncturing the roof, and is now cantilevered off the main house.

It isn't safe to poke around, and Caleb's truck isn't here either, so I head into town to check if everyone is gathered there. There's a felled redwood blocking the road about a mile from the town center. I reverse until I come to a fork in the road and head up to Camp Colibri on autopilot, dodging debris and a section of asphalt that collapsed into the hillside.

My adrenaline has worn off, leaving me jittery, edgy, and with a bone-deep fatigue.

Camp seems deserted, but something tells me to stop, although I'm barely able to take in the damage and chaos. My voice is raw from calling Caleb's name when I hear rustling from the trail that leads to Colibri Peak.

"Caleb!" I yell before an overzealous howl calls back in response. I run toward it, gasping in relief when I see Houdini charging me, nearly tackling me on the patio in the welcome court.

But Caleb doesn't appear, and it looks like Houdini's here alone. Worry rises like a tidal wave. Houdini is trembling and drooling but burrows into me as I wrap my arms around his torso.

"Houdini, what's wrong? Where's Caleb? Abby?"

He whimpers in response, and really, what was I expecting?

"Caleb?" My voice is tight from panic. I stand, running aimlessly, trying all the locked doors of the lower camp, screaming Caleb's name into windows. I start up the way Houdini had come to search the upper camp, but when I glance back, he isn't following. "Houdini." I pat my thigh.

He glances at me over his shoulder but runs toward the parking lot. "Houdini!"

He stops, but only to see if I'm coming.

I jog farther up the trail and am met with an urgent howl. An incessant, earsplitting racket. I put my hands on my hips, watching him wail beside my passenger door. I need to think. If Caleb is here—inexplicably, without his truck—it will take me hours to find him on my own.

But why on earth would Caleb have been here during the earthquake in the middle of the night? The dog wouldn't lead me away from him if he were trapped and bleeding out, right? Houdini's naughty, sure. But he's nothing if not loyal.

With a resigned sigh, I trudge down the path. When I get close, Houdini paws at my car door, trying to flip the handle. I shake my head at him for being predictably ridiculous and at myself for following his lead.

I let him in, and he jumps to the passenger seat when I slide in, circling five times, knocking the glove compartment open with his tail. Piles of disorganized paperwork spill to the floor. This dog. I clutch his face between my palms, kissing him on the nose.

"You are the worst dog. But the best boy. Now tell me where Caleb is." He looks back at me with his chocolate puppy eyes, cocking his head to the side.

I want to scream. To cry. But I don't have time for those luxuries. I've tried all the obvious places. Knowing Caleb, the town would be well versed in evacuation routes, gathering spots, and contingency plans.

Wait, yes, I do know Caleb. And he did educate the town on all those things—the weekend I came to town. I cup my forehead, trying to remember any part of that day before Mom's fall and ambulance ride.

I ran into Abby. She was handing out town maps as coloring pages. I didn't take one, though. Then Caleb and I argued. Mom fell. I drove Abby to the hospital.

Abby.

The clock in my head is stuck, ticking at the same moment over and over. Before my conscious mind figures it out, I glance to the floor of the passenger seat, spying a crushed origami crane and a fortune teller that just tumbled from my glove compartment, the ones Abby made while on the way to the hospital.

I gather them in my fist—as Houdini gives me an opportunistic kiss on my cheek—and unfold them, flattening them against my thigh. The crane is a fire-preparedness handout, and the fortune teller is a list of emergency supplies to keep on hand. I lean across Houdini again, grabbing a folded star—and bingo—the town evacuation routes and meeting zones.

And there, in the left column, is my answer. AFTER AN EARTHQUAKE, GRAND TREES WILL SET UP AN EMERGENCY COMMAND CENTER SO RESIDENTS CAN CHECK IN, RECEIVE SUPPLIES, AND CREATE AN ACTION PLAN. RESIDENTS SHOULD MEET IN THE TOWN SQUARE. IF IT IS INACCESSIBLE, THE HIGH SCHOOL GYM WILL SERVE AS THE BACKUP.

I grab Houdini by his scruff and kiss him again. "You, sir, are a genius. Don't let anyone tell you any different."

CHAPTER 39

The high school is set in a meadow on the outskirts of Grand Trees, clear of towering pines and other potential risks. The flat and nondescript building is one of the newer structures in the region. As I crawl onto campus, I notice a few folks with brooms, cleaning glass from broken windows. But otherwise, there's little visible damage.

The parking lot is packed; I'm finally in the right place. Like a beacon of light, I see Caleb's truck parked near the gym doors—tailgate down, bed loaded with supplies. What's left of my adrenaline releases into my bloodstream like rapids through a busted dam. Houdini cries, hopping into my lap as I shift into park, and busts out of the door as soon as I push it open.

"Houdini, wait!" I call, but he's on a mission.

He sprints toward Caleb's truck and leaps into the bed before releasing a loud, urgent howl.

I see Abby first, running from the gym in a flurry. She screams when she sees Houdini, who jumps out of the truck and tackles her to the concrete. They are a blur of limbs, fur, hair, and cries as they receive each other, and I stand back a pace, letting them have their moment. But then Caleb emerges from the gym and joins the fray, crouching to accept a flurry of kisses from the rogue mutt. The relief washes over me, cleaning the thick soot of fear from my frame, and I feel lighter by half.

"Caleb," I choke out and run toward him. He rises to his full height but is otherwise rooted in place, blinking as if he thinks I'm a mirage. I launch myself at him, wrapping my arms around his neck, and all the air leaves him with a low whoosh. It takes him a moment, but then his hands come to my hips, and he pulls back, still holding on to me with a viselike grip.

"What in the actual hell are you doing here? Are you insane?"

I get a good look at him for the first time. He has a black eye and a cut along the bridge of his nose—it's red and badly swollen.

"What happened to you?" I reach toward his face, but he winces and tilts his chin away.

"Eden," he growls. "How the hell did you get here?" I'm getting the pit bull today, and I'm kinda here for it. I want to weep in relief. There's no amount of hostility that can dampen my mood. He's alive. Abby's alive.

"Is everyone okay?" He has to give me this, at least, before launching an indignant inquisition.

"Everyone will be, yes. Now answer my damn question."

"I drove," I say, knowing it'll irritate him further, but his fingers lengthen on my hips, grabbing more of me, and I clasp my hands tighter around his neck.

"There could have been fires, landslides, or aftershocks. You could've been killed. You drove through a disaster checkpoint, toward a place people are trying to evacuate from?"

"Yes."

He drops his head with an exasperated sigh, but it means our foreheads are kissing. He's acting outraged and rigid, but his body is receptive and pliant. He shifts closer until his legs are bracketing mine. "Please tell me you didn't bring your mom."

"Of course I didn't."

"How'd you get here so fast?" he whispers, pulling me closer still. I can feel the rise and fall of his exhale.

"The earthquake woke me up," I admit.

He pulls back until I get a good look at those inquisitive eyes, marred by the midnight hues blooming beside his right eye socket.

"In San Francisco?" He cocks a brow and then winces in pain. That shiner is inhibiting his ability to be as Caleb as he wants to be.

"Yep."

He shakes his head but finally, finally, pulls me into a hug that feels like salvation.

"I had to come. I was worried about you, and I know you don't like earthquakes."

"I fucking hate them," he says, and for some wild reason, we laugh as we hold each other in the midst of a disaster zone. I tighten my grip, clambering to get closer than our clothing or skin will allow.

"So, on my way here, I was thinking—"

"Doubtful, since you didn't turn around and go home to safety like you should've."

"Shh." I laugh, so grateful to be in his arms that no amount of attitude will deter me. "About how I promised to run to you if the world were ending."

"But you should have stayed put. Your world was perfectly safe—"

I talk right over him. "Because it dawned on me that you are the person that I'd want to spend my last moments with, so why would I live the rest of them without you?"

He hugs me so tightly that my feet leave the ground before he whispers, "Hell if I know."

Houdini burrows between us, pushing us apart to place his paws on Caleb's chest. Abby eyes me dubiously but reaches in for a hug. "I was going to say hi earlier, but I didn't want to interrupt this awkward parental PDA thing you two had going."

I laugh and kiss her cheek as Caleb asks, "Where did this wild dingo come from?" His words are annoyed, but he's crouched and giving the wild dingo belly rubs.

"He hitched a ride with me. I went looking for you both at your house and then Sonny's. I tried to go to town but it was blocked off, so I went up to camp, and there he was."

"Oh my poor puppy," Abby squeals. "He ran all the way to camp?"

"He was probably searching for you like I was."

Dogs. We don't deserve them.

"Then he shouldn't have run away from me in the first place," Caleb grumbles.

I turn to Abby, who is miraculously uninjured—and older. She's losing some of her sweet-cheeked baby face. "What happened to your dad? He won't tell me."

She giggles. "Because he's embarrassed. He ran into a tree branch. It wasn't even earthquake related."

"Is this true?" I bite back a smile when I glance at Caleb.

He scoffs. "It was the damn dog's fault." He's still scratching said dog's belly, betraying his outrage. Houdini's on his back, limbs askew, his tongue lolling to the side. "In the middle of the night, he woke me up by busting out of the back door. I had to chase him in my slippers. But yes, technically, I was whacked in the face by a branch right before the earthquake hit. See the sympathy I get for trying to save her dog?" he says, as Abby laughs some more.

"Her dog?" I wave toward the lovefest before me. "Maybe he ran to camp since that's where we hunkered down after the last quake."

"Or he's just a pain in my ass," Caleb grumbles.

"Well, he's the one who led me here, so he gets some hero credit today." When I poke my head up, Adelaide is charging toward me, on a mission. I wave, but her expression is stern. And before I can go to her, Abby jumps in. "Umm, are you here to ask my dad out? This is really weird timing, and it took you long enough."

Caleb and I make eye contact. He bites his bottom lip. "Nah, I beat her to it. She was just swinging by to give me her answer finally."

"So?" Abby asks. "I know he doesn't look great now, but I've heard he's not hideous."

"In that case." I grin and glance at Caleb, who stands, brushing Houdini's fur from his jeans, and slides his hand around my waist. "Yes, I'd love to go out with you." *Marry you, have your children, never let you out of my sight.* But we don't need to get technical.

"No one's going out with anyone anytime soon." Adelaide strides up beside us like she's not the least bit surprised I'm here. "We have work to do."

I hitch my thumb over my shoulder. "I came with supplies."

Adelaide grabs my hand and squeezes. "And finally came to your senses, I see."

She's right. Despite the sober circumstances, I feel a deep sense of calm wash over me as I plug into the rescue efforts over the next brutal hours. I think of Abby's love of hospitals and her certainty that when she's there, she's in the right place. Over the last few months, I've felt pulled between the two halves of my heart. But I only have to peer across the gym to where Caleb—safe, whole, beautiful—is directing volunteers to know I'm where I am supposed to be.

Adelaide's also right that there's nothing romantic about the work we undertake as afternoon turns to dusk, as folks come in sharing their losses. Bob had a bad fall during the quake, but he's expected to recover. Dakota was pinned under a dresser and sustained minor injuries. A few other folks were rushed to the hospital as well. There were lacerations, broken bones, and a concussion, but everyone in town made it out alive.

When the (real) Red Cross arrives to set up the emergency shelter and the high school is filled with authorities from various governmental agencies, a group of us head into town to assess the situation. Caleb and Ian lead two dozen volunteers as we triage the worst of the destruction. Goldie's doesn't look salvageable—a section of the roof caved in over the kitchen, and an exterior wall crumbled to dust. The Paper Horse didn't fare well either, with broken windows and toppled shelves, the books and toys pinned between layers of wood and plaster.

We break into groups to board up windows, clear the confetti of glass, and secure furniture vulnerable to aftershocks, amid vows to rebuild. The destroyed buildings hold my childhood memories but also contain the futures and fortunes of people I've come to care about, so I push my own nostalgia aside, doing what I can to assist as they manage their shock.

By midnight, I insist on taking Caleb and Abby home when I find her asleep in the cab of his truck. Through slurred speech, Caleb asserts he's not tired, that he'll go home for a change of clothes and come back. But he falls asleep a few moments after I start his truck.

Once home and armed with flashlights to navigate around the debris, we head inside, where it's as cold as the fall-chilled night and as dark as a starless sky. There is no digital clock to serve as a night-light and no flashes emanating from electronics. But as Caleb escorts Abby and Houdini to bed and inspects her room to ensure everything is secure, I notice one lone bar on my cell, and I step onto the porch to call home.

"Service is still spotty, but I wanted you to know I made it. Everyone's safe. And I'm helping with the emergency response. But I'll hurry home as soon as I can."

Dad clears his throat, and there's a long stretch of silence. I'm unsure whether it's the service or hesitation. "No, you won't." His voice crackles through the line, but I fill in the blanks with context clues, straining to hear. "If it's safe, you stay there as long as you need or want. Neither your mother nor I want you to sacrifice for us. That's our job, not yours."

"Dad, I'm not abandoning you guys. I'll figure out how to juggle and visit here more often—"

"We'll talk about this more later. But your mother and I spoke, and we've decided that I should be her primary caretaker."

I'm too tired for this conversation—too bone tired—or maybe I'm just tired enough, because I don't have it in me to argue before he continues, "I made a promise to her in sickness and in health. Just because that promise was interrupted doesn't mean I don't want to hold up my end of the bargain. I never stopped loving her, Edie. Never. And maybe that makes me a fool. But I missed twenty years. I don't want to miss any more."

His offer is tempting, but I can't leave Mom, not full-time anyway. Perhaps Dad and I can share the responsibility, allowing me to start the future I put on hold months ago.

"Eden?" Caleb pokes his head out of the house.

"Dad, I love you. I'll try you tomorrow if service—" But the line is dead, or maybe it's my battery. Either way, I tuck my phone in my pocket, accept Caleb's outstretched hand, and follow him inside.

We clear a path to the bedroom, where we take turns getting ready in the blinding beams of a flashlight. When we crawl under the covers in the pitch black, my body is still clinging to the cold, and Caleb wraps his limbs around me until I succumb in one last full-body shudder. The relief of him—his existence, his safety, his forgiveness—floods my bloodstream as its own heat source, and I melt against the mattress and his body.

"I'm not dreaming, am I?" Caleb yawns. "I've dreamed you here every night since you left."

"Only if I'm dreaming, too." I sigh against his neck and tug him closer as gratitude and guilt compete for resonance as I hold him. "I'm sorry I wasn't here for you."

"You're here now."

"And I'm not going anywhere."

"When you said you felt the earthquake, you meant you heard about it and felt it, like, metaphorically, right?"

"Sure." When you encounter something that you can't explain, there's no use trying.

"Eden," he admonishes. Even a drained and weary Caleb won't let me get away with anything.

"I can't explain it, Caleb. I received the alert on my phone, but I could have sworn the earthquake was happening in San Francisco. It woke me from a dead sleep, and I ran to check on my mom and called my dad. He was the one who told me it happened here, and I didn't believe him until I saw it online."

Caleb is quiet for a long time, and I wonder if he's finally given in to the forces of exhaustion before he tries, "Maybe you heard the alert and dreamed the earthquake before you were fully conscious?"

"Sure," I say again. "Or maybe Sonny was right: Grand Trees is magic and stays with you after you leave."

He chuckles.

"What?" I ask, shifting to catch his form in shadow. Even in darkness, his is my favorite face.

"That night—at your place? When I was about to leave? Cassie whispered something in my ear. It felt threatening at the time, but now seems prophetic."

That sounds like Cassie. Sometimes terrifying, but always right.

"What did she say?"

He leans in and catches my bottom lip between his, and I'm careful not to bump his injured nose, but even this tentative kiss ignites sparks as our mouths connect. "She said, 'Don't give up on her. It may take an act of God to change her mind if you leave without a fight.'"

I release a surprised laugh. "Wow. That girl does have a flair for the dramatic."

"She wasn't wrong, though." Caleb deepens the kiss. It's easy to forget everything when his mouth is on mine. But I need him to know I'm not here by happenstance. I would have come to him even if our world hadn't tipped like a snow globe.

"Maybe it sped up my choice," I say when he pulls back enough for my brain to restart. I slide my hand to his jaw and still him. "But it didn't make it for me. I was figuring it out and coming to my senses anyway. I chose you, Caleb, and I'll keep choosing you. Maybe the conditions don't have to be perfect for us to be perfect. If we have each other, that's more than enough luck for one lifetime."

He hums, and I feel the vibration in my core. "You and me," he says. "That's the easy part. But what about everything else? What happens next?"

I find his hand in the dark and lace my fingers in his. "I guess we'll have to improvise."

EPILOGUE

Nine Months Later

"Eden!" Abby waves like an air traffic controller as I enter the camp parking lot. "Over here."

I don't know where else she thinks I would go, but I'm too happy to see her to tease her about her overzealous welcome. She and Houdini are at my door when I step out. She wraps her long arms around me in a bear hug. I have to tilt my head onto her shoulder—she's two inches taller than me now.

"How's Grams? How was the drive? Was it bad? Did she do okay? Where is she?"

I giggle but don't have a chance to answer before Houdini shoves his heavy body between us and pries us apart. I dodge as he jumps on me—we have to break him of that habit—and crouch to give him a hug.

"She's good," I say over Houdini's joyous cries. "The drive was quick, and she's at the house with my dad and Adelaide."

"But we're still doing game night, right? Because I found this new card game online, and I've studied all the strategies and think I have a really good chance of beating my dad."

She chopped her hair to her chin a few weeks ago, which only makes her look older and more like Caleb. She sent me photos from the salon. She's calling it her high school hair. The world isn't ready for this one.

"Of course. Where is your dad anyway? He texted me that I should meet him here after dropping off my folks."

"Well"—she bites her lip and darts her focus up toward camp—"he had to go up to Colibri Peak."

"Oh." I can't keep the disappointment from my voice. This is the longest we've spent apart since before the earthquake. It's been six weeks since we drove to San Francisco together for Mom's surgery. Caleb stayed two weeks to help with her immediate recovery, but this is the first time I've been home since then. It's still too early to tell how effective the surgery was, but we're hopeful she'll have some relief. Last year, after she began treatment, the medication was instantly helpful. We noticed a steep decline in tremors, but the effectiveness waned enough that her doctor recommended deep brain stimulation, like a pacemaker for the brain, which should reduce her symptoms further.

In the last two weeks, she has been much more herself and insisted on coming with me to Grand Trees for the annual preseason camp party. The only good thing about the quake was that a landslide took out the temporary detour, forcing Caltrans to fix the long abandoned and neglected main road. The drive to San Francisco is now an easy five hours, and we've found a rhythm to closing the distance: a week or two for Mom here, where she thrives between appointments. Then we return, and I have time to soak up Mom, Dad, Cassie, and Cassie's new baby. At seven months old, she already has enough sass to give her mom a run for her money. It is phenomenal.

But I've never been away from home this long, and I'm anxious to see Caleb after such a draining and difficult separation. I'm greedy for him.

"When is he coming down?" I ask.

"Not for a while. Something about bark beetles and root rot?" She sighs. "You know how my dad gets when his tree babies are in danger."

I laugh. "Do you want to check out the renovations to the gym with me while we wait?"

I'm taking a leap this summer and teaching a few dance classes at camp. Caleb installed mirrors and ballet barres in the gym to my exact specifications. I'll likely be working with a dozen beginners each week, teaching them basic positions and elementary movements. But if I can introduce the beauty of dance to a child—even if it's for only an hour a week—I think I'll be doing some good. Who knows? Maybe one of the kids will be inspired to continue dancing at home. Or maybe we'll just create a memory. I've learned that joy doesn't have to last forever for it to be worth making.

"No," Abby blurts. "My dad said you should meet him up there."

"At Colibri Peak?" I glance at my shoes. I did not come prepared for a hike; I never learn.

"He might be up there awhile. I have to help Ian with the kitchen prep for tomorrow." She tugs on my hand, leading me onto the stone path. The welcome court is already decorated with white lights and paper lanterns in anticipation of tomorrow's party. I can't believe it's been a year since I danced with Caleb in this courtyard. It feels like yesterday, and several lifetimes ago.

"Are you sure?" The thought of a hike, even along my favorite trail, makes me want to curl up and take a nap in a hammock and wait for Caleb to come to me. I pull out my phone to text him, but Abby holds up her hand.

"He doesn't have service." She nudges me toward the upper trail. "And Houdini will go with you."

A hike it is. Houdini races ahead as Abby waves us on. My desire to see Caleb keeps the worst of my weariness at bay, and each time I fall behind, Houdini races back to me like an encouraging coach. I don't know how I'll find Caleb if he's wandering around looking at trees, but Houdini charges up the hardened path like a homing device.

The hillside has faded to summer's muted tones. Sage, gold, and copper grasses bow to the wind's gentle hand as we pass. Up ahead, I notice where Caleb had a crop of pines removed due to disease. Seedlings stand in their place, their hopeful little branches soaking up the sun's affection, grateful for their chance to grace the hallowed land with fresh life.

Houdini takes off at a sprint, and I know we're close. The dormant butterflies in my belly bat their dust-coated wings, and nerves take flight. I've been waiting for this reunion for weeks—or maybe longer. Maybe I've been waiting with bated breath, holding the magic of this land in my bones, during an absence far longer than this one.

Maybe I've been waiting forever.

I climb to the crest at a jog, finding my footing and fighting my fatigue, and hear Caleb's voice before I see him as he lavishes Houdini with soft praise and affection he reserves for when he thinks they're alone. The vista unspools before me as I watch them crouched at the summit, shoulders pressed together, looking out over the view. I give them a moment, drinking in the sight of him and taking a mental snapshot. The emerald branches of the redwoods frame the reflection of Grand Trees Lake fifty feet below. The sun is a beacon in the cloudless sky—bright and resolute as a spotlight across the lake's surface.

When I step forward, pine needles crunch under my feet.

Caleb turns, his smile brighter than the sky itself. "Took you long enough."

I grin back at him. "You try hiking in these shoes."

"What did I tell you about wearing better shoes?"

"And I almost thought I missed you."

Caleb stands, and we meet in the middle. He cups my jaw in both hands, resting his mouth on mine and breathing in. "I missed you enough for the both of us."

It's so easy to get lost in him—to forget that there are a million things we need to discuss before heading home, when the entire town of Grand Trees will, no doubt, descend. I don't know when we'll be alone again.

But still, those butterflies demand my attention. The nerves, the excitement, the anticipation all collide, and I pull back. "Are you done up here?"

"Not quite," he whispers against my lips, drawing me in for another kiss. I thread my hands in his hair as he trails his mouth down the column of my throat. It's then I notice the scene before me.

"Caleb?" I ask. "Did you bring a picnic?" Houdini is sprawled out on a green plaid blanket that blends into the earth. There's a picnic basket and a bottle of wine poking out.

"I thought you might be hungry."

And come to think of it, I am. Starving, in fact. I pull him over to the blanket as his hands trail to my waist, holding on to me before I slip out of his grasp.

"This is perfect," I say. "I need to talk to you anyway."

"Well, I need to talk to you first."

"Nope. Me first."

I pull him down to the blanket, and Houdini grumbles as he scoots out of the way. I dig into the basket, but Caleb stills me with a hand on my wrist.

"I really missed you." He bites the scar on his lip, his gaze traveling nervously between my eyes. For all his confidence, it's his vulnerability that defines the best of him.

"You know I was kidding, right? I missed you like crazy."

"How could you not?" He chuckles. I push his shoulder, and he leans away before grabbing both of my hands. "But I did a lot of thinking while you were away, and I don't want to go that long without seeing you again."

"I don't want to either. But you know I had to be there for my mom." It's our first night together again; I don't want to fight about the time apart. The last few weeks were hard, physically and emotionally, and I felt our distance grow as the days wore on. But I assumed it was because I was holding back, not because he was resentful of my time away. I've been counting down to this day, when I could talk to him without the telephone diluting the impact.

"Yeah, of course. But there are some things I want settled, you know? We said we'd improvise, but it's not working. We need to plan for some things, like—"

But I pull away and stand, pacing along the summit. Plan. Plan? He wants to plan? That's the last thing I need to hear right now. Just when I have to tell him that our biggest improvisation is yet to come.

"Caleb, I really need to talk to you." I turn my back to him because I'm a coward, apparently.

"Please, Eden, let me get this out." His voice is fraught, which usually disarms me. But I am a live grenade, and there's no putting my pin back. I've waited too long. Maybe I should have told him over the phone weeks ago to avoid my emotional distance from triggering his anxiety about abandonment.

"I don't think we can plan, Caleb. We said we'd take this as it comes. And I've done my best to be there for my mom and to be here with you, but this is the first time I've done something that mattered that I couldn't do 100 percent. And I'm sorry if I failed. I really was trying to make you happy—"

"Eden, look at me. I am happy. This has been the happiest year of my life. Shit. I'm screwing this up."

"No, I am." I pinch my eyes closed. I feel his hands on my waist, and he turns me to him. Before I lose my nerve, I blurt, "Caleb, I'm pregnant."

The only sounds that greet me are the whistle of the wind through the trees and the whoosh of air from his lungs. When I gather the nerve to open my eyes, he's kneeling in front of me—face pale, mouth agape—and he finally says, "And I'm proposing." We stare at each other, missing a few blinks before he tries to speak again. "Wait, seriously? You're pregnant?"

I nod. "And you were trying to propose?"

"Yes."

"You're really bad at it." Tears stream down my cheeks and butterflies rush into my bloodstream, beating their little wings and heating me to a stupor.

He reaches for the neck of the bottle. "But I brought champagne."

I laugh. "And I can't drink it."

Caleb catches me by the waist and tugs me until I'm kneeling in front of him. "We're having a baby?" he asks again, his joy beating out shock until he's grinning. He's backlit by the sun, and a halo coats him in fairy dust, diluting every line, scar, and past heartbreak. He's incandescent.

"I found out a couple of weeks ago, but I wanted to tell you in person."

He brings a hand to my belly, covering my navel with a wash of warmth, settling the low-grade nausea that's been chasing me all day. I lean into the touch. "You should have called me. While you were busy taking care of your mom, who was taking care of you?"

"You can take care of me starting now. I wouldn't mind a piggyback ride down that hill."

He kisses me then, both reverent and fevered. His hands slide to my hair, and mine wind around his waist. Between the sweet slide of his tongue and the firm press of his chest, it takes me a moment to play back those last ridiculous moments. "Are we getting married?" I ask against his mouth.

He freezes, pulling back enough to let me drink in the whiskey of his eyes. "I don't think you've answered me. You left me hanging on bended knee."

"I don't think you asked me yet, actually."

We grin at each other, and he inhales. "Eden Hawthorne, will you marry me?"

My tears fall from my cheeks to my collarbone, but I don't bother wiping them away. His eyes are red rimmed, and iridescent.

"And have your baby?"

"And have my baby."

"Hmm," I tease.

He swats my ass before grabbing it and cinching us together. "Eden," he grumbles.

"Did you ask Abby first?"

"Yes. She was supposed to be the diversion in this terrible proposal."

"Ah. Well, I didn't suspect it for a moment, so you can't blame this one on her." I sneak a quick kiss; his scowl is adorable. "Did you talk to my parents?"

"I did," he says through gritted teeth.

"When?" I kiss him again. He's surprisingly pliant even though he's about to lose his shit.

"Answer my damn question before I take it back."

He won't take it back, but his growl does things to me. It probably has something to do with how I wound up pregnant, honestly.

"What was the question again?" I laugh against his mouth.

"That's it." He nips at my lip until I feel the pleasant sting of teeth, and he lowers me to the blanket, caging me in. It gives Houdini the opportunity to swipe his tongue across Caleb's cheek. He bats Houdini's muzzle away, and I dissolve into giggles.

"Of course I'll marry you, Caleb Connell, and even have your baby."

"And live happily ever after?" Caleb is an eclipse against the blinding sun, making me tear up at the radiance of the rays surrounding him.

I'm too giddy to care whether this joy will last months, years, or a lifetime. I have it now; I'm going to hold tight to hope while relishing the moment itself. "Is that an option?"

"It is," he says. "I hear living happily ever after is just like dancing."

"How so?"

Caleb grins and leans in to kiss me. When our smiles collide, we become a tangle of limbs, tears, and laughter. As the sun baptizes us with summer rays, as the forest hovers over us as witness, and as the blessed land of Grand Trees wraps its cloak around our broken, battered souls, Caleb whispers against my skin, "The magic is in the attempt."

ACKNOWLEDGMENTS

When I was a kid, dreaming about a career as an author, I imagined a solitary, linear process. I also imagined writing the Great American Novel™ in one draft on a typewriter, sitting in my oceanfront home perched on a scenic bluff, wrapped in a handmade shawl while clutching a fresh cappuccino. It turns out being a novelist is nothing like Hollywood would have us believe, although there is a lot of caffeine required. Unfortunately, there's no picturesque writing retreat. But luckily, there's no requirement to be perfect or reclusive. A novel is the product of an iterative—and often inexplicable—process and an expansive creative and supportive team. I am blessed with the best team imaginable.

Thank you to my wonderful agent, Melissa Edwards, who is the hardest-working woman in publishing. I am so grateful you took a chance on me, enabled me to get my words out into the world, and answered a million questions along the way. Thank you to my editors who got this book over the finish line. Maria Gomez, Selena James, and Selina McLemore, I appreciate the roles you each played in choosing, shepherding, and polishing this book until it shined. I imagined working with editors who could push me to be better, and you all have done that. Thanks to Jon Ford for accepting my love of em dashes and having the patience to insert and delete all the necessary commas. Thanks to Sarah Engel for her attention to detail and thoughtfulness during proofreading. Thanks to Sarah Horgan for designing another cover that captures the spirit of the book and the singular beauty of California. A huge thank-you to Karah Nichols, Tree Abraham, and the entire Lake Union team for getting this book into the hands of readers.

Thank you to all my agent siblings who are willing to act as the unofficial publishing handbook, offer advice and wisdom, and go down the rabbit hole of regional highway naming conventions in order to ensure absolute authenticity for even the most minute details. To my critique partners—Gina Banks, Jessica Banks, Isabelle Engel, Melissa Liebling-Goldberg, Aria Garnett, Amanda Hauck, Megan Correll, Jamie Factor, and Heather Hecht—thank you for taking time to read and offer your feedback to ensure this book was as good as it could be. To the fabulous authors who invested time to read and blurb my debut—Alicia Thompson, Holly James, Sierra Godfrey, Meredith Schorr, and Lindsay Hameroff—it meant the world to me that you said yes. I'm overwhelmed by the generosity and kindness in the writer community. Thank you!

To my loyal beta readers and dearest friends, Jenn Lockhart, Rebecca Low, Marina Moore, Amanda Jacobs, and Becca Chapin, I appreciate your wisdom and feedback—and love that you always demand the next book as soon as you finish reading.

Thank you to ballet, my first and forever creative love. Everything I learned about beauty, creation, and composition, I learned from you. My first lessons about story structure came at the hands of hundreds of patient dancers who had to be my living drafts. Thank you to my Adage dancers for all that you taught me. In thinking of Eden's backstory and how losing dance affected her, it made me nostalgic for the way dance—and my dancers—shaped me. Like Eden learns, it's never really lost. And to Miss Kathy, you taught me a lot about how to dance and how to be a good human. But who knew your famous words would prepare me for the patience and urgency required in publishing: *Slow down. Slow down. And now, you're late.*

Becoming a mother has made me fascinated with plotlines about parenthood. I'm drawn to stories about complex family dynamics and the choices, sacrifices, and mistakes we make as mothers. The stakes are never higher than when we try to meet the overwhelming expectations society places on us to be everything our children need. But Mom, I promise that none of my flawed maternal characters are inspired by, similar to, or in any way about you. I will repeat this in every book I write, if necessary, to make sure you don't internalize my wild imagination. The example you gave me was pure selflessness and devotion, which is great in real life but a little boring in fiction. So you're stuck in my acknowledgments. Dad, thank you for being my hype man and for joining Mom in the crusade to be the best parents ever. I wouldn't have been delusional enough to think I could write a book if you hadn't made building my confidence your sole purpose in life.

Most people think the middle child is the unlucky one, but it's like being forever seated at the dinner table in between your favorite people—never missing the dialogue or the laughter, never having to lead or be left behind. I'm the luckiest sister of the best sisters on earth. Hil, thank you for reading every iteration and weighing in on whether that one slight change within draft 203 finally solves the plot point you've let me brainstorm ad nauseum. Heather, a huge thank-you for reading my first words and insisting I write more and for being my on-call designer. To Kel, you're all grown up and an honorary sister. The three of you have kept me sane as I reached for this scary, unwieldy goal. Thanks for reading, rereading, and passing along my books for others to read as well. Most of all, thanks for always answering my most unhinged SOS texts.

And to the family I chose and made, you've all made my life a living symphony—loud, dramatic, and sometimes off key, but always harmonious. Oliver, the original wild dingo, gets a shout-out here for serving as a bottomless well of inspiration. You are a good dog. Don't let anyone tell you any different. Thank you to Makenna, Wyatt, Levi, and Damien for giving me the empathy and life experience to write with my whole heart. I love you all to the moon and back. And to Kenny, I can only write because you are a true partner and can only write about love because you have provided such a selfless example.

ABOUT THE AUTHOR

Photo © 2024 Kevin Neilson

Mara Williams is the author of *The Truth Is in the Detours*. She drafted her first novel in third grade in a spiral notebook—a story about a golden retriever and the stray dog who loved her. Now she writes novels about strong, messy women trying to find their way in the world. When not writing or reading, Mara can be found enjoying California's beaches, redwoods, and trails with her husband, kids, and disobedient dog. For more information, visit www.marawilliamsauthor.com.